Everything I've NEVER HAD

LYNETTA HALAT

Copyright ©2013 by Lynetta Halat
Edited by Lisa Christman of Adept Edits
Cover design by © Sarah Hansen of Okay Creations
Book interior design by JT Formatting

EVERLONG
Words and Music by David Grohl
© 1997 MJ TWELVE MUSIC
All Rights Administered by Warner-Tamerlane Publishing Corp.
All Rights Reserved
Lyrics reprinted with permission.

Printed in the United States of America
First Edition: September 2013
Library of Congress Cataloging-in-Publication Data

www.lynettahalat.com

Halat, Lynetta.
        Everything I've Never Had / Lynetta Halat. – 1st ed
        ISBN-13: 978-1492206088
        ISBN-10: 1492206083

        1.   Everything I've Never Had—Fiction. 2. Fiction—Romance
        3.   Fiction—Contemporary Romance

Dedication

This book offering is dedicated to the countless men and women in
uniform who serve our great nation. Thank you.
And, more specifically, to my husband, Sean,
and my brother Jesse Dobbins.

Prologue

I'D ALWAYS KNOWN loving him was never going to be easy, and with my eyes wide open, I'd been prepared to face many battles to keep him for my own. But I never thought I'd have to fight him for his love. A crippling pain fills my soul as that realization sinks in. As if he can't stand to be loved back by me, he has taken his love from me and is pushing me away. He's punishing himself. And I know that's what has brought this on—guilt and penance. Taking a deep breath in and releasing it, I steel myself to fight for my man. When I knock on his door, my heart is in my throat.

The Kiss

AT THE FIRST heart-stopping note of one of the most sensual songs I've ever heard, my head flies up and I make eye contact with the band's rhythm guitarist. He looks like he's having a great time. I feel like I just got sucker-punched.

I lean in to my best friend, Bonnie, and shout, "I'm going to get some fresh air, OK?"

She flips her blonde hair over her shoulder, and her worried dark brown eyes meet mine. "You, all right? You need me to come with?"

I paste a fake grin on and shout back, "No, no. I'm good. Just need a minute. Keep dancing, ma belle amie!"

With one last glance at the stage, I make my way through the sea of elbows and hips. When I reach the back porch, I take a huge breath and let the lyrics permeate my brain. *Holy shit!* Was there a sexier song than this on the entire planet? *Umm...No!* And him up there strumming it. I think back to all of, what I hope were, my surreptitious glances of the evening. *Geez, he is gorgeous.* I imagine running my hands through that shaggy dark brown hair and staring into those exquisite ice blue eyes. What if I had enough guts to place my hands on his chiseled jaw and bring his impossibly full lips to mine? I close my eyes and picture what had to be the most luscious lips I'd ever laid eyes on.

Part of me wishes that he were just a pretty face with a nice body because that I might actually be able to resist, but no, he was just as gorgeous where it mattered. And that's where my problem lies—because of his kind heart and generous nature, he'd become my best friend and my confidant.

I know I'm not supposed to want him. He's my own slice of forbidden fruit—my deceased husband's outcast cousin. And with the way our families were connected, that was not something I could ignore.

My conscience takes a nosedive and picks up where I left off with my explicit daydream. I've been denying my desire for him for so long because of our complicated connections, and I've only allowed this one other time. I'd promised myself I wouldn't permit it again. But, surely, I could make an exception because of this—my favorite of favorite songs—"Everlong."

So I allow myself to imagine, me mumbling his name against his lips...Adrian...even his name is sexy. I feel a shiver course through my body. It's on this thought that I hear the screen door bump closed behind me. My eyes fly open, and I take another deep breath to collect myself and know immediately that it's him. Yes, his scent is that unique. It somehow reminds of the desert and the ocean all at once—hot and quenching. *Why does he have to be an assault on all my senses?* Wait...what is he doing out here? He's supposed to be on stage! I search frantically for some semblance of control over my body. What is the proper etiquette for getting caught in your lustful musings by the very object of your desires? Hmm...

His rich timbre reaches across the porch as he asks, "Celeste, everything good?" If whiskey possessed the ability to speak, that's what it would sound like—his smooth, sultry voice.

My voice sounds heavy to my own ears. "Umm…yeah, what are you doing out here? Doesn't your band need you?"

"They'll live. You're more important." I close my eyes and let those words fill and warm me like a fine, aged bourbon. "You streaked out of there like you'd seen a ghost. You scared me."

I spin around too fast, and my head seems to keep spinning. There he is in all his glory. Even with my heels on, I barely reach his shoulders. He's so broad that I could imagine him double-timing it up a couple of flights of stairs with me thrown over his shoulder and I'm no waif. My eyes meet his, and I'm lost. Lost to his look. Lost to this song. Lost to my fantasizing.

I stride over to him as the guitar plays out a little stalking march for me. *I'm really going to do this.* When I get close enough to him, I can see the worry in his hypnotizingly beautiful eyes. He's worried about me. I know he cares about me and my children. He's been absolutely amazing to us since my husband passed. Could he see me as more than just a friend?

I'm close enough now to breathe him in fully, and when I do, I hear Zach sing out, "'Breathe out, so I can breathe you in, hold you in.'" I take a deeper breath and my eyes flutter half-closed as his scent saturates my every pore. Even though my eyes are almost closed, I don't miss the flare of his eyes; I take this as encouragement. And that's it. The edge I was clinging to dissipates from my tenuous grasp.

When the guitar rift hits its crescendo, I watch helplessly as my hands dart out and pull his face down to mine just like in my fantasy. Maybe I'm still fantasizing? My doubt is quickly erased as his lips are softer than anything my feeble imagination could ever come up with. I move my lips over his in what, I hope, is an enticing way. I'm not sure yet because he hasn't responded. But he hasn't thrown me off, so I continue my assault. I slant my head to the side a little more and my tongue, apparently with a mind of its own, darts out to help itself to a taste. Mmm...but his taste can barely register because as soon as my tongue touches his lips he opens his mouth under mine.

That's all I need. Desire like I've never felt before wars with my good sense. I feel his tongue move with mine hesitantly; nonetheless, it moves. *Thank God!* Oh my...this is...everything. Everything I've never felt, everything I've never tasted, everything I've never had.

When the song breaks off into what I call "the voices in my head" section, my conscience decides to make itself known again; and I wrench myself free. Adrian wasn't holding me. I was holding him, but I was suddenly overcome with self-doubt, which was quickly followed by self-preservation. I can clearly see any scenario other than friendship ending in disaster for us.

As I back away slowly, my frantic eyes assess his equally frantic eyes. Then, his look changes, and he looks downright unhappy. I clear my throat and offer, "Adrian, I'm so sorry. I...I don't know what I was thinking." My hand trembles as I push my hair back off my face. "I wasn't thinking, I guess."

He stares at me like he's never seen me before, and it scares me. Panic seizes my throat. He's been amazing to my boys and me. We can't lose him. I'm such a fool. I open my mouth to continue groveling when that damn stalking rhythm starts up again and all of a sudden Adrian is the one stalking toward me, but he looks...pissed. I lick my lips, swallow hard, and stumble back until I feel the porch rail behind me.

This time when the crescendo hits it's Adrian who assaults me, but I am a more than willing participant, so that when his hands run down my back, my body melts into his. Even though I feel melded to him, it's not enough for Adrian because his big hands keep going until they clasp my behind so hard that my right leg springs up to rest around his hip. Oh my God! I thought it was great the first time, but his kiss puts mine to shame.

I moan in time with this new knowledge as Zach sings the Foo Fighter's lyric, "You gotta promise not to stop when I say when." One realization crashes into another as I realize I never want this to stop. I never want to stop kissing him. Squeezing my eyes shut and tightening my grip on him, I throw myself even more into his soul-stealing kiss. Mmm...his hair is just as soft as I thought it would be. I pull it through my fingers roughly. When I do, he groans into my mouth and deepens his kiss momentarily before completely throwing me by pulling back a little and softening it. It's excruciatingly tender. I'm torn—I want to savor the sweetness but also want him to devour me again. Greedy—I feel so greedy. How can I want more when what I'm getting is already so good, so perfect?

When he pulls back to place closed-mouthed little kisses on my lips, I fulfill my fantasy and mumble, "Mmm...Adrian." Adrian's shudder reverberates through me, and he pulls back to grasp my hands and pull them down from around his neck. I hear the song come to its beautiful end and Zach tells the crowd they'll be back in ten.

The kiss I never wanted to end has ended and I feel bereft. I finally open my eyes to stare into his most expressive ones. His eyes are filled with regret.

I gasp at the sudden sharp pain that pierces my heart. I snap my mouth shut, drop my leg from around his hip, and pull my hands from his. "Adrian—"

"No, that's all on me, Celeste. I'm..." He runs his hand through his hair, proving what I thought impossible by making himself even sexier with mussed hair. "Shit...I'm sorry. I'm a shit. It's just..."

"I've had too much to drink," I blurt out. "This is the first time I've been out, and...I was just having fun but started feeling lonely, and I had too much to drink." So, about one-third of that statement is true. I had only had one glass of wine, and I did not feel lonely. I can't tell him that though. Best he think I'm inebriated and missing my husband rather than know the truth of the matter—I want him for my very own.

He pulls his hands down over his face and massages it for a second. Blowing out a deep breath and intoxicating me with his essence a little bit more, he insists, "Yeah, and pig that I am, I took advantage of all that."

"You're not a pig. As a matter of fact, you couldn't be any further from that if you tried," I protest. "And, to be honest, I really needed to be kissed. So...thank you." Did I really just thank him for kissing me? *I. AM. SO. PATHETIC!*

He scrunches his face up a little bit. "So, we're good then. No, uh, awkwardness?" He asks me with a look of disbelief crossing his features.

"Of course. I'm not one of your simpering groupies. I promise not to stalk you and demand any more kisses," I joke. None of what I said sounds funny, though, so we just kind of stare at each other for a couple of awkward beats.

His hand comes up and the look on his face tells me he's going to console me or something. I pull back a little. I can't let him feel sorry for me after that. Not to mention, if he touches me again, I may actually beg him to never stop. He lets his hand drop before putting them both in his pockets and rocking back on his heels a little. When he does this, he, unfortunately for me, draws attention to his nicely toned pecs. "You ready to come back inside then?"

"Umm...I just need another minute. I'll be right in, OK?" I give him a small, albeit shaky, smile.

"OK," he agrees. He makes his way back to the door before turning back to tell me, "See ya inside."

"Yep," I lie. The second the door snaps closed, I yank out my cell phone and fire off a text to Bonnie and Farah telling them that I got a cab and would talk to them tomorrow.

There's no way in hell I could go back in there, and I punctuate that thought by hitting my lock button. I snicker—a lock button—if only it were that easy for me.

-Two-

This Isn't Going to Be Awkward at All

I WAKE UP to the sound of a lawnmower. I'm typically an early-to-rise person—with three rambunctious boys usually running around, waking up early is the only way to get any quiet time. And as amazing as my boys are, oh, how I love my quiet time. Sounds like I won't be getting any of that this morning.

I laugh as I recall my and Adrian's argument over my yard. I'd always taken care of it because I was extremely particular about how it was done. When I became a single parent, I'd mentioned to Adrian that I needed to hire someone to manage it, which made me cringe when I thought about how they would surely butcher my wildflowers and the fragile plants that were in need of some extra TLC. He said that he'd be happy to do it. I insisted that he didn't have time for that. Adrian argued that I was OCD when it came to my yard and he knew how I liked it and that that was that. He'd been taking care of it ever since.

He's not supposed to mow my grass until next Saturday. I know this because I know every single solitary detail of his schedule. I've memorized it over the last year and a half although it wasn't really that hard to do considering a great deal of his schedule revolves around my sons.

Since my husband passed away, Adrian has become a fixture in my boys' lives much to the chagrin of my husband's parents and brothers. You see, Adrian had the misfortune of being born to the middle son—the one who clamored to be noticed and appreciated. Most of the time, the notice Adrian's father had garnered was embarrassing, of course, and the family had cut all ties to him. Unfortunately, the sins of the father had trickled down to include Adrian, but I'd never seen any proof of his supposed black sheep reputation.

But none of this matters to me because Adrian has been an absolute angel to my boys. No one, on either side of our families, has stepped up the way he has. Never once have I had to ask him to do anything for us or with us. He integrated himself into our lives seamlessly and without any prompting or invitation.

At first, it worried me a little. I knew his reputation wasn't that far from his father's. I didn't want the boys to get too attached to him just to have him drop out of their lives when something better came along or when he decided to start his own family. It became quickly apparent, however, that he had no intention of letting my boys know what life without him would be like. I was impressed, which is also why I completely suck. By attacking him, I've probably ruined one of the best things that has ever happened to us.

Since my muscles are screaming at me from all the dancing I did before my humiliating faux pas, I gingerly roll myself out of bed and stretch. How in the world am I going to look him in the eye this morning? Why is he even here? It would be different if the kids were here to act as a buffer, but they are at the family compound this weekend.

I go over to the vanity and yank my toothbrush from the holder as I stare myself down in the mirror. What was I thinking? I shake my head and watch my unkempt black hair cascade around my shoulders. I'll deal with that mess in a second.

I shove the toothbrush into my mouth and start scrubbing vigorously. Squinting my eyes at my dreadful reflection, I level with myself. Thinking I would fulfill the only real desire I've ever felt and kiss the only man I've ever truly been attracted to, I threw myself at Adrian. My husband was attractive and I loved him, but we'd grown up together, and he was more my best friend than anything else. This was different. I wanted Adrian with every fiber of my being and had since I'd first met him a few years back. I was so ashamed at the way my body reacted to him back then, but I'd quickly realized that I had no control over the physical pull I felt toward him. However, I could try to control my actions and thoughts; and I had been so very good at it too.

I roll my eyes at myself. I blew that last night, though. It was that damn outfit that Bonnie and Farah convinced me to buy and wear for my first night out. I thought back to the fitted, collared halter-top and scary-short short shorts. I'd paired that outfit with some tall espadrilles, and I'd felt incredibly sexy. I never felt sexy. I felt cute sometimes, other times even pretty, and usually stylish. But never in my thirty-seven years had I felt sexy. I thought about how I saw myself in the mirror before I left last night. I had left my raven hair down and in soft waves that fell about midway down my exposed back. I'd made my dark brown eyes extra smoky—something I'd only experimented with in the privacy of my own boudoir but never had the guts to leave home wearing. My dark skin contrasted quite nicely with the all white outfit and gold bangles and hoop earrings. Yeah, I'd been asking for trouble.

It'd felt so good to be dressed up and shirk my responsibilities for the night. That's what it was—I wanted him and I had felt sexy and free—a lethal combination. Yep, that's all it was. I was acting purely on physicality last night.

OK. Now that I know how I'd allowed myself to veer terribly off course, how do I go about explaining that to Adrian? That admission would be mortifying. Although, I'm pretty sure how I feel about him physically is no longer a mystery after those two kisses last night. I take a deep breath and push it out forcefully. He'd have to be utterly oblivious to not have realized how my body responded to his last night. *Why, oh why, does he have to be off limits?* I ask myself for about the thousandth time.

That's good. I roughly run the brush through my hair. Just admit that you're physically attracted to him and that it can go nowhere and that you're sorry you're such a floozy and that you will control yourself from now on.

I give myself a bright smile, toss on my glasses, and grab my fluffy white robe that will cover my silky pajamas. *Here goes nothin'.*

I STEP OUT onto my back deck and immediately see him heading away from me with the push mower. He towers over it so he has to hunch himself over to maneuver it. Of course, his hair is saturated with his sweat, making it look almost black. At only eight in the morning, a sweltering heat is already upon us. Usually, Adrian takes his shirt off when he is working outside, but he's left it on today. I can't help but wonder if he's protecting his virtue around me. *Great!* His camel brown shirt is not too far away from being as wet as his hair. I watch as his back muscles extend and stretch as he works. Who knew mowing grass could be so hot?

When he nears the fence, he turns to head back toward the house. As he turns, his gaze meets mine and he gives me a glorious smile. I let out a deep sigh. With my heart beating in my throat, I return it with one of my own. We can do this. We can get through this.

He kills the mower right then and there and starts making his way toward me. I watch as the boys' dog, Shaggy, enthusiastically greets him by jumping on his leg and trying to lick him in the face. Adrian rubs him down and coos at him for a minute, simultaneously delaying my curiosity and prolonging my pain. I'm loath to have this conversation, but I'm also dying to get it over with.

I swallow hard and move toward the patio table. This is good. This is our ritual. Every other Saturday, Adrian brings us coffee, and we sit and enjoy it while he takes a break. This is, however, our first time since I attacked him. I cringe and not just a little.

"Mornin'." His liquid voice exudes the word. He has that accent that I find incredibly attractive—that delicious mix of southern and Creole.

"Good morning," I reply. My own voice sounds raspy. I try to clear my throat quietly.

I sit down and motion for him to join me. As I reach to hand him his iced coffee, his hand darts out and our hands come to rest on the cup at the same time. My hand is under his so I can't jerk it away like I want when I feel the little jolt of energy bolt its way through me. This is bad. Very bad. I'd always had that forcibly dormant attraction to him, but now that I've tasted him and felt him, I doubt my ability to force it into a state of lifelessness again.

Ever so slowly Adrian's eyes work their way up my hand, my arm, my neck until his eyes meet mine, practically leaving the path to my face a smoldering cinder. Finally, he slowly removes his hand, releasing me. His next words seem to have to punch their way out of him. "This is why I'm here. We need to talk."

I nod my head and agree, "You're right. We do need to talk. I'm so embarrassed about last night. I—"

He quickly cuts me off. "I need to explain something to you," he says and shifts in his chair minutely. "Something I think you are aware of now, at least partially. I don't want us to be embarrassed by it. It is what it is. And we can either let it ruin us or let it make us stronger. I vote for stronger because I can't imagine my life without you or the boys."

A vice tightens around my heart and my eyes fill with tears. I vote for stronger too, but can I be stronger? I look down and arrange myself in my chair. He's giving me a moment to collect myself. After a minute, I look over at him and murmur, "I don't want to ruin us either."

"Good," he replies immediately. "I think you figured out last night that I'm attracted to you. As in really attracted to you." My mind starts to race. *He's attracted to me? Really attracted? And since when?* He seems to read my mind because he starts answering all my questions, even ones that haven't fully formed. "I have been since the first time we met. I was relieved beyond belief that you never seemed to clue in to that. I kinda consider myself a great actor now," he brags with a chuckle. I love the way the skin around his eyes crinkles when he smiles. "Three years of pretending that I didn't want you...it nearly killed me." His profession nearly kills *me*. "Last night, when you reached out, I shouldn't have kissed you back. It was wrong of me and I'm sorry. I think you're attracted to me too, but I also think that we'd be crazy to act on it any more than we already have. My family...well, our family, would make things... umm...difficult, to say the least, if they ever found out. I just can't risk that. I can't risk losing y'all."

Three years I've known him. I've never heard him say so much at one time, especially unsolicited. Suddenly realizing my mouth is agape, I snap it shut. I don't know how long I am entranced, but entranced I am. I shake my head a little to clear my stupor. "Adrian—" I begin.

He cuts me off again. "Celeste, I'm begging you not to kick me out of your lives. I'm not too proud where y'all are concerned because I don't know what I'd do without you. Can you forgive me? Forget about last night?"

"I don't think I can forget, Adrian," I tell him honestly.

Blowing out a breath, he sits back and folds his arms behind his head. "I was afraid of that. Do you need time apart from me? I'll do whatever you want. I just don't want it to be permanent."

I consider exactly how truthful I should be with him. He was so truthful with me. I owe him that much, don't I? "Adrian, I don't need time apart. You're my friend and you're amazing with the boys. They love you. I would never deny them your presence. I just...I just need us to get back to normal as quickly as possible. I...I am attracted to you. I have been for a while. But that's all it is—a physical attraction." On these words, I see his eyes narrow ever so slightly. I turn my head quickly and vow, "But I promise to control myself." I allow my eyes to find his again. "I don't want to lose you either."

He studies me for a minute. Just as I find myself about to squirm under his intense gaze, he releases me. "OK, Celeste, that settles that. Back to normal. We'll both behave. This physical thing between us will pass. No harm, no foul. Right?"

"Right," I say with a smile.

Standing up, he turns to go back to his mowing, but then he spins around and comes back to tower over me. My head flies up, my gaze searching. I open my mouth to ask him what's wrong, but he beats me once again.

"Celeste, just so you know," he says as he tilts my chin back further and runs his calloused fingertips up my cheek to tuck a strand of errant hair behind my ear. His hand fits itself along my jaw. "That kiss...that kiss was exceptional, and I'll never forget it. As I stand here and as long as I live, it was the best I've ever had, the best I could ever have."

Since my heart has lodged itself firmly in my throat, he's gone before I can speak or even form a coherent thought for that matter. Slowly, I shake my head at his retreating back. We'll never get back to normal if he keeps touching me and talking to me like that.

-Three-

It's Just Physical

"I CAN'T BELIEVE you called me over here after the night I had," Bonnie complains as she slams my door.

"And good morning to you," I say happily as I wrap up my latest blog post.

"Are you working?" She says this like one would ask, *"Are you crazy?"*

Rolling my eyes at her endearing theatrics, I respond with not a little sarcasm, "Um...yes, dear. Why is that so surprising?"

She flings herself and her oversized purse onto my perfectly arranged cushioned couch, bringing my attention to the crystal blue pattern on the pillows which immediately remind me of a set of gorgeous troubled eyes. I jump up to get us some refreshments. "Oh, right!" she yells after me. "You left early. Girl, you have no idea how Bourbon Street was jumping last night. I haven't seen it that crazy in forever. I really wish you would've stuck around. I can't remember the last time I've drunk that much. I was in rare form."

I snicker. When she drinks, she's not that far off from her regular personality. Just a little louder about it. "It's been a long while since we've been out," I remind her. I make my way back into the living room with our drinks.

"Thanks," she replies skeptically as she squints at her water. "What the hell is floating in my water?"

"Cucumber slices," I say with a shrug.

"Who puts cucumber slices in their water?"

"I do," I reply with a smirk. "Just shut up and drink it. It's delicious."

"Yeah, it's been too damn long since we've been out. I think guys have morphed into more macho, more badass versions of themselves. Geez, did you get a look at the Dog Tags' drummer last night? You think Adrian can introduce me?"

"To Garner?"

"Is that the drummer's name?" I nod. "Yeah, him."

"I don't know. Are you gonna let the ink dry?" I ask her with a quirked eyebrow.

"Pssh...we've been separated for years. The papers were just a formality."

I frown at myself. "I know. I'm so sorry. That was rude of me. I know how torn up you were over your marriage ending."

She waves a hand at me. "It's all good. I know you didn't mean it like that."

"I really didn't. Let me pose that question a little more delicately—do you think you're ready to date?"

"Yes, honey. I'm ready to date; however, I'm not looking for anything more than a good time, which is why that drummer is perfect."

Sudden laughter bubbles out of me with that statement. She's looking for something fun, not something serious. I totally get that. Wouldn't ever seriously act on that impulse myself—but totally get it. Last night doesn't count because it wasn't pre-meditated. *Time to get rid of this*, I think. "I did something stupid last night," I confess.

Giving me an inquiring look, Bonnie angles her head ever so slightly. "This doesn't have anything to do with Adrian, does it?"

She knows me so well, too well. "What do you mean? Why

would you say that?"

"Well, just before the band was headed back to the stage, Adrian asked me to go check on you. I told him you messaged me that you were leaving in a cab." She narrows her eyes at me, assessing me. "And he seemed kinda pissed."

"What?" I gasp.

"Yeah, he told me," she drops her voice an octave or two and throws her hands up in air quotes, "'I should've fucking known better.' I didn't get it, and when I tried to question him about it, he told me not to worry and that he would check on you tomorrow."

"Hmm...well," I take a deep breath, roll my shoulders, and begin, "I guess he was pissed because he kissed me."

"He what?" she practically shrieks.

"Technically, I kissed him first, but he took my simple, spur-of-the-moment kiss and turned it into something entirely different; and now he's mad at himself about it because he's full of regret and fear."

Bonnie just stares at me with her mouth open for a moment. She looks over at my arrangement of photos for a couple of beats and finally looks back at me. "Are you freaking kidding me? You kissed Adrian 'freakishly amazingly beautiful, broody, black sheep, I could take your clothes off without ever moving a muscle' Hebert, and then he kissed you back?"

"Yes."

"Screw the monosyllabic answers, Celeste. I want every single, solitary detail. Be very, *very* specific. Specificity is the name of the game here, understand?"

"Yes, Bonnie, I understand. I wouldn't dare leave out one single detail for fear that you would hack into my computer and give me, all my fellow bloggers, and all our faithful followers viruses of Homeric proportions." I then proceed to tell her every sordid detail of my little back porch tryst with Adrian. The irony is not lost on me that this is definitely a first: she was always the one entertaining me with her antics when we were in college.

"So," I sum up, "it was obvious that he regretted it and tried to console me then and there. I wouldn't let him. How could I? I'd just had the most amazing kiss of my life. And he's been so wonderful to me and the boys. He's been there for us like no one else, Bon, and I can't imagine my life without him." I shake my head and groan a little. "I lied to him, Bonnie. Told him that I'd had too much to drink and that I'd been feeling lonely. That's not like me, but I was afraid if he knew how much I wanted him we wouldn't have stopped. And that would be a mistake...a huge mistake."

Bonnie hadn't moved a muscle during my detailed, vivid description of my little exploit. Now, she focuses her eyes on me and that never fails to scare me. *Oh, no!* I'm in trouble. She has an uncanny ability to see beyond words, beyond composure to read your exact thoughts, sometimes reading thoughts you hadn't even fully realized yourself. She's excellent at this with everyone. She's a master with me. "Celeste," she says my name so seriously it scares me a little as does the fact that she's grabbed my hand, "you're in love with him."

"Wh...What?" I stutter and give a high-pitched giggle. "No. No, I'm not. I told you it's just physical. Purely physical. And I can control my actions from here on out. I just needed to get it off my chest. That is the only confession I'm making here. I'm *not* professing my love for him."

"You don't have to profess it, sweetheart." Her voice is sugary sweet, meaning she's not buying a word of what I'm saying. "It's written all over you. It was tangible with every word that you just uttered."

Her words give me pause. Am I in love with Adrian? He's amazing. He's pure hearted. He's gorgeous. It's true I do love him but as a friend, and I can't picture us having a relationship. It would never work. I shake my head at her. "Look, I know you're typically an expert on how I feel, but you've got it all wrong this time. I'm attracted to him, but I'm not in love with Adrian. I love him, yes, but as a friend, not romantically or whatever." My hand punctuates this stance with a careless wave.

"No, darlin'. That's how you felt about Tripp."

I snap back like she just slapped me. "No," I state.

"Yes," she insists, "you made the best out of an arranged marriage."

My voice snaps like a whip with indignation. "I was not in an arranged marriage!"

"Maybe not in the strictest sense of the concept, but I can't think of anything closer. You knew from the time that you were old enough to know what marriage was that you were expected to marry Tripp, did you not?"

"Yes," I mumble.

She doesn't let me off the hook. "You weren't in love with Tripp, Celeste. You married him because that was what was expected of you." Her voice gentles. "Tell me I'm wrong."

"Don't say we didn't have love. We had love," I protest weakly.

"You had a lovely respect, which was respectfully lovely; however, you didn't have a love like married couples are supposed to have, Celeste."

"If I admit that, it's like admitting my children weren't formed out of love, Bonnie. I can't do that."

"Fine. I'll rephrase—you did love him, but you loved him like a friend. Your friendship with Tripp was unbelievably wonderful, and he was a good guy. But neither of you were in love with one another. I think you know that deep down. I think that's why you slept with Scott during college even though you knew it couldn't go anywhere since you were practically betrothed to Tripp. You had the hots for him and it could've been more if you'd let yourself explore it. You knew you'd never feel that way for Tripp, so you reached out and experienced that little bit of passion before settling in with Tripp."

Holy shit! This woman! My mouth forms a tight line and I give a little shake of my head. I tsk, "You're right, Bonnie, about everything—except for your misguided insight into my feelings for Adrian. It really is just a physical thing."

The cat that ate the canary, she grins slyly at me and asserts,

"Famous last words..."

"Seriously. Drop it."

"If it's only physical, why don't you get it out of your system?" she challenges.

"Umm...that would not be a smart path to pursue. You know as well as I do what happens when you complicate relationships with sex. Besides, we couldn't be together even if we wanted to."

"And why on earth not? You're both consenting adults. You've both been in relationships and are mature and would treat each other with respect."

"One word—family. Tripp's family would not tolerate that. They would make things difficult for my family. It would be bad all the way around."

Bonnie purses her lips for a moment before asking, "Why would they care? Who would y'all hurt?"

"They would care because of who his father is. It may not make sense, but that's the way they operate. Adrian is finally working his way back into the family fold and sleeping with me is a surefire way to get him compared to his father and ostracized further. I wouldn't put that on him. They're finally starting to accept him, and I know that's something he wants. That's the whole reason behind his reaching out to Tripp a few years back."

"Ah...You never really went into detail on that."

"Well, it's important to him. Even though he wants nothing to do with the family business, he wants to know his family, and when he decides to have his own, he wants his children to know their heritage. So Tripp stepped in and championed him to get the family to open up to him. Adrian's done the rest on his own, though."

"So why not a little hidden affair? No one would be the wiser except for me. You know I would keep my mouth shut."

A cynical laugh escapes before I can control it, and I roll my eyes at her ridiculousness. "Umm...did we just meet? Because you know my family. Hiding anything in my family is as far-fetched as an Oasis reunion tour. Shoot...my family makes the Ewings look like the Cleavers."

Bonnie has the nerve to freaking chuckle at me. Like I'm over-exaggerating or something! "You're so right, girl! What was I thinking? Why would they care, though?"

"They care about everything that has anything to do with image and public opinion."

She leans in and stares me down. "I know you've been programmed not to question your family, Celeste, but they shouldn't be in charge of your entire life. And I know there's a little rebellion hiding in there, girl!"

That's because questions could end you. "Me? Rebellious? You've known me since we were eight. When have I ever been rebellious?"

She ticks her fingers off as she counts the ways. "I've already offered Scott as exhibit A. Exhibit B I don't see any little Charles Andrew Hebert the effin' fourth running around here—not one of your kids has a pretentious name. C, you drive a freakin' red MINI with racing stripes and three kids in tow. D, Rock 'N' Roll blares out of your speakers when you're in that overly priced private school pick up line, and…I forgot what letter I was on, anyway, you weren't just a little trophy wife. You've made your own way on your own terms."

Well, damn, when she puts it that way, I guess I have been a little rebellious. "Trophy wife? Me? You know what that term means, don't you?"

"Get over it; you're gorgeous! Everyone knows it, and you should too."

"I'm not ugly; I know that. We'll just leave it at that, all right?"

Her tone becomes dreamy as she insists, "Celeste, you're young and beautiful. You had to deal with one of the most excruciating things a person, a wife could ever have to deal with. I can't even imagine standing by and watching someone you care about being eaten away by cancer and that rapidly. But, as usual, you put your-self aside and did everything you could for him and for your family.

If anyone deserves to have a little fun and get what they want in the meantime, it's you. You need a little adventure—"

Ready to end this conversation, I throw her my Hail Mary of protests, "He's not even thirty years old, Bonnie!"

"So...how old is he exactly?"

"Um...that doesn't matter! He's not even thirty and I'm thirty-seven. Hello? Freakin' cougar, anyone?"

She rolls her eyes at me. "Cougars are old bitches with leathery skin, lips like an overinflated raft, and a plastic surgeon on speed dial. Your mother? Perfect cougar material." I laugh, thinking we have changed the subject. I should've known better. She asks between her teeth, "How old is he exactly?"

"He's twenty-nine," I mutter petulantly.

Her laughter causes my eyes to cut over to her swiftly. "When's he gonna be thirty?"

"Not for several months."

She throws her hands out as if sensing victory. "So, y'all are eight years apart. That is NOT a big deal, especially when you're in your thirties."

"Which. He. Is. Not. And it *is* a big deal when you're a woman, and he is younger than you, and he is surrounded by gorgeous, conscienceless women who he could take home any time of any day."

"So is that the real problem? Is he a womanizer?"

I scrunch my face up in protest. "No, he's not a womanizer. I haven't even seen him with a woman since he's been home."

"Really? Sounds like someone else is pining away..."

"No, no, no, no. When we talked on the porch this morning, it was obvious that it's only a physical attraction for both of us." At her raised eyebrow, I concede a little, "Strong attraction—we are strongly attracted to one another. His exact words were that he was *really* attracted to me." She gives me a knowing glare and an even more knowing grin. "Shoot! What am I supposed to do with that? What do I even say to that?" My voice gets higher with each word.

"Well, what did you say?"

"Nothing. Absolutely nothing." I shake my head a little, remembering. "And when he tucked a piece of my hair behind my ear... mmm..." I mentally shiver. "It's obvious that I'm in real trouble."

She sits back and drapes her arms across my pillows. "Yep. A lot of things are real obvious right about now."

An Offer I Can't Refuse

IT WOULD HAVE been much easier to resist my Adrian-fueled impure thoughts if he wasn't such a mass of contradictions because those very contradictions were what made him so unbelievably intriguing to me. On the one hand, he was macho and reserved. On the other, he talked to me like there wasn't anything he wouldn't ever tell me and played with the boys like he needed that as much as he needed his next breath.

Having been a performer since a young age, he was adept at making music, partying with the guys, fending off the girls, or sometimes not fending off the girls. *Just the thought of that makes me cringe.* Yet, contrary to all that, he was perfectly content to spend a quiet evening at my house watching movies with the boys and me or to load us all up and go hit baseballs at the batting cages and eat tons of ice cream afterward.

It was almost as if, despite all the things I was supposed to hold against him, he was the perfect man. In my world, the ideal man was supposed to wear suits, argue in courtrooms, and have brandy after dinner while playing a gentleman's game of cards. They didn't attend football games for fun. They didn't eat hotdogs with gusto. And they certainly didn't throw little boys around in the air and give them rides on their shoulders.

All of that and more—that was Adrian. A mass of endearing contradictions, a direct affront to the way both he and I were reared.

We had settled back into a nice little routine. He and the boys and I did practically everything together. Anything I needed, the boys needed, he handled it. Not only did he handle it but also relished in it. I was attached—real attached—to the way he took care of us and cared for us. Craving his presence, his wisdom I never thought to distance myself from him.

I even started going out with him and his band more and more. Bonnie and her drummer, which is what she usually calls him, had long since been dating. They are actually really good together. I'm starting to wonder if she's realized that they had passed the point of just having a little bit of fun about fifty dates ago.

The first night Adrian showed up with his eye-candy was the first night I started to question our little arrangement because feelings of jealousy instantly consumed me. From the second I saw his arm around her shoulders, I wanted to rip the bleach-blonde hair right out of her head. Then, she spoke to me. I realized very quickly that eye-candy about covered all that she was good for. She was completely self-absorbed and fake and vapid. Adrian had to be dating her just to date her. Yes, those are the verbs of my choosing. I don't want to consider any of their other activities. I only had to see *her* once; however, he started to "date" carbon copies of her every weekend thereafter. I couldn't believe that was his type. To each his own, I guess.

After a couple of months of living this safe, enjoyable routine, you can imagine how shocking I found the next series of events.

I'D BEEN SUMMONED to my father's office, which makes me apprehensive as the only two times he's ever asked to see me here were unwelcomed announcements and proclamations. Even though both had been while I was in college, they were firmly entrenched in my memory. The first was to tell me that my dog, Settler, had to be put down due to old age and many debilitating problems. The second, well, was to tell me to quit fooling around with Scott. The first broke my heart. The second humiliated me.

Having no idea what to expect from my father, I dressed to the nines. My crisp linen navy blue sheath dress was topped by my pinstriped high cut, long-sleeved shrug of the same material. I had on my nude Louis Vuitton with the three-inch heels. I'd perfectly coifed my hair and my make-up was flawless; I looked beautiful and powerful but felt everything but that. Like a piece of petrified wood wondering what happenstance would come along to tote it away, I had my hands folded on my lap and sat straight up in my chair with my legs crossed at the ankles. My back is nowhere near touching the leather chair in the illustrious and legendary law offices of Hebert & Hebert.

As I am sitting here wondering what fresh hell my father has to bestow upon me, my second-most feared father figure waltzes in and walks straight to me. I crane my neck to see him because he doesn't give me enough room to stand up. No big surprise here. I think he does it to intimidate me.

"Ah, my favorite daughter-in-law. How are you, Celeste?" Chip Hebert asks me. I stare up at his chiseled good looks and wonder how his wife, Patrice, didn't see past all that for about the billionth time.

"I'm good," I respond.

"The boys? Eating you out of house and home yet?"

"They're doing well. And yes, eating anything that stands still long enough." He chuckles at that and brushes a lock of hair from my shoulder. It takes everything I've got to suppress a repulsive shudder.

"Ms. Hebert, Mr. Hebert will see you now." Saved by my father's secretary and not for the first time.

"Excuse me, Chip. Can't keep my father waiting," I state. Finally, he gives me the space to stand up, and I will myself to meet his eyes as I rise. Capable of smelling fear, I'm determined not to let my dear old father-in-law sense mine.

"Good to see you, Celeste. Will I see you in the country this weekend?"

"Of course, see you then," I return. As I pass Gladys, I give her a tight smile; and she gives me one decisive nod.

Closing the double doors behind me as I enter my father's massive office, I allow my eyes to graze over the plaques, pictures, and Navy paraphernalia. My father—so decorated. As was Tripp's for that matter. This was how they met. Two Heberts far from home, almost identical Naval careers. The name Hebert was like Smith around these parts, but everywhere else it was a rarity. This was how they'd bonded and how they'd groomed their younger brothers and eventually their sons. The only one it didn't take with was Adrian's father. Oh, he'd gone through all the motions—college, law school, Jag Corps, respectable practice back home in New Orleans. However, along his path, he'd left a trail of debauchery, debt, and devious undertakings. That was not to say that Tripp's father and mine had not indulged in nefarious deeds. No, they were just quiet about it, making them all the more dangerous.

"Celeste, thank you for coming by," my father says. *Like I had a choice*, I think.

"Of course, Daddy. How are you?" I smile brilliantly.

"I'm doing well. Your mother has me on a new diet, though, so I'm starving," he says with a chuckle.

"Well, you're certainly looking fit," I tell him.

"How is Archer?" My father always starts with the oldest first.

"Archer is doing well. His grades were terrific last year. Seventh grade," I say with a disbelieving shake of my head. "He got picked up for the fall baseball league. Oh, and he's decided he wants to be a nuclear physicist."

My father's eyes widen at this. "No law school?"

"I'm sure he'll come around; he's only twelve," I say with a slight smile.

"Paris?"

"He's fantastic. Just got a new turtle, who he's dubbed Skip. Of course, no one knows quite why that is." I smile at the thought of my nine-year-old's eccentric nature.

"And Finn?"

"Finn." I chuckle a little. "Finn is great. He is bound and determined to follow in his father's footsteps. He's playing first-string quarterback in his recreational league. All boy, that one."

"Ah. Good, good. And how is mom doing?"

"I'm doing well." I briefly considered telling him about my latest news with all the photo shoots being booked at the house and my design advice being sought after but quickly decide against it. He hates talk of all that.

"Well, that's good. I'm not going to beat around the bush, Celeste." I brace upon hearing these words. "We've decided that it's time you brought a father figure into the boys' lives."

My heart beats triple time while I ponder exactly how to handle this with poise and not let myself get railroaded. "Daddy, I'm not really ready for that. I haven't met anyone I'm interested in—"

"You don't need to meet anyone. Chip and I've decided we'd like for you to consider William."

"What?" I blanch. "William is married, and he's Tripp's brother. Don't you think that's a little strange? Even for us?"

"Not at all. What do you mean 'even for us'? There's no blood between us. Anyway, we're allowing William to divorce Vanessa since she had an affair and there are no children involved. William is your age, and he's expressed an interest."

I feel my face wrinkle due to the fact that I am not and have never been attracted to William in the slightest. As a matter of fact, I find him repulsive. "Daddy, I'm not marrying William," I state.

"Young lady, you'll do what is requested of you. Or have you forgotten your upbringing?" I open my mouth to speak, but he cuts me off. "I would appreciate it very much if you at least considered him. It would be perfect to have an Hebert rearing my grandsons and teaching them how loyalty and honor are valued in this family."

"I'm an Hebert, Daddy," I remind him.

He gives a condescending laugh at my little insistence. "A man, Celeste. A man Hebert."

"Of course, Daddy. Would it be too much to ask for some time to consider this request?" *And to consider a way to get out of this.*

He pauses and takes me in for a moment, his gaze searching. "Not at all. It really is a request, Celeste. If you were to meet someone say in the next few weeks and show some interest, we may be able to leave it at that." He raises his eyebrows at me slightly and reaches for a file on his desk. I've been dismissed.

An about-face? My father is offering me an out. This is unheard of. Does he not want the merger either?

I say my goodbyes to my father and his secretary. My legs are trembling as I enter the elevator and make my way across the expansive lobby to enter the parking garage, but otherwise I'm pretty sure I'm covering well. *Almost there, almost there*, I chant as I see my MINI in the midst of all the dark SUVs.

When I get into my car, I take a deep breath, but it doesn't help, I immediately start bawling. If those two Heberts wanted something, nothing would stop them. It was why we had more money than God. It was why I'd married Tripp in the first place. It was how I'd had three boys. One would think that would be uncontrollable, but not so much. It was why I knew I was screwed if I didn't find interest in someone posthaste.

I FIND MYSELF sitting outside of Bonnie's townhome. Having a few hours before I had to pick up the boys from school, I blew off all of my other errands, figuring a new, undesired betrothal was a good reason to hit up my best friend.

Knocking on the door, I'm caught off guard by Garner. "Oh! Hey, Garner! I didn't realize you'd be here. I can come back if I'm interrupting."

"Nah, Celeste. It's all good, girl. Bonnie's throwing some clothes on. She'll be right down. I was just about to head out."

Oh, yes. They had rehearsals shortly. "Right. Well, how are things going?"

"Good. We've been learning some new material, gearing up for our big show. It's crazy. We're about to play the House of Blues."

His enthusiasm is catching. "I'm so excited for y'all. I think this is going to be great for the band. You guys are going to get some offers—I just know it."

"I hope so. This is all I've ever wanted." I envy his passion. I smile at him as Bonnie makes her way down to us. She's beaming as well.

"Good afternoon," I tell her with a raised brow. "How are you?"

"I'm great," she practically purrs as she places a full-fledged kiss on Garner's lips. He grabs her hips and grinds his into hers, simulating what I'm sure I just missed. Directing my eyes to the ceiling, I start mentally arranging my balcony for tomorrow's photo shoot.

"Hey, Celeste!" Bonnie calls. "I'm walking the drummer out. I'll be right back."

"OK. Sure thing. Bye, Garner. Good to see you!"

"Yep, you—" he tries to say goodbye as Bonnie playfully bites his neck while directing him to the front door. I chuckle at their fervor for each other. I'm ecstatic to finally see it being reciprocated for Bonnie's sake. Her ex-husband was one cold fish. I make myself comfortable by slipping off my shoes, making myself a glass of iced tea, and curling up on her sofa with my iPhone and my design app.

I hear the door slam, and I lock my phone, placing it on the coffee table. "What are you doing here in the middle of the day, Celeste? What's wrong?"

"It's bad," I tell her.

"What do those asswads want this time?" I blink real slow and grin.

"How'd you know?"

"There are only two people who can upset you this much."

"And I thought I was hiding it so well."

"No way, babe. Spill!"

I recount my conversation with the Fathers Hebert. She seethes and shakes her head almost the whole time. I get more and more animated as I go, talking with my hands, pacing the room. When I stop, she just asks, "What the hell are you gonna do?"

"I don't know. I'm...I'm—"

"Good Lord, Celeste, if there was ever a time to say the fucking *f* word, it's now."

"I'm fucked." I say stoically. "I'm so fucked!" I shriek.

"Thank God!"

Chuckling, I ask, "Don't you think it's a little odd to thank God for my saying the *f* word?"

"Nope, not at all. It helps a lot. And you need a lotta help."

"I know, I know," I say as I stop to stand in front of her French doors, crossing my arms over my middle.

"Can you just tell them no for once? Put your foot down?"

"Not only will they trample all over my foot. They'll trample all over my whole life. My boys' lives. I've watched them do it, Bon. It's gruesome."

"Geez. It's like they're some kinda corporate mafi—"

I spin and pin her with a look. "Right, we don't say that word. Sorry," she mutters petulantly. They are exactly that, which is why we don't say it. Silent tears start to make their way down my cheeks. I didn't want to cry again, but I really was at a loss.

"Oh, baby girl," she coos. "We'll figure something out. You've

30

got plenty of money, right? You're not dependent on them in that way."

"The money is the least of my issues, but, yes, I do have plenty of it in my own right."

"I have the perfect solution. I know who you can marry, and," she says stretching out the word 'and,' "you're in love with him already."

"Not this again," I mutter as I rest my head in both my hands.

"I've been watching you two. Y'all have it so bad for each other."

"OK," I slap my knees with force, wincing. "This conversation just ceased being helpful. I have a few things to do before going to get the boys, so I'll see you later."

She rolls her eyes at me. "You're an idiot, ma belle amie."

"Yes, I know. You know how I know? 'Cause you've told me about a billion times over the past couple of months," I state acerbically.

"Oh, oh! So touchy. Me thinks thou protests too much." She has the audacity to giggle at me.

I quirk my eyebrow at her and look down my nose at her as I calmly state, "Me thinks you forget who I'm related to. It's there under this calm façade. Don't push me," I warn her.

She throws her hands up in mock protest, "Oh, yes, ma'am. Princess of the maf—" She cuts herself off at my look. "I'm done," she concedes.

-Five-

My World Shifts

THE BOYS AND I arrive home after guitar lessons, MMA lessons, and French lessons— Archer, Paris, and Finn respectively. I'm utterly spent, but I paste a smile on my face because Adrian is here with pizza and a movie. It's my favorite day of the week. Well, it was until the Disastrous Duo struck.

"Hey, Adrian!" Finn shouts as we clear the door.

"What's up, Adrian," Archer gives him a chin lift as he makes his way to feed the dogs.

"Hi, Adrian," Paris mutters before going to check on Skip.

"Finn, he's four feet away, son," I half-heartedly chastise him, getting exactly why he's so excited—Adrian's just awesome like that.

"Hey, bud," Adrian returns with a fist bump. "How was school?"

"Sucked," Finn replies flippantly.

"Really, Finn," I try. "We've talked about this word. I *loathe* this word."

"I know, Mom." He scrambles onto a barstool and slaps himself on both cheeks, resting his head in his palms. "But everybody says it."

I open my mouth to give him the-everybody-does-it-so-does-that-mean-you-have-to do-it-too speech, but Adrian puts his finger up, motioning for me to let him give it a shot.

"All right, bud." Adrian leans across the bar on his elbows, and it takes the willpower of a hundred nuns not to check out his nice, tight butt. I'm thoroughly impressed with myself and my ability to resist—for the most part. "So here's how it goes—girls don't like ugly words like that. It makes you look like a jerk when you say those things in front of them. Girls like gentlemen. Do you hear me say those kinda words in front of your mom?"

"No, sir." Finn snaps to attention.

"That's 'cause I save 'em all up and let 'em loose when I'm with the guys," he reasons. I had been grinning ear to ear, but my mouth falls slack upon that piece of handy advice. Adrian turns to me and winks and grins like he's just figured out how to solve world hunger.

My mouth closes and tilts to a half-smile of its own accord. "You were on a roll for a minute there, Adrian."

He just chuckles and turns back to Finn, "All right, so do we have a deal? Don't talk like that around moms and girls and stuff. Save it for the locker room."

Finn wrinkles his face up and states seriously, "I don't have a locker room."

"It's a figure of speech, bud. But you get me, right?"

Finn jumps off his stool, squares off and gives Adrian a salute. "Yes, sir, Adrian, sir!"

Adrian leans in and ruffles his wavy dark brown hair, "At ease, Marine." My father would die.

"Finn, go wash up, please."

"Yes, ma'am," he yells with a sprint to the bathroom.

"Man, that kid has got some energy, huh?"

"Yes, he does."

His glacial blue eyes meet mine, and I forget what we were talking about when he abruptly changes gears on me. "What's wrong with Paris?"

"You noticed that, huh?" I take a sharp breath, debating whether or not to tell him what Paris told me on the drive home.

"Yep, so what's going on?"

I look around to make sure there are no little ears lurking. Seeing the coast is clear, I confess, "He's upset because some jerks at school keep calling him 'gay,' and he hates it."

"Kids can be fucking assholes," he states sagely.

"No kidding," I agree. "But I thought we didn't talk that way in front of girls," I joke, trying to lighten the mood. My hand twitches to smack him playfully because I'm a touchy-feely kind of girl, but I fight the urge. I haven't touched him since the morning of the talk.

"Sorry about that," he says but doesn't sound sorry. "It was called for, though. I fuckin' hate a pussy bully," he says as if to prove his point for the need for profanity.

"Well, OK then," I quip. "Please don't use that kind of language in front of the boys, Adrian."

"Babe," he says flatly with a raised brow.

"Yes?"

"Babe." Same tone. "Really."

"Fine. I get it. You don't talk like that in front of the boys."

"Sure as hell don't."

I chuckle, "All righty then. Did ya get it all out of your system?"

He throws his head back and replies, "Yes, ma'am," with a laugh. Mesmerized, I watch as he runs his hand over his scruff and looks slightly contrite. "I got your favorite," he tells me, trying to distract me. It works. I'm starved.

"Oh, thanks!" I snatch the box from him, snap the lid open, and inhale deeply.

"I don't know how you eat that crap," he says with disdain as he starts to pour ranch dressing all over his pizza.

"I don't know how you eat *that* crap," I retort, eyeing his ranch-saturated pizza. "That's disgusting."

"Ranch makes everything better," he says.

"Hmm…" I direct my attention back to my pizza. "Mmm…it

smells so good." I moan and close my eyes as I take another deep breath. My eyes fly open as I realize what that just sounded like, and I chance another look at him. His face is frozen with a look that can only be described as heated and hungry. My mouth goes dry and I pull my lips in to moisten them with my tongue, which makes me think of his mouth, which makes my eyes dart to his mouth. I try to pull my eyes away and make a joke or something, anything, but I seriously cannot. You could literally hear a pin drop in my kitchen right about now, and there's nothing I can do about it. All I can think about is how amazing his scruff would feel against my soft skin and how wet his full lips would make mine.

Before either of us can do anything stupid, I hear a snappy little bark as Ruby bounds in the kitchen. She deftly avoids Adrian's ankles as she makes a beeline for me. I jerk out of my stupor and exclaim, "Hey, baby girl," louder than I normally would. Saved by my Maltese. *Thank you, Ruby.* "There's my pretty girl," I coo as I scoop her up and cuddle her in my arms. She tries to lick my face but settles for my throat as I throw my neck back in an effort to escape her wet tongue. I try, I really do, not to look at Adrian but can't resist a quick peek. He's staring at my throat like he wishes it were him doing the licking. *Oh, how I wish it too, Adrian.*

After our pizza and movie, Adrian picks up a comatose Finn to tote him to his bed. Plays hard, crashes hard. That's my Finn. I smile at the sight of him cradled on Adrian's shoulder so lovingly. Feeling a fissure run through my heart and quick tears spring to my eyes, I quickly avert my face and rustle up Archer and Paris.

Following Paris to his room, I tell Archer I'll be right there to tuck him in.

"I got Paris tonight, Cel," Adrian decrees.

"All right. Give me a kiss, Paris," I tell him as he scuttles back to lay one on me. "Muah!" I smack loudly. "Love you, sweetness."

"Love you too, Ma," he tells me.

After I get Archer tucked away and check on Finn, I make my way into the kitchen to tidy up real quick. Adrian enters the kitchen not long after me with a huge grin on his face.

I can't help but smile back. "What?" I ask him around my smile.

"That kid. He's an old soul." His eyes gleam with admiration of my Paris.

"I know, right? He's pretty amazing."

"They're all pretty amazing," he finishes. Another fissure. *How could I not love someone who loves my kids so much?* I startle at that thought.

"Well, all is done here, I'm gonna head to bed. Want me to walk you out?" He grabs his stuff and gives me a nod.

As we're walking to the door, Adrian is filling me in on his upcoming gigs and plans for the next few weeks. I'm trying to focus on what he's saying, but, suddenly, my stomach is wreaking havoc on my entire body. My hands and face are instantly clammy, yet I feel like I'm burning up. When my stomach clenches in a most vicious way, I know this is not going to be pretty.

Adrian turns toward me as he reaches the door, and his eyes register his shock at what I can only imagine he sees written all over my face. "Celeste—"

I throw my hand up at him, spin, and make a mad dash for the closest bathroom. His following closely on my heels registers slightly as I consider how horrifying this moment is about to be, but I have absolutely no control over my body right now. I fling the toilet lid up, and the contents of my stomach violently eject themselves. I feel my hair being swept off my shoulders and know that Adrian is holding it in a makeshift ponytail for me. *That's incredibly sweet and incredibly embarrassing*, I think. This is not a quick purge. This is violent, unrelenting heaving.

After what seems like forever has passed, my stomach shows some mercy on me and seems to settle. Adrian runs his hand up and down my back for a minute. Then I feel him reach for a washcloth. He never releases my hair as he wets it and then places it on my brow. "Cel, geez, baby. It's that shit pizza you love. I tried to tell you not to eat that crap."

My stomach pinches upon hearing his endearment. He hasn't called me that in a while—two months to be exact. He's right. Spinach, mushrooms, artichokes, and alfredo sauce taste delicious going down. Not so much going in the other direction. "It must have been, but it's never made me sick before. You don't feel ill do you?" I say weakly.

"No, come on let's get you to bed."

We make our way into my bedroom, and he helps me ready my toothbrush. "Thank you so much, Adrian," I tell him. "I think I've got it from here."

"I'll just stay for a little while and make sure you're good, all right?"

"No, really. I'm fine now," I insist. I would prefer to put this memory to bed as quickly as possible even though he's being so gracious.

"What if one of the boys wakes up sick and you're too sick to help them?" he asks. "Just let me stay and make sure y'all are good."

He has a point. "OK, thank you," I grimace as I feel my stomach clench painfully again. This trip to the toilet isn't nearly as long, but it's still just as humiliating.

Making a move toward getting up, I feel myself being lifted in the air. I want to protest, but I can't muster the strength. Instead, I relish his carrying me. I bury my face in his shirt and breathe deeply and feel him shudder against me. I can't believe I just did that! I have no shame where he's concerned.

I feel Adrian scoot onto the bed and prop himself against my headboard. Nuzzling into his lap, I promptly pass out.

AFTER MONTHS OF seeing Adrian with the Buxom Blonde

Brigade, you can imagine my shock at seeing him with what could be a carbon copy of a certain wavy black-haired widow.

We're attending my favorite party of the year—the firm's annual Make-A-Wish Soiree. It's a charity that has always been close to my heart; I've always thrown my all into making it a successful event. All of the who's who in the law field attend and we raise a ton of money.

Enjoying myself and greeting newcomers with Farah, my second in command, I chat and direct them to the different events being hosted around the room. But when Adrian strides in with my doppelganger, the knife that is still lodged in my heart from his rejection twists. I'd gotten used to watching him with the airheaded eye-candy, but this is too much. She's class. She's young. She's a more beautiful version of me. And I can tell from the way her eyes move from him to the people around her that she's intelligent.

I swallow hard as they are almost upon me. Again, that unfamiliar feeling of jealousy engulfs me, and I just want to...I just want to punch her in the face. Then I want to give him a kidney shot. *What the hell is wrong with me? I cannot be with him. Why can I not find peace with this and just accept it?* I stiffen my resolve to see him as a friend only. But when I make eye contact with those ocean-blue eyes of his, images of kissing him, joking with him, him playing with my boys, him holding my hair back while I was sick all come rushing to the forefront. All my emotions are jumbled with these memories. Like seaweed they weave their way through my brain and tangle themselves so thoroughly with everything that I am that all I can see is love when I look at him—and it's not friendly love or familial love—it's all-encompassing, I-want-to-spend-the-rest-of-my-life-loving-you love.

As this realization dawns, so does the fact that I'm holding someone's hand in a handshake. I pull myself together from my internal confession and focus on another pair of startling blue eyes that are busy taking me in. They're not Adrian-startlingly beautiful, but beautiful in their own right.

"Hi, thank you so much for coming out—" As I start to go into my spiel, I'm interrupted by Mr. Blue Eyes.

"Celeste Hebert?" he asks with a dimpled smile.

"Um...yes, and you are?"

"Bradford McKinnon," he replies again with the dimples. I find myself smiling back. "I'm a friend of your brother. He invited me to join you in raising money for your favorite charity." Those dimples never disappear.

I laugh lightly. He has to be a friend of Louis's; my other brothers don't have a clue about me. "Oh, I have three, you know? Which one has the pleasure of your acquaintance, Mr. McKinnon?" *Oh my gosh!* I can hear the flirty tone of my voice, but I can't seem to help myself. He's charming. I chance a glance and see that Adrian is a few feet away from me and is frowning at me.

"Please call me Bradford," he insists. "I'm a friend of Louis's."

"Oh, the cheeky brother," I tell him and grin.

He throws his head back in laughter, "He doesn't quite seem to fit the mold, does he?"

"No, definitely not," I agree.

We both feel Adrian breathing down on us at this point, which causes us to turn and take in his look of extreme displeasure. Awkwardness pervades the atmosphere.

To try to make things less uncomfortable, I introduce Bradford and Adrian to one another. Unfortunately, it doesn't help; in fact, it seems to make things worse. I can feel waves of anger radiating from Adrian.

With a raised brow at Adrian, Bradford relieves us from what has gone from awkward to downright hostile. He turns back to me with a grin. "Well, Celeste, I enjoyed meeting you. Perhaps you'll save a dance for me later."

"It would be my pleasure, Bradford," I reply. I can't focus on him completely, though, because Adrian is making somewhat of a spectacle of himself. He's shoved his hands in his pockets and is rocking back and forth on his heels, staring up at the ceiling, and pushing his breath out in a perturbed manner. I quickly avert my gaze and watch as Bradford makes his way into the main room with my eyes following him.

I'm a little nervous about looking back at Adrian and the better version of me, especially since I've finally admitted to myself what I truly feel. Will he see my love for him written all over me? *And what the hell am I supposed to do about it?* Finally, I turn back to find him towering over me and staring me down.

"Adrian, are you going to introduce me to your date?" I ask sweetly when what I really want to do is strangle him for putting me through all of these conflicting emotions.

"Um...yeah." He glances at his date as if he's just remembered she's standing there.

"Jennifer, Celeste Hebert, my cousin." I raise my eyebrows at him. He's never introduced me as his cousin but his friend—always his friend. *Lovely how that little related-by-marriage fact works when it's convenient for him!* "Celeste, Jennifer Wilde, my girl-friend," he mutters petulantly. Both Jennifer's eyes and mine shoot toward his as he gives Jennifer a grimacing smile. My eyes shift toward her face as envy rages with disbelief. She's even more beauti-ful now with a face-splitting smile. *Great!*

We make a little small talk before they make their way into the throng. I sneakily steal as many glances as I can as they make their way around the room. She never takes her hand from his arm and every time his hand moves to the small of her back I feel a biting pain infiltrate my heart.

Finally, my greeting duties subside and I make my way into the main ballroom of my absolute favorite hotel in New Orleans. Old World chandeliers meet with New World flair. The music is elegant. The food is decadent. The champagne is overflowing. Yet, my eyes constantly seek out Adrian.

Elegantly gliding her across the floor, Adrian looks amazing as he stares down at his date; but as soon as his eyes meet mine, he glowers at me. So I glower back. *Why is he upset with me? He's the one who showed up here with a freakin' girlfriend!* No heads up, no warning, nothing.

Spinning on my heel, I decide to put a little distance between Adrian and me. Plucking two glasses of champagne off a waiter's tray, I make my way to one of the anterooms that doesn't contain a crowd and move even further away by sliding through the French doors to the balcony.

-Six-

I Love Him, Now What?

QUICKLY DOWNING BOTH glasses of my champagne, I immediately feel a little rush. A running joke in my family is that I'm a lightweight: one glass of wine and I'm giggly. Not drunk, mind you. I don't do drunk, but one glass and I'm feeling good. So when I down these two glasses, it goes straight to my head. I grin at myself and give myself the Fonzie nod. *Good call*, I think.

Hearing the volume kick up on the jazz band's Harry Connick, Jr. number, I realize the doors behind me have opened, and it startles me. I whirl and there he is. I shake my head and narrow my eyes at him. "Nope! We are *not* doing this again," I proclaim.

He snaps his head back and wrinkles his brow at me. "Doing what exactly?" he asks, clueless to inner turmoil.

"Making out on a porch," I throw my hands out, which I realize are still holding the empty champagne glasses, "or balcony or whatever. Not going there again."

He chuckles at me. "Celeste, I didn't come out here to make out with you. I don't want to make out with you." I must make a God-awful face because his softens and he says, "I didn't mean it that way, Cel."

I move toward him, "Get out of the way, Adrian."

"What the hell, Celeste? What's with the hostility?"

"Are you kidding me?" I shriek. I push his chest with the back of one of my hands. He doesn't budge. Worse than that—my hand freaking tingles at the contact. *Ugh! Control thyself!* I take a deep breath and release it. Carefully, I set the glasses down on the bistro table.

"No. I'm. NOT," he enunciates each word clearly.

Turning back to him, I take a deep breath, close my eyes, and exhale. "Please, Adrian, move out of my way," I try with sweetness, a bobbing of my head, and an even sweeter smile.

"Not until you tell me what you're pissed about."

My eyes fly open and I stare a hole in his chest. *How can he be so oblivious?* "I'm upset because you brought a date, a girlfriend, and you didn't even tell me you are seeing anyone much less that you have a girlfriend!" My eyes jerk up to meet his. As always, I get lost in them. They are soft and piercing at the same time. *How does he do that?*

"I'm sorry, Celeste, but I don't see how that's really any of your concern," he tells me.

My mouth drops and I snap it closed quickly, only to let it fly back open with, "What? How that's any of my *what*?" I'm utterly astonished.

"Who I see isn't any of your concern," he lays it out for me.

"Oh, OK," I puff. I feel tears spring to my eyes and not a few. That hurt. A lot. "I thought we were friends." *I'm back to sounding pathetic. Fabulous!*

"We're family, Cel. We're cousins," he says without feeling.

"We are NOT related. If we were related, I wouldn't ache for you the way I do." *Please, God, tell me I did not say that out loud.*

I hear his sharp intake of breath and know for certain that I did. He stuffs his hands in his pockets. "Celeste, don't say shit like that. I'm trying to do the right thing here. I've moved on from that."

"Mmm...doesn't sound like someone *has* moved on so much as

someone is *trying* to move on." I lean in and run my fingertip down the front of his shirt. I jerk my finger back and shake my head a little. What am I doing? Who is this woman? "Adrian, I'm sorry. I'm so sorry. I don't know what's wrong with me. Please let me pass. I just need to go get my head together."

"What do you mean 'get your head together'?" I look up and watch his brow draws together. He reaches out and runs his fingertips over my gathered brow. His folded hand rests on my temple for a minute and neither of us says a word. "I don't want to hurt you, Celeste. I never wanted to hurt you. I care about you too much."

"I care about you too, Adrian. I care about you so much," I admit. Again I feel tears spring to my eyes. This time they don't stop though. They spill over and he catches them with his thumbs. I feel his hands grasp the back of my head as he tries to clear my tears. I close my eyes and lose myself in his touch. Feeling his calloused fingertips move over my skin is at odds with his gentle caress. "I don't know what to do," I whisper.

"What do you mean? What to do about what?" My eyes fly open and he startles at what he sees there, what I can't hide anymore. I feel his grip intensify. "I don't know what to do either, baby. I'm trying to move on."

All those little fissures that have been hanging on by a thread splinter and cause my heart to crack. It's a slow breaking, which I now deem worse than a fast one. "What if I told you I don't want you to move on?" I whisper brokenly.

His eyes slide to the side of me and his hand moves to hold the back of my neck. "Don't, Celeste." His voice is as rough as the hand that grips me.

"Don't what, Adrian?" I feel myself being moved to him even as he tells me no. I lay my forehead on his massive chest and breathe deeply. His scent further intoxicates me. God, I'm an addict. I crave the smell of him.

"When you breath me in like that..." I barely hear his whisper, but I hear it.

"What?" I ask as I tilt my head a little to the side to peer up at him. "When I breathe you in like that what?" I repeat.

He bends his head slightly and places his lips on my forehead, kissing me softly. "I want you. I want you so damn much," he murmurs against my forehead.

I tilt my head back further even though he has a firm grip on my neck. I lick my lips and glance at his to see a little smile resting there. "I still know what you taste like," he tells me. I almost come undone. "I still know what you sound like when you say my name when you're turned on." *Oh. My. God.* I swallow hard and inch up a bit on the tips of my toes.

"Celeste?" *Oh my God!* "Hey, are you in here?" I hear Farah call. I freeze as does Adrian.

"Stay here for a few minutes," I tell him.

"I'm going to have to," he murmurs darkly. I bite my lip at that piece of information. "I'll…uh…see you later."

"OK. Later," he agrees.

FINISHING WITH THE auction—what used to be my favorite part of this event until it kept me from exploring what was going on with Adrian and me—I head off the stage and move into the crowd. I haven't seen Adrian the whole time. Trust me, I looked. My eyes continue to scan the crowd as I look for him. Realizing that I'm absolutely famished, which is probably yet another reason I felt the champagne so quickly, I move over to one of the waiters and ask for a plate. When I finish speaking with him, I look back into the room and see Bradford headed my way with a huge grin on his dimpled face. I smile a small smile. I'm afraid I may have led him on a bit earlier. I'd better fix that.

"Celeste, I have to tell you, you looked gorgeous up there," he states unabashedly. At my expression, he quickly apologizes. "Sorry for being so forward, but really you have to know that I couldn't take my eyes off of you." He gives me a half grin. I can't help but smile back at him. He seems so different from this set. Stating exactly how he feels, smiling at me, not holding back—these are not things our crowd are known for.

"Bradford, I trust you're having a good time," I reply, hoping for a friendly, not flirty, tone.

"I wasn't until you took the stage," he tells me. *Uh oh! Danger, Will Robinson!*

"I was just about to head over and get a drink to go with my dinner that I forgot to eat earlier," I say.

"Oh, I'll walk with you," he says amiably.

We move toward the bar and I chance a glance over at the ballroom. Everyone is having a great time. Spending lots of money, I hope. *Who am I kidding?* I'm looking for Adrian. We really need to finish our conversation or whatever was happening on the balcony. I'm about to turn back to Bradford because he's just asked me a question when my eyes fall upon Adrian and Doppelgänger. They are tucked away in the tiny hallway that leads to one of the kitchens. She is pushed up against the wall and he is...devouring her. I'm pretty sure that's probably how I looked on the back porch a few months back. Her leg is up around his hip. His hands are on her ass. She is clinging to him and holding on for dear life, which is pretty much what you do when Adrian's kissing you.

And that's that. A fast break. It overwhelms me, and I almost crumble with it. I close my eyes and sway a little. I feel Bradford grab my elbow. "Celeste, you OK?" he asks in a worried tone.

My eyes snap open. They still haven't come back up for air. I glance down and look around at the floor as I try to recover from having my heart ripped out while surrounded by hundreds of people. "Oh, yeah, I don't know what that was," I tell him. "I did forget to eat, though."

"Come on, honey. Let's get some sustenance in you," he tells me. I glance at his hand on my elbow and then at his smiling face. I feel myself smile a little at his kindness and that kindness suddenly makes me wary.

"Why are you being so nice to me?" I ask.

He looks a little taken aback. "Well, I'm...uh...a friend of your brother's."

I tilt my head a little and repeat, "Yes, but why me?"

He shifts a little and seems slightly uncomfortable. Feeling like I'm on to something, I don't relent. "Why me?" I repeat.

"Well, I guess I feel like I know you." His thoughtful eyes shift to my shoulder, and he moves a lock of hair from my shoulder. "Louis told me a lot about you."

"Oh. Really?" I relax a little.

Meeting my eyes again, he says, "Yeah, and what he told me coupled with what I've seen tonight has made me...more intrigued than ever."

I swallow hard. He's a good-looking man. I didn't miss the fact that I wasn't the only one checking him out earlier. "Intrigued?" I ask as I start moving toward the bar again.

"Yes, intrigued. As in I've been wanting to meet you for a while now."

"Oh?" Once we reach the bar, he asks what I'd like to drink and motions for the bartender to order my drink.

"Yes, I'd really like to get to know you, Celeste. I was going to try to play it cool," he says with a laugh, "but I guess I'm not good at that. I'm more the see something—or someone in this case—and go out and get it kind of guy. But I know you've been through a lot, so I wanted to give you time."

"Give me time before what?"

"Making my intentions known, asking you out on a date, asking you out on a second date...I think you understand where I'm going," he tells me.

"Oh." I've got nothing else at the moment. I haven't been asked out on a date in...in over fifteen years.

He frowns at me. "I see I've scared you a bit. That's exactly what I was hoping to avoid."

"No, I'm not really scared of going on a date with you. What's scary is the realization that I haven't been on a date in over fifteen years. I don't even know how to date."

He blows out a deep breath. "Well, that's easy enough. I'll say something like...Celeste, how about I pick you up for dinner and a show? And you'll say something like...'That sounds like fun.' See? Simple."

I grin at him and his comforting nature. That actually does sound like fun, especially since Adrian has his tongue shoved down what-her-face's throat. "Well, since you've got the first part worked out, when and where will you pick me up?"

I'M PACKING UP some of the nicer decorations that I want to recycle for another event when I sense a set of eyes on me. Hesitatingly, I glance over my shoulder and find a slumping William staring at my backside. I straighten up quickly and frown at him.

"What's wrong, Celeste?" he asks with a slur.

"What are you doing in here, William?" I counter.

He sits up a little, rakes his hand through his unruly blonde hair, and lazily moves his stare up to meet my eyes. "Just getting it together before I head out."

"Oh, well, you could've let me know you were in here."

Quirking his brow at me, he asks suggestively, "And ruin the show?"

I smirk and turn back to finish with my last box without bending over.

"Actually, I've been wanting to catch up with you. You don't come out to the country near as much now that Tripp's gone."

"It's hard, William, being a single parent. I have a great deal to take care of."

"That's what I was hoping I could help with."

"What's that?"

"You and the kids. I was hoping to help around your house."

I should've never given him an opening. "Oh, no, William. That's not why I told you that. I'm fine really."

"Adrian's help is enough then," he practically sneers at me.

I spin around and pin him with my glare. William never says anything in passing. He's made this remark for a very specific reason. "Adrian has been a great help, William."

"Yeah, but he does spend an awful lot of time with you and the kids. Is that really necessary?"

"They adore him."

He shifts his head slightly to the left and then back to the right. "Yeah, I bet they do," he grits out between his teeth.

Losing my patience, I snap, "What is that supposed to mean? What's your problem, William?"

He springs out of his chair and advances toward me and I resist the urge to tuck tail and run. He's always had this effect on me. I delight in the fact that I'm able to hold my ground. "My problem, Celeste, is that Adrian is bad news. He's up to something with you and the kids. I just know it."

"Yeah," I spit out, "he's up to taking them where they need to go, caring for them when they need it, listening to them tell about their day, making sure they feel loved and cherished—"

William cuts me off as he reaches me and grasps my elbow, "You don't want to get smart with me, Celeste. You have no idea what I could do with that smart little mouth of yours," he warns me.

"Get. Your. Hand. Off. Of. Me," I grit out. I have every reason to fear his father and mine, but I refuse to fear this slimy bastard.

He drops his hand quickly and immediately looks contrite.

"Sorry, babe. That guy just pushes my buttons. Always has."

"You barely know him."

"What I know, I don't like."

I shake my head at him a little. "William, you should just go. Do you need me to call you a cab or something?"

"No, I can handle that. I'm just upset about this whole Vanessa thing."

I guess the Vanessa thing he was referring to was the fact that he repeatedly and flagrantly cheated on her and just expected her to get over it. Vanessa thought that what was good enough for him was good enough for her, and she started fooling around until she found someone who actually loved her.

"I'm sorry about your marriage, William, but that's still no excuse for your behavior."

"You're right." He hesitates briefly, reaching out to run his fingertip up my arm. It is soft and directly contradicts the touch I'm yearning for. "I had a little too much to drink and was already in a pissy mood. I apologize."

"It's fine, William. I really need to get going, though. I have a long day ahead of me tomorrow."

"Of course, Celeste. Shall I walk you out?"

"No, Farah and I are leaving together. I'm good. Thanks anyway."

He leans in and kisses my forehead but only briefly because I quickly but subtly move my head back and turn back to the box. "Goodnight then."

"Goodnight," I return.

I hear him moving toward the door, and I turn to watch his retreating frame. This is not good. This is so not good. I'm on his radar now. Just like back when we were growing up. An involuntary shiver makes its way up my back. I'm afraid I may have just gotten myself in a little bit of trouble.

-Seven-

The Trouble with Men

"SO, WHAT YOU'RE saying is Adrian is going to babysit your children while you go out on a date with Ole Miss?"

"Yes, Bonnie. For the fifty-eighth time, Adrian and I are trying to get past this whole attraction thing. Part of us doing that is dating people. I especially need to date because of that little threat hanging over my head if you'll recall."

It had been a couple of weeks since the soiree. Bradford and I had been on our awkward but sweet first date. And Adrian and I had had our strictly awkward conversation about the lines of our "relationship". I still cringe when I recall it.

We'd all been hanging out for a while now. It was really neat to have expanded my social circle to people I actually enjoy hanging out with, even fit in with more so than any of my usual crowd. I love the Dog Tags. Each and every one of them is unique and awesome in his own way. They had all been in the Marine Corps at one time or another, hence the name, and have an enviable sense of pride and loyalty and honor. They rock it out and have a ton of groupies but aren't disrespectful or entitled. Determined to make it on the local music scene, the band works hard but still plays hard.

Part of this playing hard is their weekly football game they play every Saturday in Audubon Park. It attracts quite a crowd probably more so than their shows really. I mean, how could it not? Ten shirtless, hot guys running around the park, oblivious to their surroundings, enjoying their freedom, playing football with abandon—there is nothing better than that.

It was a couple of days after the soiree at one of these games during half time that Adrian pulled me aside and decided to talk to me about the balcony incident. This conversation was vastly different from our first. Rather than apologize or worry that I would do something rash like throw him out of the boys' lives, he set me straight. I was mortified. I was crushed. I wanted to crawl in a hole.

I had been cheering our boys on alongside Bonnie and the other girls when we took the lead right before half time. I cheered for the guys and leaned in to the girls to start gabbing about girl stuff when I felt myself being wrenched from my chair. Startled, I looked up to see Adrian looking over at the girls, not at me, to tell them he needed a minute with me. I could feel, not see, the same startled look from the girls. This was a new Adrian and one I didn't much care for. No, that's a lie. It turned me on. I'm pretty sure anything and everything about him turns me on. Aw...and he'd put his shirt back on.

After Adrian made his apologies to the girls, he tugged me along until we were standing in between his motorcycle and my MINI. He didn't get to ride his bike often because he was usually hauling my boys from one place to another. But when he did—wow. It was...wow. I was distracted by those thoughts, so when Adrian cleared his throat and gave me that look, I asked, "What?"

"What do you mean 'what'? It was a pretty simple question, Celeste," Adrian replied bitingly.

He'd never snapped at me like that before. I flipped my hair over my shoulder, pushed my sunglasses up on my head, folded my arms across my breasts, and stood up a little taller. "Adrian, why are you being rude to me? I just lost focus for a minute. Could you repeat your question, please?"

He took his fingers and bridged his nose with them before running his hand through his damp hair. "Celeste, are you trying to drive me crazy?"

"No, why would you ask me that? Just ask me what you wanted to ask me," I snapped back. Now I was getting irritated.

"I just did. So for the third and final time: are you trying to drive me crazy?"

"No, I'm not trying to drive you crazy. What are you talking about?"

"Balcony. You. Me." He glanced around. "Almost going at it. Again." He raised his eyebrows at me.

"Oh. Well, I thought we were just going to forget that happened."

"Forget it...forget it happened?" he asked me incredulously.

"Well, yeah. Like last time," I seethed. Why was he bringing this up? Why did we have to rehash this issue?

"I can't forget it. I can't forget you. Damn, woman. I—" I knew it. I knew he felt the same way. Maybe he'll listen to me in the light of day, so I make a hasty decision to lay it all out for him now.

I grasped both sides of his shirt and fisted my hands in it, automatically pulling him closer. Tears were already swimming in my eyes when I whispered, "I saw you making out with her right after we had our...moment. How could you, Adrian? I was thinking maybe we could—"

He cut me off this time. "Thinking we could what? Are you insane? My uncle..."

"Chip? What about him?"

He shook his head at me. "Nothing. Nothing. Look, nothing is going to happen between us. Do you understand? It's no good."

I tightened my hands in his shirt, swallowed the huge lump in my throat, and forged ahead. "Adrian, I think we could be good together. I think we're crazy to deny how we feel about each other. I think what's going on here is more than—"

"I'm with Jennifer now. I'm happy with her." He said this while he simultaneously unfisted my hands, dropped them, and backed away from me.

My gaze flew to the ground. I cleared my throat and leaned against my MINI. Finally, I dared a glance back up at him. His look shifted so quickly, but I could've sworn it'd said regret—regret for hurting me, or regret for not returning my feelings? I honestly didn't know. I blew out a breath. "I have to go. Will you make my apologies to the girls, please?"

"Celeste...sure, I'll tell them," he agreed.

I jerked my keys out of my pocket, grateful that I hadn't brought anything that I had to go back for—it was only my heart and my pride I'd been leaving behind. And I was pretty sure I wouldn't be getting those back for quite some time.

Bonnie's look of disgust and her exclamation pull me back into the present. "Ugh...How could I forget? William. What a little perv!"

I shake myself my heartbreaking memory and another unpleasant one takes its place. "I know. I think I may have inadvertently offered him a challenge too," I say with a grimace.

"What do you mean?"

I hadn't really wanted to acknowledge what had gone down in the ballroom that night, so I hadn't told her yet. Even now, I recoil with the retelling. There is just something so off and so creepy about him. I conclude with telling her that he'd used about every medium to contact me over these last few weeks. The only place I was safe was on Facebook and that's only because he didn't know I was on it.

"Shit, Cel," she says with an exhale, "why didn't you tell me sooner? Did you forget what he pulled with you when y'all were kids?"

"No, of course not," I reply more calmly than I feel. "I didn't want to make it more real," I admit with a shrug.

"Here, try these." She thrusts my black peep toe stilettos with the zipper on the heel. "These are badass and go perfectly with the rocker chic look you've got going on."

Bradford was taking me to a concert tonight. I was a little

surprised at first, but he said he was representing the band and had been planning to go for a while. Of course, I jumped at the chance to hang out with rock stars and enjoy some music.

"Ooh...yes, these are perfect," I coo.

"So, back to Don Douchebag," I snicker. Oh, her nicknames are the best! "Seriously, Celeste, what gives? What are you going to do about him? I'm thinking you need to go ultra-bitch mode on him."

"I'm not sure yet. I'm afraid if I go 'ultra-bitch mode' he'll see that as a challenge too. If I try to reason with him, he'll see that as a weakness. Either way he'll hone in for the kill. I'm thinking my best move here is to continue to date Bradford and ignore him."

As I'm putting on my second heel, I hear Adrian enter and the wrestling and vying for his attention commence. I grin at how much my boys adore him and stand to take myself in. My hair is big and sexy, and I've done the smoky eye thing again. I turn sideways to take in my backside. I have to remember not to bend over in this thing. The black dress, which is more like an oversized t-shirt, barely covers my behind. It's simple but says so much with its v-neck, fringed sleeves and fringed bottom hem. I'd wrapped a silver chain belt around my waist. I throw on my silver bangles and hoops and spin around to face Bonnie.

"Whatcha think?" I ask.

"I wish I were as tiny as you because this sweater dress is to die for," she says, her voice muffled. She peeks out of my closet and does a double take. "Damn, woman. You look hot! I'd totally switch teams for you. If I didn't like di—"

"Yeah, OK, I get it!" I yell, willing her not to finish that statement.

"—ck...so much," she finishes quietly.

We exit the bedroom and enter the family room still laughing over her response to my look. My eyes search the room for his and land on his beautiful blues almost immediately. He's frozen in place with Finn dangling from one ankle behind his back. Hair disheveled, clothes askew, taut abdomen showing, he's never looked sexier or more undeniable. I want him so bad it physically hurts. As soon as I realize that my face probably shows all of this and more, I reroute my gaze to take in the room. Pillows everywhere, ottoman pushed out and over, three little t-shirts thrown here and there. Everyone freezes and follows my gaze.

"Sorry, Ma," Paris pops out first. "We'll clean it up."

"Yeah, Mom, our bad," Finn screeches.

"Adrian, you may want to release Finn. It sounds like he's depleted his oxygen reserve," I kid.

"Yeah, Adrian, lemme go," Finn squeaks out.

Adrian spins around sending Finn's shaggy brown hair and appendages flying out and says, "Finn? Where did Finn even go?" This immediately results in some pained laughter on Finn's part, and I just stare in wonder at them both. Then Adrian stops and bounces up and down a few times, causing Finn to spurt with laughter, which immediately causes me to laugh. I feel Bonnie elbow me in the back.

I turn slightly to take in her frown. "What?" I ask.

"Stop gawking," she whispers.

"I know. I'm sorry."

"So, Adrian," Bonnie pipes up, "what's been going on with you?"

"Oh, the usual." He grunts as Finn's small fists start pummeling his back. He makes like he's going to drop him and swings him around to catch him, putting him on his feet. We all laugh as Finn staggers around dazedly.

"Mom, I'm drunk!" Finn declares.

"Finn, you don't even know what that means," Archer says, not hiding his big brother disdain.

"Yes, I do too! I took a gigantic gulp out of the communion wine once. My head was all cloudy!" Finn yells back.

"Oh my gosh, Finn! At least you'll have something for your next confession," I joke and then switch mom gears immediately. I clap my hands. "All right, boys, just make sure you get this mess cleaned up before I get home," I manage to say rather sternly.

We head into the kitchen, leaving the kids to exact destruction on my house.

"So, Adrian how stoked are you about the big gig at the House of Blues?" Bonnie asks as she plants herself at the bar.

"Very. It's gonna be cool. I've been going there my whole life. Never thought I'd play there."

"You guys are so talented and hot! Of course, you're playing there!"

Adrian laughs. "Well, we're just opening, but it's still gonna rock."

I've busied myself with making drinks for the boys' pizza night with Adrian. I've managed to get myself out of pizza night for the last few weeks. It's just too straining to be around him. I miss him. So much. I have to remind myself that Bradford is nice. Bradford is cute. Bradford won't annihilate my heart.

"Cel, what do you say?"

I start at the mention of my name. "About what?" I ask.

"About us all going to support the guys at the concert. Do you think Bradford would like to go?"

I glance at Adrian and can't get a read on him, except for the slight tightening of skin around his eyes. "I'm not sure, but I'll ask."

I turn around to put the pitcher of tea back in the refrigerator and hear Adrian grunt which is followed by a swift, hard verbal response. "Celeste, go change." I gasp and spin around. Bonnie starts laughing hysterically.

"What? You want me to change my dress? What's wrong with it?"

"First off, it's not a dress. It's a t-shirt pretending to be a dress. Second off, I just saw the bottom of your ass when you bent over. Go change. Now."

I take a deep breath, but even with my effort to try and calm myself, I feel my eyes shooting sparks at him. Bonnie slaps the countertop, diverting our attention. "Well, with that telling, yet Neanderthal, comment I'm going to go. Garner is picking me up in a little while." She moves around the bar and kisses me on the cheek. "Have fun tonight! Tell Bradford hi for me. And do everything I would do."

I give a stilted laugh despite my anger, "Love you, Bonnie. Thanks for your help. I'll call you tomorrow."

Bonnie turns to Adrian and whispers something in his ear. I see his eyes widen a bit, and he gives an impatient little laugh. She squeezes his arm and then throws a mischievous little smile at me.

After Bonnie shows herself out, I finally feel calm enough to address his command, "I'm not changing. I temporarily forgot not to bend over. It won't happen again. I promise."

He folds his arm across his chest. Is he trying to intimidate me? "You're damn straight it won't happen again 'cause you're changing."

I grit my teeth and keep my voice contained since the boys are in the next room. "I'm NOT changing. And you have no right to tell me to change anyway. You have no right to anything about me. And while we're on the subject of rights and wrongs, I really don't like the way you've been talking to me lately. You're either mean like you were at the park, distant like you've been every other time I've seen you, or overbearing like you are now. I don't like it, and you need to remedy that immediately."

He just stares at me for a minute like I've lost my mind. "You are clueless. Do you have any idea how many men are going to try and have a go at you?"

Of course he ignores my comments about his behavior. "That's ridiculous. No one's going to mess with me. I'll be with Bradford anyway."

"Exactly what I'm worried about. Don't you care what he thinks of you? What's he going to think of you looking like that?"

My mouth drops. No he did NOT just go there. I open my mouth to respond but he abruptly walks past me to enter the hallway. "Where are you going?" I'm spoiling for a fight now.

"Let's continue this conversation somewhere else, yeah?"

"Oh, yeah, let's," I agree vehemently.

My heels click-clack as I stomp after him and follow him into the laundry room. I enter the room and spin to see him closing the door behind us. "Celeste, I'm not trying to be a jerk. I'm just telling you that that 'dress' is gonna get your ass in trouble. If you had any idea..."

I narrow my eyes at him. "Any idea of what?"

"Nothing." He rearranges his face to a more pleasant look and gives me a little smile. "I guess I went about it the wrong way. Let's try this...Celeste, will you change your dress before you leave?"

"No."

His face falls from his patronizing little smile. "No?"

I give him a slanted smile and raise my eyebrows. Fighting with him is fun. I don't know that I've ever fought with anyone except Bonnie. "Yeah...No."

He runs his hands through his hair and places both his hands on his hips. "No," he repeats, seemingly in awe of my refusal. He's probably used to us women just doing whatever we're told. I laugh a little at this realization. I've had my fill of being told what to do. "There's nothing to laugh about here. If you only understood that I'm trying to protect you. This is for your own good."

My blood boils at this comment. "If you had any idea how often I've heard that line , you'd never say that to me again."

"What do you mean?" He furrows his brow in concern.

"Everything that anyone's ever done for me or to me has been for my own good, Adrian. Except it never turns out for my benefit." I bristle as I realize that he's starting to treat me like every other male in my life. "You know, Adrian, I thought I knew you. I liked how you were different toward me. Not like all the other overbearing men in my life. Now, I wonder if this is the real you. Just like the rest of our Hebert men—arrogant, misogynistic, self-serving—"

"Misogynistic, self-serving? Do you have any idea what I've done for you? No, I guess you wouldn't, would you? The point was to protect you from all that shit."

"What are you talking about, Adrian?"

His voice is back to dripping with venom. "Nothing. The only thing I'm talking about is that fucking dress, and the fact that you're not leaving here in it."

"This conversation is over. Get out of my way." I start to walk past him, but when I do he grabs my arms and guides me back to the wall. "Adrian, what—"

Adrian runs his hands up my arms and shoulders until they grasp both sides of my neck to tilt my head back so that I'm staring straight into his arctic blue eyes. I immediately start trembling, and it's not with fear. That whiskey-laden voice drips with passion. "Celeste, I'm begging you not to leave here looking like that. You look gorgeous, babe, but I can't sit here all night wondering who's hitting on you, who's imagining moving that scrap of fabric over to get a glimpse at what is..."

"What is what?" I breathe heavily.

"What is underneath it all?" His brow wrinkles, and I feel his hands tighten their pleasurably painful grip. "What is underneath it all?"

"Just me, Adrian, just me," I breathe. "That's all."

"So everything then. Just like I thought." He removes one of his hands to run it up the back of my thigh. My eyes widen and I swallow hard.

"That's not a good idea," I whisper. His hand wraps all the way around my thigh, his fingertips coming to rest along the crease of my left cheek. My thigh pulses with fire.

"Why not?" His fingertips tease back and forth a little. Even though it's a light touch, it feels like his calloused fingertips mark me.

My voice is strained. "Why not? Look at us. We can't even have a civil conversation for everything that has passed between us, and you want to further complicate it. What you're doing will further complicate matters."

His hand stills. He exhales loudly and lets his head drop on my chest. "You do this to me. I don't act like this. That day in the park, watching you cross and uncross your legs. Throwing your hair over your shoulder. Laughing without a care in the world. Cheering me on like it was your favorite thing to do! It killed me. Killed me. I've never wanted a woman the way I want you. Never."

His words rain down on me like fiery drops of lust. I close my eyes and rewrite that memory. I thought he was just being an ass, but his unexpected anger was because he was yearning for me. I bite my lip, open my eyes, and shake my head. "It's just because you can't have me, Adrian. I'm nothing special."

"Oh, baby, you have no idea." He runs his nose up my throat, scenting me as he goes. I lean my neck back, giving him more access even as my brain screams at me to run—not walk—out of this room. But when he says, "You're everything to me." My head falls back even further and my eyes close again as I feel him slant his head and attack my jaw, throat, and neck with closed-mouth kisses. I hear myself moan and give myself one more little jolt to try to spare myself from this delicious torment that will only end in frustration.

Adrian works his way back up my throat, but this time, it's his tongue that leaves a scorching path of devastation. I feel as though I've been flayed open and am just a quivering pile of nerve-endings. "Oh my God, Adrian, what are you doing to me?" I manage.

"I could ask you the same thing," he murmurs against my throat. "You're driving me insane. We shouldn't be here. Doing this. Yet, here we are again. And I can't stop."

I shiver at his words and will myself to move. I feel his fingers twitch on my thigh, and I ache to bend my knees a little to help his fingers reach their intended destination. I would give anything to feel those fingers on me, inside me. "Adrian, I need—" Right about that time, I hear one of the boys shuffling around in the kitchen, complaining about starving to death. "Adrian, let me go," I tell him. There's a double entendre to my statement and my eyes pool with unshed tears. He jerks his head back and pins me with his gaze.

"All right, Celeste. I'll let you go," he acquiesces. Yes, he gets it. I press my lips together hard, barely containing a pained moan that builds in my chest and threatens to erupt. He eases back but only slightly, dropping his hands and throwing his head back to look at the ceiling. I move toward the door and look back at him. He's braced himself on the wall and let his head fall forward. I pat under my eyes with the sides of my fingers to dry any escaped wetness. I exhale, stand up straight, and go out to check on my starving children.

After I see to them, I realize Adrian still hasn't come out of the laundry room. I contemplate going to speak to him. Chickening out, I whisper to Archer to go and tell Adrian that I'm leaving.

Securing the door behind me, I walk briskly to my MINI. I play with a couple of buttons and P!nk's "So What?" blasts through my speakers. "Perfect," I snap. This will help me get out my pent up frustration before I meet Bradford. Bradford who will not twist me in these knots. Bradford who will not drive me freakin' insane. Bradford who will not cause me to lose myself. Yes, Bradford.

This One or That One?

"I REALLY WISH you would let me pick you up for our future dates," Bradford tells me.

I give him a small smile. He is quite gregarious, and I'm enjoying being with him. "I know you would like that, and I appreciate that. I think it's better this way until I'm ready to introduce you to the boys."

"So you told me all about them on our last date, and I can't wait to meet them. One thing you didn't do much talking about was you, though." He gives me a half-smile. He's really adorable and sweet. I'm very fortunate he's shown interest in me since he's quite different from my other "options," which are, for me, non-options.

"Umm...what do you want to know?"

"Everything, anything that you're willing to share." I take a sip of my Pinot Grigio and nod my head, collecting my thoughts. Bradford signals to the server, and he's quickly there refilling my glass.

"Well, what do you already know?"

He surprises me by not mincing words. "I know that your

husband died relatively quickly after being diagnosed with cancer and that you haven't dated anyone. I know that your family is pressuring you into choosing someone to help you raise your children."

My back stiffens at this last little tidbit, and I raise my eyebrow at him. "Really? What do you know of that?"

"Louis told me a little. I don't fully understand it, but I know enough to know that Louis is worried about you."

I nod my head a little, taking this in. "My family is very... protective. That's why Louis talked me up to you, playing matchmaker." I nod my head as I begin to put the pieces together. "Makes sense."

"Well, I'm glad he did. Even if he did have a hidden agenda, I think it was a noble one." He smiles warmly and reaches out to cover my hand with his. I glance at it and am immediately thrown to the all-too recent memory of another hand on another part of my body. It takes a mammoth amount of effort on my part not to pull my hand away.

I give him a little smile. "Me too, Bradford. You're very nice."

He removes his hand but not before running his thumb over mine, causing a slight tingle. "Ah...nice? The kiss of death. Women don't like nice guys."

My brow furrows. "That's not true. I was married to a very nice man for quite some time."

"So...you had a good marriage?"

"I did. We grew up together. He was one of my best friends. And he was a great dad. My children and I were very fortunate to have him while we did." Tears pool in my eyes. I may not have been in love with him like a wife should be in love with her husband, but I did miss him when I thought about our friendship and the love he had for our children.

He reaches across the table and tucks my hair behind my ear, cupping my neck for a moment before releasing me. It's a possessive gesture, and I surprise myself by liking it. "I'm sorry. I didn't mean to make you sad. I brought it up because I know you haven't dated anyone, so I was wondering just how you felt about moving on."

I take him in—his sincerity, his charm, his good looks. He's the whole package: successful, kind, and intelligent. His light brown cropped hair is slightly wavy, and he has gorgeous blue eyes except that they immediately cause me to think of my favorite blue eyes. *Damn it! I'm a freakin' mess!* "I'm good," I tell him with way more calmness than I feel. "I'm ready to move on, ready to date. But I think taking it slow is best for me."

He gives me a half-smile. "I can do slow." His words and the way he says them cause me to shiver a little. Maybe if I give him a chance and quit comparing him to Adrian, this could go somewhere good.

We finish the rest of our meal with mainly small talk about me. I tell him how I got into the decorating business. How I dream of nothing more than becoming a designer. How I thrive on making the things around me pretty yet functional. How I started way back when I was in junior high. I joke that I was on every organizing and designing committee known to man. I had to get it all out of me, for in my own home, I wasn't allowed to touch anything around me. My mother was meticulous and paid top dollar to the best in the business to decorate our home, the compound, and the firm. Even my own bedroom wasn't mine to personalize. I think that's why I let my boys run wild around my house. It may make for a messy home, but they love it and feel comfortable at home. It was the best thing I could ever offer them because I'd never felt that way.

"OH, THIS BAND is amazing!" I shout in Bradford's ear. The band is unlike anything I've ever heard. I love them! They are Dave Matthews Band meets the Foggy Mountain Boys.

"I'm glad you like them," he whispers back as he moves in for a slow number. He pulls me close, and I can't help but have my pulse speed up. Bradford's hips move in time with mine, and the warmth that seeps out of him and into me is refreshing and comforting. My hands rest on his forearms, and he pulls his arms back to take my hands in his and brings them up and around his neck. Running his fingertips down the underside of my arms, he causes a path of fire to quickly spread throughout my entire body. I look up at him in surprise, and he gives me a knowing grin. He continues his sweet torment by running his hands down my sides until they come to rest on my hips. He leans and places a soft, little kiss by my ear and tells me, "I'm really glad you're here with me and that you wore that amazing dress. Every guy in here hates my guts right now."

I give a nervous little laugh. How can I want Adrian so badly yet be so affected by Bradford's words and touch? Am I that starved for attention? I feel confused all of a sudden. I swallow hard and lean back to take him in. "I don't know about that, but I do consider myself very lucky to be here with you," I admit.

He gives me a glorious smile and then dazes me by leaning and resting his lips on my forehead before giving me a sweet, lingering kiss there.

As the concert wraps up, we make our way backstage. I'm about ready to jump out of my skin I'm so excited! I have a not-so-secret appreciation for rock stars.

We're escorted into the VIP room to wait for the budding rock stars, and I'm in awe. For all my money, I've never had this kind of access before. There isn't a surface in the entire huge room that isn't covered in some kind of swag—giant vases of every flower imaginable with huge metallic balloons in the shapes of musical notes and instruments, t-shirts from every vendor in New Orleans, platters of food, champagne, lots of champagne—which is my weakness—and tons of other stuff. And these bands were just starting out in the States.

Bradford places his hand on the small of my back as he escorts me fully into the room. I feel him lean in and his warm breath on my neck sends shivers down my spine. "Will you be all right here for just a second?"

"Oh, sure," I assure him, "I'm going to grab a glass of champagne.

His hand moves to my hip to give it a light squeeze. My eyes meet his and he smiles big at the *Wow!* that I imagine is written all over my face. "Good. Be right back."

"K," I murmur as he moves away. I watch him walk away, and it's a mighty fine view. I'd seen him in a tux, a suit, and now in his relaxed look. And he looks good every single way. Today, it is dark jeans that fit him perfectly with a tight, white Henley that draws my attention. I shake my head at myself and my thoughts. Again, I'm amazed that I can be drawn to two men simultaneously. I'm not quite sure how this makes me feel about myself.

I make my way over to the champagne-filled table, and as I'm approaching, a guy turns quickly from it and almost plows into me. I have quick reflexes so I'm able to dodge him before he makes contact.

"Oh, sorry," he starts and then we make eye contact. He switches gears almost immediately. "Or not. Hey there, beautiful," he says with an English accent. He gives me what I can only describe as a licentious grin.

"Umm...hi," I can't help but grin back. He's gorgeous and every visible square inch of him is covered in elaborate tattoos. I want to study them.

"Sorry about damn near running you over, gorgeous. Where you headed?"

"Just beyond you. I'm after some champagne." Oh, geez! I can hear the flirtatious tone in my voice. *What the hell is wrong with me?* Maybe it's the fact that I haven't had a man in so long. My libido has graduated from tapping me on the shoulder to bypassing the filter between thought to speech.

"Here ya go, love. It's the least I can do for making you move like that." He hands me his just-poured glass and turns to pour another. "Did you enjoy the show?"

"I really did. The opening act was amazing. I'd never heard of them, but I'll definitely be hitting up iTunes when I get home."

"Yeah, you liked 'em, huh?"

"More like loved," I admit. "I love discovering new talent."

"Well," he spins and taps his glass to mine, "To you and your mission of discovery. I'm ready and willing for your venture to start with me."

"Huh?" I giggle.

I feel a hand on my lower back again and glance over to be sure it's Bradford. With all these horny rock stars roaming around, you never know. "Drake, you flirting with my girl here?" Bradford winks at me. *His girl?* Hmm...has a nice ring to it. "Celeste, the man who is unabashedly hitting on you is the drummer for the Rising Sons. Drake, this is my date, Celeste."

Drake slaps Bradford on the shoulder. "Damn, mate, you shouldn't have left her alone for a second back here. What in the bloody hell were you thinking, man? Another thirty seconds and she would've been leaving with me tonight."

I roll my eyes heavenward, laugh again, and say, "Drake, you really need to work on that low self-esteem of yours, you know? You really have a lot to offer a girl. No need to be so hard on yourself."

"Yeah, babe. Hard is—"

"All right, all right, I can see exactly where this conversation is headed." Bradford laughs and I feel his hand move around to rest on my hip. Yep, very possessive. I just hope it's the good kind of possessive. "Drake, I just talked to Brian. The contracts are looking good and tight. We'll get those over to your room in the morning to be executed before y'all head out tomorrow."

"Whatever, mate. I'm just here for the free booze and," he winks at me and grins, "the hot women." I can't help but laugh at him.

Bradford claps Drake on the back and nudges me toward the crowd. "Come on, Celeste, the rest of the band is a little more civilized." We say goodbye to Drake and make our rounds around the VIP room. The rest of the band has made its way down as has the main act. Bradford seems to know a little bit about all of them and is easy-going in their midst. I even get to talk harmonies with the lead singer and main songwriter for the band. It's an amazing night for an aficionado like me.

After too many glasses of champagne and getting hit on by every male in the room, even though Bradford never left my side, we say our goodbyes and begin to head out. I turn to go out the way we came in, but Bradford gently guides me in the other direction. I raise a questioning brow, "I thought we were heading out?"

"Not quite yet. I have something I want to show you, though," he says with a mischievous little grin.

He guides me to an elevator, and we ride up a few floors until the elevator opens on the rooftop. When the elevator opens, I'm treated to tons of lit candles and a rooftop garden that's to die for. "I think this is the real VIP area. What about you?" Bradford breathes from behind me. I can hear all the sounds of New Orleans floating up to us—the jazz bands, the street performers, the impatient drivers, the rambunctious revelers, the sirens. I wouldn't trade this city for anything in the world. You couldn't make this kind of thing up. I turn into Bradford's embrace, for his hand still hadn't left my hip. When I do, his hand drags across my entire back, leaving goose bumps in its wake.

"You did this? You set this up? For me?"

His pretty baby blues focus all their intensity on me. "Yes, you seem surprised by that notion."

The truth tumbles out of me before I can help it. "I am. No one's ever done anything like this for me."

His voice turns raspy. "I'm sorry to hear that because you," he says as he brushes a piece of errant hair from my forehead, "deserve this and so much more. But I will say I'm not sorry that I was the first do to such a thing."

I give him a slight smile and back out of his grasp to turn and take it all in. It really bothers me that I can feel this attraction to Bradford when just a few hours ago Adrian had his hand up the back of my dress and I had been dying for so much more. It made me feel...like a cheat. And I'd never felt like a cheat before. "Hey, you all right?" I walk a little and turn back to him. He looks uneasy now. He raises his arms. "Is this OK?"

Nodding my head, I tell him, "It's more than OK. It's wonderful. I just don't feel that I deserve this, I guess."

"Why don't you let me be the judge of that," he says with a grin. "Come here." He guides me over to the wicker loveseat and helps me sit down, lowering himself in front of me. "These shoes are sexy as hell. But your feet have to be killing you." He runs one hand down the back of my calf and the other over the top of my foot, giving me an inquiring look. I nod and he slips my shoe off and begins massaging my foot. I relax back into the loveseat as much as I am able because it feels amazing. More than amazing after a moment. Whatever part of my foot he is rubbing has a direct line to my libido. I actually moan when he slips my other heel off to work his magic on that one.

"That feels amazing," I tell him. "I didn't think my feet were bothering me until you got a hold of them."

"You are amazing. I admire you so much, Celeste, and you deserve to be treated like a princess." His look turns serious and he smiles warmly. "I'm sorry to sound so serious, but I was raised by a single mother. So I can appreciate your situation."

My heart pinches and I smile wide. "Thank you for saying that, Bradford. Your mother did a fantastic job, by the way."

"Anyway, I thought you might be a little hungry after all the dancing and cocktails, so I ordered us up some oysters. Kind of a midnight appetizer if you will." Suddenly, I feel ravenous.

"Yes, I'd love some," I tell him. He slips my shoes back on and lifts himself out of his crouched position to a table that contains beverages and, apparently, oysters. He brings the tray over and I see it's raw oysters on the half shell.

"Madame," he says as he presents me with the tray.

"Oh, my favorite, thank you!" My energy level has suddenly revived itself. I get so giddy over food that it's ridiculous. It was one of the major transgressions my mother had scolded me for most of my life. "Sorry," I tell him. "I just love raw oysters."

"Don't apologize. I love your enthusiasm."

"Thank you. And thank you for a wonderful night, Bradford. I've loved every second of it."

"Even getting hit on by all those rock stars," he jokes.

"They were harmless," I say.

"Yeah, only because I was there. If you'd have been by yourself, you'd have been in trouble. Believe me. They were going easy on you." I laugh at the thought of Drake and the other guys turning their full charm on me. He's right. I wouldn't have stood a chance. "I think you like the thought of all those rock stars fawning over you, you naughty thing."

I gasp at exactly how accurate his comment is given my earlier line of thought. My mouth falls open as I think of a way to protest but then I snap it shut. *She doth protest too much and all that!* "Whatever," I say eloquently.

After squirting them with lemon juice and Tabasco, we get quiet as we devour the oysters.

Bradford is the first to break the comfortable silence. "You have to be getting tired by now? I know those three little boys keep you on your toes."

"Do they ever. And yes, I'm starting to become quite tired. I've had a lovely night, Bradford, really. Thank you so much."

"It was my pleasure, Celeste. Thank you for the wonderful company. Would you mind if I followed you to your house? You know, to make sure you get home safely and all?"

"Oh, sure. That'd be fine, but I don't live far from here at all. Just off Carrollton."

"I know, but I'd feel much more chivalrous." He gives me that dimpled grin again. Boy, I bet that grin has gotten him his way a lot over the years.

"All right then. Ready?"

"I've never been more ready," he replies, and I tremble. I give him a tilted smile and let him help me from the loveseat.

AS I PULL into my driveway and get out of my car, I give an idling Bradford a wave. I'm so grateful that he respects my boundaries. I'm just not ready to take things any further than our few innocent touches and glances and foot massages. Not until I've firmly pushed Adrian from my mind.

I slip my shoes off and begin to make my way up my porch steps. I'm nearing the top when I hear Adrian's voice cut through the somewhat still night. "Have fun?"

My hand flies to my throat as I gasp. "Adrian, you frightened me. What are you doing out here?" His elbows are planted on his knees and his head rests on his fists as he sits on my porch swing not moving.

"Oh, nothing. Just enjoying the night. It feels good out here. Why don't you come sit with me for a minute?"

"Umm…"

His voice turns husky. "I promise I'll behave myself." *Yeah, sounds like it,* I think. Of course, that's the crux of the problem. I don't want him to behave.

"Uh, all right. Let me go change." I know my limits. There is no way I could sit next to him in this dress.

"Hurry back."

Eager to get back to Adrian, I dash into my house and into my bedroom. I'm yanking my belt off as I traipse through the living room. As my door is closing behind me, my dress is over my head and off. I grab my favorite Loyola hoodie, a pair of panties, and yoga pants from my bureau. I quickly put them all on and am heading back out when exactly what I am doing and thinking hits me. *Shit!*

I turn back into my bathroom and give myself a long hard stare. "You can't have him," I tell my reflection. Closing my eyes and shaking my head at my own stupidity, I reach out and grab my contact solution, case, and glasses. After popping my contacts out and putting my glasses on, I throw my hair up in a bun. Smirking at myself in the mirror, I think, I've made myself less attractive. I'll just go and enjoy his company. Rushing back to my bureau, I grab my favorite fuzzy, warm socks—definite defense mechanisms.

Making my way out to the porch, I catch Adrian leaning over the railing. His arms are splayed wide and his head is hanging down slightly. As I gently close the door, he turns toward me, leans against the railing, and folds his arms across his chest. I'm mesmerized by his every action. He gives me a little grin as he takes in my appearance. His eyes run up to my bun and down my body to my socks.

"Cute socks," he says with a laugh.

"Cute and warm. It's starting to get a little breezy out here." Crossing my arms over my chest, I move over to the swing—my absolute favorite place to sit in the world. I could sit here and look over my neighborhood all day long. The large, sprawling oaks, the wrought iron, and the wisteria, when it blooms, are all utterly magnificent. Getting lost in all that for hours is instant, effective therapy.

"So you never answered my question. Have fun?"

"I did. Thank you. Only a few rock stars hit on me," I joke.

His jaw ticks a little as he stares at me.

"I'm kidding, Adrian." Well, not really, but he doesn't need to know that.

"Do you see things getting serious with Bradford?" he asks.

I swallow the lump in my throat. "Maybe. He's a nice guy."

"That's what Louis said, and I trust Louis."

"Thanks for trusting me," I snap.

"That's not what I meant. I just meant I'm glad that someone I trust knows him. I'm sorry," he murmurs. He runs both his hands over his face and up into his hair.

I decide to change the subject. "Your hair's getting long."

"Yeah, I guess it is," he says as he grabs at it a little. "I can't seem to keep it short since I got out."

"Do you miss it?"

"The Corps? Yeah, I do and I don't. I miss my unit, the camaraderie. I don't miss the shitholes I had to go to. And I damn sure don't miss fighting for a cause I don't believe in."

"You don't believe in our latest mission?"

"Nope. When I went to Afghanistan, I believed whole-heartedly in taking down terrorists. When I went to Iraq that first tour, same thing. We needed to be there based on the intel. This latest thing is straight up politics. And you know how I hate politics."

I do know that. We'd talked long and hard about his return to the family. He didn't want to get involved in all they were involved in, but he did want his family back. He wanted his future children to know their cousins. Heck, *he* wanted to know his cousins. "It is a mess. A mess I'm not sure we'll ever get out of. I feel like it will plague our children long after we're gone."

"I do too, Celeste. It's even worse over there now than when I was there."

"I've heard."

"Yeah, well, I still have friends there. Hearing it firsthand—it's some scary shit. The shit nightmares are made out of, except those guys have to live it."

"I'm glad you're not there," I whisper.

He finally moves to sit down beside me and grimaces a little. "Me too, mostly. I do wish that I could be there for my guys, though."

His sincerity overwhelms me, and my eyes tear up a little. "Adrian—"

The sudden warmth on my leg cuts me off from speaking as he has placed his hand on my knee and is rubbing up and down a little. I glance down at his hand and let it rub back and forth for a moment before placing my own hand over his. I curl my hand around his and squeeze, staring at our intertwined hands. He squeezes my hand and releases it.

"Thanks for listening, Celeste. I've gotta get going, though. And the boys will have you up early tomorrow."

"Yeah, that they will," I say with a laugh. It must be nearly two a.m.

"See, this is what I don't want to lose. Your friendship means the world to me. I want that back."

"Yeah, me too."

"Good. I'm going to try really hard not to attack you again, OK?"

I hold up my right hand and vow, "And I will endeavor not to attack you and/or instigate attacks by you." A laugh bubbles out of me. This is kind of ridiculous. Anyone else would just give in and go for it. Why do things have to be so complicated?

"Night, Celeste."

"Night, Adrian." I grin up at him as he starts to leave.

"Will you go in and lock up before I go?"

"Yes, Adrian."

"*Now* she cooperates."

"Don't push it, sir."

His chuckle follows me into the house as I close and lock the door behind me. I lean back on the door for a minute and let myself return to my laundry room. My eyes drift closed for a few seconds as I fantasize about what almost happened, what I wanted so badly to happen. I have so many "if only's" running through my head, but that's not going to do me any good. So I make a deal with myself. When I move away from this door, I'll no longer fantasize about Adrian. That little deal makes me stay here longer than I'd intended.

Marveling over how we'd found a new way to deal with our

slip-ups, I think this one works best—just pretending—pretending like it hadn't happened, like we weren't affected. Groveling and fighting about it just plain…sucked.

I reach up to my bun, release my hair, and comb my fingers through it. Straightening from the door, I take a step to go to fetch a glass of water before heading off to bed. A knock on my door has me spinning back and throwing it back open wide.

"Did you—" My words and smile die on my face as I look into William's obviously drunken one. "William, what are you doing here?" I say in my sternest voice. I move to go out on the porch but I'm not fast enough. He's in my house and stumbling to my couch before I can protest.

"Celeste, you don't look happy to see me? Why? I'm not Adrian? You looked plenty happy to see him," he slurs just about every word.

I ignore all of that. "William, why are you here?" I demand.

"I don't know, Celeste. I just know I had to see you. I've screwed up. I've screwed up again."

"What do you mean? What did you do?" Flashbacks of a drunken William bombard my memories as if they happened only yesterday. Blitzed out of his mind, he used to come crying to Tripp about every little thing there for a while until I'd told Tripp exactly why his presence was not welcomed around here.

He's moved over to plop himself on my couch, so I move closer so that he doesn't raise his voice and wake up the boys.

"I think it's pretty obvious, Celeste. I fucked up because you're the one for me, and I let Adrian get to you first."

I shake my head at him and sit on the arm of the couch. "William, nothing is going on with me and Adrian. We're friends and that's all. But nothing's going to happen between you and me either. You can understand that, right?"

"I understand that Adrian," he sneers the name at me, "will never settle for friendship. You don't know what kind of trouble you're inviting there. He's after everything this family holds dear.

He wants it all. That's why he's back and he's set his sights on you. He may display that sensitive musician side to you, but he's got one hell of a mean streak and is definitely the love 'em and leave 'em type. He has never committed to any woman before. And you're deluding yourself if you think he will start with you, sweet Celeste."

Warring with my temper, I maintain control over myself. This piece of shit sure has a lot of nerve to come into my house and criticize a man who has been nothing but wonderful to my kids and me. But he's drunk and already an unreasonable person, so I know better than to try to reason with him or argue those points. I have to knock my baser senses to the ground. It kills me not to defend Adrian and not to mention that even though William may be willing to commit, he still wasn't willing to be faithful. Me arguing any of these points will result in nothing but forcing me to endure his company longer.

"Now see, there's where you are wrong because I desire nothing more than Adrian's friendship and he feels the same. That's all." I hesitate and let out a long sigh. "I think it would be best if you left now, William. The children are asleep and it's getting really late."

I can tell I've said the wrong thing as his eyes darken and his mouth curls up with hatred. He's practically in my face as he bites out, "You can try to sell that shit somewhere else, Celeste. I saw you two on the porch. That's not friendship,"

I'm not doing this. I no longer have any allegiance to William and I'm not putting up with his crap anymore. "OK. That's enough. Let me—"

Before I can utter another word, William has pulled me down on the couch and has one of my arms pinned beneath his leg. I move to slap him off me with my other hand, but he grabs that hand and jerks it on to his own crotch and suddenly I'm twelve years old again. And I freeze. *No, no! Not again!*

"If I remember correctly, you like it rough, Celeste," he coos as he moves his hand so that I'm massaging him. He begins rocking himself into me. I hear a whimper escape me, and I spiral. My mind spins out of control, but I clutch at what words will get him off of me. I come up completely empty. I literally cannot think beyond how much I loathe him and loathe the fact that he stole my innocence at such a young age. "Oh my God, Celeste. Do you feel how hard I am for you? How bad I want you? All I have to do is think of you and I'm ready for you. This won't take long, baby. Your hand feels so good. Oh yeah..."

His head falls forward to rest on my forehead, and I'm reminded of the sweet kiss that Bradford placed there as our date wound to an end. I feel William under my hand and I'm reminded of Adrian gently caressing my hand on my porch swing as he shared his thoughts on war and comrades. And suddenly I'm no longer frozen. I'm enraged. I'm livid and I want this pervert off of me. I can feel his movement getting more erratic and more furious as if he's starting to find release and when I feel him shudder I know I have to act.

Tilting my head back, I lock my eyes with William's depraved ones and bring a smile to my eyes. He responds immediately. "Yeah, baby. Oh yeah. You like that don't you. Help me out now, and I'll return the favor in just a minute. I'm so close."

I let my eyes fall to his lips and feel my stomach revolt at what I'm about to do. "Kiss me, William," I mutter hazily, lick my lips, and meet his gaze again.

"Fuck yeah..." he murmurs as he slams his lips on mine. The second they touch mine I open my mouth and bite hard. A metallic taste floods my mouth immediately. "Fuuuck," he sputters. His hand loosens a little but mine tightens to a vice. I squeeze as hard as I can and bite even harder as I do. *Oh yeah is right, baby!* I'm really feeling this now. This bastard deserves to pay. Pay for what he's doing now and pay what he did to that twelve-year-old girl.

William whimpers and releases me enough so that I can spring from the couch. As I try to get around him, I misjudge my proximity to the coffee table and attempt to jump over it but slam and drag my shin along on the coffee table trying to get away. Pain shoots through my entire leg, but I stifle my yelp as I certainly don't want my boys to wake to this mess.

Jogging to the front door, I throw it open and slow my retreat as my leg begins to throb. I limp down my stairs and out into my yard and turn, spitting his blood from my mouth as I do. And I wait. I wait for that bastard to recover and follow me out.

He doesn't make me wait long. "You fucking bitch!" he snarls at me. "You were never anything more than a little cock tease." He's seething and stumbling down my stairs.

"I bet your stupid ass is sober now," I say with a laugh. I'm so damn proud of myself, but I stop short of doing a little jig cause my leg is killing me and I still need him to leave.

"I can't believe you did that shit, Celeste," he whines, wiping at his mouth and holding his crotch.

I laugh. "Really? You can't believe I stopped you from sexually assaulting me?" I scream. "That's rich, William. Get the hell off my property before you have more than a busted lip and a sore dick."

"Listen to yourself. He's already corrupted you. You used to be a lady."

"If being a lady means letting you get off on me while I am freaking out and sobbing, then I'm thrilled to relinquish that title. Now, get the hell off my property, you low life bastard."

"What would my brother think of you talking to me like that? You think my brother would let you throw me out of his home?"

"If only I knew what your brother thought of all this. But I bet it would be pretty close to what he thought when I told him what you did to me all those years ago. I was too weak to fight you off then. But not now, William."

"Wait…what do you mean about Tripp? You told him what we did?"

"What *we* did?" I screech. "You attacked me, held me down, and made me masturbate you! Yes, I told him. And he hated you for it. I wouldn't let him do anything because—"

"You little bitch!" He rages and pales right before my eyes. "You probably made me out to be a pervert when all it was just me being a horny teenager. A lot of people do it. You need to let it go."

Is he freaking kidding me? "How can I let it go? You never once apologized to me. Never once asked for my forgiveness. You acted like you had a right to do that to me. And fool that I was, I let you get away with that." I take a calming breath and change my tone to one that I pray implies strength and sincerity because I mean every word of what I'm about to say. "Hear me now when I say this, William. If you ever lay your hands or any other part of your anatomy on me again, I'll fucking kill you." I lean toward him as I snap out my threat, but I don't get any closer than that. I don't want to breathe the same air as he breathes.

"Whatever, bitch. I'm done with you," he mutters and moves around me.

Not taking any chances on what else he'd do to me, I spin and follow him with my eyes. When he staggers far enough down the street, I feel myself sag with relief.

My eyes burning with unshed tears of relief and my heart burning, I turn to head back into my house. I feel beads of perspiration break out on my forehead and under my arms. Adrenaline. Thank you, God, for adrenaline. As my foot lands on that first step, I feel a shooting pain radiate up my leg. I bend and pull my pants up to assess the damage. I gasp as I realize just how bad it is. An eggplant—the blood that has gathered has formed something that resembles the shape and size of an eggplant on my shin. *Great! I just had to have a sturdy table that the boys couldn't move around, didn't I?*

A faint whisper pulls me from my inner tirade. "Did he do that to you?"

My head flies up and I freeze. Archer is in a fighting stance with a baseball bat extended from his rigid form. He's not even looking at my face but at my leg.

"Archer, honey…" I drift off. I don't even know what to say. How much did he see? Oh, God, how much did he hear? Not only had that bastard stolen my innocence, but now he's also claimed my baby's. To think, I was just wondering if it were possible to hate him more than I already do. I push my pants leg back down and climb the steps to put my arms around him. Resting my chin on his head and turn and run my cheek over his soft, dark brown hair. "Come on, honey. Let's go inside."

I get Archer settled on the couch, tell him I'll be right back, and walk down the hall to check on Paris and Finn. After I ascertain that they've remained blissfully ignorant to all that has transpired and thank God for small favors, I return to Archer and sit beside him quietly. I think it best to let him talk it out rather than start making assumptions and telling him what and how to feel about all that has happened. Grabbing his hand, I sit and wait for a few minutes. It's killing me. I begin to think maybe he's in shock and decide I should start talking when he says one simple thing that shatters my heart into a million tiny pieces.

"Dad would have never treated you that way," he whispers raggedly. He finally turns and makes eye contact with me. Kind dark brown eyes that mirror his father's are brimming with tears. "I miss Dad."

He becomes blurry as my own eyes water. "Sweetie, I know you do. And you're right. Dad would've never treated me that way. What Uncle William did was not very nice." *Understatement of the year!* I think.

"Don't call him my uncle," he says coldly.

"All right, honey. William is mixed up between right and wrong, and he drinks too much. What he did was wrong. He'll feel bad about it tomorrow." I almost choke on the lie, but what do you tell your twelve-year-old son about a twisted person whom they happen to be related to?

"I've never liked him. Now I know why," he says sagely. "I was about to come after him, Mom, but I saw that you had him under control." I wince as I imagine him "coming after" William. That would have been bad.

"I'm so sorry that you had to see that. Please know that it will never happen again. I promise to only surround us with good people."

He chews on that for a moment. "Adrian would never treat you that way either."

My heart does flips as I hear him say this. He loves Adrian so much, and he's such a good influence on him. "You're a good judge of character, sweetheart. Adrian wouldn't treat me that way either."

I give Archer a kiss and bring him back to his room and tuck him in. I make my way through the house, turning off all the lights, double-checking all the locks, all the while feeling something building inside me. It's ugly and scary and reminds me of the Devil himself. I'm terrified by what I feel right now, and I can't even put a name on this emotion.

Easing myself into the shower, I begin to wash the extraordinarily long day away. What a naïve little fool I am, thinking I could have a little something for myself, whether it be Bradford or Adrian. What was I thinking?

Closing my eyes, I feel my tears mix with the water that cascades over my face. Thinking back to that scared little girl in that dark closet who was forced to help a depraved young man masturbate, I turn my face up to the water and bite my lip hard as whimpers start to bubble from me. I open my mouth to release them but all that erupts is a silent scream. Bending over, I start gagging. I grasp my abdomen as the contents of my stomach swirl around the drain. I close my eyes and purge myself. Finally, I succumb to all that I'm feeling and I'm on my hands and knees, heaving and crying and praying.

-Nine-

A Bittersweet Cocoon

STANDING AT THE island, I roll my eyes as my mother asks me yet another invasive question about Bradford. Popping another piece of cheese into my mouth, I grant myself a reprieve from answering her. Just being around her causes me to regress about twenty years.

"Celeste, dear, you've had enough cheese for now, don't you think?"

I roll my eyes again. When I'm finished reacting like a moody teenager, my eyes fall on Bonnie and Farah. Their reactions are so different it's priceless. Bonnie is mocking my mom by pulling her skin taunt and narrowing her eyes at me. Farah's eyes fly down to the most interesting head of lettuce she's ever shredded. I laugh aloud at all of our ridiculousness. How a parent can instantly take away your adulthood and make you feel as small as a child is beyond me. I hope I never have this effect on my kids.

My mother spins from her place beside Maureen and cuts a look at all of us. "I don't see anything funny about watching your figure. I don't weigh anymore today than I did when I was in college."

This elicits a whole new round of laughter from Bonnie and me. Farah is still too young to be irreverent. "Mother, no one should weigh what they weighed in her twenties. I was a stick then. I quite like my curves, thank you very much." I punctuate that by popping another piece of cheese into my mouth and humming, "Mmm…"

"Really, girls," she chastises. "And you never did answer my questions," she reminds me. "Maureen, make sure to slice those cucumbers real thin, now. Celeste, Bradford?"

"Yes, Ms. Claire," she says as she exchanges a knowing look with me. I love that woman. She may be my parents' live in house-keeper, but she'd been there for me more than my mother ever had.

"Bradford went to law school at Ole Miss. He practices enter-tainment law and does quite well. He's never been married and is thirty-five," I spit out.

"Ole Miss," she replies with contempt. "Are you two serious?" she asks. I roll my eyes again. *Let's focus on the fact that he went to a rival college, shall we?*

"They haven't even kissed," Bonnie offers.

"Thanks, Bon," I say sarcastically.

"Why haven't you kissed?" Farah asks. "He obviously likes you. Do you not feel the same?"

I busy myself with taking Adrian's ranch out of the refrigerator. I can't believe my mother hadn't thrown it out. It was a good ques-tion. One I, unfortunately, didn't have the answer to. I couldn't tell them that when I was with Bradford I felt like I was cheating on Adrian. How could you cheat on someone you couldn't be with? "We're taking it slow," I reply. "That's why he drove out with Louis, and we're kind of keeping our distance. I want the boys to get to know him on a non-threatening level for a bit before I introduce him as someone I am dating."

"I think that's wise," Farah says. Bonnie knowingly cuts her eyes at me.

"Well, in my day, there was none of this sneaking around and taking time sort of thing. You were either together or you weren't," my mother says.

"We're not sneaking around, Mother. And it's different. I have young, impressionable children depending on me. I have to be careful."

"Dear, I know it may seem strange because Tripp and he are brothers, but have you considered William?" My movements freeze upon hearing William's name. He was out there somewhere today on this very property. It's part of the reason I didn't want to be here. But it was our annual Labor Day celebration, so I felt obligated to attend. Slowly, my eyes search out Bonnie's and she gives me a sympathetic smile. "Celeste?" My mother prompts. It had been three days, and I still hadn't told Bonnie about William's latest endeavors to win me over. I was so embarrassed. "I mean who better to rear Tripp's children than his own brother?" My eyes shoot over to my mother's, and I see eyes that mirror mine in color and shape. I could only pray that that look had never been exuded from mine—cold, calculating, shrewd, manipulative.

"Mother—" I'm cut off by the boys excited voices heading this way. "I don't want to talk about him, Mother, not now, not ever. Do you understand?"

My mother gives a jaded, little laugh. "Really, Celeste, that was—"

"I mean it, Mother. Don't."

About that time, the boys reach the kitchen; and I'm distracted by Adrian removing a clinging Paris from his back. I give him a relieved smile that is short-lived when a fast-moving Finn barrels into my shin. I cry out in sheer pain as my recent injury throbs with a beating pulse. I spin toward the windows and stare out unseeing, trying desperately to control the pain coursing through my leg, the tears in my eyes, and the perspiration that has gathered on my forehead.

Maureen is at my elbow in a second. "Celeste, you all right, sweetie?" I just nod.

"I'm sorry, Mom," Finn apologizes and rubs my back soothingly. "I didn't mean to hurt you. I didn't hit you that hard, did I?"

I pinch my lips together. I want to assure him that I'm OK, but I'm not and know if I open my mouth I may start sobbing. So I take a deep breath, nod my head at him, and turn to take him in, but as I do, Archer's terrified expression catches me off guard, and a furious one from Adrian soon distracts me from Archer. Adrian slowly leans up from his folded stance over Archer. His gaze never leaves mine. And I know. I know that Archer has divulged our little secret. One that I hadn't asked him to keep but had hoped that he would.

Shaking my head at Adrian, I start to move toward him only to have him backing away from me. If I weren't a stronger woman, I would have disintegrated into a pile of ash with his scorching look. He isn't moving fast, so I don't either. I just follow him out of the room, but when I hit the hallway, he is gone. I hear the side door slam, so I take off after him.

As I hit the top step, I see him disappear into the barn. Launching myself down the steps, I wince with every jarring step; but I have to get to him. I sprint across the yard slinging the barn door open as I reach it. Wanting to maintain some privacy, I quickly close it behind me.

Breathing hard and frozen in the middle of room, Adrian has his arms extended from his sides, but his eyes are frantically searching the room like he's looking to exact more destruction. My eyes follow his to the disarray of shovels and axes and barrels and pitchforks. I'm impressed. He was able to do quite a bit of damage in the short time it took me to get over here.

"Don't come near me," he says, his voice dripping with anger. Those eyes dark and troubled as an angry ocean train themselves somewhere over my head.

"Adrian, I don't know what Archer—"

"He told me that William hurt you and that you told him William was not a nice person who'd be very sorry for what he did to you. But we both know that is bullshit. William will never be sorry for what he did on his own...but he will be sorry, Cel. That bastard will be very sorry," he promises. His eyes finally focus on me, and I see understanding there. However, his menacing tone and his scathing look have me shivering.

Being across the room from him is killing me. Without further hesitation, I launch myself at him. I hit him with such velocity he takes a step back to regain his footing. Wrapping me tightly in his strong arms, he drops his face and buries it in my hair. Breathing me in deeply, I feel him shudder under me; and I just hold on with everything I've got. I don't know how long we stand there. Me comforting him. Him comforting me. Finally, he pulls back, his gaze still seething, he asks me the one thing I'd hoped he wouldn't.

"What exactly did he do to you? And don't you dare think of lying to me and covering for him."

Nodding my head at him, I look up at what exists beyond the ceiling and pray that what I'm about to tell him won't forever mar his opinion of me. Meeting his stare once again, I tell him without hesitation and without embellishment exactly what happened. I'm surprised I'm able to finish, for his arms tighten with every single, damning word I speak until I am breathless with my final words.

His telling eyes have gone distant, and I know he is plotting vengeance. "Adrian, I handled it. Do you hear me? I hurt him. I bit his lip all the way through and hurt his...manhood. Do you understand? I took care of it."

Gazing out over my head again, he nods and releases his grasp on me a little. One hand comes back to smooth my wild hair down and behind my ear. His eyes focus on his actions. I savor the feel of his hand fisting itself in my hair. "I understand," he assures me. Finally, he brings his deceitfully tranquil eyes back to mine. "But I'm gonna fucking beat the shit of him. Do you understand that?" he asks as he narrows his eyes.

I sag with defeat. This is what I'd hoped to avoid. He releases me and calmly begins to right everything he had, just moments ago, thrown into disarray. His calm authority freaks me out more than his angry outburst. If that's what he'd decided while he was calm, then that would, in all likelihood, be what he'd go with.

"Adrian, don't you think that would make an already bad situation worse? I mean, when he left my house, he was very clear about where he stands with me. He's not going to approach me again."

He doesn't answer me as he replaces the equipment to its proper place. Placing both of his hands on the wall around the tools, he stands there and breathes for a few minutes. I wait patiently for my logic to sink in. Finally, he turns and his eyes take me in from head to toe and back again until he meets my eyes. Ever so slowly, he strides toward me until he's just a hair's breadth from my face. I lick my lips and force my eyes to stay on his. He puts his hands on either side of my face and I brace.

"Celeste, do you understand that what he did was assault? Sexual assault? Do you understand that he has no right to touch you like that? I understand that things get overlooked in this family. Chalked up to strong personalities and an overwhelming passion. But this will not be swept under the rug. You will not be forced to pretend this didn't happen."

If he only knew the whole ugly truth of the matter, I'd never be able to talk him out of gaining revenge against William. Placing both my hands on his cheeks, I beg, "Please don't do anything. I've handled it. He's not going to mess with me again. Tripp would've let me handle this the way I wanted."

"Newsflash, I'm not Tripp. Never wanted to be but in one aspect. We are very different people."

I thought the Tripp comment would win him over. He admired him so much. But I should've known better. Adrian is a strong-willed person and, like he'd just reminded me, he didn't do politics. Last ditch effort, I try, "As a favor to me, will you please leave it alone? I don't want everyone to know about it. I would be humiliated."

He stares at me and I can see the battle raging in him. "Shit!" he roars and I know I've won. I relax and think to offer him gratitude when I hear the barn door being jostled open. They're back. Adrian moves away from me, and I move in front of him.

It's all of them—my father, my father-law-in, my brothers,

Tripp's brothers, and Bradford. It looks as though the kids have already gone in, and I thank God for that little blessing. Now, get me through these next few minutes as I try to get us all out of here without it all going to hell.

Louis breaks the awkward silence that has ensued by finding Adrian and me alone together. His brow is furrowed as he strides forth to stand in front of me. "What's going on here? Celeste, are you all right?"

I guess the tension was that thick because even Louis could feel it and he'd just arrived. I open my mouth to assure him and everyone else that everything was fine, but William beats me to the punch. "She told you," he states. "Unbelievable. You won't be happy until everyone hates me, will you?" He sneers the last comment at me and my eyes meet his. Unfortunately, his are trained on Adrian's and I turn to take him in. Remember what I said about those expressive eyes? Well, they're trained on William and William should be the pile of ash now. "I'm curious to see how you've twisted the story to make yourself seem like the victim?"

"Told him what?" Louis asks me.

He beats me to the punch again, and his words ignite a fire of indignation in me. "She told him that we fooled around. That things got a little out of hand. No worries, she put me in my place." He walks around our fathers and stands behind Louis. "I don't see how it's any of your business what happens between me and Celeste anyway, Adrian. I'm pretty sure you agreed to—"

"That's enough," Adrian barks and I can feel his anger radiating out from his chest and into my back as he moves closer to me. "And 'what happened between you two' comes nowhere near describing what you did to her."

Louis spins to face William. "What did you do to her?"

"Nothing she didn't like at first. I can't help it if her regrets cause her to view things a little differently after the fact."

Adrian's chest bumps my back with every word he fires at William. "You ass. You forced yourself on her. You fucking sicken me. You always have, but this goes beyond anything I've ever thought you capable of. And beyond forgiveness. You've pulled that shit for the last time, cousin."

William raises his eyebrows at Adrian and his eyes widen in disbelief. The four of us have ended up practically on top of one another. My eyes shoot to my father's, imploring him to stop this, but he just stands there, transfixed by what is happening before him. I allow my eyes to drift over all the other male counterparts, and they're all staring at me as though I'm the one causing all this drama and they'd like nothing more than to squash it— and me—out. When my eyes meet Bradford's, I see tenderness and questions. I'm pulled from looking at them with William's next words. "It wasn't the first time she begged for it, cousin. And I can assure you it won't be the last."

I barely let out a gasp as a fist slams into William's face. It's not the fist I'd expected, though. It's Louis's and he's not stopping there. "Is that where you got your busted lip from, William?" Louis bellows as his next blow glances off of William's chin. "You're sick, man. I happen to know Celeste doesn't want shit to do with you! You attacked her and you're gonna pay." Louis has William backed into a stall and is pummeling him before anyone can get to him and pull him off. The sickening thud of fist on face actually thrills me. The fact that William is getting the shit kicked out of him actually makes up for the mortification I was feeling about everyone knowing everything now.

Adrian darts around me to pull Louis off of a slumping William. "He's good, brother. Ya did good," he congratulates him and pounds Louis on the back as he turns him and guides him out of the stall. When Louis reaches me, my eyes fill with tears and I throw myself at him.

"Thank you," I whisper. "I'm so sorry. I'm so sorry."

Louis is breathing hard and he squeezes me tight as he assures me, "You didn't do anything wrong, baby girl. That's all on him. You're going to put that behind you. You'll be stronger for it." He stops abruptly and leans back and narrows his eyes at me. "And you're gonna tell me if he or anyone else ever tries that shit again. I know you're my big sister, but it's my job to look out for you."

"Louis," I whisper as I wipe a little of William's blood from his cheek.

"What is going on in here? Everyone can hear you all." My mother's shrill voice cuts through our tender moment. The brothers Hebert are helping William out of the stall as my mother takes him in. "William, what happened to you?"

"I had to teach William some manners, Mother. It seems he didn't know how to keep his hands to himself where Celeste was concerned."

My mother's eyes, currently shooting darts out of them, cut to me. "You told them. After all this time. You TOLD them," she accuses.

"No, Mother," I try.

But my father finally intervenes, "Everyone out! Now! Essential parties only." Most everyone moves to leave. I feel Adrian close in on me again. "Adrian, you too. This doesn't concern you."

"Everything about her concerns me," he replies with quiet firmness. I thrill at his little declaration and I give him a little smile that, I hope, conveys my gratitude.

My eyes shoot an apology over to Bradford as he turns to leave. He gives me a lingering look before his eyes glance over to Adrian and then back to me. I try for a tentative smile before focusing my attention back to the involved parties. After most everyone has exited, my father takes control of the situation, "How do you know about this, Claire?" my father demands.

"They were very young," she starts, "I told her that it was just normal teenage hormones and not to be alone with him for a while. Leave it to Celeste to dredge up old misunderstandings in a most melodramatic fashion." Her cold resolve makes me shiver. She didn't care then and she doesn't care now. As that reality slaps me in the face yet again, I shake my head, dazed.

"What are you talking about, Claire? This incident just transpired."

Finally, my mother looks shaken, but only because she's just discovered that she's ratted herself out. "I don't know what you're talking about."

I move from Louis's embrace and Adrian's quiet support to stand before her. "They're talking about the fact that William attacked me again, Mother. He forced me to get him off," I spew, taking great pleasure in being so vulgar in her presence, "when I was twelve years old and he tried it again a few days ago. He didn't get so lucky this time," I sneer.

My father's steely voice slices the thick air in two. "You little bastard," he says to William. "And how dare you, woman? How dare you keep this from me and force our daughter to keep that secret."

"That's not exactly—" William tries but one look from Louis has him cowering where he stands.

"Don't speak to me like that," my mother says. "You know what I've endured for the sake of this family. And it's quite sanctimonious of you to pretend otherwise." Wow! I was really impressed with my mother for standing up to my father. He was one of the most intimidating men I knew. She must have something really good on him because he doesn't say any more.

Chip finally intervenes by telling William that he should leave and keep his distance for a while. *How about forever!* William storms out but not before kicking the recently rearranged barn tools to the ground. His brother and father follow him out.

My father moves to stand in front of me. He places his hands on my upper arms and pulls me to him slightly. I get lost in his expression for a moment, mesmerized by the look of regret and compassion that I'm fairly certain I've never seen from him before. "Please know that we will deal with William. He will not hurt you again, and you won't be forced to further endure his presence. Do you understand?"

"Yes, Daddy," I murmur, grateful, but is this really what it took for him to finally get it? "Thank you for supporting me." It feels awkward to thank him for something that he should have done, but honestly, I was that surprised that he had sided with me. He just gives me a nod and leaves me with Louis and Adrian.

Louis pulls me to his side and kisses the top of my head, rubbing his hand up and down my arm in silent support before he follows the rest of them.

I'm afraid to look at Adrian. He knows the whole ugly truth. Will he see me as a damaged, defiled woman? One he has to tiptoe around and coddle? That would kill me. I like how unpredictable and unruly he is with me. Nothing needs to change between us. *Wait! All that needs to change between us. Back to just friends. And not this twisted back and forth. Friends only! That's the plan, right?* I groan with frustration, and I hear him chuckle behind me. Yeah, I was totally lost in my own head for a minute there.

Spinning around, I take him in. All confidence, leaning against the barn wall with his arms folded and one leg kicked out over the other. I swallow hard as his pure, overwhelming masculinity hits me all at once. Faded jeans, scuffed up cowboy boots, faded navy, button-down Oxford with folded sleeves, disheveled dark brown hair, those unbelievably brilliant blue eyes...*How am I ever not supposed to want him?*

Shaking my head slowly at my dilemma, I remark, "I can't believe you can find any humor whatsoever in this situation." I try to mask my grin, but I just can't because he's so freaking adorable with his smug smile and his laugh lines.

"You're right. Nothing about that situation was funny, but I know what you're thinking, and that's damn laughable."

I quirk my brow at him. "Really? You know what I'm thinking, do you?"

"Yep, you're wondering if I'm going to hold this whole mess against you. Think about you differently. Treat you differently."

Damn! He's good. Well, pretty good. He's missed all my wayward thoughts about how irresistible he is. His comments sober me up a bit, and I nod my head at him seriously.

"Celeste, I didn't think it was possible, but I admire you more than ever—your tenacity, your strength, your independence." He pauses for a second and runs his hand over his stubble for a second before continuing. "I had a friend in college who experienced something similar. It was date rape, though. And it happened to be someone I'd considered a friend who assaulted her. Anyway, I knew something was wrong and had to pull it out of her and convince her to do something about it. Not to make light of what happened to you, but she wasn't able to fend him off, so it went way further for her and she didn't deal with it well. But the one thing she worried about more than anything else—looking weak and being embarrassed in front of everyone." He runs his hand through his hair, seeming to try to shake off his bad memory. "Anyway, we didn't need to attack William. You'd taken care of him all on your own. I'm just happy we were able to do it. The one thing that pisses me off, other than the fact that it happened, was that you didn't confide in anyone."

My heart aches for his friend and rejoices at his kindness. "I'm so sorry about your friend. In many ways, I was fortunate that he didn't take it farther. And, well, I did confide in someone—my mother—when I was a child, and she told me that it was a woman's duty to see beyond male weakness."

He blinks rapidly and leans his ear toward me as if he'd misheard me. "Excuse me?"

"Yes, could you imagine being a twelve-year-old child and being given that little gem of advice when someone has held you down and used you in that way?" My voice falters a little as I remember feeling so disgusting and so used and so distraught, yet my mother brushed it off like it was inconsequential.

My eyes had drifted closed, but they spring open with his gruff command. "Why are you still standing way over there? Come here," he orders. My feet move without any prompting from my brain. I don't stop until I'm completely enfolded by his warm, strong embrace. The few tears that escape are dried by the heat seeping through his shirt. After a few minutes, he releases his hold on me.

"Jesus, that woman is a piece of work. I'd always known she was…cold. But that's just heartless. I'm sorry, Celeste."

"Me too. But I think it actually feels good to have it out in the open. Maybe Chip and my father will quit with their interest in me and William becoming a couple."

"Yeah, that's definitely gonna happen. Don't you worry about that, OK?"

My brow furrows a little at his reassurance because I don't see how he can really stop it. My appreciation for him grows with his promise, however. "All right."

"I don't want to give you anything else to worry over, but we should probably discuss this now. Does Archer know the details of what happened?"

I blow out a relieved breath. "No, he only knows that William scared me and caused me to run into the table. Oh, and that I yelled at William in our front yard."

"Thank God for small blessings, right?"

"Yes, those were my sentiments exactly."

He laughs suddenly. Again, I wonder how he is able to find humor in almost every situation. "I'm hoping one good thing will come out of this."

I wrinkle my brow. "Like what?"

"It would make my fucking year if you could verify this." He pauses and his eyes dance with mischief. I want to keep him paused right here until I can get my fill of him, which would probably never happen. "Please tell me that the reason William is such an entitled asshole is because he has a little dick."

I gasp. "Adrian!"

"What? Cel, come on," he cajoles. He holds his fingers close together. "Does he have a tiny penis?"

"Oh my God, Adrian!" I take him in. His laughter. His humor. His ability to make me feel better, and I decide to make his effing day. "Yes, he has a small penis."

"I knew it!" He punches his hand. "I knew that little bastard had penis envy!" I can't help but join him in his laughter.

We've both subconsciously drifted toward the barn doors. "I guess we should get back to the festivities," he says.

"Yeah, I guess so." I reach out and grab his arm and give it a little squeeze. "Thank you for everything, Adrian."

He looks out over the yard for a moment, and I wonder where he's gone. When he suddenly turns toward me, I see a look he's never given me before; but I can't put a name on it. "Babe, anything for you." And before I can respond, he's gone.

I turn and lean back on the barn door. My hand finds its way over my heart and I massage it as I realize his words and his actions over these past couple of years have found a way to weave their way into my heart, creating a cocoon of knitting that has pulled tighter with each endearment, each look, each action. Sometimes it pulled painfully. Sometimes it pulled delightfully. Most of the time it was a mixture of the two—making the cocoon a bittersweet thing because his protection and his comfort were things I could never really have.

-Ten-

And That's My Final Decision

I REACH THE landing and throw my hands out to hold myself up while I pretend like I am stretching. The truth of the matter is, I am completely winded since I haven't been able to run or really do anything strenuous in a couple of weeks. My shins are already protesting even without the smaller version of the eggplant bruise I'm sporting. I lean out and deeply inhale the pungent smell of the mighty Mississippi. I absolutely love running along the riverfront. The sites, the sounds, the weirdoes…it's home, it's comforting. As if on cue, a sax player starts up his sad tale of misery and woe. Popping out my one ear bud, I enjoy his song for a moment.

I stretch a little more and decide to continue my normal route even though I am in pain. I have to exercise since I love to eat. A fast walk was going to have to suffice, however. Unzipping my iPod case, I grab a dollar and toss it into the open saxophone case. The player gives me a slight nod of thanks. As I leave hearing range of his beautiful tune, I put my ear bud back in and crank up my T.I. Usually, he works wonders on ridding me of my troubling thoughts, but today seems to be the exception. I keep replaying Bradford's comments about Adrian, and it's driving me insane.

Our conversation had started out innocuously enough, he asked about the incident, of course. I tried to downplay it as much as possible, and then he wanted to know about our family dynamic in general. It seems he got a pretty clear picture of how things worked in my family. Bradford wondered aloud why I wouldn't take legal measures against William, but I assured him that my family would deal with him as they saw fit. And I was fine with that. Talking about them and how they treat me and each other wasn't what made our conversation uncomfortable, though. It was black and white to me and crystal clear where I stood within the fold of my family. When he brought up Adrian, that's when the conversation turned murky and became quite awkward. I still wasn't sure what to do with it.

When I finished explaining Adrian's role in our lives, Bradford surprised me by saying outright what I knew deep in my heart and what Bonnie knew and had a hard time keeping quiet. "You and Adrian have feelings for each other." Simply said, complexly explained.

I spat and sputtered a bit before confessing, "Yes, we do. We've gotten close since Tripp passed. He's become my best friend."

Sounding thoughtful, Bradford's voice turned raspy when he said, "It's more than friendship for Adrian. I saw the way he acted toward you and looked at you. You don't look at a friend like that." He cleared his throat a little. "Anyway, I can get beyond his feelings. What I need to know, though, is if it is more than friendship for you?"

Of course it was more than friendship for me, but there wasn't squat I could do about it. I wanted to be honest with Bradford. I really did, but it was just too painful. So I sucked it up and boldfaced lied. "I'll only ever see him as Tripp's little cousin. We are close but only through friendship."

He'd seemed satisfied with my response. I guess I did have a bit of my mother in me after all. I figured my lie was for a good cause, though. I liked Bradford enough to try to explore a relationship, and

I could never have Adrian. Now if only the rest of my being would accept that.

Making my way past the French Market, which never fails to remind me of my great-grandfather making his living as an immigrant here, and over to Esplanade, I end up sprinting across Decatur because I'm not really paying attention to where I'm going. As soon as I get to the other side, I look back to see how close I had come to becoming road kill. When I turn back, I'm staring at a wall made of hard lines and a black suit. Glancing up, I am greeted by a pockmarked and somber face.

"Umm...excuse me," I mumble. I try to move around him but he grasps my elbow. *What the hell?* There are people everywhere. What is he doing?

"Ms. Hebert." He's not asking. He's telling.

Reaching up, I pop out my ear bud. "Umm...yes?" My voice is shaky even to my own ears.

"I'm a friend of your late husband. You mind if we talk in my car for a moment."

My chuckle surprises me. It's loud and cackling. "I don't think so, Mr..."

"My name remains mine to know until you need to know," he states. "When you need to know, it'll be because you're in trouble." I shiver at his words despite my desire to be tough. He releases a deep sigh and glances around before he says, "If it helps, Tripp told me to tell you 'cream cheese and salsa with Triscuits and many late night runs to get them.'"

"Oh..." No one and I mean no one knew about this otherwise disgusting craving I'd had with all three of the boys. I didn't even tell Bonnie. I knew she'd never let me live it down. "OK."

He guides me over to his Town Car, makes me slide across the back seat, and then gets in behind me. "I'm going to keep this short and to the point. I'm not here to upset you, however, your late husband made provisions for you beyond the financial. I'm an 'associate' of his and I was tasked with keeping an eye on you and certain individuals in your life." I simply nod. "It seems some people in your life don't have your best intentions in mind, Ms. Hebert. Your husband was well aware of this and gave me some vital information that could cripple these individuals if they choose to try to harm you or your children in any way. Do you understand what I'm saying to you?"

Again, all I can do is nod my understanding. "Excellent. I'm not here to give you that information just yet. From where I sit, things look warm but not boiling. I don't want to risk your getting too close to that fire, mind you. So I wanted to give you this." He pulls out a black business card. Only it's not really a business card. Just a single phone number printed in white with the initials OG below it. "Now, when you feel yourself too close to that flame, you'll give me a call immediately, won't you?"

I don't answer either way. Instead I ask, "Tripp asked you to look out for me, so you've been watching me for almost two years?" I'm a little amazed by this news.

"Not really, no. More like watching those around you to make certain moves. These moves have been discussed with growing frequency the last few months, but it seems as though there has been some reluctance in going forth. Regardless, if you feel any more pressure from your family, you are to contact me as per your husband's request. The one thing they seem dead set against is your association with one Mr. Adrian Hebert. It seems they've got something on him as well and are prepared to use it should he become problematic."

I nod my head again and thank him as my head reels with all of the information he just gave me. Something on Adrian? What could they possibly have on Adrian? He gets back out of the car and motions for me to follow. As one of my feet hits the pavement, his parting comment causes me to look up briefly, "You're well aware of who you're up against should they decide to push matters along, aren't you, Ms. Hebert?"

My grim smile is probably quite telling but I assure him, "Yes, I certainly am. Thank you again."

Dazed, I begin to make the trek back home. Only I'm completely robbed of energy and stunned beyond belief. Why that is, I couldn't say. I know what they are and what they are capable of. I knew that Tripp knew. I didn't know that Tripp wanted to protect me from that so badly. This causes me to smile briefly. I'd always felt so alone in my large, boisterous family, but lately, that had completely changed. When I finally hit St. Charles, I decide taking the streetcar back home is an excellent idea. At the rate I'm going, I won't make it home in time to get ready for the show tonight. Typically, riding the streetcar is one of my favorite things in the world. Today, however, I barely notice all that is going on around me as I ponder just exactly how close to igniting I should let myself get.

"YOU LOOK BEAUTIFUL," Bradford tells me upon picking me up. I'd let him pick me up at the house but only because the boys weren't home. I look down and grimace a bit at my outfit. I hated wearing long pants to a concert. New Orleans was sweltering enough without additional clothing weighing you down. But I have to admit this outfit is gorgeous, and the side slits running up the legs will allow for some airflow. The blood-red genie pants could either be worn as smocked pants or pulled up and worn as both a top and pants, exposing my shoulders. I'd opted for that look, thrown my hair into a French twist, and paired it with my Louboutin leopard heels and lots and lots of gold "jingly" jewelry as Finn called it.

I glance up and get lost in Bradford's look of sincerity for a moment. "Thank you. Would you like me to show you around before we go?"

"Yeah, absolutely."

I lead him through the living parts of the house and avoid the bedrooms. When I show him my office, he gets really interested. My heart expands and glows from within. "Celeste," he says as he fingers my sketches tacked all over the board, "you are really talented. These are amazing. And your whole house is just beautiful. I don't know much about design, but yours has a homey feeling, yet it's aesthetically pleasing as well. If that makes any sense."

I laugh and tell him, "It makes perfect sense because that's exactly what I was going for."

As I lead him back out and to the main part of the house, he continues, "You seriously need to look into how to get started with your own designs. Those few that I saw are inspired. Really."

Could this guy get any more perfect? I beam. "Thank you so much. That means a lot to me."

WHEN WE ARRIVE at the House of Blues, we meet up with practically everyone I know. We are that excited about our guys, our homegrown heroes hitting it big time. Bradford fits right in with everyone. He'd met most of them before. Even Louis and a friend have joined us. I happen to know Louis hasn't gone out in forever—being a junior associate certainly puts a damper on your social life. It's so good to see him loosen up.

After taking a sip of my mojito, I grab Louis's arm and drag him to the dance floor. "So who's your friend, honey?"

"Oh, yeah, just an associate at Teller and Brooks."

"He seems nice and funny too." I bite my lip a little as Louis throws a look over his shoulder at Lance.

"Yeah, he's a good guy."

Searching Louis's dark chocolate eyes for moment, I can clearly

EVERYTHING I'VE NEVER HAD

see how uneasy he is, so I switch topics. "It's good to see you out, enjoying yourself. You work too much."

He bobs his head in time with the music. "Yeah, you too, Cel. It's good to see you have a little fun. How about you and Bradford? He's a good guy. You see it going anywhere?"

Now I'm the one feeling uneasy. My eyes fly to Bradford's and the scorching look he's giving me causes me to falter in my step a little. Umm...wow! Taking a deep breath and giving him a little smile, I turn my attention back to Louis. "I like him. He reminds me of Tripp in many ways, but he's extremely thoughtful. Not that Tripp wasn't, you know? He was just very busy. I just mean his easy-going demeanor reminds me of Tripp. Bradford is really sweet, though, Lou. He'll send me text messages in the middle of the day for absolutely no reason. We're taking it slow, you know? But one day I told him I was exhausted from photo shoots and running the boys. Shortly after I got home, there was a knock on the door—delivery from Pho's." I raise my brows and grin.

"Nice. He's got tricks."

I smack Louis on the chest. "They're not tricks, Louis. He's thoughtful and considerate."

"And only that way in hopes to get that one thing."

I smack him again. "That's not true, Lou. Not every guy is after that."

"Umm...yes, yes we are. If we're not thinking about it, we're dreaming about it. If we're not dreaming about it or thinking about, chances are we're doing it."

I chuckle and grabbing his chin, give it a shake. "Louis! Why are you being so inappropriate?"

"What? You're almost forty years old. You should be well aware of how we operate."

With that little comment, my face falls and I no longer care what guys think—ever. "Did you just say I'm almost forty?" My voice rises an octave with each word, and Louis's eyes widen.

"Aww...shit!"

"You better be glad we're in the middle of a club, Louis Mathias Vigier Hebert," I say with a laugh, "or I would claw your eyes out."

Louis's eyes shimmer with mirth. "I'd like to see you try. I'm your baby, remember?"

"Aww...Lil' Louie...Yes, I remember." I grab him and hug him tight. He was my baby. I'd been seven when my parents had brought him home. I've doted upon his cute, little self everyday since. When he went off to the Naval Academy, I'd felt like a piece of me had died. "Love you, baby boy."

I hear him groan at my endearment, which causes me to chuckle and hug him tighter. "Love you too, Cel."

About that time, I hear them announce our boys. "Ladies and gentleman, the House of Blues is proud to present local talent and rising artists, the Dog Tags!" I quickly release Louis and spin around, clapping with everything I've got. When that's not loud enough, I form a megaphone with my hands and shout into it.

I feel hands on my hips and turn to take in Bradford. I smile at him before my eyes drop to his lips. They move in and he places a lingering kiss just under my ear, causing me to shiver. He grins against my skin, and I relish the feel of his hands giving me a tight squeeze. I lean in to him as the guys make their way onto the stage.

Garner is the first to take the stage, so I turn and give Bonnie a huge grin and a thumbs up. She, of course, barely glances at me because she's so mesmerized by the sight of him. He is good look-ing. Well over six feet, he towers over the rest of the Dog Tags. And I'm still astonished at the fact that he can get his mohawk to stand that high. He's clearly in his element as he jogs onto stage and then starts a rousing drum cry for the rest of the band to enter to.

Next up, Tracy, the bassist, appears. Clearly out of his element, he just gives a little wave and heads straight for his instrument. He's so adorable. I chant his name a little like I did Garner's and spot a blush spreading over his face.

My laughter dies and my breath catches as my favorite Dog Tag and obvious obsession graces us with his presence. And that's exactly what it looks like. He saunters downstage, doing his little praying bow; and I feel like I'm going to hyperventilate. Just by entering the room, he's sucked all the oxygen out of it. I just stare. I don't chant his name. I don't look as Chris and then Zach take the stage. I can't look away. I watch him strap his guitar on and warm up the crowd and am just enthralled. He has on his signature faded and frayed blue jeans and a tight, black, v-neck t-shirt. He's wearing his black scuffed up boots. And his only embellishments are his heavy crucifix necklace and dog tags. I love the way his hair flops around as he bounces his head in time with the music. They've already spoken to the crowd a bit and begin the intro to their first song when I finally break the spell he unknowingly has over me.

When I feel Bradford moving in time to the music behind me, I close my eyes and chastise myself for being such a horrible person that I could have a good man's arms, around me and be fantasizing about another man—and an unattainable one at that. Looking over to the side at our little group, I see his date, the doppelgänger. She's blown away too, and she gets to go home with him. Jealousy licks its fiery tongue all the way up my body and tears spring to my eyes. *What the hell?* I've never been jealous of anyone. And I am OVER feeling like this about a man I cannot have.

Spinning in Bradford's arms, I lace my hands around his neck and give him an inviting look. His look of surprise isn't lost on me. I know I'm acting out of character, but I can't seem to help it. My survival instincts have kicked in. I have to do something about all this...this angst. I let my eyes drop to his lips, and I lick mine. When his lips crush mine, I moan and tighten my hands in his hair. Coaxing my lips open with his own, I feel his tongue, insistent and warm, thrusting against mine, and I try to lose myself in his kiss. I swallow his groan and savor the feel of having him inside my mouth. His kiss catches me completely off guard as it is unexpectedly delicious. Then I'm not trying to lose myself. I have lost myself.

Making out like teenagers in the middle of a dance floor is a new one for me. I try to pull back a little, but Bradford's having none of that. His hands snake from my hips all the way around me until I'm pulled tight against his front and evidence of the effect I'm having on him is quite clear. Finally, his kiss changes to a slow, sensual one and I let myself go and enjoy it for what it is and who it's with. "Geez, Celeste," he murmurs against my lips and places another sweet little kiss on the corner of my mouth. "What have you done to me?"

I open my eyes and find his pretty blue eyes, heavy with arousal, staring at me and realize I don't deserve him. I don't deserve this good man giving me this incredible look like I'm this amazing person. I whimper a little at this revelation. If he knew I'd kissed him because I was so turned on by Adrian, it would hurt him, and I don't want to hurt him. I can tell he's falling for me, and falling for him would be as easy as putting one foot in front of the other if I didn't already have the heavy weight that is Adrian pressing down on me. I envision myself walking out of here hand in hand with Bradford and not seeing Adrian again, and my heart protests violently. *I'm starting to piss myself off!* I need to figure this out and quick.

"About a hundred emotions just passed over those gorgeous eyes of yours, Celeste. So which is it? Are you happy? Do you want us to pursue this? Or is it one of the others? Regret? Fear? Anger?" he asks perceptively.

Unfisting my hands, I smooth his hair and run my hands down his shoulders; his muscles jerk as I do. "What's wrong?" I ask.

"It feels good. Too good." He laughs. "You're making me nervous."

So honest. And I'm such a liar. "I think it was a terrific first kiss, so I'm hopeful. But, like you, I'm nervous."

"I would say you can trust me. But isn't that the first thing that someone who can't be trusted says?" He gives a slight laugh before he continues, "How about I say that I'm completely into you and haven't been into anyone in a very long time. I don't do casual, and I don't play around."

I hear my sharp intake of breath and squeeze his arms as I respond, "I can't believe we're talking about this right here, right now."

"Yeah, me either. It wasn't how I saw it playing out in my mind, but I don't want you to be scared of this, of us. And the kiss we just shared scared you. You can't be rehashing that and coming to false conclusions before we have a chance to sort things out." When his hold tightens on me possessively, I make a split-second decision. My heart crumbles with it, but amidst the rubble, the potential in the ruins for it to come back together into something beautiful with Bradford shines bright.

I run my hands back up his arms, his neck, and to his jaw. Bringing his face down to mine, I kiss him with everything I have. Every thought, every part of me focuses on him and this kiss. I hope he's as intuitive as I think he is.

When he pulls back, I see nothing but relief and acceptance on his face. He understands. I spin back around in his arms as the band strikes up another song, and I don't look at their rhythm guitarist for the rest of their set.

WHEN THE DOG Tags thank everyone for coming out, I'm ready to go. My feet are hurting, and my leg is throbbing. What was I thinking wearing these shoes? And now, I'm curious to spend some time with Bradford now that all of my attention is focused on him and him alone. Bradford has other ideas as does the rest of my group. They're in it for the long haul. I need some air and the restroom so I head toward that area. Of course, when I make my way through the throng, the line for restroom is spilling into the hallway and the door says emergency exit only. Standing with my back to the hall, I decide I'll wait in line and just people watch. One of the naughtiest songs ever comes on while we're waiting for the main act, and I can't help but move my hips in time with the rhythm.

Maroon 5's "Kiwi" lyrics permeate my brain and flood it with vivid imagery as I wonder what it would feel like for me to make him moan. No, no, not *him*. I shake my head. I'm done with that. I try to lose myself in the music and forget about him and all that makes him *him* when I feel his warm breath on my neck and his rough hands on my thighs through the slits in my genie pants. My head falls back and a throaty moan escapes my lips. "Adrian, no," I half-protest. "We can't—"

"I know, Celeste, I know," I hear him mutter. "Babe, I couldn't take my eyes off of you all night. Don't you know that I know. I don't…don't want to want you like this. But geez, babe, I'm only human and watching you dance with him when I knew you were thinking of me…"

My body moves and sways with his and my hands find their way around his neck as I hold him to me. When I feel his hands move toward my center, my eyes fly open; but they are unseeing as I would give anything if we were alone and not in this crowd.

"Adrian, I want to…"

"What, baby? What do you want? Whatever it is…whatever you want. I'll get rid of Jennifer and Bradford. Is that what you want?"

I can't speak as his tongue plays behind my ear and he runs little kisses up and down my neck, moaning and groaning as he goes. "These pants, babe. All I could think the whole show was how I wanted to rip these things off with my teeth. Fuck me," he grinds out against my skin. And that's exactly what I want. I whimper. "I'm gonna turn those whimpers into screams. Do you hear me, Celeste? You'll be screaming my name."

"Adrian, I…I want you, please." He removes his hands from my thighs and grasps my hands tight. I feel him being jostled into me a bit. Then I hear him being slapped on the back.

"Adrian, dude, that was a great show," says Louis. I squeeze my eyes shut tighter, willing Louis away. I feel Adrian tense and I bury my face into his side and try, unsuccessfully, to melt into the wall. "Aw, man, sorry," he says when he discovers Adrian is not alone. "I didn't mean to interrupt."

He moves around us to give us our privacy, and I think I'm in the clear until I hear his muttered curse. Then louder he says, "Man, what are you thinking?" Mortified, I finally chance a glance at him. He's gone pale. "Celeste, how long has this been going on?"

I feel like a teenager getting caught making out by her parents, and I want to die. I try to speak but nothing comes out. I clear my throat. "Louis, nothing is going on. There were just...just a few stolen moments."

"You two are insane. Adrian, I think you were pretty clear on where they stood. If they find out—"

"I know, I know," Adrian says, cutting him off. "It was a mistake. I got caught up. It won't happen again." I swear I can feel his temperature and his voice drop by ten degrees.

"Look, y'all get this shit straightened out. I'm going to go talk to Bradford. Damn, Celeste. Bradford doesn't deserve this."

I can only nod. Louis stomps off, leaving me with Adrian. I turn and dash down the hall with Adrian close on my heels. He grabs my hand and pulls me into a smaller hallway, and we stand there and stare at each other for a few beats until it empties out.

"I thought we'd agreed. Your girlfriend and my...boyfriend are out there. Why did you do that?"

"I know. Shit, I'm sorry. Why the hell are you wearing that damn outfit? And you wouldn't look at me. What the hell was that about? The whole time I was playing I was watching you. Watching you dance with him, rub on him. And it killed me. And there isn't shit I can do about it. Then I walk out, determined to ignore you, and there you are shaking your ass in those non-existent pants."

My blood is boiling. He's made it out like I purposefully set about to seduce him with my choice of clothing and dancing. *Did I?*

No, I dress for myself. I like this outfit and didn't think of him once when I chose it. "I didn't wear this for you, Adrian. I wore it for me. I can't help if you can't keep your imagination and your hands to yourself."

"Did you wear it for him or me or both of us? Are you done teasing the two of us? Toying with us?"

"What? I'm not toying with you." And I'm not. That indicates pre-meditation. And these feelings are not pre-meditated. They just are. "I'd made a decision tonight. A final one. I'd decided that I was done having 'moments' with you. I'm done lusting after you, wanting you. And then you…you ruined all that with one touch. You have to stop! I can't do this anymore! You're killing me!"

"*I'm* killing *you?*" He pauses while he tries to catch his breath, and I can see him collecting his thoughts. He's breathing hard like he's just climbed the stairs to the Eiffel Tower. Completely worth it, completely exhilarating, completely energy zapping. But something once you've done it, you know you'll never do it again. Would it be that way with us? A one time thrill to be had and remembered with fondness because you'd probably never have it again. "I'm…hear me when I say this...please. Why are we killing each other? We're grown ass people. Do you know how many times, how many ways I've tried to come up with for us to be together? What if we say fuck them and be together?"

The roller coaster that my heart was on comes to a screeching halt. Isn't this what I wanted? Adrian saying screw the conse-quences? Let's be honest about how we feel and be together. Then I recall the scary enlightening conversation I had with Mr. OG today. Whatever they're holding over him must be big. They don't want us together. And they'll stop at nothing to ruin both of us, right? Hot tears spill over my lashes and I watch as they hit the cold, gray concrete beneath my feet. I raise my eyes to his, and I see his own tears mirroring mine. It took a lot for him to say what he just said to me. I can see that. I can also see *them* tearing him apart, and I whimper aloud at that thought. I can't let that happen. I can't be that selfish. God knows I want to. A little run of pleasure isn't worth the destruction it will surely inflict. I draw myself up, wipe my tears away, and meet his expression head on.

"Adrian, I may be physically drawn to you, but it's not worth hurting everyone I care about for a little physical pleasure." I steel myself and conjure my inner bitch that I pray I inherited from my mother. "And I've decided that I'm over you."

The rapidness with which his tears dry should've been my first clue to run, but I don't listen to my instincts and the ugliness that Adrian spews at me I know I deserve, but it's still hard as hell to take. "Over me? You're over me? You're physically attracted to me? And I'm not worth it?" *Oh my God, no! I'm in love with you, damn it!* He sneers a laugh at me. "Over me? To be over me, babe, you'd have to have been under me. And if you'd ever been under me, there'd be *no* getting over me." He takes a long stride and his arms come up to pin me in. "You are fucking chicken. You care about me, but you're not a big enough person to do anything about it. Either that or you're the biggest cock tease in existence. So which is it, Celeste? Which offense are you guilty of?"

"What do they have on you, Adrian? You tell me. What did Louis mean by 'they' don't want us together? What offense are *you* guilty of?" I shout my questions back at him so that I'm mere centimeters from his face when I'm done. I feel like I've just swallowed ten thousand razorblades and they're slicing up my insides as they make their way through my body. I hurt everywhere, and all I want do is curl up in his arms because I know he could make all that go away. I'm hurting myself and him, yet I can't do anything about it. I want to touch him, but I know I have to be stronger than that.

And at that precise moment of my almost faltering, I thank God for a crowded club and good friends. "Umm…Celeste, are you OK?" It's Farah and I'm so grateful I could kiss her. I turn my head and say, "Yes, I'm fine. I'll be even better when Adrian lets me go."

Taking a deep breath, Adrian throws his arms out dramatically. "Oh, I'll let you go. No problem." I stifle another sob and feel yet another razorblade slice, and it cuts deep.

"What's going on here?" Farah asks incredulously.

"Nothing," I say, "absolutely nothing. We're done here."

"I thought you two were friends. Why are you yelling at each other? You both look like you've been crying too."

"I found out what Adrian's been up to is all. And I've asked him to keep his distance," I lie. Well, I guess now I have asked him to keep his distance.

His jaw clenches as he watches me walk away, leaving him with Farah and my shredded heart.

When I exit the hall, I grab the wall and bend over, clutching my stomach and fighting back tears. I need to get it together.

If only I'd made it further. I can't move when I hear Farah say, "Adrian, what was happening between you two?" Adrian only grunts in reply. "You have to know that Celeste loves you, right? I know it may seem like I don't know much because I don't say much, but I know that. I'm an observer so to speak. And what I've observed is that you love each other and care about each other deeply. She's just scared, but you can't give up on her." My eyes almost bug out of my head. How in the world does she know all that? My quiet Farah.

He exhales deeply. "Farah, you're a nice girl. So I don't want to offend you in any way at all, but if I loved Celeste I'd be a dead man 'cause she'd chew me and spit me out with gusto. I've finally come to the conclusion that Celeste is my cross to bear. We all have them. Mine is just weighing heavily on me right now. But I'll get it figured out—"

I don't stick around to hear anymore. I can't take any more heartache or heartbreak tonight. I stumble to the now empty restroom since the main act has made their way to the stage. I take a few minutes, fortifying my walls both mentally and physically. I fix my make-up and my hair and take calming breaths. Taking one last look at myself, I decide that that was the one and only time Adrian Hebert, or any man for that matter, would make me hurt like that.

THE RIDE HOME is quiet. Bradford keeps trying to engage me in conversation, and like Teflon, it all just beads up and trickles off on impact. I just can't do it. And it's not fair to him nor is it fair to me. When he pulls in my driveway, I take a deep breath, unbuckle my seatbelt, and turn toward him as he turns to face me. He's so handsome and wonderful. I'm an awful person. But I'm about to fix that on one point.

"I don't like the way you're looking at me, Celeste. And I don't understand where things went wrong. One minute we're dancing and kissing and enjoying each other. The next I couldn't even put my hand on your back without getting freezer burn. So what gives?"

"Bradford, you are such a nice guy." He groans and I hear his head *thonk* as he dramatically drops his head on the window glass. "But I'm feeling very conflicted and overwhelmed right now."

He surprises me by grabbing my hand and kissing my knuckles. "Well, that's not exactly a break up, is it? Are you saying you don't want to see me or you don't want to see anyone?"

"I can't see anyone yet. I'm not ready."

"This may seem crazy to you since we haven't know each other long, but I'll wait, Celeste. I'll wait till you're ready."

Again, why can I not get on board with this sweet guy? "I can't ask you to do that, Bradford."

"Celeste, you're the first person I've been interested in, much less cared about, in years. You're not asking me to do anything. If you're interested in me the way I am you, I'll give you some space."

I nod my head. He's perfect for me. He's everything I should want. And on some level I do, but if there are a hundred levels of interest, Adrian's volcanic effect has overflowed onto all my levels so that Bradford is hanging on around fifty. And pursuing this while

I'm so conflicted and indecisive wouldn't be fair to either of us. Maybe I do just need time to get Adrian out of my head.

Nodding my head, I say, "If you're willing to give me a little time and space, I'll be in touch when I'm ready to date. But if you meet someone else, I don't want you holding out for me."

He laughs loudly like that's the funniest thing he's ever heard, grabs me by the back of my head, and kisses me hard. And I do get lost for a second. When I realize I'm losing myself, I pull back gently.

"See? It's there. You just have to be open to it. I know you feel it too."

I give him a half-grin, let myself out of his car before he can move, and walk quickly to my porch. Turning, I give him a smile and a wave. Time and distance...I hope that's all I need.

-Eleven-

Everybody Hurts

IT'S LATE. I'M exhausted. I'm miserable. I've cried enough tears to last me a lifetime. Rolling over, I grab my phone and pull up Facebook to see if anyone else is still up at three o'clock in the morning. Yep, look at all those insomniacs. After a few minutes of scrolling through status updates and funny pictures, I toss it down and reach for my book. I try to read my latest romantic thriller to no avail. She's an annoying lead who won't confess her true feelings for the man she's obviously fated to be with and that hits a little too close to home for me right now. My own indecision and lack of self-control is going to drive me to drink, so I don't need any help from what should be my escapist reading therapy.

Lying there staring at the ceiling, I feel my phone vibrate. Hoping no one's hurt or in trouble, I reach over and grab it. My eyes almost bug out of my head.

I'm sorry I'm such an ass. Can we meet tomorrow? Talk?

Still as a wooden plank, I lie there for a minute just staring at it. I know what I have to say but don't want to say it. Not responding is not an option, though, because we have the same phone and he knows I've read his message. *Be strong, be strong!* I chant. Even though he can be kind of a jerk, he can also be incredibly sensitive. No matter which personality I get, I love them all because they're what makes him so genuine and unlike anyone else. And, of course, I don't want to hurt him—but it has to be this way. Like removing a bandage this must be done quickly to avoid inflicting even more pain. Here goes.

I think it best we don't see each other for a while. I've repeatedly proven I'm just too tempted when it comes to you.

So...what I fought so hard to keep from happening is happening anyway?

My poor, tattered heart slows. How will it ever recover?

I'm so sorry that I'm not stronger. I'm not saying forever. I'm just saying for now.

I know he's seen it, but I have to wait a while for his response. Every time I touch my screen to keep it from going to sleep, I offer a silent plea that we'll be all right.

I understand. Does this mean I can't see the boys either?

My response is quick and fervent. **Absolutely not! Of course you can see the boys. They adore you.** And so do I, which is why I have to let you go.

So I can just text you then to make sure we're on the same page or not as the case may be?

Yes, that'll be fine.

A full minute passes before his tenderness takes another swipe at my heart.

I'll miss you.
Me too.

THE NEXT FEW weeks are pure torture. The boys know something's not right. My friends know. I don't go to any shows with them. Bonnie is even being sensitive and not bringing up Adrian at every turn like she had been. Louis is pissed at me because I hurt Bradford and he knows why. The boys are confused because Adrian's not coming around to hang out like he used to. So in total, I've made all our lives fantastically miserable.

I keep waiting for this pain to go away. And it just won't. I don't know if it's because I've never been heart-broken or rejected or rejected anyone, but it just hurts. All the damn time. I can think of it and nothing else, and I feel like such a fool. I want to challenge our family and go after what means most to me, but then I recall Adrian's venomous statements that night and remind myself that, even when he was that upset, he wouldn't say things that didn't have a little bit of truth to them.

How can I risk everything for someone who doesn't fully return my feelings? Yes, I know Adrian likes me, admires me, wants me. But that's not enough for me. I know this because during this silence I've been able to recognize and admit something significant—I'm in love with Adrian Gabriel LeBlanc Hebert. Love without condition. Love I cannot escape. As in even though his feelings are only fleeting or physical or shallow, he dates a woman who looks exactly like me, and can make me angrier than anyone I've ever known, I adore him, desire him, need him. The intensity of all those emotions, emotions I've never felt at this level or all at once completely overpowers me, which is why, no matter how hard I try, I cannot resist him.

So I go about my business of taking care of the boys and working and trying desperately not to think of him and what could be. And pretending that my heart doesn't resemble crackled glass every time I hear the doorbell ring, knowing it's him here to pick up the boys.

I'm making the boys their favorite breakfast treat because it's tedious and will keep my mind somewhat off what's going on when I hear Paris hit the bar.

"Good morning, baby. How'd you sleep?"

"Good, Ma. Mmm...beignets. How about you? Do you feel any better?" he says as he rubs his hands over his face and ruffles that wavy brown hair. I meet his sleepy dark brown eyes and see so much heart shimmering there. My Paris—so wonderful.

"I'm good, sweetie. I feel fine."

"Everybody knows 'fine' is girlspeak for not fine, but don't ask," he retorts.

I burst out laughing. He's so right. "Where'd you hear that, crazy boy?"

"It's on an episode of *Full House* that Finn has played about ten times lately."

"Oh goodness. Y'all watch too much TV."

He puffs out a little sigh of exasperation. "We don't even have cable, Ma. How can we watch too much TV?"

"You know what I mean. Videos are still TV. And I really am fine. Don't worry about your mom, OK?"

"And the first thing to do when someone says don't worry—is worry," he replies sagely. Shame on me for coaching my kids to always look below the surface of what is offered. *Total backfire!*

I'm saved from anymore awkward verbal dodging when Archer and Finn enter the kitchen. Archer piles up next to Paris at the bar, but Finn makes his way to me and buries his face in my side. "Mmm...the beignets woke me up, Mom. What's the special occasion?" Archer asks.

I put my arm around Finn's shoulder and give him a squeeze. "No occasion. I just felt like making them."

"You usually make us beg cause they're bad for us. And they make Finn act like he's on crack," Archer jokes.

"You boys are full of jokes this morning." I squeeze Finn a little more. "Hey you, you're quiet. What's up?"

"Nothin'"

I give him a final squeeze. "Go put a shirt on for breakfast, sweetheart. It's almost ready."

"I don't wanna." He hesitates and then mutters, "I'm too sexy for my shirt."

"Huh?"

He lifts his head and I see mischief dancing in there. "I'm too sexy for my shirt," he starts singing and moving around the bar, "So sexy it hurts."

"Oh, yes," I say with a laugh, "there's my Finn. I knew the quiet was too good to be true."

"You'd be bored if I was quiet," he says as he runs out of the room to get his shirt, singing Right Said Fred at the top of his lungs.

"Wow!" I clap my hands and roll my eyes. "OK, boys, eat up. Louis will be here to get you soon. We've gotta get you packed for the weekend."

"Are you coming up?"

"Umm...I may. I'm not sure yet. If I do, it'll be Sunday afternoon." I'm not jumping to spend time at the compound. And I didn't know if Adrian would be there. "Who wants to do the powdered sugar first?"

"Meeeee!!!!" I hear Finn all the way from the back of the house. I drop my voice to a whisper. "Geez...that boy has excellent hearing."

"I heard that," he shouts again.

AFTER I GET the boys packed and off with Louis, who barely gave me an acknowledging nod, I get cleaned up and spend the day taking care of various errands. Tonight is girls' night and I'm thrilled. While I'm out, I pick up everything to make cosmos. I'm in dire need of a little distraction. Getting home late, I run around the house throwing all my distractions in a tote—Scrabble, chick flicks, my recent photo shoot proofs. Running into my bedroom, I change into my comfy yoga pants and favorite threadbare Saints t-shirt. I'm planning to have a nice buzz, so I trade my contacts for glasses, throw my hair in a high ponytail, and slip on my flip-flops.

Dashing out the door, I decide to walk the four blocks to Bonnie's. If I'm too inebriated to walk home, I'll just call a cab. As I pass the block that Adrian's apartment is on, my steps falter and I slow, glancing down his street to see if I can catch a glimpse of him. Willing myself to keep walking, I imagine what he's been up to these last three weeks. It's pure torture because, while I've been distracting myself with cooking and the kids and work, I can picture the black-headed, brown eyed distraction he's had wrapped around him.

I promised myself I would stop these musings, but it's so difficult. Feeling like a lovesick teenager, I chastise myself for the millionth time. Steeling myself, I straighten and walk with purpose. As soon as I focus my gaze ahead instead of behind, I see him exiting a corner store with the little lookalike tucked into his side, and I feel myself fold in like a falling house of cards.

His arm is thrown around her casually, and she is looking up at him like he is the greatest thing since stilettos. He's looking down at her and laughing a little at what she's saying. They are picture perfect, and it's just too easy to imagine myself there in the curve of his arm. I freeze and do just that for a moment. Snapping out of it after a few seconds, I panic. Frantically, I glance around, looking for a place to hide, and figure I probably have ten seconds before I'm spotted.

Just as I move to hide behind a rack of tie-dyed t-shirts, Adrian's eyes fly up and zero in on me. I see him stiffen and watch his arm drop. I move to stand behind the rack and drop my head, pretending like these are the most interesting t-shirts I've ever seen. I pray that he just keeps moving along. I don't want the awkward conversation, nor do I need any more fuel for my already flaming desires.

As he passes me, I can't help but look over. His gaze looks like it's never left mine and it's full of hurt and questions. He looks... wounded. I send him an apology with my eyes, and we maintain eye contact until he rounds the building and starts down his street.

Releasing a shaky breath, I collapse against the wall and try to calm my erratic heart. He looked so good. He had a little growth of facial hair and his hair was a little longer than usual, but he looked so good. I close my eyes tight for a moment. My appreciation of his aesthetically pleasing nature doesn't last long before my brain switches to jealous mode.

Is he serious about her? I mean, honestly, I thought he was using her as some sort of replacement for what he couldn't have and that he'd be over her by now. And shouldn't I be happy for him? It's good that he has someone. Someone who obviously makes him happy. This should make me happy for him, not stung because it's not me. It can never be me, the rational part of my brain insists. Logically, I know this. Breaking this to my emotions is another issue, though. They do protest.

Finally, I pull myself from the wall and start to head toward Bonnie's again. The shopkeeper gives me a dirty look for spending so much time and not buying anything. I just shrug and hurry my steps along.

Raising my hand to let myself into Bonnie's, I'm surprised when the door is wrenched open from the other side and a furious Garner almost barrels over me. "Whoa, Garner, are you OK?"

He runs his hand over the top of his mohawk and pins me with his bright green eyes. He puts his hands on his hips for a moment before beginning to gesticulate wildly. "Your friend is a lunatic. I can't talk to her. She's just...just crazy. What is wrong with her? I'm dying to know. I didn't break her, yet I'm paying for whoever did. Is that fair? Is that right? Damn, I've been patient but this is ridiculous. It's been months, Celeste, months. I don't know how much more of this shit I can take."

I blink rapidly, trying to process all he's just said. I've never heard him speak so much before and certainly nothing more than a few pleasantries and a few inappropriate comments about what he wanted to do to my best friend. Before I can formulate a response, he's folding himself into his bright red Camaro and taking off.

Wondering what mess I'm about to walk in to, I gingerly enter the kitchen to find Bonnie calmly preparing snacks for tonight. "Hey, Bon. What's up?"

"Just dumping all this store bought crap into serving dishes so that you'd think I made all this. I guess I wasn't quick enough," she says with a shrug. To anyone else, this would all seem and sound perfectly normal. Me, I can see the tightness around her eyes and hear the hurt in her tone.

"Bonnie, what happened with you and Garner?"

"Oh, the usual." She waves an impatient hand through the air.

"And that would be?"

"You know...wants to introduce me as his 'girlfriend,' let everyone know I'm his, introduce me to his parents." She sneers the word "parents" like it's the most offensive word in the English language.

"What a jerk!" I exclaim sarcastically.

"I know, right? I keep reminding him we're having fun, and he keeps trying to spoil it."

About that time, I hear a timid knock and Farah calling out to us.

"We're in here, Farah. Come on in!"

Farah rounds the corner taking in our expressions. "What's wrong?"

"Men suck," Bonnie explains.

"Ah..." is all Farah says because she is married to a gem of a man.

"Don't start with me Farah. You married perfection," Bonnie snaps, pointing a chicken salad-covered spoon at Farah.

"Hey, just because I married perfection, doesn't mean I don't know heartache. I know heartache," Farah snaps back.

"OK! Whoa! Bonnie don't snap at Farah because you don't want to admit you have feelings for Garner. And Farah cut Bonnie a little slack. She's in love with Garner and wants to have his little rocker mini-me and can't admit it."

I hear Bonnie gasp when I call her out on her true feelings for Garner, but when I say she wants to have his baby, I hear her slap her hand over her mouth. When I turn back to Bonnie, her eyes are wide and she is shaking her head.

"Yes, you do, sweetie. Nothing has ever been clearer to me than that. And I've known you forever."

Farah backs me up. "I haven't known you forever, but I see it too, Bon."

Tears quickly fill Bonnie's eyes and she dashes them away. "I...I know," she says as her voice breaks.

Farah and I both round the bar and surround her in a group hug. I feel Bonnie's shoulders shaking. "It's going to be all right, Bon. We'll get through this."

After we have our little moment, Bonnie piles up all the snacks that are still in their original containers on a tray; and I make my famous cosmos. Farah turns on some music and spreads a bunch of square pillows around the coffee table for us to pile around. We laugh and chat and ignore all the heartache in the room while we eat our fill of take-out and, Bonnie and I drink our way through two pitchers of tart deliciousness.

Farah finally braves the topic of Bonnie's relationship hang-ups. I'm incredibly proud of her because Bonnie can be a little scary when cornered. "Bonnie, I don't understand why you're holding back with Garner. He's crazy about you, and he's a good guy. A little rough around the edges but, ultimately, a good guy. Don't you care about him enough to admit this to him?"

Tilting her head back a little and losing her balance a little in the process, Bonnie says, "Of course, I care about him. I don't want to hurt him, but I honestly only want to have some fun. I can say with absolute certainty that I have no desire to get involved in a serious relationship. And not just now but ever." Her gaze shoots forward to pin both of us. "I know what y'all are thinking, but I'm serious. I'd rather end things with Garner now than end up like that."

"But why?" Farah asks with pure wonder.

"Farah, I was married to a man who didn't love me."

"Bonnie—" I start.

"No, Celeste. He didn't. He didn't love me, he didn't respect me, and he didn't care if I knew or didn't know that. He had affairs right under my nose. Never caring how that made me feel or how that hurt me."

"God, Bonnie. I'm so sorry," I whisper.

"You tell me everything, Celeste. But I never told you the half of it," she admits with a sigh.

"Why, Bonnie? You know you can talk to me." It hurt that she hadn't told me.

"I know that. But the worst of it went down when Tripp was dying, and I couldn't burden you with that." Taking a deep breath, she confesses, "I walked in on him once screwing his secretary. She was riding him in our bed, and he glanced over at me like he was annoyed with me. He just grasped her hips harder and continued all the while keeping his eyes on me. What did I ever do but love him and try to make him happy? Nothing and everything and all that lies between, that's what." She downs the rest of her drink with one gulp. Farah and I sit in stunned silence for a moment. I knew that they weren't happy, but I'd had no idea it was that bad.

I pray that God gives me the words to help her because I have no idea what to say. "You do realize that that is a reflection on him and not you, Bonnie. Someone who would treat another person like that...it's clear that he is an awful human being who was undeserving of your love and that you're one of the most generous and deserving people I've ever known. And just because he was a selfish fool doesn't mean that all men are."

Farah chimes in with her two cents. "Yeah, and just because Matthew is a wonderful husband doesn't mean we don't have our share of problems. All I've ever wanted to be is a mother. I know that may not seem like a lofty aspiration these days. I know you two have careers. But I never wanted that. I always saw myself as a wife and a mother. And..." she pauses to take a steadying breath. "Matthew doesn't want to have children. And it's killing me, y'all. I love him so much and he's so fantastic. But how do I move on from that? It's huge. It's everything."

"Geez, Farah. Why doesn't he want kids? I mean, does he never want children or does he just not want them right now? I don't understand. Isn't that something you would've talked about?" I ask her.

"Yes, we did. Of course, we did. He told me that he wanted them down the road. That he wanted me and his career to take priority early on our marriage. That he wanted me to be able to travel with him and support him without being divided by the responsibility of having children. I always thought this made sense and was the responsible thing to do. So I was fine with that. Well, last year, I started talking to him about the fact that I was getting older and that his career was stable and we should start trying."

"And?" Bonnie prompts her.

Farah closes her eyes, blows out a deep breath, and reopens her eyes. "And he told me that he really liked the way our life is now. And that he was thinking of making a bid for senator. That was a year ago. He was hesitant, but not decided, so I waited him out a little. When I broached the conversation again, he was no longer hesitant but definite." She looks down for a moment before sighing deeply and bringing her tear-filled eyes back to ours. "He told me that, under no circumstances, does he want children now. That he was a different person than when we first married."

Bonnie and I exchange a troubled glance. If that had been her dream all of her life, to have children, how is she supposed to move past that? Can she move past that? "I don't even know what to say, Farah. That's a huge...point of contention. What are you thinking?"

"I'm thinking that as much as I adore my husband I can't

imagine going through this life without having what you have. I know you lost your husband and haven't had it easy, and you've been a rock. But those children...they're so precious and loving, and I can't imagine not having that. I often ask myself why Matthew can't be enough for me. Why can't I just be with him since I love him so much and he's so good to me? I don't really have an answer for that other than I just can't. I want to be a mother. I think it's the greatest thing I'll ever do as a human being. If I put all that aside and accept our relationship on his new terms, I'm afraid that down the road I'll end up resenting him, and we'll be over anyway."

Bonnie clears her throat a little. "I'm sorry that I've been such a bitch to you lately about having the perfect husband and relationship. I was just jealous of what you had and felt like you couldn't relate to what I was going through. I should've known better. We all have our own hurt, our own pain even if it's not obvious to the world. You'll make the right decision, Farah. You're intuitive and caring and loving. You'll make the right choice for yourself and for your family."

"Thank you, Bonnie. You're forgiven. You weren't too horrible and I knew you were hurting." Farah slaps her thighs, jerking me out of my little stupor of watching my best friends make up. "So two problems discussed. Now what are we going to do about Celeste's problem?"

"Oh no," I protest. "We're not discussing me. I'm great. I'm fine."

Farah rolls her eyes at me. "You're not great. You're not fine."

"She's in love with Adrian," Bonnie declares. "And she can't get over it."

"And he's in love with her," Farah adds. "And he can't get over it either."

My mouth falls open. Snapping it back shut, I glare at them both for a few seconds. After everything they've just confessed, I owe it to them to be honest. "Y'all are right. I am in love with Adrian. Bad. We're talking all-consuming, all-encompassing love with him. But there's not a damn thing I can do about it." Blowing out a deep breath, I continue, "But, Farah, you're wrong. Adrian may want me and have some feelings for me, but he's not in love with me." At the shaking of her head, I reiterate, "No, he's not. Lust is not love. Caring is not loving."

Farah narrows her eyes at me and I visibly blanche. "Are you done? Because I happened to have had an extremely enlightening conversation with him. I know what I'm talking about, Celeste. Adrian loves you. Not familial, not obligatory love. I mean true blue love."

"I heard what he said, Farah. I was eavesdropping in the hall. He said I was his cross to bear and that if he loved me he'd be dead because of my vicious nature. That's not love, honey, that's regret that borders on hatred because of feeling a little something like love."

"Again, are you done?" she asks unperturbed. "Your eaves-dropping skills need some work. You should have stuck around and heard our whole conversation. Because what he said after I called bullshit on those statements, would've changed your life."

"What do you mean? Tell me then if it's so life-changing."

"I can't. I swore to him that I wouldn't. And I know you're my best friend but his reasons for your not being privy to those thoughts were sound. I'm just hoping that you'll both come to see reason before I have to intervene."

"Intervene now, damn it!" I say half-jokingly.

"I can't. I...I can't say anymore right now. Only that, I think he's struggling to figure some things out for himself and that I'm not giving up on the two of you just yet."

Bonnie finally chimes in while I mull this over. "Ugh...that's because you're a hopeless romantic, Farah. They both have their reasons for not being able to overcome whatever they're up against, and we should respect that."

"You make us sound weak and our problems trivial."

"If the shoe fits..." Bonnie chimes.

"Oh great! You two make up and then turn on me. I get it. I'll be your punching bag for this bonding moment, but I promise I won't do it for long."

"Aww...honey, you're not our punching bag. We just want what's best for you. And we both think that Adrian's what is best for you."

"So you've been talking about me behind my back?" I cry disbelievingly.

Farah shakes her head no, but Bonnie pats me on the hand and says, "Of course, we have. But it was for your own good."

"Great," I mutter. "Look, even if Adrian feels a little something for me, the forces that we'd be up against," I shake my head, "they'd ruin us. Both of us. I have my children to consider. If they bring me down, my boys go with me. Do you understand that?"

Bonnie nods her head yes. Farah shakes her head no. "No. No, I don't understand how your family can be so cruel and manipulative."

I throw up my hands. "You know, me either. I don't understand it. I've just come to accept it."

"OK. Our party just got really depressing, but I'm about to change this vibe," Bonnie decrees, jumping up and swaying a little with the movement and the cosmos.

While she does whatever she needs to do, I run into the kitchen to pour up another round. I drain the contents of my glass quickly and refill us both. "Farah, you sure you don't want one?" I call.

"No thanks," she calls back. "I'm just not in the mood for alcohol tonight."

I'm no lush, but how could you not be in the mood for a cosmo?

"Okey dokey," I singsong.

Suddenly, our quiet music fades out and I hear the opening horn for one of my favorite songs blaring. I abandon our drinks and dart back into the living room in time to see Bonnie grab Farah and pull her up for a little dance. We twirl around for a minute, but as the chorus strikes up, we line up and belt it out in sync, "I love you baby, and if it's quite all right..." We know every single word, every single intonation, and hit it all on cue. When it slows back down, we sway and serenade each other until it fades and then we collapse on the couch and dissolve in a fit of giggles and tears.

"Oh my gosh, Celeste, please tell me you brought *10 Things I Hate About You.*"

I laugh again. She knows me so well. "What do you think? May I interest you in a little Heath Ledger?" I wiggle my eyebrows at her.

"I knew I loved you. Go get the drinks and I'll get it going."

"Yes, ma'am."

Farah follows me into the kitchen and fixes herself a glass of tea while I finish up with our drinks. "This is fun. We need to do this more often. It's like a slumber party. Do you remember those?"

"Yes, they were so much fun. Do you remember making the sign-in book where you listed all your favorite stuff and hopes and dreams and passed it on to the next person to do the same? It was like old school Facebook."

"No, we had MySpace."

I groan. "I keep forgetting you're a dang baby!" I nudge her and we load up and make our way back out. When we hit the living room, we both come to a screeching halt. Bonnie's face is bunched up like she's in pain. My eyes follow hers to find Garner standing in the open doorway staring her down. I start to back out of the room but I'm not quick enough. And it's like I'm invisible anyway because they are so intent upon one another.

"I'm here to tell you that you're not my girlfriend." Well, that doesn't sound good. "I don't give a shit if you ever meet any more of my friends, or my parents, or anyone else. I'll never introduce you as my girlfriend, and I'll never acknowledge you in public. I've been miserable all night, damn it. You're the one I want, and if it has to be on your fucked up terms, then so be it. Thinking about carrying on without you was like wondering what it would be like to try to carry on without oxygen. My chest burned at the mere thought of it. I can't do it. I *won't* do it." He pauses and takes a deep breath before continuing in the most serious tone I've ever heard him use. "Bonnie, queen of my soul and imprisoner of my heart, will you do me the honor of being the woman I bang on a regular basis, the woman I flaunt at my gigs as the hot piece of ass I get to go home with every night, and the woman I'm honored to hang out with if she's got nothing or no one better to do?"

I blink rapidly at his unconventional "proposal" and look toward Bonnie. Her eyes have filled with tears, and she's nodding her head up and down. Before she can say a word, Garner is across the room, hoisting her up in the air, and pulling her head in for a kiss while simultaneously whisking her up the stairs.

He pulls back only slightly to murmur against her lips, "Tell your friends good night."

Not taking her eyes off his, I barely hear her mumble, "Good night."

Turning toward each other with identical expressions of astonishment, Farah and I burst out laughing. We head back into the kitchen and straighten up quickly, all the while giggling and shaking our heads at our quirky lovebirds. Whatever works, I guess.

"Will you drop me at my house on your way home?"

"Yeah, sure," she agrees.

Locking up behind ourselves, we head down to Farah's car and start toward my house. When Farah starts the car, I reach over and turn the song up, "Oh, I love her."

"Me too. 'Breakaway' is my favorite too."

After listening to the lyrics for a minute, I feel a pull unlike any other, I put my hand over hers as it rests on the gearshift. "Will you do me a favor and not ask any questions?"

"Umm...yeah, of course."

"Will you drive down Willow?"

"I don't know if that's a good idea." She shakes her head at me.

"You said—"

"That wasn't a question. It was an observation," she says as she puts her signal on to turn.

"Thank you, Farah."

As we near his apartment, I ask her to pull over and wait here for a minute. I don't really know why I'm stalking him, but I'd always wondered what it would feel like to do this kind of thing. I'd heard it was a popular thing to do when you were young and crushing on somebody. I really don't see what all the fuss is about. I'm staring at a lifeless building.

That thought dissipates rapidly as I see him move out onto his balcony. Holding his cell to his ear, I see him take a swig of the beer he's holding and make that face like it's his first sip. I swallow hard as I take him in. *Why am I doing this to myself? Stupid, stupid idea!* I'm about to ask Farah to pull out when I see *her* come out to try to sidle up next to him. He shakes her off and motions for her to go back in. She does, albeit, in a pout.

"Let's go, Farah. You were right. So not a good idea. Furthermore, it was stupid and immature. I'm regressing constantly these days, I swear."

"Celeste," Farah says as she pulls back onto the street, "I really think you need to decide what it is you want and go after it. If it's Adrian, great. If not, move on. All this...indecision is not good for you."

I laugh a little too loudly. "I've been cursing myself for that very thing. The kicker is I have decided to move on several times, yet I can't seem to make my heart get on board with my head. And every time I think I've got a handle on it, I have a relapse."

"I know, honey." She pats my hand. "It's easier said than done. I guess you just need some more time, or you need to make a different decision. Seems to me, if you're having that hard of a time fighting it, maybe you shouldn't be trying to resist at all."

"I'm stuck with this decision. It's just...it has to be this way."

"I don't get that either."

"I know. It's...complicated. My family is..." I take a deep breath. How do I explain them? "They're evil, Farah. Can we leave it at that, please?"

"Of course. I don't mean to push, but I hate seeing you this miserable. What you just said about your family I've suspected. There are rumors about all that. I can't even imagine."

"No, you sure can't," I whisper.

-Twelve-

Everything Changes

IT'S THAT MOMENT. That moment when we think everything is happening on course. No ripples, no waves. We're just trying to get through another day, feeling like all the little things overwhelm us and they do because they end up making up our day. We get so focused on the little things that we forget the bigger picture. Sometimes we forget to appreciate the things that truly matter because our vision is so clouded by all of the mundane. The here and now become our obsession, and we forget the concept of our finite state because with all the little things vying for our attention it feels like we'll go on forever.

Then tragedy strikes and shakes our very foundation. We wonder—how did we not see this coming? How did we not sense that something life-altering was closing in on us? How did we not know that our entire world was about to be rocked, rattling everything we know and changing everything about us?

That's the way of it, though. If we did think like this, we'd need to be heavily medicated just to get out of bed. We wouldn't be able to function if we considered all the what-ifs life can and does hurl at us. Our fears would completely incapacitate us. Thank God for tunnel vision because if I'd had time to consider how my life was about to change I wouldn't have survived it.

After Sunday Mass, I run a couple of errands that I know I won't have time to run once the boys come home this evening. While I am taking care of this, I ponder last night's conversation with Farah and begin to wonder exactly what the mysterious Mr. OG has under wraps on our local criminals. I come to the conclusion that now is probably the time to find out what kind of insurance policy he possesses to help me out of my predicament. Maybe I could use that leverage to get Adrian out from under their thumbs as well. I don't know what they have on him, but I do know that they will do anything to protect their own hides, and if I could get both myself and Adrian off of their tenterhooks with the same bit of information all the better.

Adrian out from under their control. Me out from under their control. A win win. If what Farah said last night holds any merit and Adrian's feelings do run deeper than his libido, maybe we can explore that without fear of being destroyed by them. I'm running through my plan on how to do this as I'm putting away the groceries when that devastating call comes in. The one you hope you never receive, but chances are, you will receive one form of it at some point in your life and most likely when you are completely un-prepared.

I hear the distant ringing of my cell phone coming from my purse, so I act quickly, not sure how long it has been ringing. When I look at the screen, I can see that I have several missed calls, voice mails, and texts. A sliver of dread runs down my spine. And I know—I just know.

"Hello?" I ask warily.

"Celeste. Are you at home?" my sister-in-law asks.

"Umm...yes, is everything—"

I hear her muffled comment to someone else. "Tell him she's at home."

"Natalie, what's going on?"

She adjusts her phone. "Honey, I'm so sorry, but there's been an accident. We think he's going to be just fine. As a precaution, they've airlifted him to Oshner's. Louis is with him. We're all headed there now. We've called Adrian; he should be there in just a moment to pick you up and get you there safely."

I'm trembling with every word, waiting for her to tell me exactly what is happening, and not just the logistics of the situation. "Is it Daddy? Did he have a heart attack?"

"No," she whispers and her anguish is tangible. "It's Archer." Icy dread washes through me and tears fill my eyes immediately. "He had a swimming accident. He was underwater for a couple of minutes, but they were able to revive him immediately."

When she says the word "revive," I cry out and throw my hand over my mouth. I can't speak. I hear knocking at the door and then a key. And all I can think is that I wasn't there. *I'm not there!*

"Celeste, we think he's going to be absolutely fine," she says in a strong voice. "He was responsive but sluggish. He ingested quite a bit of water, so to err on the side of caution they wanted to get him to a trauma center." I'm nodding but still can't fathom what to say. My mind runs through all possible scenarios. None of them good. One thread ties all these thoughts together—*I'm not there*. I feel the phone being slipped from my hand and then a hand comes to rest on my shoulder.

"Natalie?" I jump at the welcome sound of Adrian's voice. "I've got her. We're on our way." I hear my phone lock, feel my hand being pulled, and see my purse being grabbed. "Come on, baby. Let's go see about Archer, all right?" I finally pull my eyes up to focus on his and they look calm and reassuring, which actually does make me feel somewhat calm and reassured.

"OK. I'm OK. Let's go." I nod vigorously so he sees that I can do this.

He doesn't waste another moment, and he never lets go of my hand.

THE DRIVE IS so silent for the first few minutes that I'm a little scared to speak. I don't know what to say, and I'm terrified of the thoughts running through my head. "Do you know what happened?" I finally whisper.

"Apparently they were fishing and playing around on the pier while Louis and the guys were getting the boat ready to launch. Your mother was with the boys. They said Archer was running around for some reason and slid off the pier. The other kids waited for him to surface for a moment because they know he can swim.

"When he didn't, Paris jumped in and tried to find him while Finn tried to get Claire's attention. Finally, all the commotion got Louis's attention and he jumped in and fished him out. He was able to perform CPR and get him revived. The fire department called in an airlift right away; being a child and being our family, they didn't want to take any chances." His gaze is focused forward the entire time. He gives me the facts straight and without embellishment. I appreciate this trait of his so very much right now.

"Is Paris OK?"

"Yeah, baby, he's good."

When we reach the hospital, he drops me off by the emergency doors so that he can park the car while I get to Archer. As swiftly as my legs will carry me, I make my way in and find the information desk.

"Hello? My name is Celeste Hebert. My son Archer Hebert was brought in on an airlift a little while ago. Can you tell me where he is, please?"

"Yes, Ms. Hebert. If you'll just go to those double doors, I'll buzz you in and walk you back. They're just getting him settled now."

I glance back at the entrance. I really don't want to face this without him by my side. I don't know if I can do it. I move toward the doors, hoping that he'll beat me and we can go back together. When he strides through that door and his gaze locks with mine, I send up a little prayer of thanks. *I'm counting on you for the big prayer now.* I offer a small smile and motion with my head that we're to go back. He joins me at the door, his hand comes to rest on the small of my back. It may just be a hand, but everything that is attached to that gesture feels like a pillar of support at the moment.

The door buzzes and we enter, following the nurse as she quickly makes her way through the corridors. I release a deep breath. I know I need to be extremely calm right now. When we reach his room, the door opens with a swoosh. My eyes search the room to land on Archer's wide ones. He's asking the doctor how long can someone be underwater before not being able to be revived. *Always so curious!* I let out a relieved chuckle. His gaze flies to mine and a little smile lights his face.

"Mom?" He asks hoarsely.

"Archer, baby, are you OK?"

"Yeah. I'm just tired. I'm sorry, Mom."

"You have nothing to be sorry for, honey." I glance over and see Louis worrying his bottom lip and give him a small smile. Entering the room, I set my purse down in the chair and move to the side of the bed. Leaning down, I bring my lips to his forehead. I kiss him about five times consecutively before looking up at the doctor. I feel Adrian move in behind me, and he runs his hand up and down Archer's arm before resting one hand on Archer's shoulder and one on my lower back again.

"Is he going to be OK?" I ask the question the doctor's probably heard a million times before.

"Right now, we're preparing to run tests to make sure his lungs are clear and there are no obstructions. What we're most concerned about is pneumonia. We're going to observe him until this evening to make sure he's in no danger of developing that. Other than that, he will be lethargic and probably doze on and off for the next several hours."

A nurse enters the room and they explain that they're going to wheel him for a couple of tests and will be right back. I kiss Archer and promise him I'll be right here when he returns. Adrian ruffles his hair and tells him he loves him.

"Celeste?" I hear Louis call me. "I'm so sorry."

I turn and take in his haggard look. He looks like he's aged five years. "Louis, you saved my son's life. A few more seconds and he would've drowned. Why are you sorry?"

He blows out a tired breath. "Mainly, I'm sorry for not paying better attention to the boys. But I'm also sorry for being judgmental. You've never done anything but accept me, and the first time you need me to be understanding, I throw it in your face and turn my back on you."

Walking over to my baby brother, I throw my arms around him and kiss him and make him look at me. "Louis, I love you so much. Thank you for saving my son's life and for always being there for me and my children. Yes, you've been a bit of a jerk lately, but I've also been quite frustrating," I say with a smile, "so you're forgiven. OK?"

He nods and hugs me back tight. I hear the doors open and turn to see if Archer's back already. In waltz my mother and father.

Before I can fully process her arrival and the look on her face, I feel Adrian move in behind me and pull me in close, resting his hand on my hip.

My mother takes in Adrian's possessive stance and narrows her eyes at him before she asks, "What is *he* doing here?"

"Mother—" Louis starts.

I pat him on the arm. "No, Louis, I've got this."

This is the person I'm upset with. "*Adrian* is my family, Mother." I feel Adrian's grip intensify and watch as her eyes widen at my tone. I figure by the time I'm done with her, they'll have bugged out of her unnaturally nipped and tucked face. "He's been here for me and the boys like no other, so I won't be denying him." I narrow my eyes at her and tilt my head. "What I want to know is where were you when my little boy fell into the water and nearly drowned?"

Clearing her throat, she straightens and says, "I was just up from the water."

"What were you doing when my little boys were calling for your help?"

"I was on the phone with my doctor."

My rage barely suppressed, I ask, "When you heard them calling for you, what did you do?"

"Celeste," my father warns.

"No, Daddy, I want to know." My eyes never leave hers. "What did you do when they begged you for your help?"

"Celeste, I thought that they were horse-playing. I had heels and a suit on, for God's sake. I got to the water as quickly as possible."

"As quickly as possible? Did you bother kicking off your thousand dollar shoes and throwing that designer jacket on the ground while trying to get help for my children? My two children who were in the water fighting for their lives?"

She strengthens her resolve before she tells me, "Celeste, you're overwrought. I understand because I'm also a mother and would be terribly upset myself had this happened to one of you. However, I will not take the blame or the verbal abuse you seem intent on dishing out as I do not deserve it, especially since you continue to defy your father on important matters. You, my dear, have not a leg to stand on in this family, so I'd watch myself."

I open my mouth to speak but before I can get anything out, Adrian's voice booms from behind me. "Get out."

"Excuse me?" my mother says.

Adrian continues in that scary calm voice, and I can't believe my mother doesn't tuck tail and run. "Get out. Your daughter almost lost her son today. She's already lost her husband. She continues to try to appease this family to her own detriment. Her son needs her to be calm and focused right now. You're not helping. Get. Out."

"You're going to let *him* speak to me like that?" Her gaze flies from me, to Louis, and back to my father. "You're going to let him speak to me like that," she states incredulously. She turns and points at my father. "I think it best if you remember what's at stake here."

I just roll my eyes. My mother and her threats. I'd been listening to those all my life. Her heels clicking and clacking down the hallway are the only sounds for a moment before my father turns back to me. He signals me over. I try to move toward him, but I'm immediately pulled back into the brick wall that is Adrian. I put my hands up helplessly and laugh a little.

My father shakes his head and moves toward me. He picks up one of my hands and proceeds to blow my mind. "I've never been as scared as I was today, Celeste, watching helplessly as my grandson had to be revived." His voice breaks slightly. "You've never done anything for this family except what has been required of you. I'm here to tell you no more—I want you to be able to live your life in peace. You're my daughter and I'm proud of you and…I love you."

I throw my arms around my father even though Adrian's hand stays anchored to my hip. Four times. Four times in my whole life had my father told me he loved me. I don't tell him I love him back. I can't. I'd been rejected too many times by him, so I hug him tight and nod my head. Maybe one day we can get there.

He moves over and hugs Louis before leaving. I feel sorry for him because now he has to go deal with my mother. Feeling weak from the whole evening, I feel my body exhale and Adrian pulls me in to hold me tight.

ADRIAN AND I climb the steps wearily. He carries a sleepy Archer all the way up the stairs while I cradle the other two boys next to my hips as close as I can get them. After Adrian tucks in Archer and I tuck in Finn and Paris, Adrian and I cross paths in the hallway. He reaches out and grabs my hand, holding on until we can't any longer while we switch rooms to kiss the boys goodnight. A not-so-little thrill shoots through me.

Archer is almost dozing off again as I sit down beside him. "I'm going to let you go to sleep as soon as I tell you this, honey. I don't know what I'd do without my Archer. You are so special, so important to me. I can't even find a word grand enough to tell you how much I love you and how much I need you in my life." We are both sobbing when I get finished, so I wrap it up quickly. "You and your brothers are my heart, Archer, and I need you to be very careful with my heart. OK?" He nods his head profusely. "I love you. Sleep tight, sweetie."

"I love you too." He blows out a little breath and sighs before continuing. "Mom, I'm sorry I scared you. I don't want you to have anyone else that you have to live without every day. I see how sad you are sometimes, especially when Dad died. I don't want to be the one to make you feel that way. Ever."

"Oh, sweetheart, thank you for saying that. I'm much better now though, don't you think?"

"I think you were for a while but not lately."

"Ah..." Adrian strain. "I loved your father, Archer, but I'm doing OK. I need you to understand that you are my heart and soul. No love compares with what I feel for you and your brothers. No love ever will, so I need you to take care of yourself and your brothers. Do you understand?"

"Yes," he whispers.

"OK. I'm exhausted. You're beyond exhausted. Good night, love." I brush his hair to the side and kiss him for probably the hundredth time of the night.

"Night."

When I exit his bedroom, a vision stands before me—a beautiful beacon of a vision. He was my rock tonight, and I'm not going to give that up. Whatever we have to face is worth it, and if he's by my side for it, I can handle it. He doesn't say a word, just gives me a small smile and grabs my hand again. Much to my delight, he has not stopped touching me since he whisked me off to my son this afternoon. Would it always be this way between us?

I snap the lights off and close the door to the hallway as we make our way to my sunroom. I'm so glad he's in the lead. There's something I need right now, but I don't know that I would know how to ask for it. When we enter the sunroom, he closes the door behind us and leaves his palm on the door for a few beats before he turns to me, causing my heart to skip in anticipation. When he finally does turn the love that I see shimmering in his blue eyes is unmistakable and heart mending. Tears pool in my eyes a bit before he releases my hand to move both of his hands to cup my face, and I swallow hard.

I know where my heart lies, and I suspect his is there as well. Are we finally on the same page? I'm afraid to ask. He just holds me there in place and I finally see the answer to my unspoken question shining in his eyes. Ever so briefly, I smile.

When his lips brush over mine gently, I fight the urge to close my eyes and lose myself to his touch. His stare is so intense and makes me feel so precious that I don't want to miss a moment of it. When his tongue darts out to tease my lips, my eyelids finally flutter closed, and my mouth opens for him immediately. Feeling his tongue softly dance with mine, I let myself go. Moving my hands to his hips, I pull him tightly into me. His answering groan is all the encouragement I need. Running my hands up his back, I feel his taut muscles tremble a little. I smile through my kiss. We've shared a few kisses, each one unique and wonderful, but none of them have been this meaningful, this sure.

After a few moments, he pulls back but doesn't stop placing little kisses all over my mouth for another moment. "You are so strong, so beautiful. You have no idea..."

Tilting my head a little, I kiss one of the hands framing my face while he rains kisses over my neck. "No, Adrian, you have no idea," I say with a smile. "I don't know what I'd have done without you today. You are everything I need. I'm so grateful. I don't know what I did to deserve to have you, but I hope I never have to experience it without you again."

Pulling my lips back to his, he gives me a long chaste kiss before pulling me over to the wicker loveseat. Sitting down first, he guides me to his lap so that I'm draped across it. He's so smooth and quick that I don't have time to question it. I pull my legs up on the couch and curl into him, relaxing into his strength and warmth. All those weeks of our refraining from touching are completely erased from my memory as I absorb him into me.

Running his hands through my hair and down my arm, he rubs up and down for a second, before he asks, "You know what this means, right?"

"Yes, I know. I'm ready. Let them try to inflict whatever damage they wish." My voice shakes with indignation as I declare, "You're worth it. I'm worth it. My children are worth it. You mean so much to all of us, and I can't imagine denying ourselves any longer. So let them try to stop us." I take a deep breath and struggle with how much I should admit right now. Not knowing how serious he wants to be with me is difficult, but I need him to know that what I feel is not a fleeting interest. "They're not going to come between us, though, because I'm crazy about you and have been for a *long* time."

His gaze, still so intense, hasn't left mine for a second. I watched as his eyes tightened with each word I'd just proclaimed. *Was I wrong in thinking this is where his heart is?* Tipping my head back, Adrian leans in and places a sweet kiss on my lips. "That's not good enough for me," he whispers against my lips. I still, thinking I've read him all wrong. "Although," he says playfully with a smile, "being crazy for me is a good start." His smile fades as he sobers up again. "It's just not enough for me since I happen to love you." My mind goes blank and I just stare at him wide-eyed as he places more sweet little kisses all over my mouth and chin, nudging my head back and continuing that sweet torment down my throat.

"You love me?" I struggle to say. My voice is strained.

"I've loved you since you spilled cocktail sauce on my favorite pair of jeans," he says with a laugh. "You were so cute and sweet. You made me change, and you must have washed those jeans three times before I left. You gave it your all, but I got news for you—the remnants remained. There was only one problem. You were married to my favorite cousin. A good man and a good father and, as far as I could tell, a good husband—and I felt like a complete scoundrel."

"Scoundrel?" I ask with a laugh. "You didn't do anything wrong, though. I'd forgotten all about that part of dinner. Thanks for reminding me. I was so embarrassed." *To tell the truth or not?* He'd been honest with me. "I'm not normally a klutz but I was so... affected by you, and I'd never experienced anything like it." He pulls back to look at me. "Never," I reiterate. "I didn't mean to feel that way, and the guilt that ensued was tremendous. One glance at you and the pull I felt just...consumed me. Like you were the one person who could hold me to this universe if my body ever felt the desire to float off—an anchor. That's how I've always viewed you. My anchor. I can't believe it's possible to be this attracted and this drawn to someone. Sometimes I think the way I feel about you is crazy, Adrian." I shake my head in awe. "I love all of your emotions —moody, carefree, protective, grouchy, sensitive, domineering. Everything about you is precious to me." I reach up and rub his scruffy cheek for a second while he takes in everything I've said.

"You have no idea what those words mean to me, Cel. I've been so...torn. The biggest part of me wanted to cling to you and make you mine while the other part felt like I had to push you away in order to protect you."

"I understand. I do. And I said all that so you would know that I mean this—I love you too, Adrian. I've known it for a long time too. That night I kissed you for the first time, deep down, that was it for me. I convinced myself I was acting on a whim of attraction, but it was so much more than that. The only reason I didn't want to admit it to myself or you was because I feared the hailstorm I would bring down on us."

"You're right to be afraid. It's not going to be pretty. That night you kissed me, so sweet, so tentative...I wanted you so badly for myself but knew I couldn't have you without serious consequences for the both of us. I was willing to accept them, but I didn't want that for you or the boys. I've always wanted better for you than me."

"What? What do you mean? You're the best thing for me. I've been beyond miserable since the concert that night. It's more than just attraction with you, Adrian. I mean you're beautiful and I feel physically drawn to you, but you've also become my best friend and so much more. I'd already been so miserable, but to have to hurt you like that, it killed me. I was just afraid of all that they might do, and I still am. I'm just not fearful enough to let it stop me anymore."

"We'll figure it out, Celeste. I know they're powerful, but we'll find a way."

I want to ask him what they have on him, but I don't want to ruin this moment. There's plenty of time for the drama that will ensue later, so I tackle a less stressful topic. "I feel funny asking you this, but what do you see happening between us? I mean, if I'm going to bring the wrath of my father and father-in-law down on me, I want to know what I'm getting in exchange."

"Celeste, I've only told one other woman I've loved her, and I'm almost thirty years old." My heart plummets with that knowledge. On the one hand, one's not bad. On the other, I'd like to strangle the one who beat me to the punch of being the recipient of Adrian's love. "I think it's safe to say that I'm not going anywhere. You think I would invite this kind of trouble if I had doubts about us lasting?" I smile with this sentiment. I can see us lasting.

"OK," I whisper.

"By the way, that other woman who's heard those words from me..." He pauses and I nod my head, encouraging him to share more. "She's biologically engineered to love me back," he says with a grin.

My brow furrows as I try to figure out what he means. After a second, I gasp. "Your mother?"

"Yes, I've only ever told my mother I loved her. Others, I've said things like I care about you, you're amazing, love ya—"

"OK! I get it!" I say, nudging his shoulder a bit. "Have you been with a lot of women?"

"Hmm...what's a lot?" he asks.

"I don't know. I've only ever been with two men and was married to one of them for fourteen years. A lot to me would be five."

"Then, yes, I've been with a lot of women."

"Got it."

"But you're the only one who matters. The only one who matters forever."

Forever—my heart rejoices. "It's a little soon to talk forever, don't you think?"

"If that scares you, I won't talk like that; but, no, I don't think it's too soon. Our past might have been rocky, but I think our future's inevitable."

Our forever is inevitable—my heart exults. A sudden thought causes my heart to stop. "Ugh...I hate to bring this up but...what about the doppelgänger?"

"The what?"

I laugh at my little inside joke. "Oh, I mean, Jennifer. What about Jennifer?"

He furrows his brow at me. "What about her?"

"I've never been the other woman or cheated or anything along those lines. I don't like all that."

He laughs at me. "Oh, well, that's good to know."

I squeeze his arm. "Don't laugh at me. I'm serious. I don't want to be *that* woman."

"Ah...you could never be *that* woman when you're *my* woman."

"Your woman?" I choke out.

"Yeah, you gotta problem with that?" His voice drips with

arrogance.

The look he gives me takes my breath away. It's a compliment, not an affront to my independence. I level with him and myself. "No, I like it," I say simply.

"Good, because that's the way it is now."

"And Jennifer?" I remind him. I'm not letting this go. I don't want anything to mar our being together.

"There is no Jennifer. We ended things last night."

"You did?" I mentally clap my hands together.

"Yes, after I saw you on the street, I realized I couldn't pretend with her anymore. It wasn't fair to either of us. I figured I just needed time to get over you and that I didn't need to use someone while doing that." Pulling me closer, he continues, "When I saw you yesterday and realized that you didn't want to see me or speak to me, it hurt. I've never hurt so bad in my entire life. I went back to the apartment and kept replaying it. That look on your face as if I was the last person on this earth you wanted to see. I fucking hated it. I didn't know what I could do about it, but I hated it. After a while, I realized that I needed to end it with her and..."

After a few seconds of waiting for him to go on, I prompt him, "And what?"

"And I decided to leave town." I inhale sharply. "I had decided to move on, literally—that I couldn't take it anymore. Then I got so pissed. Pissed that I wouldn't be a part of your life or the boys' lives. I called myself every name in the book, drank a bunch of beer, and...if you ever tell anyone, I'll deny it—cried like a freakin' baby."

My heart clenches. I'm thrilled that he cared enough to have that reaction, but I ache for the pain I've caused him. "I'm so sorry, Adrian. I hope we never hurt each other like that again."

He runs his fingertips across my cheek. "I'm sorry we hurt each other too. Then, tonight with Archer." He releases a deep sigh. "I realized that I can't live without y'all. Y'all are my world, and I'm done letting others refuse us our world. All I want to do is hold you and protect you and love you. Will you let me do that, no matter the consequences?"

I nod in total agreement of all he's said. "Yes, that's all I want too. We can't let them get between us. It's what they do—make you question your own sanity."

"I'm ready for them. I feel like with you by my side I can take on anything, anyone."

I smile before his lips reach mine again and tell him, "We can, Adrian. And we will."

-Thirteen-

Turn Me Inside Out

ADRIAN AND I decide that it would be best if we keep quiet for a little bit regarding our relationship. His argument: the sooner we say anything, the sooner they start trying to rip us to shreds. I had my reservations, but I have to admit it's actually kind of fun having a secret relationship. No one else's bias gets in the way. We can get to know each other on that level without all the drama. A few days after our decision to be together, we plan an afternoon with the boys at the zoo. Our zoo is absolutely one of my favorite places on earth.

We have lots of junk food. Finn rides the elephant. Paris feeds the monkeys. Archer is...quiet. I try to get him to join in the fun, but he just gives me a small smile and half-heartedly obliges me before succumbing to his own thoughts once again.

I sit on one of the wooden benches a little ways back from the lions and admire how good Adrian is with the boys. He's got Finn on his shoulders, which seems to be his favorite seat. Paris is leaning into him and whispering excitedly, glancing up at Adrian to make sure that he shows some kind of response to each of his comments. And, although Archer hasn't said much, he stands next to Adrian. Every now and then I see Adrian squeeze Archer's shoulder. I'm wondering what's going on in that thoughtful little head of his.

After several minutes, Adrian scoops Finn from around his shoulders and deposits him next to the other boys before joining me on the bench. "I'm worried about Archer," I tell Adrian once he gets settled.

"Me too. He's usually the quieter of the three but never this quiet. What do you think's going on?"

"I don't know," I say with a sigh. "He just seems to be doing some heavy thinking. I'll talk to him about it tonight."

I glance down and smile when I see our hands resting next to each other. One more millimeter and we'd be touching. He follows my gaze and laughs. "You have no idea how bad I want to touch you right now. Damn, pretty much all day, I've been dying to touch you."

I laugh with him. "I think I have a pretty clear idea about how desperate you are if it's anything like what I'm feeling."

"So when do you want to tell the boys? And do you want me there when you tell them?"

I glance back at them before answering. "I don't know all the details of what and how I want to tell them, but I want them to know soon. I don't like keeping them in the dark."

"Yeah, me either." He glances toward them now, and the look he gives my boys melts my bones.

"We haven't even spoken of the possibility of my dating. I know they are sensitive, loving people; but I have no idea how they're going to react."

"Try not to worry about it too much. I think they'll be OK with it."

"You do?"

"Yep," he grins a knowing grin.

I fall right into it. "What?"

"About four months ago, right after you kissed me that first time—"

"Hey, we kissed each other!" I protest.

"You kissed me first, though," he says with a laugh.

"Yeah, and don't you forget it," I whisper.

"Mmm...I want to you kiss you so bad right now," he says in that husky voice that drives me mad.

I glance over at the kids and back again. Heat surrounds us like a tangible thing. "I interrupted you," I'm barely able to say.

He shakes his head a little and focuses his gaze on the boys while he rehashes their conversation. "Yeah, so about four months ago, the boys and I were headed to baseball practice, and we got caught in some traffic. We started talking about everything under the sun. I don't have to tell you that they are great conversationalists." I smile and nod my head knowingly. "Finn started talking about his friend who was getting a new step-dad, and that led to them wondering aloud how long it would be before you started dating. I let them meander their way around the topic before finally asking them how they would feel about it."

"And...?"

He blows out a breath and says, "They said they'd be good with it on one condition."

"Really? What condition?"

Finally, he looks back at me and pins me with his beautiful blue-eyed gaze. "They said they'd be good with it but only if...you dated me."

"Really?" I manage to squeak out.

He nods at me, his look becoming even more intense. "Finn said he wanted me to be his dad."

My eyes well with tears immediately and I seek Finn out in the crowd. That crushes me in more than one way. Part of me is over the moon to know that they'd accept my and Adrian's new relationship. But another part aches that they don't have their father and that they are missing out on that. No matter how amazing and generous Adrian is, he could never replace their father, and having Adrian help out the way he has been isn't even a close second. But what we're building, it's going to be beautiful.

"That breaks my heart," I finally tell him. "It's sad that they have to go through their whole lives without their dad."

"It is, but they're doing remarkably well. I think we've found a good balance for them, don't you?"

I look at him and take in his sincere expression. He really cares about what my boys need and how they feel. It was one of my great fears when I considered how I would move forward after Tripp. "The way you care about them, Adrian, is just so...unexpected and wonderful. I'm so grateful for you."

About that time, Finn bounds without warning into my lap. "I'm ready to go see the snakes," he says as he pulls my face to his by my cheeks.

"Oh...snakes," I whisper with tears brimming my eyes again. Watching his big brown eyes light up with excitement after everything Adrian and I just discussed is overwhelming. "I'm not crazy about snakes. Maybe Adrian could take you in and I'll wait outside."

"Yeah, OK. Adrian, will you take us to see the snakes since Mom's being a girl?"

This causes me to giggle and my tears become happy ones. "I'm always a girl, Finn."

"Yeah, but you're acting like one now. There's a difference."

This causes us all to break out in laughter. "My funny man," I say as I ruffle his hair.

Adrian picks up our zoo paraphernalia, rubs Finn on the head, and says, "Let's go, little man."

Finn pops his tiny fists up, dances around like a fighter, and says, "Who you calling little? I can take you. Let's go."

"Haha, not now. Maybe later. Let's go, boys."

I smile as I watch the boys with Adrian again and feel my whole countenance rejoice. They are talking to him animatedly like they hadn't spoken in years. He hangs on their every word.

THE BOYS FALL asleep in Adrian's truck on the way home, and I barely live ten minutes from the zoo. We ate at the café before heading out—full bellies and worn out little bodies—all in a day's work. That's good because Adrian and I could get to what had quickly become our ritual and the favorite part of my day.

After getting the boys tucked in, I make my way to my bathroom to freshen up and change my clothes. I decide to take a quick shower, so I call out and get Adrian's attention. He walks over to my door where I have only my head hanging out for modesty's sake. "I'm going to jump in the shower real quick. I feel gross," I tell him.

His eyes darken and he whispers huskily, "Please don't tell me you're naked behind this flimsy door."

I glance down at my body, look back up at him, and answer, "Umm...OK, I won't *tell* you that I'm naked."

Placing his hand on the door even with where my chest rests, he groans and leans his forehead on the doorjamb. "Ah...Celeste, you're killing me. I'm trying to be good here."

Bringing my lip in, I bite it in frustration before I ask, "And why are we being good exactly?"

He draws back like I've slapped him, his brow furrowed. "I figured you would want to wait."

I gasp. "What made you come to that conclusion? I've never wanted anything more in my life."

He chuckles at my candor. "I don't know. You're a good girl. Good girls like to wait for milestones and shit."

I raise my brows. "Milestones and shit?"

"Yeah, like after the third date and stuff like that."

"Oh," I whisper. "Maybe I'm not a good girl."

"Oh, yes, you are."

"I'm thinking I must not be because I don't want to wait."

He runs his hands through his hair and over his scruff. "Are we really having this conversation while you're standing there naked on the other side of a door?"

My head falls back with the force of my laughter. "I guess we are."

"What if I said that *I* want to wait?"

"Do you?" My eyes widen.

"I do. I want us to be...different."

"Me too," I agree.

He flicks this thumb toward the other bathroom. "On that note, I'll hop in the other shower while you tidy up."

I groan a little at the thought of us showering so close yet so far away. "Fine. Do you think there'll be enough hot water?"

He starts to walk away, throwing over his shoulder, "No worries. Mine's gonna be a cold one." My laughter follows him down the hall.

After showering I throw on some comfy clothes to include a bright blue camisole, which reminds me of Adrian's eyes, and a stretchy pair of white short shorts. Tossing my glasses on, I make my way out to the sunroom. Adrian is playing on his phone and is already seated on the loveseat—the piece of furniture that had become the location of our make-out sessions. I'd never really made out with anyone; it is great fun if a lot on the frustrating side.

"Hi," I whisper.

He looks up at me with a smile and tosses his phone on the table. "You look so sexy in those glasses," he blurts out.

"What?" I gasp. "No I don't." My hand flies up to adjust my horn-rimmed ovals.

"Yeah, you're my hot for teacher and naughty librarian fantasies come to life and all in one package," he says with a look of barely contained lust.

"But I'm not a teacher nor am I a librarian," I barely manage to say.

"Doesn't matter. You look like one. Why are you standing way over there?"

"I don't know."

"Well, come here."

I smile and move to sit beside him. Abruptly, he stops me midway down and hauls me into his lap. I laugh upon impact. One of his arms snakes around me to pull me close while the other comes to rest across my knees. "What are you doing?"

"I don't want you that far away. I have to erase all the distance that was between us today," he murmurs as his lips find mine.

My fingers lace themselves around his neck as I pull him closer in, reveling in the feel of him in my mouth and under me. Running my fingers through his hair and massaging him, I manage to pull him in even closer.

All of my senses are diverted from our kiss as I feel his fingertips run ever so lightly up my thigh. So far all he'd done is kiss me senseless during our make-out sessions. I feel a change coming on.

I wiggle in his lap a little at that thought. He groans into my mouth and his fingertips disappear for a second before I feel his whole hand alternately kneading and pulling at my thigh and moving up quickly to do the same to my behind. I can't keep kissing him because I'm out of breath and can't seem to get any oxygen to my brain. I pull back and angle his head so that I can run my lips over his clean-shaven jaw. I place wet kisses all along his neck and work my way up and down his throat while he works his way up my body with his strong, supple hands.

He seems to switch gears a little, and I delight in the loving touch I feel as he softly massages the little knobs of my spine. Leaning my forehead on the side of his neck, I smile against his throat.

"What?" he asks me in that gravelly voice that I love.

"That feels so good," I admit.

"It's my mission to make you feel good."

"That's better than good actually—fantastic."

"Mmm...mission accomplished," he murmurs against my throat as he attacks it with enthusiasm. "You taste so good. Like the ocean."

I feel one hand move to my face as he pulls his lips from me. "That would be my coconut and lime body wash." He traces my cheekbone with his fingertip, eliciting a little laugh from me. My eyes spring open. "That tickles."

He licks his lips as he brushes my bottom lip lightly with his fingertip. I watch as his entranced gaze follows his fingertip as it trails down my throat, over my collarbone, and back and forth over the seam of the top of my camisole before finding its way down to circle my nipple. I can only groan as I feel my nipple form a tight bud.

"Does that feel good, baby?"

"Mmm...hmm," I moan. He continues his sweet caress for a moment before running his fingertip back and forth over the bud. The shudder that overtakes me is unexpected and a little frightening. I squeeze my thighs together to try to alleviate some of the tension gathering there. It doesn't help, and I'm nervous that this little touch elicits this much of a reaction from me. I can only imagine what I'll feel when he touches me in earnest.

His lips find their way back to mine, and he kisses me until I am weak and no longer able to worry. His entire hand massages my breast for a moment before I feel my camisole being pushed down and under it. The action not only exposes me but also lifts my breast like an offering to him. He rubs it for a moment, teasingly and lovingly, before he pulls his lips from mine.

"Lie back," he orders in a whisper.

Thoughtlessly, I do as he tells me. I open my eyes and watch with fascination until I can't watch anymore and I lose myself in the sensations he wrings from my body as he teases me with his tongue and then devours me with his mouth—first one breast and then the other. When I feel like I absolutely can't take any more and am a writing mass in his arms, he nips at them before kissing them tenderly and pulling my camisole back over me.

Turning that tender kissing to my mouth, he kisses me into oblivion before pulling back to say the most incredible things to me. He murmurs, "I love the way you respond to me and my touch. Your body is my temple. Mmm…you taste incredible. You are so perfect."

My eyelids flutter open to drown in the beauty that is him. I know what he means, but I have issues with this word. "I'm not perfect," I whisper.

"You're perfect for me. Other than the fact that you like to show off this delectable body of yours, you are absolute fucking perfection. Made for me, babe. Made for my lips," he says before nipping at mine with a little force. "I've never known such a feeling of complete contentment than when I am with you and the boys. Do you know how huge that is for me? To feel peace and acceptance and love? I've never had that."

My heart aches for him, not out of sorrow, but pure empathy. "I do get it, Adrian. That's how I felt my whole life. Always on edge, always looking for love and acceptance." I shake my head back and forth. "But never really finding it until I found you."

"I still feel on the edge with you," he confesses. "But it's different. Exciting. Like being on the edge of an amazing turning point . I've always liked my life other than the fact that I felt estranged from my family. Babe, you and the boys make me *love* my life. And while I enjoy one moment, I find myself looking forward to all our moments together, and I can't wait until the next one unfolds." He buries his face in my neck before he says, "Look at what you do to me. Turn me inside out. I'm not making any damn sense."

I pull his head up from his hiding place and give him a long, yet chaste, kiss. When I pull back, I see so many emotions swirling in those beautiful eyes of his—love, desire, fear. "Adrian, you make perfect sense. I love how honest you are with me—always. You never hold back how you feel. Even when you're torn or conflicted you show me everything, make me feel everything you feel. All my life I've been forced to tiptoe around my emotions to avoid their bubbling out of me accidentally. And it didn't even matter which ones they were, we were not allowed to express them overtly because being emotional was an 'undesirable' character trait. I made sure that the people I welcomed into my life were people who felt free to express themselves and let me express myself. When my boys were born, I promised myself that they'd never have to go through that. That they'd always feel comfortable being themselves and expressing themselves. I love that you don't hold back with me, and I wouldn't want it any other way."

"You don't mind my emotions even when they're scary or make you uncomfortable?"

I shake my head at him. "Being pushed outside of my comfort zone is living. And I love living."

He draws my forehead to his lips and places a light kiss there. "I love you so much, Cel. I didn't think it was possible, but every day that we're together I fall more in love with you. I...it blows my fucking mind."

I turn my lips to find his jaw again and kiss the line of it until I find his ear. I nip at it for a second, causing him to shudder underneath me. "I love you, Adrian Gabriel Leblanc Hebert. All of you. Every piece of you."

-Fourteen-

Whatever It Takes

MY WHOLE LIFE I'd wanted this, yet I'd never thought it possible. In between the gigs, photo shoots, and running the boys to and fro, Adrian and I had found a perfect peace. I am thrilled, but a part of me, kept waiting for the other shoe to drop. We knew we couldn't keep our relationship a secret, and frankly, we didn't want to.

We were both dying to tell the boys and had decided that that's where we'd start with our "coming out." I was looking forward to bringing them in on things, and we'd decided tonight after the talent show would be the ideal time to tell them.

Looking over at Adrian chatting with Louis, the butterflies that are already flitting around in my stomach intensify before settling in for a nice humming routine. As soon as my eyes start roaming over him in an appreciative manner, he nods at Louis and looks up to fix me with his gaze. I can't help the little smile that instantly forms, so I bite my lip a little to refrain from grinning like an idiot. He gives me a half-smile and shakes his head at me. I just shrug and continue staring at him before Louis notices Adrian's distraction and follows his stare to me. Louis gives me a little wave before turning back to Adrian and continuing their discussion.

My nerves exist for a multitude of reasons. The boys are all performing tonight—Archer's first. We, of course, are planning to talk to them about our relationship. And I'm not sure how well I'll be able to fake *not* being in love with Adrian with some of my friends and family being around. I know for a fact that my brothers and sisters-in-law will be here. Bonnie and Garner will be here as well. We've been around them a bunch, but it's been when the guys have been performing and that's very different from us all sitting in an audience together and then maybe going out to dinner.

I'm pulled from my internal musings as Bonnie cuts into my line of vision. The annoyingly perceptive woman immediately follows my gaze before it dawns on me to avert it. She tsks at me and walks over to join me.

"Lord, woman. You're never gonna learn," she chastises me.

"I'm a glutton for punishment, I guess," I say with a sigh.

"Oh my word...you're pathetic!"

"I know." I sigh again.

She grabs my arm, forcing my attention to her. "Geez, Cel, get a grip."

"Maybe I don't want to," I say with a shake of my head.

"What's that supposed to mean?" she asks with a furrowed brow.

I finally snap out of my Adrian-induced stupor. "Oh, nothing." My hands flit around erratically. "Please ignore me. I'm just..."

"A glutton for punishment," she finishes for me. I nod. "I'm thinking of pulling a scene from one of our romantic comedies and locking you and Adrian in a closet until y'all come to your damn senses. Would you hate me?" Before I can answer, she says, "Cause it would be for your own good, honey. This is getting exceedingly ridiculous."

I want to tell her so badly, but I want the boys to know first. Fortunately, Garner interrupts my almost-confession. "Hey, baby. Wanna get a seat?" he practically purrs in her ear. Mmm...to have that kind of openness. She turns her face toward his and rubs it along his in a loving gesture. My jealousy licks a fiery path up and down me for a moment before I feel immediately ashamed. She deserves this, and I'll have it soon enough. She went through hell with her ex-husband. I tamp all that down and give them a smile.

Adrian touches my elbow for a second before motioning me to join him in finding our seats. I wave to my family, and we all settle in to watch the children perform. Adrian casually throws his jacket between our two chairs, covering my arm. I glance up at him and smile before attempting to move it out of the way when I feel his hand work its way down my arm and grasp my hand in his. Again, he gives me that sly smile of his before turning his attention back to the stage. I practically melt in my seat before I'm able to swivel my head around for the first performance.

As the opening acts perform, Adrian shifts and threads his fingers through mine before using his thumb to run back and forth over my palm. It's really not fair that he can turn me on like this. My senses are firing in every direction.

When Archer takes the stage, he settles down a bit, which leads me to believe that he knows exactly what his touch was doing to me. I turn and smirk a little at him, eliciting a little laugh before he turns back and whistles at Archer.

Archer perches himself on his stool before speaking into the microphone with the utmost confidence. "Hello, everybody. I'm Archer Hebert, and I'll be performing 'Bridge Over Troubled Water' by Simon and Garfunkel. I've been working on this for a couple of months now with my cousin, Adrian. I hope you like it."

Tears populate my eyes immediately, and my gaze flies to Adrian. I had no idea. "Really?" I whisper.

He leans over and whispers, "He wanted it to be a surprise."

My sweet boy, playing my absolute all-time favorite song, I can't believe it. He adjusts his guitar before strumming that first note, and my respect and pride bubble from me and I give a nervous, little giggle. I'm more nervous than he is.

Flawless—his performance is flawless. The crowd is so moved

that they are stunned into silence a moment before erupting in a cacophony of cheers and clapping and whistling. I feel a single tear escape me just before I feel Adrian scoop it up. Turning to him, I watch, mesmerized, as he sucks it from his fingertip.

When we settle back down from Archer's rousing performance, I steal back under the jacket to lace my fingers through Adrian's while we await Paris's performance.

So many emotions course through me, and so rapidly, that I can't pinpoint them long enough to name them, and I can't believe how fortunate I am to have these three beautiful children and this beautiful man in my life.

I see the piano being wheeled out from upstage and Paris entering left, so I give Adrian's hand a brief squeeze before letting go in order to welcome him. He, like his brother, announces himself but only his name. His nerves are shimmering just below the surface.

When I hear the opening notes to Lennon's "Imagine," I look over at Adrian and mutter, "Are they trying to kill me?" He just grins real big at me.

Turning back, I tear up all over again as I listen to his beautiful instrumental rendition of this classic that speaks volumes about my sage little man. He is indeed a peacemaker and the song fits him so well. My heart surges with joy and a little heartbreak as I know one as sensitive as he will struggle in this world.

When Paris wraps up, he garners as much of a reaction as Archer did. If Finn comes out and does something of this nature, I don't think I'll survive it. I lean over and whisper that sentiment to Adrian. Then I realize something else. I tap Adrian to get his attention. "They weren't supposed to do those songs. They had other songs all picked out and had been rehearsing them. Is this your doing?"

"Maybe," he says with a cheesy grin.

"I have to say I'm thrilled with the changes. Those are fantastic songs," I say.

"Well, I just played them for them and let them choose. I may have swayed Archer a little bit."

"Mmm hmm," I mumble as the next act comes out.

We enjoy a variety of other performances. My nieces even do a little ballet routine. In my completely unbiased opinion, none are as good as my little virtuosos. The principal pops out to tell everyone that Finn Hebert will be the last performer of the night, and we all clap loudly as my adorable seven-year-old traipses on stage.

"So, yeah, I'm Finn, but I think everybody knows that by now cause Mr. Fitzpatrick just said it." He has the audience laughing in seconds and eating out of the palm of his hand. "I'm not singing or playing anything, but I think you'll like what I've got for you. How many Michael Jackson fans do we have out there?" He cups his hand to his ear like he's entertained hundreds on a regular basis. I'm dying, as is Adrian. I catch Louis's eye and we both roll our eyes at our little ham.

"Yeah, that's what I thought," he says when the applause dies down. "Well, I hope you like this number 'cause I worked real hard on it."

The lights die down for a moment before a single, white spotlight finds Finn on stage. He has on a fedora and it's tilted over one eye. As soon as the beat starts, he starts moving those hips and those arms. I'm flabbergasted. I've seen him dance around the house for fun, and he's always really adorable. But this is choreographed and inspired. When he does that kick twist that MJ does, I can't help but clap and cheer. This little move causes almost the entire crowd to hop up and start dancing with him including Louis and me. Adrian stands and claps along but refrains from moving his hips like Finn.

He's wrapping it up, and the crowd is in awe of him. But when he does the Moonwalk, we all lose it—lots of catcalling and whistling and laughter break out. He only does it for a few seconds, but it's so good. When the music cuts off, the spotlight does too. Then the stage lights cut back on, illuminating a bowing Finn. The crowd goes nuts, and I've never been prouder of my three boys for working so hard and doing what they love.

After the show, Adrian and I make our way backstage to gather the boys for dinner. I know a little shortcut from helping with props and stage design, so we cut through that area. I'm leading Adrian through all of the props and fabric and things that make a show go, when I feel him pull at my elbow, which causes me to stop and look back over my shoulder at him.

Running his hand over my breast and up my neck, he pins me to his chest. His strong fingertips push on my jaw so that my lips meet his. I melt into him while he kisses me tenderly and lovingly for a second. His kiss quickly turns scorching, but before I'm able to absorb all those sensations, he reins it in and places little kisses on my mouth. I smile against his mouth and murmur, "What was that for?"

"For being irresistible," he murmurs back. I lean in further and give him a quick peck before starting us on our trek again.

Just before we pop out from our hidden location and our stolen moment, I'm stunned to hear a young voice say, "I knew you were gay, dude, but really? A piano solo?" The boy asks with disdain. "You should've played some Elton John or something that would be more your deal, right, guys?"

I hear some boys laugh, but I'm even more stunned to hear my Paris respond and deny the claim.

The knowledge that Paris is on the receiving end of the vitriolic comments shakes me from my frozen state to remedy the situation, but before I can emerge completely, Adrian halts me with his words. "Hold on, Mama," he breathes in my ear.

I look back at him with a frown. He just nods at me to listen to what's going on. Turning my head back, I hear Paris laugh before he says, "The only reason you're trying to pick on me is because you have low self-esteem and don't like yourself."

I gasp, wondering what the boy will do. I peek out and see not one but three boys cornering him. Shooting a nervous look over my shoulder, Adrian just nods at me and joins me in peeking out.

"What are you even talking about, faggot?" The ringleader asks.

My blood boils.

Paris keeps his cool and responds, "I'm talking about that the fact that you're overweight and hate it, and instead of dealing, you try to make others feel bad. Like when you pick on Jamie for being so skinny or on Josh for being so small. None of us can help the way we are including you. By the way, people don't really like you, but it's not because of something you can't help. It's because you're a jerk with a bad attitude." I mentally clap my hands together. *Go Paris!*

"Now here's the thing," Paris continues when his brief pause is met with silence, "I like who I am. I like who Jamie is and who Josh is too. I'm even willing to overlook our differences and be friends with you too. Only you have to stop being a jerk to everyone."

I hear the bully sputter for a second before he threatens, "I can kick your ass."

Paris just snickers before he says, "You can try, but that's not gonna happen. I would never start a fight with you, but I will finish it with my black belt in tact."

"You," the bully sneers, "have a black belt?"

"Yep. MMA. Mixed Martial Art. You know, Jiu-Jitsu, Muy Thai, wrestling?" Paris had leaned forward with each one of his words so that the bully was the one who was leaning back now. You've heard of them, right? Basically, everything I need to know to defend myself and incapacitate you."

My eyes widen and I glance at Adrian as I hear him rubbing his hands together as if spoiling for a fight. I raise my brows at him and he shrugs at me. "I'm kinda hoping they hit him. I want to see him wipe the floor with their asses."

I gasp and smack his arm. "Adrian," I admonish.

I lean back out to see Paris going off in the other direction with the two other boys and I get nervous all over again until I hear one of them say, "Dude, MMA? That's cool. I've been trying to get my mom to sign me up."

Leaning back against Adrian, I release a long breath and relax my shoulders. "Being a kid sucks sometimes."

He kisses my cheek and runs his hand over my hair. "Yeah, but I'm proud of him. He handled that well."

"Yes, he did. It sounded almost...rehearsed." I turn and raise my brow at him.

He just laughs and nudges me from our hiding place to go and gather the boys.

DINNER IS A reasonable affair considering we have about fifteen of us and more than half is made up of children. The kids are still high from their performances and everyone cajoles Finn into showing the server some of his moves. It doesn't take much to get him to do that.

The boys are still talking animatedly as we arrive back home. Once they've taken care of their chores and I've gathered up a little nerve, I call them to the living room. I sit on the couch and pull Finn onto my lap. Adrian sits on the loveseat with Paris, and Archer plops down across from me.

I make eye contact with all of them and tell them again how proud of them I am before I get to the fun part. "Boys, Adrian and I have something we want to share with you. I hope you'll under-stand—"

Before I can say another word, Finn cuts me off. "Adrian's your boyfriend."

I gasp. Paris and Archer giggle while Finn does his obnoxious snorting laugh. Adrian starts laughing with the boys. "Finn Thomas Hebert."

"What? We know he is."

"Yeah, Mom," Archer agrees.

"Really?" I ask Paris when I see his head nod. He nods again.

"Yeah," he agrees with his brothers.

"And you guys are good with that?"

"Yes," they say in unison.

"Why didn't y'all say anything? And how did you know?" I ask, still incredulous.

Finn answers, "It's gross how we know. I'm *not* saying it." He swipes his arms in safe motion. I guess that makes it final or something.

Paris pipes up, "We saw you kiss when we were at the park a few days ago. We came from fishing from the other side of the lake, so we just turned around and headed back in the other direction."

I know my face is blood red; I'm so embarrassed. "I'm sorry, guys."

With an eye roll, Finn says, "Mom, we're not babies."

I squeeze him tight. "I know that, but I'm sorry that I didn't tell you and that you found out that way."

Archer looks over at Adrian and takes him in for a minute before he asks, "So what are your plans with our mom?"

"Archer!" I squeak.

"It's OK, Celeste," Adrian reassures me before looking back to Archer. "I think it's important that you boys understand how much you and your mom mean to me. I consider y'all my family, and I have for a long time. And, to be honest, I've never had a family like this." He looks from boy to boy and then finally to me. "I plan to protect that with everything I've got. And as for your mother," he says as he makes eye contact with me again, "I plan to marry her if she'll have me." I feel my jaw drop but that doesn't slow him down. He releases me from his stare to look at the boys with a wicked little smile. "Maybe you guys could help me think of a cool way to propose."

Paris doesn't miss a beat, "I think you just did." We all laugh out loud.

I think he just did, indeed, and if I hadn't been so shocked, I'd have probably said yes on the spot.

AFTER OUR REVEALING little chat, we settle in to watch a movie. Usually Adrian sits on one of the chairs with one of the boys and the other two boys and I will sit on the couch or they'll curl up with the dogs on the floor. Tonight, however, he sits on the couch with me but still a respectable distance away. Archer and Paris lie on the floor using Shaggy, their Collie, as their pillow. Finn has his head on my lap and his feet in Adrian's. Ruby is curled up next to me. I haven't watched the movie at all because Adrian's hand has never left my hair and his beautiful blues have never looked away from me.

ADRIAN LET ME tuck the boys in tonight so that I could have a private conversation with them about how they felt about our being a family. I told the boys that they are the first to know and that I'd appreciate them allowing me to tell everyone else. The boys assured me they were more than OK with it. In fact, they loved it. They told me repeatedly that they love Adrian. When I assured them that Adrian would add to our family and make it whole in a new way and that he wasn't trying to replace their dad, they practically laughed at me and told me that that wasn't something they were worried about—mature little things.

After I put the little ones in bed, Archer called me back into his room and told me that he'd been worried about what was going on between me and Adrian. He didn't like the idea of someone, even Adrian, dating his mom without knowing what that person's

EVERYTHING I'VE NEVER HAD

intentions were. Once again, I'm floored by one of my thoughtful sons, and I'm so grateful I didn't screw everything up.

I'm still grinning when I hit the living room ready to make my way to the sunroom for a little private time with my man when I see him still in the living room leaning over the piano playing a couple of quiet notes. I sneak behind him and wrap my arms around him. Burying my forehead between his shoulder blades, I inhale deeply all that is him—strength, masculinity, compassion.

He continues to play for a few seconds before he asks, "Did I scare you with the marriage talk?"

I swallow hard. I'm not scared—I'm petrified. But not of the things he thinks I'm afraid of. "I love that that's where your heart is. Truth be told, I can't imagine my life without you. I think we still have some things to figure out, don't you?"

After a minute of listening to him tinker around, he says, "We do. We need to talk. How about the front porch tonight?"

Loosening my arms to allow him to turn into me, I tilt my head back and take him in. Worry mars his features. I run my fingertips over the frown lines around his eyes. "You all right?"

"Yeah, just some things I want to tell you. I don't want to get distracted on that loveseat," he says as he leans in and proves his point by giving me a deep kiss. His hands slip behind me and overlap each other on my behind as he pulls me in tight before releasing me.

"Mmm...OK...I'll meet you out there."

Once I make my way to the porch, I'm a ball of nerves. I've an idea what he wants to share and it terrifies me. What if what they have on him is so bad that we can't be together? That it would affect the boys for us to be together? I can't even wrap my mind around the concept of living my life without him. I know we've only had a couple of weeks together, but what we've been able to carve out is everything I've ever needed. I'm not ready to give that up. I'm certainly not ready to give him up.

He pats the swing beside him, and I barely get settled before he jumps right to the matter at hand.

"I've done some things I'm not proud of, Celeste, but you have to know that I did them to protect you and the boys from William and the family. I'm afraid that what I'm about to tell you will scare you off, but I hope not. I want you to know I'm done with it. I won't be doing them any more favors. If you know the truth, they have nothing to hold over my head. That's the only thing that was keeping me in play." Pausing, he looks at me and I can see the fear swimming in his eyes.

I'm scared too, but I reach out and run my hand up and down his jaw for a moment. He leans into my touch and closes his eyes as if gathering his strength.

Without opening his eyes, he begins after a deep sigh. "Did you know they picked me up and brought me in to harass me after I started helping you with the boys?" I murmur my no, but I'm not surprised. I knew how much they had hated him. "Yep, they were ticked that you were spending time with me and were trying to scare me off. Of course, they weren't successful. Anyway, it wasn't too long after they started talking to me about joining their ranks. I was able to keep them at bay, telling them I wanted to focus on my music career and possibly go to law school." His eyes pop open, and I can see his sincerity. I give him an encouraging nod. "When I found out about their plan to marry you to William, I went to them and told them to back off. It was worse than just William. If he didn't work out, their back up plan was to marry you to another cronies' son." I swallow hard, and if possible, come to despise them more. "They were insistent for a while but finally implied that they would leave you alone if I'd be willing to help them out. That was my condition—you and the boys were untouchable. I didn't consider what they would want from me. As long as I was protecting y'all, I didn't care. At first, it was little things—errands and such. Nothing illegal, just unethical mostly. But that didn't last long. It escalated pretty quickly to me becoming a collector. Do you know what that is?"

Closing my eyes slowly, I nod my head slowly before reopening them. "Please don't cry, baby," he pleads as he wipes my tears from my face. I didn't mean to start crying, and I didn't even realize I had, but the thought of him hurting other people to protect me rips my heart out.

"Did it escalate from collector?" My voice sounds dead, but I can't muster any strength because if he did more than collect we are in trouble.

"No, but they're wanting it to. I'm going to talk to them tomorrow and come clean with them. Let them know that they can't threaten me where you're concerned any more. Honestly, I don't care where this puts me, but I know it's going to hurt you. I know they're going to try to make you pay."

I feel my shoulders relax because I may have our way out of this whole nightmare. Nodding, I take a deep breath before I launch into telling him about my meeting with Mr. OG. His blues run the emotional gamut before I finish—anger, fear, disbelief. "Do you think that would work? Me getting that information before you talk to them and having it accessible in case they threaten us further?"

He runs an impatient hand through his hair. "Well, I'm not crazy about you meeting with this OG guy but if Tripp trusted him then we probably can too." I nod my agreement. "I think it will help put us on an equal playing field. Though, I wish Tripp would've shared that information with you rather than doing all this."

"He probably thought that everything would be fine. He always tried to see the good in everyone, you know? And he would've never seen this thing with William coming. *I* couldn't have predicted that, but I'm not surprised by their underhanded means and compulsion to control my life. That's always been the case."

"I know how they are with the men, so I can imagine how tough they were on you."

I take a deep breath to prepare myself to tell him something I'd never told another soul. Not even Bonnie knew the whole story. "I got a wild hair while I was in college and had a short-lived fling with a guy named Scott. He was a handsome, nice, normal guy. Not connected. Not a threat in the world we live in. Anyway, before I began school, I was informed that I was to marry Tripp after graduation and that I was to save myself for him." Suddenly uncomfortable, I shift on the swing and will myself to say these words aloud. Adrian squeezes my hand in silent support. "When they found out about Scott, I was summonsed to the office and told that I would be cut off from the family and kicked out of school if I didn't end things; furthermore, they would have Scott's scholarship pulled for his 'drug use' and his family's small business would have 'faced troubling times' if I didn't end it without a fuss. The worst part—they made me apologize to Tripp for sleeping around. He was so good to me about it. You know, sometimes I think that the whole reason he went along with their plans and married me was because he felt sorry for me. If he'd said no, there's no telling who I would've ended up with. He knew that too."

Adrian brushes my hair behind my shoulders and runs his thumb over my cheek. "I'm sorry, baby. About the threats and humiliation that is, not about you having to end things with that guy. And Tripp respected the hell out of you. Nothing was clearer to me than that."

I give a little laugh. "He really was good to me. Anyway, I'd thought for a brief moment that if I pushed, if I questioned I might be able to escape their rule, so I gave it a little try. But I was just too scared to follow through." Looking up at him, I promise, "But not now. I'm not scared anymore. I'm not going to let them destroy us—any of us."

He leans back in the swing and brings me with him. I curl into his chest and, bringing my legs up under me, settle in. Adrian pushes off with his feet and swings us slowly. He exhales a deep breath. "I'm sorry, Celeste. Sorry that I acted on impulse. You're going to lose your family over this, over me," he says as he rubs my back soothingly.

Leaning back a little to capture his eyes, I tell him, "I'm not sorry that I chose you over them. That incident? Nothing new. All they've ever done my entire life is use me and hurt me and the people I care about. I know that I'm not exactly suffering in the grand scheme of things—I have everything anyone could ever want —but all that doesn't compensate for the emotional hell they've put me through. I think that's why I'm kinda over the top with the boys. I never want them to doubt for one second that I love them for exactly who they are."

Tenderness battles with fierceness in my heart, before I confess, "Being with you, Adrian, it's everything I've ever needed. Tripp protected me and loved me in his own way. But, with you, I feel like you love me for me. Not for what I have to offer you or what you can acquire or who you can make happy by being with me. And the things you make me feel—I thought I'd never be free to feel, so I don't regret us. I'll never be sorry for loving you."

He doesn't say a word, just grabs my jaw and ravages me. I cry out a little in surprise as he bites my lip a little to get me to open up to him. Once I do, his taste, his scent, his strength assail me so that I feel only pleasure at the little assault he exacts on me.

When he releases me, I lay my head on his chest to try to gather my wits and my breath.

After several beats, I do tell him what I regret. "I'm sorry that you had to compromise yourself to protect me."

"I've done far worse than that, babe. You forget where I've been and what I've done. I've been on the frontlines of many wars. I've watched lives end right in front of me. I've even been the one to end some of those lives."

Tilting my head back, I whisper fervently, "That's different."

"Hmm...is it?"

"Yes, you were fighting for your country and protecting her citizens. What you did over there was honorable."

He doesn't answer me. Instead, he places a light kiss on the end of my nose and nudges my mouth up to take me again. And take me he does. Our disturbing conversation recedes from my mind like the ocean during a tsunami.

-Fifteen-

Never Saw It Coming

I CONVINCE ADRIAN to wait until the weekend and until we get to the country to enlighten the family about the change in our relationship, arguing that being in a more relaxed setting might help our case. Since he agreed, we have a few more days of peace before all hell breaks loose. I don't doubt for a second that that's exactly what it'll be like either.

Hearing my front door open and my best friend shouting for me jerks me out of my pensive state. She's the one person I'm dying to tell. She's going to be so happy for us and so supportive. I pop out of my bedroom to catch her checking herself out in my full-length mirror. Her eyes are currently roving over her behind.

I gasp. "You look amazing." She has on a hot pink jumper that is sleeveless and very, very short. Gold jewelry accents her waist, her throat, and her wrists. The high-heeled booties make her legs look even longer. "Wow. Bonnie, you always look great, but I've never seen you look so..."

"Hot?" she finishes for me.

"Yes, hot. You are exuding confidence, and you wear it well, honey."

174

"Thanks, Celeste. That means a lot coming from you. You look fantastic as usual."

I look down to my turquoise dress. It's one of my favorite pieces. It's a one shoulder billowy number that makes me feel like a princess. I'd paired it with lots of silver and leather. Even my stilettos were black leather—platform with fringe. They were sexy as hell.

I lean and give her a kiss on her cheek. "Thank you, sweetie. You want a quick drink before we go? I'd love a glass of wine."

"Yeah, sure. Where are the boys tonight?"

"Their friend, Collin, from school is having a huge weekend birthday bash. I think they've rented out every attraction in the city for it. The boys will be over there today and tomorrow." I pour our small glasses of Pinot Grigio.

"Oh, nice. Mama could use a break."

"Yes, she could. So how is everything?" I ask before sipping my wine.

She takes a gulp of hers, however, before refilling it. "Everything's good."

"Really?" I ask with a raised eyebrow.

"No, not really. But I'm not ready to talk about it yet."

"OK," I say because I can completely understand that notion since I'm hiding Adrian from her. "I hope you know that I'm here when you're ready."

She gives me a look that screams "Duh! Of course!" then she actually says that. I laugh so hard I bring tears to my eyes.

THE JOINT IS jumping tonight. It's so crowded, and I fear that our Dog Tags have outgrown these small venues. They are playing more and more original music. So much, in fact, that they only do a few covers now. Looking around, I watch in awe as people sing their lyrics back to them. Then I have a startling thought: what if they get picked up by a major label and have to leave for a tour? They're young and talented. None of them have anything holding them back. Could Adrian and I handle a long distance relationship? Could I handle knowing he was out there surrounded by beautiful and willing women? It's bad enough here with the women fawning all over him. I can't even imagine battling the unknown while he was out there living it up.

I shake my head a little at my runaway freight train of frightening thoughts. I am getting a little ahead of things. Focusing my attention back on my guitarist, I take him in as he plays a Hendrix number. He is absolute perfection. He'd cut his hair a bit, but that didn't stop the unkempt, dark brown locks from bouncing as he played. I liked the one-day stubble he was sporting. And don't even get me started on those eyes—those gorgeous blues that seek me out every few minutes and drink me in.

When Bonnie and I had arrived by cab, he'd ushered us in and set me up at a table just to the left of where he stands on stage. We'd gotten here early so that when Garner and Bonnie had slipped off to get us drinks there was hardly anyone around to witness what he'd done next.

Turning me on my stool, he'd spun me to face the stage and stood between my legs. When he had me positioned how he wanted me, he ran both of his hands up my dress and curled them under my thighs, resting his fingertips just below my center. My eyes widened and I gasped. How did he do that? Catch me completely by surprise without my freaking out as I'm sure I would've if anyone else had dared to do that me, especially in public?

Leaning forward, he whispered in my ear, "Celeste, you look so damn sexy. And all I wanna do is shout from every rooftop in New Orleans that you are mine and claim you in front of everyone." I purred. I literally heard myself purr. I tried to muster up some shame for our reactions to each other but to no avail. "The best I can do until the world is in on our little secret is park you right here in front of me and make you promise."

I waited a beat before I asked, "Promise what?" even though I was thinking I'd promise him anything, anytime, anywhere.

"Promise me that you're mine. Mine to watch." He pierced me with that gaze. "Mine to kiss." He leaned in and placed a quick kiss on my lips. "Mine to love." His hands tightened on my thighs.

Swallowing hard, I promised, "Yours. Yours for everything, anything."

"God, I love you," he'd responded.

Before I could say another word, he released me from his spell and stepped back toward the stage. It took a few seconds for me to register that it was because our friends were headed our way.

I feel him staring at me again, and it shakes me from my reverie. I smile at him, and he winks at me. Wrapping up their song, Zach gets my attention as he announces, "My man, Adrian, is gonna sing a little something for you tonight." Shocked, I glance back over to Adrian who is readying himself with an acoustic guitar. I've never heard him sing before—not lead anyway. "Adrian's gonna set a little mood for you lovers out there, and then we'll take a little break before our second set."

Adrian situates himself on his stool and clears his throat before speaking to the crowd. "How y'all doing tonight?" The crowd hollers back with enthusiasm. "Good deal, y'all. Well, as you know, I don't usually sing." The enthusiasm of the girls takes over, and I hear one comment above all the others. "Yeah, Adrian! We love you, baby!" It's everything I can do not to turn around and give her a death glare, but I'm not about to take my eyes off of him or let her distract me from this moment. "Yeah, love y'all too!" he says with a blush. Aw, he's not used to being the center of attention. I love that.

"Anyway, how many of you have ever been in love?" Lots of hooting and hollering. "Yeah, well, this one is about the kind of love that compels you, that takes you on a ride like no other. The kind of love that wraps you tight in its embrace before it sinks its teeth into you." Lots of catcalling and whistling. "Yet you gravitate toward its hold and scream with joy from its sweet torture, knowing you wouldn't have it any other way." The bar is a riot of emotion, and I'm blown away by my otherwise quiet leading man.

He puts his finger up and shushes everyone. I, along with the others, am mesmerized. As he strums the beginnings of what I'd deemed to be "our song," I melt on my stool. I'm so glad that no one is sitting in front of me because there's no way that I could hide the love that must be radiating from my expression. This song is all about waiting on that all-consuming force that is love and finding it and never letting go. It's simply brilliant.

When he hits the chorus, his gaze swivels to mine and never leaves it. With his song, he asks me a series of questions: "If anything could ever feel this real forever? If anything could ever feel this good again?" When he sings, "You gotta promise not to stop when I say when," I feel myself nodding in agreement. I'll never stop, never let go.

He ends on a quiet strum, but the bar erupts. I hear some Sublime click on over the loudspeakers, and he's sitting there and staring at me. A few of the guys go up and shake his hand and congratulate him on an awesome debut. I can't really make him out too clearly any longer, but I can't stop staring either. I'm mentally chastising myself for being so obvious when I hear some chastising come from none other than Bonnie.

"Tsk, tsk, tsk. How long have you been sleeping together?" she asks near my ear. I spin around on my barstool and meet her shit-eating grin.

Trying to suppress mine, I answer her question with a question. "What makes you so sure we're sleeping together?"

Before she can answer me, I feel my hand being lifted and pulled. I catch a look of complete astonishment on her face before I hear Adrian ask her to excuse us.

I barely have time to find my footing before I'm being pulled behind him to the back. When we exit the back to the alleyway, I'm immediately pushed up against the door that he's slammed behind me. Grabbing both my hands, he pins them to the door with his. His grasp is so strong, so true. He holds my hands beside my head and ravages me. His tongue pushes into my mouth without any encouragement, and he feasts on me while I hang on for the ride. I feel my leg spring up and rest around his calf. It's the only means of control I have. I push my center toward his and feel his own excitement as he groans into my mouth. After what seems like forever, he frees me but not before sucking and biting at my lips. My mouth feels so swollen and so damn good.

Releasing a shaky breath, I ask, "What was that for?"

"I've never sung in front of a crowd before. I don't know why I just never felt the urge. I had to sing for you. I wanted you to understand. Do you understand?"

At the wild look in his eyes, I nod ever so slowly. I get it. He makes me want to do the craziest things too—like challenge my family and marry a thirty-year-old and make out in alleys. "I understand."

"Do you understand that I've never needed anyone like I need you? I can't keep you a secret anymore. When that guy walked over to your table while we were getting ready to play, I wanted to smash his head in with my guitar. No asshole would dare hit on you if they knew you were mine."

"Is that why you've marked me?" I barely breathe the question. I know my lips are swollen and red.

"Maybe," he half-admits as his gaze drops to them. "We're telling them Sunday. Got it?"

"Yeah, I got it. Bonnie's on to us, by the way." His eyes widen before he nods his head.

"I was pretty obvious with my performance, I guess. Sorry about that."

"She'll get over the fact that I wasn't the one to tell her because she's going to be happy for us." He's still holding my hands up. I don't even think he realizes it at this point. "I want to touch you. Will you let me?"

"I might shatter into a million pieces," he grinds out but drops my hands.

"I'll put you back together again," I promise. I lightly run my hands up his forearms, over his biceps, and up around his neck. Pausing there for a moment, I massage him a little. His head drops back, and I'm in awe of what I can make him feel and of how he shows me what he feels because I've never experienced that before. I lean in and run my lips over his jaw and down his neck and suck there for a minute, hearing his breathing become even more erratic. Using my fingernails, I trail lightly down his chest and circle his pecs for a minute before moving my mouth there to nip and tease. He laughs under my ministrations.

He groans before he proclaims, "Shit, I don't want to go back in there. I want to throw your fine ass over my shoulder and take you home and do dirty things to that troublesome little mouth of yours."

I gasp and my head flies up. "What?" I sputter.

His look is priceless. "Not a fan of dirty talk?" he asks.

"I...I don't know," I sputter again. My brain is just reeling.

He narrows his gaze at me. "What do you mean 'I don't know?' You either are or you aren't." Realization dawns in his eyes, and he grins wider than ever. "You've never had anyone talk to you that way, have you?"

"Umm..."

He runs his knuckles over my burning cheekbones. "Fuck. You are so innocent."

"I'm not innocent. My three children didn't arrive by Immaculate Conception, you know?"

"Yeah, that's not what I'm talking about and you know it."

I close my eyes and whisper, "We never talked about what we wanted or how we wanted it. We weren't...close like that."

"Look at me." I immediately comply even though I'm mortified. "I want us to be open with each other. I want to be able to tell you what I want and I want you to tell me too. Can you do that?"

I swallow hard. Just *talking* about talking about what we want is making me nervous. "I'll try."

"You will," he says with confidence. "I like the thought of taking a prim and proper thing like you and making you bad and dirty just for me."

My tongue darts out to wet my suddenly parched lips. He doesn't miss my action and leans to take a swipe across them with his own tongue before exploring my mouth again and at great lengths. "Mmm...I gotta go," he breathes into me.

I nod and deepen our kiss before pulling back and moving to follow him inside. We're not in the hallway for two seconds before I hear Bonnie say, "Oh, no you don't. Adrian, get your butt up on stage. I'll bring your lover back in a second."

Adrian's hold tightens on me, so I assure him I'll be fine before Bonnie's grabbed me and tugged me back outside.

She doesn't waste another minute. "How could you not tell me? Is he amazing? Are y'all just messing around or y'all going to try to be a real couple?"

"I'm sorry. We haven't been together long and were just giving it a little bit of time before we faced my family's wrath. He is amazing, but we haven't slept together. And...we're going to be a real couple. This is not a casual relationship for either of us."

"Wow," she breathes in wonder. I see tears gather in her eyes. "I'm so damn proud of you."

"Thanks," I say with a grin. "Bonnie, he's wonderful. I can't even...I can't even properly put it into words. You know how good he's always been with me?" She nods. "He's like that now, too, sweet and understanding and tender but rough and demanding and sexual. Like all the time. Whenever he can, he's touching me. Though, not always in a sexual way. Sometimes it's just a caress or a massage. And then he's just so honest. He tells me whatever he is feeling and wants to know what I'm feeling. I'm just blown away by it all. I never thought I'd have any of that. I've never known a man like that."

"Babe, your pool of men was pretty shallow, but I get what you're saying. I'm loving this side of him; he sounds so amazing," she says with a sigh.

"*So* amazing, and the boys are thrilled beyond my greatest expectations. They love him so much." She smiles and nods at me. "I'm just...it's just overwhelming, but in a good way. You know?"

She reaches out and pulls my hair. "Yeah, I know. You sound like a teenager, experiencing all that lust and love for the first time. I'm happy for y'all."

"Thank you, honey."

"Let's get back and listen to our guys."

"Yeah...our guys."

SINCE THE CAT was out of the bag, Adrian and I enjoyed a dance together at the bar before calling it a night, and then we left together. Sunday would be here before we knew it, and we'd come clean with the family.

We'll be at my house in a few seconds, so I finally muster up the courage to ask him what I've wondered about all night. "Adrian?" I call to get his attention.

"Right here, baby," he grins at me and kisses the knuckles of the hand he's been holding on his thigh.

"Will you stay with me tonight? You can park your truck in my garage?"

He grins and winks at me. "I like the way you think, but your dirty talk needs some work, sweetie."

I gasp and jerk my hand from his while he laughs at me. "That's not what I was talking about," I mutter.

"I know. I'm sorry, babe. I couldn't resist. You're so damn cute. Now give me my hand back."

I begrudgingly give him my hand. "I hereby rescind the offer," I state with a glower.

"No you don't," he teases.

"Fine, I don't but you're going to have to make up for embarrassing me."

"Don't ever be embarrassed with me, baby."

I melt in my seat. He's going to have to scrape me out of his truck.

Surprisingly, I'm able to extract myself in order to open the garage. I wait for him to join me before I use the keypad to shut it. He's still chuckling at me. I smack him before he pulls me in and kisses me deep. Finally releasing me, he pulls me by my hand toward my front porch.

We're climbing the stairs, when I hear someone clear his throat from my porch. I try to snatch my hand from Adrian's, but he holds me fast. "Louis," he says evenly.

"Adrian, I sure to hell hope you know what you're doing."

"We do," he replies.

When we get to the top, I take in my little brother who's leaning on the post next to me. I give him a one-armed hug, seeing as Adrian still hasn't let go of me. I think he must be in protective mode, but we have nothing to fear from Louis. "Louis, I'm sorry you found out this way," I say. It seems we're not really as stealthy as we'd like to think.

"Celeste, you know I want you to be happy, but do you know what he's been up to?" he asks, gesturing at Adrian.

"I do, and we're going to handle it. Sunday, as a matter of a fact. I promise you have nothing to worry about."

Louis scrubs his hand over his dark mane. "I wish I could be as sure as you. I have nothing against the two of you being together, for the record." He looks from me to Adrian. "I respect the hell out of you, Adrian. I know how good you've been for them. I just worry what they'll do."

"We have a plan, Louis," Adrian tells him. "I would never go into this lightly. I'm not going to risk Celeste or the kids getting hurt."

"I trust you two to do the right thing. I'll be there Sunday as back up," he assures me as he rubs my arm up and down for a moment.

"Thank you, Lou," I whisper. "That means a lot."

"Night, Cel. Night, Adrian," he says as he turns to go.

"Wait! You were here for a reason. What's up?"

"Oh, nothing that can't wait. I'll talk with you later."

"Are you sure?" I feel awful. He hasn't dropped by just to hang out in a long time.

"Yeah, we'll talk Sunday."

"OK," I agree as I watch him move toward his car.

"That could've gone worse," he murmurs behind me.

"Yeah, do you think we'll actually get a chance to tell anyone or that we'll just keep getting busted?"

He just laughs at me.

WE AGREE TO meet back in my room after our separate showers. I'm a ball of nerves once again. I am desperate to spend the night with him, but I'm afraid one night will never be enough for me.

After slipping on my loose fitting, deep purple, silk cami and shorts, I exit my bathroom and lose my breath at seeing him sitting on my bed. His shirt is on hiatus, and I'm thrilled to see all that skin just for me. As if pulled by an invisible string, my nerve-endings bolt upon seeing him and propel me to make my way over to him. His arms slip around my waist while I circle his shoulders with mine. I lean in and give him a chaste kiss. He mumbles something against my lips that I don't understand.

I pull back a little. "What was that?" I ask.

"Silk—I love you in silk."

"Really?"

"Yeah," He runs one hand under my cami and then back over the silk. "I can't tell where the silk stops and your soft skin begins. You feel so good." He begins caressing my skin in earnest.

"Mmm...Hold that thought, Mr. Hebert," I say as I shake myself from his hold and his spell. "Let me dry my hair."

He lets his arms fall dramatically to the side and falls back against the bed. "Tease," I hear him murmur behind his hands scrubbing over his face. I laugh lightly.

Flipping my head over, I dry the underside of my hair quickly. As I flip back up, he's standing over me and a startled shriek wrenches from me. He just laughs as he takes the blow dryer from me and motions for me to sit at my vanity. With one hand he smoothes a lock of hair while running the blow dryer down alongside his fingers. My gaze drifts from his actions to his face. The look of concentration on his face is adorable. For someone who has never been in a serious relationship, he's surprisingly good at the wooing because I'm thoroughly wooed. His blues finally come up to meet mine in the mirror, and I give him a grin.

"What?"

"Nothing," I say with a laugh.

"You don't like it?"

"No, I love it and you. I love you."

He drops the dryer for a second before bending down and running his tongue up the side of my neck to my ear where he nips a little before he says, "I love you, Celeste. Like crazy love, like I can't sit across the room from you and watch you without wanting to be a part of what you're doing. Does that turn you off? Am I suffocating you?"

I'm just on this side of whimpering from his beautiful

confession, so I just shake my head side to side in a *no*.

He straightens up and finishes drying my hair while I ogle him. I watch his skin stretch over his taut abs and muscular chest while he moves the dryer around. I let my gaze drift over his biceps and up to his chiseled jaw that's held tight while he concentrates. When my wandering eyes meet back up with his, those blues hold a smile.

"See something you like?" he asks as he cuts the dryer off and lays it on the counter.

Instead of answering him, I spin on my stool and grasp him by his trim hips. Looking up at him, I lean and place kisses all along his stomach, circling his belly button with my tongue. Releasing a swift rush of air, he buries his hands in my hair while I worship his body with my tongue. When neither of us can take a second more, his hands find mine, and he leads me over to my bed. Turning me so that my back is to the bed, he nudges my lips until I let him in and nudges my body until I'm scooting up on the bed. He follows me up, and I lose myself in his kiss, my nerves effectively forgotten.

Pulling back, his lips trail down my neck, over my collarbone, and down to my breasts where he suckles and nips until I'm a writhing mass. Just when I think I can't take this build up of pressure anymore, he runs his hand up my loose-fitting shorts. His head shoots up when he realizes I don't have anything on underneath them, his blues turning dark and turbulent.

"I want to make you feel good. Do you trust me?" he asks, his voice turned raspy. I fall into those beautiful blues and nod my agreement. He pulls me in for a mind-numbing kiss while one of his fingers finds its way to my nub of exposed nerve-endings. It takes me by such surprise that I yelp. I try to conjure up some embarrassment at my raw display of ecstasy. He doesn't let up, though, and I can do nothing but focus on the pleasure he brings me. When he has me so worked up that I feel I'm about to explode, I feel another finger slip inside of me. This time, instead of yelping, I lean up and kiss and bite at his shoulder while my orgasm rockets through me.

"That's it, baby. Give it all to me. Oh, you're so wet and so eager." I bite at him in earnest and hear him growl, but I can't help myself because I'm riding out the tempest that's tearing through my body.

Just when I think it can't get any more intense, he inserts another finger and twists them simultaneously. I lose focus with what I'm doing with my mouth and I fall back. "Adrian," I say desperately. My poor body doesn't know if it should give in or resist.

"I've got you baby. Let go."

I don't let go so much as shatter all around him. "Mmm..." is all I can manage as I ride out wave after wave of pleasure. He slows down and strokes me languidly as my body goes soft like jelly and then removes his fingers, licking them clean before grinning at me.

He kisses my chin and rearranges my clothes before flipping on his back and pulling me in tight. "You are amazing," he tells me as he plants kisses on the top of my head.

How am I the amazing one exactly? He made me come twice in about three minutes. I would tell him that, but that would be way too humiliating. "You're not turned off by how, umm, easy that was?" I ask.

"Uhh...no, the exact opposite actually."

"Oh good," I breathe. I feel bad. He didn't get any pleasure, and he's nestling like he's about to doze off. "What about you?" I blush upon asking that.

"What about me?"

"I want to make you feel good too," I admit.

He gives me a lopsided grin. "You do?"

I bite my lip and nod.

"What do you want to do to me?"

"I want to touch you."

"How?"

Grinning, I bite my lip harder and shake my head. Oh, he's not going to make this easy on me. I lose the smile and tell him, "I want to wrap my hand around you and stroke you until you feel as good as I do right this very second." I feel my cheeks burn, and it's everything I can do to maintain eye contact with him. His grin widens, and he brings my face up to his and kisses me deeply while I trail my hand down his chest and abs.

I play a little at the edge of his shorts before diving my hand in and grasping him. Adrian releases a shaky breath into my mouth, and I feel encouraged. Running my hand over his length a few times before circling him in my grip, I begin to massage him in earnest. I run the tip of my thumb over his tip to gather the wetness and smear that to help me in my quest.

Adrian throws his head back and clenches his eyes tight as I work him with my hand. His hooded eyes open to watch me and that turns me on even more. "That feels so good, baby," he says all gruff-like.

After only a few minutes, he strains and bucks and finds his release. I gather it and spread it over his length to finish the job while he moans under me. I lean up and capture his lips with mine and give him a long, lingering kiss while he comes back down.

I give him another couple of pecks before getting up to get a washcloth. I warm it and bring it over to clean him. "I can do that," he says as he comes back to me.

"I want to," I assure him.

When I climb back in bed with him, he holds the covers back for me while I nuzzle into his side.

"Adrian?"

"Yeah, baby?"

"Does it worry you that I'm older than you?"

"You're older than me?" he asks, feigning surprise.

I smack his chest playfully and grab at his chest hair a little. "Does it?"

"I never even consider it," he assures me.

"Well, that's actually what worries me—the fact that you're all wrapped up and not thinking about the ramifications of our being together." I hesitate for a second before telling him my true concern. "You've told me before that you want children."

"Yeah, so?"

I lean up and prop my face in my palm before stating the obvious. "My youngest child is seven. I'm thirty-seven. I don't know that I'll be able to have any more children if that's what you want. And, to be honest, I don't know that I want any more children because of my age. It would be...difficult."

He swipes a lock of hair from my face and rubs it between his fingers, watching the action before looking back at me. I see pure conviction steeling my beloved blues. "Baby, I only want to be with you for you. I don't want to be with you for what you can or can't offer me. Right now, what you're giving me, is more than I ever dreamed possible, and it'll be more than enough for the rest of my life."

I smile big before I tell him of my musings from earlier. "You're really good at this, you know?"

"Good at what?"

"Being in a relationship, the wooing."

"The wooing?"

"I'm so wooed I can't see straight," I joke.

"Really?" he asks with a raised brow.

"Mmm hmm," I confirm.

His face becomes somber again, and he grasps my neck a little as he pulls me in to him. "You and the boys are enough for me now and forever. I mean that with everything I am and everything I'll ever be. Do you understand?"

A massive knot has lodged itself in my throat so that I'm only able to nod fervently before he kisses all thought from me once again.

IT HAD BEEN an eventful weekend that's for sure. Adrian and I had spent all day Saturday ensconced in the little cocoon we'd carved out for ourselves before picking the boys up from their friend's house that night. When we'd gotten the boys home, we played cards and games with them until they became whiny due to being overly exhausted. Adrian helped me get them tucked away before slipping away to his place.

After spending one night with him, I was already bemoaning the prospect of having to sleep without him. He must've sensed that because he pulled me to him on the porch before he promised, "You won't have many more nights without me by your side." I think I actually growled. He chuckled, kissed me, and shooed me back inside with a command to lock up.

He'd picked us up for Sunday Mass the next morning before driving us up to the country. I wondered if our family would notice that we'd driven out together. We'd never done that before.

We'd had lunch and walked the grounds a bit before the bottom fell out of the sky. Now, we are holed up in the family room because of the torrential downpour. The kids are being fabulous. The adults seem edgy. My mother, my sister-in-law, and I sit on the couch looking over some designs. My mother had never shown any interest in my work, but since the accident and our falling out, she'd seemed determined to play nice with me—a blessing in disguise. I still don't trust her completely, though.

As surreptitiously as possible, I steal as many glances as I'm able of Adrian and the younger boys. He's held them all enthralled as he's showed them how to play some songs on the piano. I'm pretty sure he's played every Elvis song under the sun. My father and father-in-law sit next to the older boys regaling them with Naval battle stories. My teenage nieces sit in the far corner with their phones out, laughing and giggling over God only knows what. Louis and my older brothers sit and discuss law stuff. How boring.

Reflecting on this peaceful familial setting, it's all I can do not to laugh aloud at the bomb Adrian and I are about to drop. The irony is not lost on me that my nefarious family can live the life they do and appear like the ideal family. Not to mention, commit their reprehensible acts without batting an eye, but they are going to lose their shit over my choice of husband. Maybe it won't take us too long to get back to our sense of normality.

My mother asks me a question about some fabrics I'm considering using for the throw pillows of my next shoot when I hear the soothing sound of the piano cease. I look up to see Adrian taking a call. Putting the room at his back, he walks the short distance over to the windows. I hear her ask me another question, but I don't answer as I've noticed Adrian's stance get taller and tenser with his conversation. I think it may be my imagination, but then I catch a glimpse of his white-knuckled hold on the phone. I pass the book to my mother as I begin to go to him. But before I can stand, he hits the end button and spins toward me, his gaze searching as it meets mine. I see trouble brewing in those eyes of his. I can't even imagine what could make him look like this.

I worry my lip a little as I wait for him to make a move. Never releasing me from his gaze, he takes a deep breath before he finally says, "Kimberly?" I hear my niece respond. "Will you and the girls take the kids into the playroom for a little while?"

Adrian has never asked anything of them, so I would imagine this triggers alarm bells for everyone because the room becomes silent and the kids start moving toward the door without any prompting. "Sure thing, Adrian," she replies as she ushers them from the room, leaving only the adults.

Paralyzed, I sit in wonder at what is going on. I can't make myself move even though I want to go to him and comfort him. Is it his father, his mother? He doesn't make me wonder long. "My unit has been activated," he says, "and we're being sent back to Iraq."

A sob erupts from my throat. I feel my mother startle and turn her eyes to me. I still can't look away from Adrian. I see him swallow hard a couple of times, fighting off emotion. I hear my brothers start muttering about fucking politics, and I hear my father and

Tripp's father commence to discuss duty and the call to protect. I don't think about any of that. All I can think is how messed up the situation is over there now and how my man is being sent over in the thick of it.

Finally, I'm able to pull myself from the couch, stumbling a little as I feel quite light-headed. Adrian's brow furrows, but he doesn't make a move to help me as I right myself pretty quickly.

Moving behind the piano, I run my hands up his chest and around his neck, bringing his forehead down to mine. I close my eyes and bring my lips to his, kissing him with everything I have in me. I hear a few startled gasps, but I can't be bothered to care.

After a minute, I pull back and place little kisses on his lips while I murmur, "You're going to be fine. We're going to be fine. You're so amazing at what you do, and I'll be right here waiting for you when you return. I love you, Adrian. Do you hear me?" He nods at me. "We're OK." He nods again.

I'm so impressed with my family because it takes them a couple of minutes to break us up. Of course, it's my mother's voice that I hear. "Celeste, do you care to tell us what exactly is going on?"

I'm not the one who answers though. Adrian's found his voice again and says what he's been dying to say since day one. Spinning me around in his arms, he wraps them around me before he says, "Family, Celeste and I are getting married."

I feel myself chuckle. I can't believe he just said that. *What happened to breaking it to them gently?* Louis moves in to shake Adrian's hand and say congratulations while my mother just sits in stony silence next to my sister-in-law, who waits for my mother's reaction to determine how she'll react. My brothers do much the same as they move to stand behind my father.

Tearing my glance from my mother, I seek out my father, who looks quite shocked but not angry as I'd feared. Maybe that's to come later. He breaks our gaze, and mine follows his to my father-in-law. Ah, there's angry. If I were a lesser woman, I'd wither up and die on the spot.

Chip looks toward my father and I hear him mutter, "Fix this. Fix it now," before storming from the room.

My father stands and walks over to me. "Is this who you want, Celeste?"

I bristle at his use of that rude pronoun. Adrian has a damn name. He's not a *this*. But a temper tantrum might not be helpful right now. So I answer his question. "*Adrian's* who I want, who I need, who I deserve, Daddy."

"So you've been sneaking around behind our backs then?"

Adrian answers for me. "No, not really. We've only been seeing each other a couple of weeks and were all set to tell you today—just not like this."

"And you've already decided on marriage?" he asks disbelievingly.

"Daddy, we've been falling in love with each over the last couple of years." I hear my mother's startled gasp upon that confession. I look over to her. "I'm sorry, Mother, but it's true. I wasn't in love with Tripp, and you know it. Not that you cared. Either of you." I meet my father's gaze again. "Adrian and I didn't jump into things, however. We were there for each other as friends until recently when it became more." Adrian's arms tighten around me before releasing me and asking to speak to my father alone.

I'm left with my mother who beckons me over to the couch to sit beside her before proceeding to shock the hell out of me. "I'm turning over a new leaf where you're concerned, Celeste. If you want to be with Adrian, who am I to stop you? I only want for you to be happy, so I will support you."

"Thank you, Mother." She doesn't reach out and hold me like I would if it were one of my children, but it's the warmest feeling she's ever given me, so it's good enough for now.

Our ride home is quiet. The boys sense something is up. Adrian holds my hand as usual. The only difference being his thumb has numbed mine with the little path he's worn with its constant movement. I don't want to give this up. Not for even a moment much less however long I'm about to lose him for. Leaning my head back on the seat, I look over at his profile and smile. He glances toward me and gives me a tentative smile of his own. I mouth, "I love you."

He mouths, "Thank you."

It's kind of an odd response, so it makes me grin a little wider. His eyes find their way back to the road.

Once we talk to the boys and explain how Adrian will be leaving us in four days, we make our tired way out to the sunroom. I'm really impressed with how well the boys took it. Of course, they don't know the full extent of what is going on over there. Like true developing men and patriots, they are proud that Adrian will be going over to support his unit. Archer even said he couldn't wait until he could join the Marine Corps. Again, my father would die. Finn jumped out and defended my dear old dad's branch by declaring that he was going to be a Seal. Paris was quiet but smiled in all the right places. He's a thinker that one, and I'm sure I'll find out all about those thoughts real soon.

Adrian follows me into the sunroom and starts massaging my shoulders before I can make a move to sit down. Reveling in his touch, I lean back into him and moan. God, that feels so good. I utter that exact sentiment without thinking, eliciting a chuckle from him.

"You're so easy to please," he says as his expert hands make their way down my back in a soothing, rhythmic pattern.

He relaxes me enough that I'm able to say what I feel is all. I turn and grab his hands in mine. His stare focuses on my hands, so I crouch down a little to get his attention. "What are you thinking right now?"

Kissing the backs of my hands, he releases them and strides over to look out over my back lawn. I allow him to have a minute to himself before sliding over and snaking my arms around his middle. Laying my head between his shoulder blades, I focus on breathing in and out for a few minutes and let his scent saturate my every pore.

Pulling back, I repeat his techniques from earlier as I wait for him to disclose what's going on in that beautiful head of his.

I hear him draw in a shaky breath after a few minutes, and it startles me. He finally turns to me and pulls me to him almost violently. His hands and mouth are everywhere, and like a leaf clinging to its branch in a storm, I latch on tight and take him.

He shudders under me before pulling back and grasping both sides of my face, his frantic gaze seeking mine out.

"You're scaring me," I mutter. I've never seen such a wounded look in someone's eyes before, and I can feel the pain and restraint emanating from him.

"I'm sorry," he chokes out. "I don't mean to. It's just what I'm about to say is killing me, but I have to say it. I don't want to hurt you anymore than I have to, though."

Rubbing my hands up and down his arms, I say, "I'll be fine. I just need you to talk to me. We're going to be fine."

"I...I don't want you to wait for me." I try to pull back on those words but he doesn't let me, his hands pressing in hard. "You don't deserve that after everything you've been through. You watched your husband die a slow, painful death and struggled to make it own your own with your boys. And you did, but that was hell. I don't want to be the one causing you pain, Celeste. You don't deserve to sit here and worry about me and wonder when or if I'm coming home. That's not fair."

Even though his hands make it difficult for me to speak, I can't get my next words out fast enough. "Adrian, I love you. Period. End of discussion. I will wait for you to come home so that we can be together because I *cannot, will not* have it any other way. Neither of us deserves any of this, but you'll go and serve our country because that's who you are. And I'll be here waiting for you to come back to me because that's who I am."

His hold relaxes; his forehead falls to mine. I close my eyes and breathe him in before he pulls back and places a series of kisses on my forehead. "What did I do to deserve you? We've barely been together three weeks, and you're willing to wait on me for six months? We haven't even slept together. Do you even know what you are waiting for?" he asks with a chuckle. Oh, thank goodness, my Adrian is back from that dark place that suggested he leave me.

"It's like I told my family—I've been falling in love with you for a long time. This is not a casual relationship for me. I'm not in this to have a good time."

His brow furrows before he asks, "You're not having a good time?"

I laugh in earnest now at my sweet man. "Oh, yes, worrying about our *delightful* family, fighting off your various groupies, and watching you try to break up with me is all great fun."

"Geez, so much drama. I hope he's worth it," he says as he leans in to suck my bottom lip into his mouth.

"Oh, he's worth it all right," I'm able to mumble before he consumes me.

-Sixteen-

Shades of Blue

SIX MONTHS, I tell myself for the millionth time. Six months. Not even the length of a school year or a pregnancy. I can do this. We can do this. I shouldn't even be feeling sorry for myself. Adrian is the one who has to go to the front lines and fight in a war that he doesn't believe in and all without me. I get to stay here and live my posh life. Yeah, I'm definitely getting the better end of the deal.

Four days. Four days is a remarkably short time period. When it's the bulk of a workweek, we're talking about, it seems like forever. When it's all you have with the love of your life, it's nothing. Time has that uncanny ability to speed its ass up when you're begging it to slow down, and to slow its ass to a crawl when you're begging for it to speed up.

I'm trying so hard not to dwell on the elusive bitch that is time. Yes, I'd taken to using more profanity than ever but only in my head. Adrian's plan is to prepare to leave and spend as much time with us as possible before he has to ship out. The first two days he dedicated to running the legal and logistical errands that he had to get squared away while doting on the boys as much as possible.

When he leans over me while I am doing the dishes and

whispers in my ear that he is taking me away for those last two days, I almost weep with relief. I can't wait to get him to myself. *Sorry, boys.*

While he ran his errands, I ran mine. He wouldn't tell me where we were going only that I wouldn't need much in the way of clothing, which caused my stomach to do acrobatics of astounding feats. So I bought lots of silk—red silk, emerald silk, and my favorite, aquamarine silk that reminded me of Adrian's eyes. He did ask that I pack one dress that I wouldn't mind wearing for photos. I was too excited to ask questions.

After dinner the night before we are to leave, I turn in surprise when I realize he's followed me into my room as I go to change. I gasp. "What are you doing?"

"I want to see what dress you've chosen to bring. Will you show me?"

"Do you want me to put it on?" My curiosity is piqued, but I'd do anything for this man so I don't question it.

"No, not yet. I'll just have a peek if you don't mind," he says with an eyebrow wiggle.

Blushing, my voice turns soft when I tell him, "No, I don't mind." I go into my closet and remove the black v-neck dress hanging on one of the hooks by the door. It's my go-to dress and, since he won't tell me what it's for, I figure it will do in any situation. I bring it out with a flourish, twirling it in front of me. "What do you think?"

"I think you're...I mean...it's gorgeous. But it's not what I have in mind. Do you have anything lighter? Like more 'summery'?"

"OK, you definitely need to work on your ability to describe clothing," I joke before I disappear into my closet. I sort through and find a "summery" dress even though it's going on Halloween. I pop back out, brandishing a flowery ensemble.

He squishes his face up and shakes his head. *OK, this could go on all night.*

I go back in and come out with three dresses—a light pink billowy, a yellow sleek, and a gray seersucker apron. All to which he screws his face up and shakes his head.

He jumps up from the bed, snatches the dresses from me, and sits me on my bed. "Let me see what I can do, madame," he tells me. I laugh and shake my head at his antics. What is he playing at?

I study my nails for a moment, thinking I really need to get them done, but there's no time. Then I pick up my phone and play with it for a minute. Finally, I pick up my book and read a scene before calling out, "You all right in there?"

"Yep, be out in a minute," he calls back. I read another scene.

I see some movement out of the corner of my eye and turn my head toward him to see what he's found. "You have a lot of damn clothes," he complains.

"I know. I collect," I say without a qualm.

Finally, I look over to what he's holding. "Really?" I ask without a little shock.

He just grins at me. I shrug. It's one of my favorite pieces, but I'd never had the occasion to wear it. I'd never have expected him to choose it, but I'd wear a brown paper sack for him if I had the right shoes to go with it.

GETTING BONNIE SETTLED in with the boys is no easy task. They're thrilled beyond belief to have her come and stay with them, and she is running around my house like a madwoman. They'll have a great time together so no worries there.

As we are leaving, Bonnie calls out, "How am I supposed to get in touch, just in case, you know?"

"You can call our cells, and we won't be too far," Adrian assures her.

She leans in to hug me goodbye and whispers, "I'm loving all this mystery. Keeps you on your toes."

"No doubt. And Garner's not staying over, right?"

"No, Mom, I didn't forget how uptight, uh, I mean traditional you are."

I just smirk before kissing my boys goodbye with promises of prayers and toothbrushes and sleeping tight.

Pulling out on to the road, I wave goodbye to my little family with tears in my eyes. I hadn't left them in a long, long time. As we pull onto Carrollton, Adrian says, "Hand." I giggle and slide my hand into his waiting one. He pulls it up and places a sweet little kiss on my knuckles before resting our intertwined hands on his thigh.

We ride in companionable silence for a couple of miles before he passes Highway 90 and then the best way to get to Interstate 10. I don't say anything because this trip is his baby, and I know men hate to be told how to drive. When we're headed into the French Quarter, I get really confused. When he pulls into the valet area of Hotel Monteleone, I have to turn to him and ask, "What are we doing here?"

"You love this hotel," he states with a shrug.

"Yes, but I thought we were going away."

"This is away. I've thought of much better ways we could spend our time other than riding along beside each other in a vehicle. What do you think?"

"I think that's brilliant," I say with a laugh as the valet opens my door.

After getting checked in to this magnificent hotel, we head upstairs to our room. It's soft blues and yellows and has an amazing view. I can't even imagine how much he's paid for us to be able to check in early and at the last minute. I'd offer to help out, but I don't want to offend him. I know he makes decent money being a musician, but I also know his family has cut him off completely moneywise.

Standing in front of the picture window and overlooking the Mississippi, I imagine what our life will be like when he returns. I see nothing but happiness and blue skies ahead for us. Is he frustrating? Yes. Does he drive me insane? Yes. Is he slightly domineering? Triple yes. Have I ever felt more challenged, more loved, more cherished? No. No. No.

I hear Ray LaMontagne's "Hold You in My Arms" start up, and then I feel Adrian's lips on my neck and his hands on my waist. He's swaying side to side, taking my hands in his as he simultaneously spins me around and under his arm. I really try to stop the sigh that exudes from my entire body but it's no use. He's so sigh-worthy.

"Do you remember the first time we heard this song?" he asks his voice turning raspy.

"I do," I whisper and lay my head on his shoulder as he moves me around the room. I'd had my satellite radio on my favorite station that was renowned for being the first for playing the next big thing. I was in the process of turning this gorgeous song up when Adrian stopped what he was doing with the boys and joined me in the kitchen, telling me to turn it up. We shared a laugh when he saw what I was doing. Staring at the information on the screen, we both downloaded it within minutes and then plugged in my iPod to the speakers and put it on repeat. I grabbed Finn up and spun him around the room. Adrian just sat and watched us dance around. Kissing the top of Finn's head, I tossed him on the couch and grabbed Paris, making him dance with me. Then, I couldn't leave Archer out, so I grabbed him up to.

"That's one of my earliest and fondest memories of you," he tells me. I lean back from my comfy position to take him in. "I remember thinking that you were the best person I'd ever met in my whole life. The way you are with your children. Your love for them is always shining through even when you're irritated with them or they're being little shits. They'll never question whether or not they're loved and accepted. I remember wanting to be a part of that, wanting you to love me like that." I swallow hard, trying not to get weepy. He laughs a little. "I even prayed about it. I asked God to show me a way that we could be together where no one would get hurt. I got nothing, though."

"Do you really think you got nothing? Because that's not the way I see it. Yes, we didn't jump right into each other's arms, but we have almost two years of memories of our falling in love with one another. That's what this time has meant to me and what has made me so sure that we'll work. I love you on so many levels—person, friend, confidant, almost-lover," I say with a blush and light giggle, "father—"

"I'm not a father," he protests.

"Are you kidding me? You may not be biologically. But, Adrian, you put our boys before everything else, you love them unconditionally, you look out for their best interests, you spend time with them, you listen to them, you respect them. That's what a father is, baby. It's not a piece of paper or even blood that declares it so. It's doing those little things every single day that add up to being everything."

"You said 'our boys,'" he says as he kisses me lightly on my nose. "And, I guess, when you put it like that, I sound pretty amazing. What a lucky girl you are," he half-jokes as he spins me out and back in.

"Still so humble," I joke back.

His face turns somber again. "You and the boys...*our* boys are everything to me, Celeste. You have been for a long time, and I'm so proud that I can let everyone in on that life-altering fact because that's what it is—y'all have changed my life. Up until now, I'd felt like an imposter or a drifter. Like I just didn't fit in with my family, and I was coasting along. I found music and the Corps, and that helped a lot, but it still wasn't enough. Then I met y'all and all of a sudden I had a purpose and was loved and accepted." I feel him tremble beneath my hands a little. "When I'd think about you meeting someone and not needing me anymore, I would get cold chills. When I saw that you weren't in a hurry to meet anyone, I thanked God. I didn't even feel bad that you might have felt lonely. Not one of my finer moments."

"I can't fault you for that. I had similar thoughts about you finding someone. It scared the hell out of me. I kept waiting for someone to see how beautiful you are—not just your looks," I say when he smirks at me. I tap his heart with my fingertips. "Here, sweetheart. You have the most beautiful heart, the most beautiful soul."

He clears his throat a little. "I don't think you were in danger of anyone seeing that because I'd never felt confident to just be myself before I met you."

"I am one lucky girl," I breathe.

"We're well-matched in luck then," he agrees with a kiss.

We're still swaying back and forth when it dawns on me the music has ended and long ago too. "The music's ended," I tell him.

He stops moving and pulls our hands in front of us before dropping down in front of me on his knees. "Our music will never end, Celeste." My heart comes to a sliding stop right in my throat. He runs his hand through his hair for a second. "Ah, I had this all planned out. A romantic lunch, a rehearsed proposal, but I can't wait. I have to do this now."

My hands are suddenly clammy and my pulse is racing. He's already told me he's marrying me, and not just once, but still. I watch mesmerized as he pulls a little box from his pocket and cracks it open. I gasp because the ring is the exact color of his eyes. "Celeste Marie Dubois Hebert, will you do me the absolute honor of becoming my wife?"

I'm nodding the entire time, tears streaming down my face. "Yes, Adrian, I would be honored to be your wife."

"Perfect," he says, sliding the aquamarine engagement ring on my finger, "because we have a date to get married in just a few hours." The grin he gives me is brilliant. I've never seen him smile so big, and I've never felt my heart plummet so hard.

Sputtering, I say, "Adrian, I...don't you think that's kind of soon? I mean three weeks. We haven't even slept together. Are we going to tell anyone? Would it be a Catholic ceremony?" I realize I'm babbling and spitting some of the same issues he'd given me a few nights ago. The same issues I'd brushed aside in favor of our staying together while he is deployed, but I'm blown away.

Adrian pulls me down to the floor with him before he pulls me close, breaks my heart, and mends it all at once with his next words. "I have to go there knowing that I'm yours to protect," he says, pausing for a second and bringing his lips a hair's breadth from mine. "Because I'd never do anything to hurt you, Celeste, including getting myself killed."

I close the small distance to his mouth and urge his lips open with mine, thrusting my tongue against his before I slow down and lightly run it alongside his until he joins me. Pulling my mouth from his, I open my eyes and meet his blues and give him another little kiss.

I let my eyes drift over to my ring that's resting on his shoulder. "The stone is the same color as your eyes, and the ring of diamonds that surrounds it is exactly like the halo of silver that surrounds your pupil."

He laughs nervously. "I didn't consider that. But it is your birthstone. And I just know you wear a lot of that color and have a lot of that color decorating your house."

"I do," I agree. "And there's one reason."

"Yeah, what's that?"

"When I met you I slowly began gravitating toward this color, the color of your eyes. I didn't even realize it until we were talking one night on my front porch. You'd just returned with the boys from a basketball game. The porch light was on and it was hitting your eyes just right, and I thought, oh my God, I've been obsessing and hoarding blue because of this man's intensely beautiful eyes."

He laughs again, this time in earnest. "That was the night I thought you'd swallowed a bug because you started choking all of a sudden."

It's my turn to laugh. "I can't wait to be your wife, Adrian."

"Is that a yes to our date?"

"Yes," I say.

He kisses my forehead, my nose, my cheek, and my mouth all the while murmuring how happy I've made him. He gets up and helps pull me to my feet, moving us over to the wingback chair near the window. He settles in with me in his lap and pulls my legs up to drape over the side of the chair. I lace one arm around his neck while my other hand runs up and down his chest so that I can shamelessly admire my breathtakingly gorgeous ring.

"I hate to be Debbie Downer, but we have to get some paperwork together. I'll have to go home and get my social security card and birth certificate at least, right?" I gasp suddenly. "That dress!" I accuse.

He looks sheepish. "Yes, that dress is your wedding dress."

"You're good, Mr. Hebert." I smile approvingly.

"And the paperwork is all squared away too. We have an appointment at Our Lady of the Gulf in Bay St. Louis."

"Why Bay St. Louis?"

"I figure it'd be best if this ceremony is just for us. I mean the family is slightly accepting of our being together, but could you imagine the spectacle if we told them we were marrying before I left? Just imagining the number of obstacles and objections make my head spin. I just want this day for us. Is that OK with you?"

"A peaceful, perfect day for us." I grin. "Yes, it's how it should be." Thinking back to all the trouble he's gone through, I shake my head, disbelieving. "How did you manage all that anyway?"

"I pulled some strings to get us married over there. I happen to know a few people myself. Bishop Bernie contacted Our Lady's priest and gave his approval. We'll still have to jump through a few hoops where the Catholic Church is concerned, but they'll let us marry there. And the rest," he hesitates with a grin, "Louis."

"Louis?"

"Yes, Louis knew where all of your documents were located in the family safe, and he's kind of a romantic."

I laugh. "He is." I'd forgotten about all our extra originals we'd stored there. "Why? Why all the subterfuge?"

"I didn't want you worrying or over-thinking things. I wanted to make it very easy for you to say yes."

I run my lips along his jaw until I'm at his ear and I whisper, "You make it impossible for me to say anything else. Yes, always yes."

STEPPING OUT OF the bathroom, I release a deep breath. I've never been more sure of anything or anyone in my life, but I've also never been more nervous. Adrian's looking in the mirror and his gaze catches mine as he rearranges his vest. His eyes light up as he takes me in.

He spreads his arms out to his sides, gives me a sheepish grin, and turns toward me. "I hope this is good. I'm not big on dressing up, but I'm pretty sure no one's going to be looking at me anyway."

I move to him and straighten the collar of his unbuttoned white shirt that provides a stark contrast to his tan skin. Running my hands down his sleeves, I take his engraved H cufflinks from his hand and fasten them for him. He laughs and says, "I never thought I'd have the opportunity to wear these."

I just smile and run my hands down his charcoal gray vest, fastening his buttons as I go. "You look perfect."

"You're not pissed I'm not wearing a tie?" He gives me a look of disbelief.

I take in his disheveled hair and day's growth—two things I'd asked him not to change as I left the room to get ready. Leaning in, I nibble at his Adam's Apple for a moment before running my tongue up his neck and pulling back to say, "If you were all buttoned up, I couldn't do that, now could I?"

He just grabs me and kisses me senseless. On a groan, he

releases me and spins me toward the mirror. He claps his hands together. "This dress...this dress is gorgeous." I look down at my ivory vintage find that I'd purchased for a steal at an estate sale. I'd never had the occasion to wear it, but I absolutely loved the floral organza material, the scoop neck, and the butterfly sleeves. It was so simple, so sheer. It floated down over my body just perfectly before coming to rest with at a swish around my ankles. Complete exquisiteness that I couldn't resist buying even though I could never imagine having the opportunity to wear it. It had been stored in the very back of my closet, almost forgotten over the last couple of years.

"You have no idea how thrilled I am that you found this in my closet. I've always wanted to wear it, but I've never had the right moment. It's vintage, you know? 1930s."

His admiring gaze flies to mine. "Are you serious?"

I give a nervous laugh over his look of astonishment. "Yes, why?"

He grabs my hand and brings it up in front of us. "This is vintage. 1930s."

"Are *you* serious?" Now *I'm* astonished.

"Yes. That's unbelievable. When I went to see the jeweler, I described you to him and told him your favorite things and that you were a designer. He just nodded at everything I said. As a matter of fact, I started getting kind of pissed because I didn't think he was listening to me. When I wrapped it up, he went to the back and came out with this. I was shocked over how much it reminded me of you. I didn't even say anything. I just nodded and handed it back to him to wrap up for me. I never looked at any other ring."

"That's beautiful, and I love it so much. It's so perfect."

"You're perfect. I love you," he counters. Smiling, he says, "All right. I think we've got the something blue covered, definitely have the something old covered." He grabs my ass and squeezes, eliciting a gasp from me.

"You better be referring to this dress, Adrian!"

"What?" Oh...shit, yes, definitely the dress," he says with a laugh.

Then he reaches behind him, and I feel him slide something around my neck. When he moves his hands around to fasten the double string pearls that are interspersed with crystals, my breath leaves me in a whoosh. "Your something new, my lady."

"I'm impressed. You've thought of everything, Adrian." Running my hands over the pearls, I can't help but say, "It's so much. Are you sure?"

"Yes, I'm sure. I don't know if you've noticed but I never spend money on anything. I'm a saver. I've still got plenty where that came from."

I feel my shoulders relax. I don't want to put him in the poorhouse. I bite my lip and nod. "Thank you. I love them. They're amazing."

"They remind me of you. Classy but modern." *I can't believe he is my man.* Again I wonder how no one had snatched him up.

Once they're fastened, I see him digging in his pocket and wonder what else he's up to. "Your something borrowed." He shrugs, puts the lace, embroidered handkerchief in my hand and says, "Actually, it's more stolen than borrowed. I lifted it from my mom's cedar chest. It was one of the grandmothers. I can't remember which one."

Laughing, I move over to the bed to put my shoes on. "Thank you. Now, you really have thought of everything."

"Don't move," he orders.

"Umm...OK," I say.

I'm holding my shoes in my hands, waiting patiently for him and wondering what he's up to now. I see him grab his jeans and sort through them for a moment before joining me. He kneels down on one knee and props one of my feet on his leg. Taking one of my ivory lace booties, he drops a penny in it, places it on my foot, tightens the laces, and ties them up. I laugh. *He's superstitious!* Placing it on the floor, he grabs my other foot and repeats the process.

"These are sexy as hell," he tells me once he has me all situated. "I'm thinking you in nothing but these tonight. You and shoes.

Mmm...the red ones with the black trim and black laces—those are my favorite." He crooks his brow at me and runs his hands up my stockings, leaving goose bumps in their wake. "Please tell me these aren't thigh highs."

I chuckle. "Why?"

"Shit! They are," he says on a sigh as he reaches the tops of my stockings. Snatching his hands back, he grabs me by the hand and pulls me behind him to head for the door. "Hurry up. If we don't leave now, we'll never leave." *That doesn't sound too bad to me*, I think. He stops abruptly, spinning so that I bump into his chest. He cups my jaw and forces me to meet his eyes. "And I'm not taking you until you're my wife," he says all raspy before whisking me away to make me his.

-Seventeen-

Mrs. Adrian Hebert

AS WE SLIDE back into his truck to head back to New Orleans from the Bay, I slide my hand into his before he can demand it. He looks over, giving me that devastating smile of his—the one that causes his little laugh lines to bunch up around his eyes, the one that makes me want to stare at him for all of eternity. I've got it so bad for him.

"I didn't have to tell you," he says. "Good girl."

I beam at his praise. "You make me so happy," I tell him. "I just want to make you happy too."

He pulls my knuckles to his mouth and rests his lips there for a minute. "Wife, you make me so happy it's almost ridiculous."

Devastating tremors make quick work of my body. "And that makes me ridiculously happy," I say with a laugh.

A sudden thought occurs to me, causing my laughter to continue to bubble from me loudly.

"What?" Adrian asks, giving me a lopsided grin.

"It just occurred to me that I've once again been granted a reprieve from the tedious process of changing my last name."

"Oh," he chuckles with me, "is that what this is? A marriage of convenience?"

My laughter dies out, and he makes eye contact with me. "The only convenience that I'm looking forward to taking advantage of is being able to have you whenever I want." Lifting his hand to my lips, I kiss it tenderly.

The rest of our short ride back to the city is quiet, so I find myself reflecting on our perfectly quiet ceremony. I wished the boys had been there, but Adrian and I decided on the way over that we'd have small ceremony and big reception when he got back for our family—whoever was happy for us could attend and no one need be the wiser about the fact that we were already husband and wife. He said we'd spring it on them at the reception. I don't know that I'll be able to wait that long.

After we'd said our vows and the church secretary had snapped some pictures of us, Adrian had taken us to a little gulf-side bistro where we'd enjoyed a light meal and spoken of some of our plans upon his return.

Just when I thought that our little moment in time was winding to an end, the server popped over with a huge slice of Italian cream cake. Adrian cut a piece with lots of icing off before using his finger-tips to gather it up and feed it to me. Unabashedly, I'd licked every drop of icing from his fingertips. First, because icing is the best part of the cake. Second, and most importantly, he'd tasted delicious and the little flare of his eyes when I scraped my teeth down his finger was priceless and thoroughly encouraging of my wanton behavior. I figured he was my husband and if I wanted to lick him and nip at him in public and he was OK with that, then that's what I was going to do.

When I fed him his tiny piece sans icing, he did much the same even though I happened to know he really doesn't like sweets.

After changing, we decide to go for a walk before calling it a night since it is a gorgeous fall evening and we don't get those for long around here—it was either sweltering or freezing. As we walk through Woldenberg Park hand in hand and speak of nothing really important, my mind drifts to considering exactly what a tour in Iraq means for Adrian, exactly what he will be facing over there. And I just feel...overwhelmed. He's talking to me about a song he and Zach had been working on and weren't seeing eye-to-eye on, and I feel like I'm about to lose it. Frantically, I search for a restroom or some place to hide and just bawl my face off, but we've just come out on the Moonwalk and there's nothing.

I feel my whole body tense and I can't swallow. I'm about to make a break for it when I realize we've stopped walking, and he's standing in front of me. My pulse is racing, and I feel slick with sweat. I try to focus on Adrian, and I watch his mouth moving and his terrified eyes searching mine, yet I can say nothing.

I'm in a bubble. I want to reach my hand up and pop it and continue my perfect day like nothing's happened, but I'm paralyzed. Finally, I feel my arms being jerked and I hear Adrian's voice, which doesn't much resemble Adrian's voice but Charlie Brown's teacher. I see a brilliant shard of light, and then I'm back.

"Oh my God," I gasp for air and grab my knees, panting for oxygen.

"Celeste, what the hell?" Adrian growls.

"I'm...I'm sorry. I—"

"You scared the shit out of me," he barks as he rights me and rubs my arms.

"I didn't mean to."

He's kissing my face, and when his lips move to mine, I taste the salt from my tears. I grab at his neck and return his kiss with fervor until we are both breathless. Laying my head on his chest, I look out over the Mississippi and the setting sun.

"Adrian, look," I say after a couple of minutes.

He turns his head and takes in the beautiful sunset with its brilliant purples and pinks and oranges. "Magnifique," he says simply.

"I'm so sorry I scared you."

He looks back to me. His eyes no longer quite as worried. "Has that ever happened before?"

"No, never."

"Baby, you froze. You were gasping for breath, your pulse was erratic, and your body temperature spiked. But you were almost ...catatonic."

"It was strange. One minute I was thinking how wonderful our day had been and my mind wandered for a moment to your leaving and what's happening over there. And I was just...gone."

"Shit," he says as he hugs me tighter to him.

"Can we go back to the room now?"

"Yeah, let's go."

I'M STARING IN the bathroom mirror, willing myself to go out to him. I've been wanting him and waiting for this moment for so long, but I'm incredibly nervous. It's been a long time for me.

Taking a couple of breaths, I study myself critically for a couple of minutes. I'd changed into my aquamarine silk gown that resembled my wedding dress in its simplicity except the gown has spaghetti straps. It was long and flowing. I'd put my thigh highs back on for him since he seemed so excited by the prospect earlier. They matched my little white lace underwear. My black hair cascades around my shoulders. The only jewelry I'm wearing is my beautiful wedding set. I hold it up again, admire it, release a deep sigh, and jump when I hear a knock at the door.

"Yes?" I call.

"You all right, baby?" he asks.

Instead of answering, I open the door with a flourish. His swift intake of breath is all the reassurance I need. I step out and into his arms. "Sorry it took me so long."

"Oh, no worries. You're worth the wait."

I hear some light jazz sounds and realize its coming from outside. He must have a window open. That's the last thought I have as he runs his hands along my backside and pulls me in closer. I moan with the knowledge that he's already hard, and I know I'm ready too.

Adrian slants his mouth over mine hungrily, and I quickly follow suit. I feel my silk bunched up around my waist, and he mumbles, "We won't be needing this any longer." He whips it over my head. He's quite talented because he doesn't disturb a single hair on my head.

His mouth is back on mine, he's moving backwards toward the bed with me in tow. My pulse races and my heart beats a frantic tattoo. I've never wanted anyone or anything more in my life. Bending, he scoops me up, spins, and lays me down. I swallow hard as he pushes off his pajama bottoms to reveal he's naked underneath and oh so ready for me. He makes me giggle when he raises his eyebrows seductively and grins big.

Inching up on the bed, his knee slides between my legs until it gets to my knees. When his eyes lift to mine, the hunger that I see there makes me moan. He sits up and runs his hands up my stocking covered legs. "I love these. So freakin' hot, babe."

Bending he kisses the exposed skin just above the lacy tops. I giggle at his light kisses. Running his nose up my leg, he doesn't stop until he places a kiss on my center, and then he buries his nose, inhaling deeply. He nips at me through my lace. I don't know how much more of this I can take. I'm already panting and gasping and trembling beneath him.

He must sense all that because he says, "Easy, baby," as he works his way up my torso, over my breasts, and to my mouth again, kissing me into submission.

Sitting back again, he eases my underwear down and his lips follows his hands until he's making love to me with his mouth. My hands find their way into his hair, pushing at him and encouraging him simultaneously until I am a bucking, writhing mass underneath him. Relaxing under him, I struggle to understand how I can feel sated and wanting at the same time.

Kissing the inside of my thighs, he makes his way up my body with his mouth until he's back to looking in my eyes. His beautiful blues are glistening and bright. I smooth his hair down a little from all of my pulling. Running his hand along my jaw, he grasps it before bringing my mouth to his. I whimper at the intimacy of kissing him after he's so thoroughly kissed me.

"I knew it," he says, grinning from ear to ear. "I knew you'd be perfect."

I can't stand it anymore. I need him, so I tell him. "Adrian, I need you. I need you inside of me now."

He doesn't make me wait any longer. I feel him nudging and I wrap my legs around him and pull him into me. His head falls to my neck where he groans and tells me I feel so good. I want those blues back.

"Blues, please," I murmur.

"Hmm?" He looks up at me.

"I don't want to lose my blues," I tell him, running my fingertips along his brow bone.

He gives me his eye-crinkling smile before his expression turns serious and he begins working my body in earnest. "My wife, my love," he says as moves in and out of me with precision. I've never felt more loved, more cherished, more alive.

"Husband, I love you," I whisper.

"My heaven, I love you," he declares as he sinks even further into me, his blues never leaving me.

ADRIAN ASKS ME if I'd like to go out for drinks and dinner. I do not. I want as much quiet time with him as possible, so we order room service and champagne. Then we veg out in front of the TV. Him in his shorts. Me in my silk. Us laughing ridiculously at *Friends* reruns.

"Chandler's the funniest." I argue as I toss another grape in his mouth, and he breaks off another slice of cheese for me. "He has that dry, clever sense of humor that I absolutely love and find so sexy."

"You think Chandler's sexy?" he asks with a smirk.

"Yes, his sense of humor makes him nerd hot."

"Nerd hot?" He grimaces. "I don't like you thinking about how hot other guys are," he says on pout.

I can't help but laugh out loud. "He's a fictional character, Adrian. You can't possibly be jealous."

"The hell I can't!"

I gasp. "Please tell me you're joking."

"Matthew Perry is real," he persists.

"Oh, yes, and if he lived around here you'd *really* have the right to be concerned," I say my voice dripping with sarcasm.

He doesn't miss a beat. "He doesn't live here, but he visits here. I've met him."

"You're not kidding," I say with shock. Springing up on my knees, I scoot over to him and push him back before straddling him. I grab both of his hands and hold them at his sides as I lean in and tell him, "You are the sexiest." Kiss. "The hottest." Nip. "The funniest." Bite. "The most intelligent." Lick. "The kindest." Long, lingering kiss. "Man I've ever known. You have no reason to be jealous—ever—even of Matthew Perry who we both know is ridiculously good looking and funny." I can't help but laugh as I place a chaste kiss on his lips.

My laughter is short-lived as he has me on my back and under him before I know what's hit me. He nips at my mouth with his teeth before running them up my jaw to my ear. "Don't start something you can't finish, Celeste," he warns me. I pull back and see his eyes twinkling.

"You're not funny," I complain. "I thought you were really

jealous. I was wondering what I'd gotten myself into."

He starts laughing in earnest. "I am jealous. I'm not kidding about that. I'm just not really mad about it. Seriously, if you run into Perry on the street, steer clear. I can see the headlines now—'Local Mafia Princess Runs Away with Geeky Funny Guy Leaving Behind Devastated Marine/Guitarist.'"

I lock my legs around him and squeeze because now I'm pissed. "Take it back," I say when he gasps for air.

"Shit! I'm sorry I forgot. You're not a Mafia Princess!"

"Not that part! He's not a geek! He's a nerd and there's a difference." I laugh and release him.

He rolls to the side. "Ow, that was just mean. Remind me to never wrestle you." I just giggle.

Propping up on his elbow, he says, "You've got way too much energy. Let's go for a swim on the roof."

"Oh, yes. I forgot they have a heated pool!" I jump up and off the bed to get changed.

"I didn't realize you liked to swim so much," he calls after me.

I poke my head back out. "Do you know how often I get to swim without children? Swimming without getting cannonballed, getting pushed in every five seconds, being told to look at every jump, and timing every held breath is like...like bliss. I think. I can't remember the last time I did it, so I'm fuzzy. Why are you still lying there? Get changed," I squeak.

BLISS. IT IS utter bliss. It's late so we have the pool to ourselves. I dive. I swim laps. I float on my back with my eyes closed, none of which I can ever do with the kids around. Finally, I get bored and swim under a passing Adrian to get his attention. I pinch at him until he comes up sputtering for air.

"I thought you wanted a quiet swim."

I give him a half-smile. "I missed you."

He takes my hands and spins himself, fastening me to his back and swims us to a spot where he can stand. I unfurl my body and paddle around to the front of him, winding my legs around his hips and my arms around his neck.

He wraps his arms around my back and lays his head against mine. We're quiet for a while before he finally breaks the silence.

"Cel, I have to tell you something. Something that's been weighing on me."

"You can tell me anything. You know that."

"I do, but I don't want to upset you. I need you to know."

"OK, baby." I lean back and capture his face with my hands. Placing a kiss on his forehead, I murmur, "I'm not going to waste any of our precious little time being upset, so spill."

He releases a deep breath, stills for a couple of beats, and tells me, "I'm not entirely sad to be leaving." He immediately tenses, so I rub his neck a little.

I grin a little and shrug. "I know that." My eyes immediately fill with tears.

"You do?" I feel him relax a little.

"Of course. You wouldn't be the man I love if you weren't willingly going to help your brothers. They may have activated you and told you to go, but you do so without hesitation or regret."

He assesses me with that knowing gaze. "And you're good with the fact that I'm actually looking forward to getting over there and helping out?"

"I'm not jealous of your brothers or this war, Adrian. I admire you too much. Am I sad to lose you for six months? Absolutely wrecked. I don't know how exactly I will do it, but I will. I'll put one foot in front of the other and all with a smile on my face and gladness in my heart because that's what I have to do, what many spouses have to do every single day." He pulls me in for a little kiss.

"You can do it. You're strong, baby."

"Just know, however, that underneath all that 'have to' is my 'want'. I'll be wanting for you every second—"

His kiss cuts me off. He whispers his love for me over and over again until his kisses turn more heated than reverential. When I feel my bathing suit being pushed aside and some exploring fingers, I tremble and look around. There's no one here, but still it feels weird.

Before I can protest, his fingers find their way inside me, and my legs involuntarily squeeze him to me tighter. Pushing the material aside with his thumb, he works my nub as his fingers plunge inside me again and again. My mouth opens to cry out, so I let it fall to his shoulder and bite down hard while my fingernails dig into his back. A growling Adrian nips and sucks at my neck as my release washes me, and I bite and claw harder until he's wrung it all from me.

I go limp in his arms as I come back down, but I can tell he's just gearing up as he presses hard into me. I'm not ready for full-fledged exhibitionism, so I whisper, "Adrian, let's go to our room."

He throws back his head in laughter. "Yeah, that's probably wise, but I think I need to take a couple more laps. I...uh...might shock some people on the way to our room."

I join him in his laughter. "Tsk, tsk, what a waste. If my legs will work, how about I walk in front of you?"

"That could work. Come on, Mrs. Adrian Hebert, escort your horny husband to your chamber."

WE MAKE IT to our room without being spotted. When Adrian closes the door behind us, I attack him. Making my incredible man feel good is my number one priority. I lavish him with kisses as he lets his towel drop to the floor and his head drop back on the door. I make swift work of removing his t-shirt and untying his shorts, running my hands alongside the band and pushing and pulling until I have enough of him exposed to do what I want with him.

"I have to say I like this side of you," he says with a groan as I massage his length from his shorts. "I had no idea you'd have all this naughty underneath all that nice."

"Yeah? All this naughty is all yours."

"Hell yeah."

Raining kisses down his shuddering abs, I slow down and place a light kiss on his tip before running my tongue over his length. His hands find their way into my hair to tangle and pull while I make a meal of him and elicit sounds from him that act as fuel for my raging fire.

"Celeste, oh *mimi*, yes," he hisses, his naughty term of endearment only serving to further encourage me. I feel him pull at my hair a little before his voice huskily asks, "Do you want me? All of me?"

I've never desired anything more. Moaning, I pull him deeper with my mouth and run my hands around to his ass to push him even further. He takes that action exactly as intended and begins to pump and drive into my mouth in earnest. I devour all that he has to offer until he ceases trembling.

I work my way back up his glorious body with my mouth until I get to his. His hands, still in my hair, tighten to the point of almost pain as he thrusts his tongue into my mouth and feasts on me.

Pulling back a little, I mumble against his lips, "Did I make you feel good?"

"Mmm...my *mimi*. You made me feel better than good. Cherished. You make me feel cherished. You have no idea what that does to me."

I laugh as he begins slipping my cover and bathing suit off. "I think I have an idea of what it does to you." I can already feel him getting hard against my stomach. I shiver.

"I'm going to go run us a bath in the whirlpool so that I can wash every delectable inch of you and warm you back up. Outside," he says, placing a kiss on my breast, "...and in." He punctuates that promise with a quick thrust of his finger inside me, and I feel weak. "You're drenched, *mimi*."

"You're insatiable," I kid.

He's bending before me now to help my suit from around my feet. "Damn straight," he says matter-of-factly. "I won't apologize for my need of you. It was torture. Fucking years..."

Kissing him lightly on the neck as he begins to straighten in front of me, I say, "I'm so grateful no one was able to snatch you up."

Those beautiful blues meet mine, and I'm in awe of the love I see shining there. I'd caught that fleeting look before over the years but had always chalked it up to other emotions because, in my mind, we didn't have any other options. I can't believe I can finally let myself bask in it.

His arms curl around the back of my knees and my back as he lifts me in his arms. His voice is as strong as his body as, he proclaims, "I was never anyone else's to have. You own me, Celeste. Always have. Always will." My heart melts, yet my fear ignites. I can't lose this. I can't lose him. Pulling him to me, I devour him as he carries me into the bathroom.

"Up you go," he says as he sets me on the counter and turns to get our bath running. I watch his strong back bend over and am mesmerized by him once again.

"You don't have any tattoos."

"Umm...nope."

"Why not? I mean most Marines have lots of tattoos. Not to mention guys in bands."

"Uh, I don't know. I guess I've just never felt that strongly about having something on my body forever. Never felt the inclination." He pours some bath salts and soaps in.

"That's plenty. Come here and I'll keep you warm while we're waiting," I tell him.

He turns and pushes his shorts down the rest of the way. His eyes never leaving mine so that he has to push the shorts off with his feet. He kicks them to the side as he begins to stride toward me.

I lick my lips in anticipation. He grabs me by the hips and pulls me to the edge of the counter. I lean back on my palms as he licks and nips and kisses. He runs the backside of one hand down my neck, between my breasts, and over my stomach as his eyes follow his hand. Running both hands down my legs, he grabs my ankles and props them up on the counter flush with my hips. "Hold the edge of the counter," he orders as he inserts a thumb into my mouth. "Suck," he orders again. I suck. Placing it on my tight bud and rotating it, he murmurs, "That was completely unnecessary, *mimi*. You're still so wet."

I can only groan and hold on as he dives between my legs and brings me to climax in a matter of moments. "Adrian," I mumble. I slide into his arms, and he lifts and carries me to the tub.

Placing me on my feet, he holds my hips and asks, "Can you stand up for a second?"

"Yes," I say with a laugh. "You have a mighty high opinion of your ability for bringing me down, sir."

"You never know." He punctuates that sentence with a slap to my behind. I stumble forward a bit. "That's what I thought," he says proudly.

"No, that's only because you smacked my ass."

"Mmm...say that again."

"Smack my ass." I tease as I bite my lip. He obliges with a chuckle.

He bends, turns the water off, and climbs in. Once he's situated, he helps me in and arranges me in front of him. The bath and he both feel heavenly. We enjoy the quiet for several minutes.

"This is something else I haven't had in a while...a bath," I say with wonder. "You don't realize how insane your life is until it slows down for a bit."

"Or until things happen that put shit in perspective for you," he says. I turn my head and give him a quick kiss.

He reaches for the bath sponge and soaps it up while I just lie there like a slug. He runs the sponge over me leisurely. He gets real leisure-like around certain parts and that has me giggling. "Sit up," he says.

I do and he pushes my hair aside and washes my back. He turns the water back on and reaches for the extender. Once he's washed all the soap from me, he says, "Lean your head back."

I push my hair back around and lean my head back as he wets it. "Hold this," he says as he hands me the extender and reaches for the shampoo.

"I can do it," I tell him. I have a lot of hair.

"I got it, *mimi*."

"OK," I can rewash it tomorrow, I think.

I hear him lather up his hands and then they dive into my hair with sureness and smoothness. "Oh my God," I say with a gasp. "That feels amazing." I draw the word out as far as it will go.

"Mmm hmm," he says, and I can tell he's smirking. "You doubted me. How could you doubt me?"

"It's not easy to wash all this hair. My apologies, sir."

It ends all too soon, and he rinses the soap from my hair. "Conditioner, ma'am?"

"Are you serious? Absolutely." He repeats the process and has me humming.

"All right," he says. "I'm washing up quick. All those sounds you were making have me hard again," he complains.

"Are you complaining?" I ask.

"Hell no, but this water's not gonna stay warm long enough for me to do what I want to you."

"Oh!"

"Yeah, oh!"

I turn around and help him as quickly as possible.

-Eighteen-

Feel This Kiss

LIGHT STRUMMING COMING from the other side of the room wakes me from a most peaceful slumber. I put my arms over my head, stretching languidly before finally forcing my eyes open. It's our last day together, and I can't waste it sleeping. I pop up on my elbows and admire him without him noticing me for a few minutes. He's wearing his faded and frayed jeans and is barefoot and bare-chested. Closing his eyes for a second, he appears deep in thought before they spring back open, and he stops his playing to jot something down. He tosses his pen down, runs his hand through his hair, and then snatches up his cup of coffee.

As he tilts his head back for a drink, his eyes meet mine and he grins around his cup. "Mornin'," he says before taking a pull on his coffee.

"Good morning," I reply as I reach for my glasses. "Did you sleep well?"

"No, not at all," he admits. "I couldn't stop staring at you."

My mouth drops. That's sweet. "I'm sorry." I'm not.

"I'm not," he says, seemingly reading my thoughts. I can't help but laugh.

"Please tell me you have more coffee."

"I do."

"Oh good," I say. "Give me just a moment." I dash into the bathroom and brush my teeth quickly. I need something before I need my coffee.

Crossing the room quickly, I bend in front of him and kiss him deeply before snatching my coffee and crawling back up on the bed. He chuckles at me and starts his strumming back up. I drape the cover over me a little since all my silk purchases had gone to waste.

"What are you working on?" I ask.

"A new song. I've been working on it for a couple of weeks," he says with a smile.

My stomach does somersaults. "What's it about?"

"You," he says simply.

My stomach has lodged itself in my throat. "Really?" I squeak.

"Mmm hmm." He continues strumming. "Wanna hear it?"

"Really?" I squeak again.

He doesn't answer just smiles and begins playing my song.

I don't know what I'm expecting, but it certainly isn't the ballad that he's written for me. Each stanza is dedicated to our unique kisses. From my first tentative kiss, to his all-consuming one, to our lust-fueled one, to our one filled with promise. Though each kiss is different, the theme remains constant—pure love and adoration.

I swallow hard. "Adrian, that was...beautiful." I stare at him at a complete loss for what to say. He starts to put his guitar down. "Wait!" He freezes. "Will you play it again for me?" He wrinkles his brow but nods. "Hold on." I hold the sheet around me and reach for my phone. I play with it until I get to the screen I want and hit record.

He plays it for me again. Again, I melt. I hit stop and release a deep sigh. "Will you play 'Everlong' for me?" He grins and plays so that I can record it. And I just want to die. This song is genius already. Acoustically it's musical nirvana. I laugh a little at that thought. I watch him for a while and then let my head drop back. I bring my knees up and stare at the ceiling while I absorb every last fading note.

After a few seconds, I hear the thunk of his guitar being set down. I feel my sheet fall to my middle and a little fingernail grazing the inside of my ankle, my calf, my knee. When it hits my knee, I look down my body and watch him. Only it's not his fingernail but his guitar pick. The silver one with "Dog Tags" engraved on it. *Oh shit!*

"This," he says as he flicks it between his fingers to face me, "is my favorite pick." Resuming his path on my knee, he keeps grazing until he is at the top of my thigh. He circles it around a little, making a playful pattern. Goose bumps populate my skin from the delightful little scraping. "My favorite pick wants to hang out in my favorite spot. Shall I acquaint them?" he asks with a raised brow.

I don't know exactly what he means by that but I don't care. I nod at him and reach to remove my glasses.

"Leave them," he whispers and gives me a naughty grin. Without further ado, the guitar pick makes its way to my clit and plays it to perfection. I mewl as sensation after sensation rocks through me.

Leaning in, he places his fingers over the corner of my mouth before kissing me gently. He thrusts his tongue in my mouth suddenly, never losing his rhythm below. Dipping his fingers over my bottom lip, he pulls his mouth back as I suck and lick at his fingertips. Those fingers find their way inside me, and Adrian renders me senseless as he works me inside and out.

Gasping and shuddering, I enjoy what I hope is one of many orgasms to come today. My poor body hasn't had one, let alone several in quick succession, in so long I'm sure it's wondering what in the hell is going on.

Adrian collapses beside me and pulls me in tight. "I just thought this was my favorite before," he says as he holds the pick above our heads and stares at it in awe. "Now, I know it's my favorite."

I laugh and burrow my face in his side while running my hands over him. "I believe that act would be considered misappropriation of a musical implement, sir."

"I should mass produce these with a stamp that reads, 'For maximum pleasure: use for purposes not intended.'" This elicits both our laughter.

"I think you may be on to something. That guitar pick knew what it was doing. It was amazing."

"OK...now I'm getting jealous," he says as he tosses it on the nightstand and attacks my neck.

Giggling, I give him the praise he deserves. "You can't be jealous over an inanimate object. You're so creative, musically and ...otherwise."

"Lately, I've been feeling especially inspired," he says as he pushes the sheet down and devours my breasts like I'm his own private smorgasbord.

"Mmm...Adrian. I'm going to miss you so much. Your talent, your hands, your mouth—how did I ever manage without them?"

He nips at me, causing me to giggle, before he lies back beside me. "I'm wondering the same thing. I knew it would be good between us," he pauses and turns my face toward his, "but this is beyond anything I'd ever imagined, ever hoped for." He runs one fingertip down my cheek, and I tear up at his beautiful words and his gentle touch.

Leaning in, I give him a chaste kiss before I tell him simply, "I love you."

"I love you too, Celeste. More than anything. More than everything." He smiles against my mouth. I love the feel of him smiling, so I run my fingertips over his lips for a moment before my growling stomach vies for our attention.

He chuckles. "Am I starving my baby?"

"Apparently I need sustenance and real coffee."

"Café Du Monde?"

"Yes! Absolutely!" The speed with which I spring from the bed mirrors my enthusiastic response. His chuckle follows me to the bathroom.

AFTER WAITING IN the perpetually long line at the café, we are shown to our little wrought iron table for two in the corner. Adrian pulls a seat out for me, and I sit facing the bushes, which I never do when I come here because I love to people watch. But with Adrian around, I have tunnel vision so that doesn't even factor in.

I'm surprised and thrilled as he grabs his chair from the other side of the table to bring it close to mine. I glance up to the server and watch her expression go from interested in Adrian to impressed with Adrian. He's gorgeous and can't stay away from me—a winning combination.

"What can I get for y'all today?"

"I'll have a café au lait, please, and two orders of beignets."

"Babe, no beignets for me," Adrian cuts in.

"Oh, no, those are for me," I reply unabashedly.

"Hon, you know those come in orders of three," the helpful server offers.

"Yes, I know," I say with a smile.

"My woman has a healthy appetite. I love that," he says, those blues never leaving me. "I'll have a black coffee, please."

I glance up to see the server staring shamelessly at Adrian while fanning herself with her notepad. Correction—gorgeous, addicted to me, encourages my eating—freaking slam-dunk.

"Thank you so much," I say, taking pity on our entranced server.

"I'll be right back," she mutters.

"So you don't think I should worry about my figure?" I question him.

He gives my whole body a deliciously slow once over with his eyes. "I like my woman with a little meat on her bones."

"Really? You don't mind my little pudge and my bubble butt?" I ask with a raised eyebrow. I know that he doesn't. He's proven repeatedly that he loves my body just as it is.

Turning in his seat a bit so that he faces me and the restaurant, his thigh lodges itself against mine. His hand slips up the inside of my thigh. "Babe, don't change a single thing about the way you are—inside or out. I'm in love with you just as you are."

Before I can respond, his fingertips slip further up and graze my bare center and his hand springs back like he's been scorched. My eyes widen as do his. I didn't expect him to actually touch me *there* while we're sitting here.

"Fuck," he grinds out under his breath. I watch fascinated as those crystal tranquil pools morph into dark stormy seas. "Please tell me that was my imagination and you are wearing panties under that tight, short fucking skirt."

Oops! Sounds like something's caught him off guard as well. "Umm…"

"Celeste, what the fuck?"

"I don't like panty lines?" I offer weakly. "I thought you knew that from the other times we'd fooled around and I wasn't wearing any," I grit out.

"I thought that you just slipped them off for convenience when we were making out. And that time in the laundry room, I thought you were at least wearing a thong."

"Well, there you go." I put my hands up as if we've just reached a truce. "Just pretend I'm wearing a thong. Is that acceptable?" It's everything I can do not to laugh in his face. He's being ridiculous.

"Babe, I cannot be over there doing what I need to do when I'm worried about your fine, naked ass traipsing all over New Orleans without me here to watch out for you. Today's the last day you get to go without wearing panties."

I have to admit I'm addicted to his bossy nature in the bedroom and about our rules of proximity outside of it; however, I draw the line at being openly told what to do with things that don't even concern him. I open my mouth to argue my no panty lines motto, but the server returns with our coffee and my beignets. Shooting daggers at him with my own eyes, we make nice in front of her.

Once she leaves, he doesn't give me the chance to counter his demand. "I'm serious, Celeste. Do not walk around this city like that. I…I'm gonna fuckin' lose it if I think about that." I see immediately that he's not exaggerating; it really bothers him. His eyes read panicked. I can't have him panicked and worrying about me when he's got to keep himself safe.

I put my hand on his thigh and lean in to him, putting my lips against his ear, I whisper, "I'll only *not* wear panties when you're around, OK?" I feel the tension seep from him immediately. "I don't want you worrying about that. I promise I will wear my undergarments. I'll wear a corset if it makes you feel better. I can't have you distracted or worrying about me for any reason, got it?"

"Hell no, you can't wear a corset. That's even hotter." He pulls back to pin me with his gaze before nodding. "Your beignets are getting cold," he says with a raspy voice.

I give him a quick peck before beginning to devour my first order of these melt-in-your-mouth French donuts.

After slaking my hunger, I glance up to find him watching me with a smile on his face. "What?" I mumble around the little bit of donut in my mouth.

Tilting his head, he leans in and runs his tongue across my lips once, twice, three times, licking me clean. He places a chaste kiss on my lips. "Powered sugar," he answers.

"Mmm…but you don't like sweets."

His tongue darts out to lick his own lips like he can still taste me there. "I like the sweet that was under that sugar."

My blood heats and pounds in my ears. How can I be wanting him already? We've just left the room. "I don't know what you're doing to me," I say barely above a whisper. "All I can think about right now is how much I want you. I've always had a healthy libido, but this borders on nymphomania."

"Lucky me," he says with a grin. "And if it helps, the only thing I've been able to think about since I touched you is the fact that if I took you behind this building I could be inside you in about a half a second."

I rub my thighs together with that thought, trying to alleviate the pressure that has built between them. It only makes the pain more acute. "That doesn't help at all actually," I admit.

"Let's go back to the room," he says.

I throw my head back and laugh. "Nuh uh...you promised me the French Market. I want to get a few things for a day behind closed doors."

He groans, runs his hand through his hair, and springs from his chair. "I'm going to pay," he bites out.

"She'll bring the check, Adrian."

"We don't have time for all that," he says as he huffs away. I can only laugh.

I really don't want to waste time outside of our hotel room either, but I can't help teasing Adrian and making him follow me like a lost puppy through the French Market. It's priceless. I look at different breads like buying the wrong one would be tragic, all the while knowing exactly which loaf I want. What's really priceless is that each time I bend over I can feel Adrian move in closer as if protecting my virtue from a wandering eye. I'm not a novice. I know how to bend and move when I'm not wearing underwear since I've been at it for years. Well, except for that one time in my kitchen with Adrian. Now I have to wonder if that was really an accident. *Things that make you go hmm...*

When the vendor asks me if I'd like the mozzarella sliced, Adrian and I answer simultaneously yet in complete contradiction to one another. I laugh and confirm my response for the vendor and turn to Adrian. "Adrian, we have to have the cheese sliced so that it's easy to eat once we're in the room."

"You didn't get the bread sliced," he practically whines.

Trying to placate him, I lean in and run my hand up and down on his chest and croon, "That's because the bread is better torn from the loaf."

"Only you can make tearing bread sound hot," he says with another groan. He leans in and whispers, "I'm hard as a fucking jackhammer, Celeste." His voice deepens but doesn't getting any louder. "You can stop being a tease and go back to the room with me now like a good girl, or I can punish you later like a naughty one."

"Excuse me?" I barely breathe out, searching his turbulent blues.

"You heard me," he says, his voice sandpaper. His hand comes up to play at my waist, slipping down and teasing a little bit.

My entire body melts into his. I'm shocked at the way he speaks to me sometimes, yet I'm turned on beyond anything else. And he knows it. I just got played.

"Mmm hmm, that's what I thought, *mimi*. Tell him to hurry his ass up." He grunts. I have to say I'm loving my new nickname.

He barely closes the door behind us when I hear the bags being tossed on the ottoman and feel my hand being grabbed. I can barely register those two things before being turned into his arms and his mouth is relentless on mine. I groan and bring my hands up to run through his dark brown mess that I'm about to shear for him. His kiss is impatient and rough before he releases me only to push me toward the door with a gentle command. "*Mimi*, put your hands on the door and bend over."

I gasp at that mind-blowing command, which renders my brain useless so that I comply instantly and rapidly. Putting my hands on the door, I bend over slightly, but he grabs me by the hips and pulls me back so that my torso is parallel to the floor. I moan, I'm already beyond turned on. I can't even imagine how amazing he's going to make me feel. When I hear his zipper, I rub my thighs together in anticipation.

My skirt is pushed up around my waist, and his knees nudge my legs further apart. "Spread your legs, *mimi*, I'm taking you fast and hard." On another groan, I immediately cooperate.

I feel him at my entrance, but he stops. I push back and feel him retreat a little, only keeping the slightest contact. "Adrian," I breathe.

"Is that what you want? You want me to take you that way, don't you?" I can only groan in response. I have no words.

"I want to hear you say it, Celeste."

I turn my head, noticing the full-length closet mirror across the room from us and almost come undone at the sight of us. His gaze follows mine, and he smiles lasciviously at us. I swallow hard before I rasp out. "Take me, Adrian, fast and hard, please."

He touches my womb with his first thrust, and I cry out with abandon. Holding tight at my hips, he never relents. I just hold on for the ride.

I can feel him nearing his climax, and then his thumb finds its way to my nub and works me so that I find mine first.

Grasping both of my hips again, he chants, "Mine…never… ever." He says those three words over and over as he spills himself into me before finally stilling and draping himself over me to plant kisses along my spine.

Straightening, I turn my head and he takes my mouth tenderly with his. He may have been rendered almost inarticulate but I understand. He's mine, and I've never ever had it this good either.

AFTER SPENDING MOST of the day feasting on bread and cheese and each other, Adrian and I finally leave the room for drinks and dinner downstairs. When we enter the elevator, he turns to me and runs his hands up my thighs until he gets to my hips, looking down and back up to my eyes. "This dress is much more acceptable," he says of my full-length turquoise ensemble.

"You like?"

"Yes, all the other guys have to use their imagination, but I know exactly what is waiting for me underneath all this," he says running a finger under the neck of my halter-top. He straightens a bit and rewraps me with my brown and turquoise paisley scarf until hardly any skin is showing. I just laugh at him and roll my eyes. "I wouldn't want you to catch a chill."

"Thank you, Adrian. You're so considerate."

"Damn straight. So I made a reservation at the restaurant after we have a drink, but I'm rethinking that. How about some Bar Bites instead?"

"I'd love that." The Carousel's Bar Bites are phenomenal, and if you order enough, they make a nice meal.

When the elevator dings, he takes my arm in his and leads me to the Carousel. It's making one of its legendary revolutions so that we have to wait a moment before sitting. Once I'm up on my red and white-striped seat, Adrian sits beside me and turns so that he's facing me with his feet resting on my stool. I reciprocate.

"Good evening, folks, what can I get for y'all tonight?" the bartender asks.

"Hi, I'll have the Goody, please."

"Can't go wrong with a classic, can you?" Adrian asks. "Hendrick's Martini with an extra cucumber, please."

"Coming right up. Are you ordering from the grill tonight?"

"Yes, sir," Adrian responds.

"I'll give you a minute to look at the menu then," he says as he hands us menus.

I give it a cursory glance, but I always order the same thing. "What are you thinking?" Adrian asks me after a minute.

"I'm going to have the Crawfish Pie and the Mini Monte Po-Boys." I'm proud that I show enough restraint to keep from licking my lips.

He gives his menu a quick glance and says, "I'm gonna have the po-boys and Blue Crab Beignets."

"Oh, those sound delicious. I've always wanted to try them. You won't mind sharing will you?"

He laughs. "What's mine is yours, babe, you know that." He picks up his coaster and spins it before tossing it back down. "Speaking of...we need to talk about a couple of things. While I was running my errands, I met with Louis and made sure that I left everything in trust to the boys should I not make it." My heart drops to my toes, my stomach lodges in my throat, and tears spring to my eyes. "You're the guardian, and I would've left it to you but I know you have a shitload of money and wouldn't have any use for it. I figured the boys were the best bet. They can access it when they're in college."

"Adrian..." I try to say something but all I can think is "should I not make it" and that makes me want to lose it.

He reaches out and cups his hand around my neck, bringing my face close to his. "I don't like talking about it either, but, Celeste, it's a real possibility and I just wanted to do right by the boys. I really don't want to talk about it anymore if that's OK with you."

I just nod.

He places a chaste kiss on my lips and relaxes his hold a bit. "It's not a lot, but it's something. I want them to have it."

I just nod again.

The bartender places our drinks in front of us, and Adrian orders our food. I pick up my Goody and take a delicate sip, letting the delicious mixture of rums and pineapple and orange play on my tongue for a moment before swallowing. Perfect—the perfect mixture, sweet yet tangy. I lick my lips to get the little that remained behind and take another small sip, delighting in it before looking over at Adrian.

He's grinning his Cheshire cat grin. "Damn, that was sexy."

Thank God I didn't have anything in my mouth because I start giggling uncontrollably. Finally, wiping tears from my eyes, I say, "Adrian, may I just say that I love that you are turned on by just about everything I do." My laughter dies and I run my hand up his jaw, back and forth for a minute, loving that scruff that he's about to shave off. "How did I get so lucky?"

Giving me that half-grin of his, he grabs my hand and pulls it to his lap. "We'll see how lucky you feel tomorrow at the airport. You get to meet my parents."

In all these years, as close as my and Tripp's fathers are, I'd never met this branch of the family tree. Apparently, the falling out between them had occurred when the boys were young. Tripp said the last time he'd seen Adrian that Adrian had been in diapers. "I'm sure they're not that bad."

"Well, my mother is lovely but a complete lush. But she loves me like crazy even though she's never been able to stand up to my father. Anyway, I imagine she will be quite dramatic tomorrow even if it'll be too early for her to have indulged." He releases a deep sigh. "My father, on the other hand, he loves taking cheap shots at me and the fact that I'm headed to war won't stop him from trying to make me look bad in front of everyone." He takes a swig of his martini as I try to process this. Raising his brows, he says, "So fair warning."

"Consider me warned. They do know how amazing you are, right?"

"Amazing?" he asks with a bitter laugh. "I didn't go to law school, Celeste. For some reason that's the standard in our family, so I'm considered subpar in their eyes. I'm definitely not considered amazing."

I narrow my eyes at him, forcing him to frown at me. "Adrian, I think it's time we both learned and accepted that our families have mixed up priorities when it comes to us and that their opinion of how we live our lives doesn't count. We're both on that slow road there. We proved that yesterday with our eloping. We just need to fast forward to the part where their disdain and rejection don't hurt anymore."

"I think we're almost there because I didn't even consider their feelings yesterday, and the only reason we're not telling them now is because I don't want the drama before I go. I don't want that lingering feeling following me to Iraq. I want the sweet memories of these last few days to follow me. I also don't want you having to deal with any fallout on your own.

"And then there's this simple fact. You and our boys—y'all make me feel more loved and more accepted than anyone needs or deserves. I feel full to the point of bursting when I'm with y'all. I never knew what I was missing out on, not having unconditional love, and I want to make sure I never *have* to know."

I lean in and pull him down to kiss me. When the carousel spins, it takes me a minute to realize that it's not just me who feels like I'm floating.

HOLDING THE CLIPPERS in my hand, I try to work up the nerve to shave his head.

"Baby, just do it. It's just hair; it'll grow back. I know you like to have something to tug on, but my hair grows fast," Adrian says as he holds the towel around his neck and peers at me in the mirror.

I give him a rueful smile. "I know. It's just...I was thinking about the first time we met. You were still active duty and had a high and tight, remember?"

"Yes, I came to see y'all when y'all were stationed in DC and I was passing through to report to my next duty station. Best idea ever to stop and catch up with Tripp."

I blush because it was then that I'd been so attracted to him, but I'd also been married, of course. "I felt so guilty over my reaction, but I couldn't help it. I'll never forget it either. I walked into the room and you were facing away looking at some of Tripp's plaques, and I felt a little...hum. When you turned around as Tripp was introducing you, it was instantaneous. My entire body sang. No thought. My body just knew that it was attracted to everything about you." I shake my head, staring at the clippers as if they held all the answers. "Once you'd gone on your way, I was able to put that physical attraction out of mind and carry on. I wasn't harboring any feelings toward you. Then, when you moved back home and after Tripp died, I got to know you, and it got harder and harder not to imagine myself with you. I'd always find my thoughts drifting there." I hear him laugh and my head snaps up to catch him grinning.

"Not just sexually!" I say with a laugh. "Men, I swear. What I'm telling you is the physical attraction I could ignore. It was everything else about you that made ignoring you impossible."

He clears his throat. "It wasn't like that for me."

"What do you mean?"

"I mean I loved you as soon as I spoke to you. Have you not noticed that about yourself? How people tend to fall in love with you immediately? First of all, you're gorgeous. That draws us in, of course. But that ability of yours to make the person you're talking to feel like the only person on the planet seals the deal. You listened to me like you were born to listen to me. That's what you do. You're completely selfless like that. So, it was different for me because I fell for you in every way possible almost immediately."

I lay the clippers down and sit sideways in his lap, running my hands through his hair one last time. Staring into my blues, I kiss him softly. "I hope you never get sick of feeling that way, Adrian, because you and our boys are the most important people on this planet and I'm never going to let you forget it." I promise.

I pretend the head I'm working on doesn't belong to him. I'm nervous but excited. Excited that I'll get to see him as I first met him. Nervous that I'm going to screw up his hair. He assured me that making him look like a Jarhead was a no brainer. I trim the little hairs on his neck and ears and step back to admire my work. Damn, I did a good job.

"It's ridiculous that you are still so good looking," I joke. I reach out and run my hand over his short, now prickly, hair. "You're head is flawless. That's crazy. It is absolutely the ideal shape. Oh, you have a little scar here." I say as I rub my finger over the indentation. "What do you think?" I ask as I set the clippers down.

He runs a hand back and forth over his head. His eyes meet mine in the mirror. "It looks great. I'm impressed. Now, for the fun part, he says as I roll the towel up with all the hair on it.

"What's that?" I look back up at him.

Mirth dances in his eyes. He wiggles his eyebrows at me. "You get to work on getting all these little hairs off of me in the shower."

"Mmm...I like the sound of that."

-Nineteen-

Quite Taken

"BABY, I NEED you to wake up," Adrian calls softly while moving his hands and mouth over me.

"Already?" I felt like I'd just gone to sleep. I pry my eyes open a little and notice the room is still blanketed in darkness. "What time is it?"

Adrian pulls back a little from lavishing my breast to mumble, "Four."

"Adrian, we don't have to get up yet. We just went to sleep three hours ago, and you need your rest," I whine.

"I want to make love to my wife, and I can sleep on the plane," he mumbles before switching breasts. His actions along with his claim have me stirring again.

"OK, baby," I say as I run my hands over his shaved head.

He pops up and whispers, "And I want to talk to the boys."

I smile. "Good plan."

I CARRY A sleeping Finn into Archer's room while Adrian follows behind me with a half-asleep Paris. I kiss Finn all over his head. "Wake up, Finny Finn Finn," I chant.

"Mom?" he mumbles.

"Yes, honey?"

He lifts his head and looks around, those big brown eyes half-closed. "Why are you waking me up at the butt crack of dawn?"

"Finn!"

"What?"

I roll my eyes. "Nothing." We'll chat about language later. "Adrian wants to talk to you before we take him to the airport, OK?"

He turns in my arms and spots Adrian. They grin at each other. "I don't want you to leave," Finn tells him.

"I know, buddy." My heart crumbles and tears spring to my eyes, so I take a swift breath in and release it quickly to keep from losing it.

"It's OK, Ma," Paris says, "you can cry if you need to."

This makes me laugh instead. "Thank you, Paris. I think I can hold it together for a little while," I say, grinning at my sweet son. Finn puts his thumbs at the corners of my eyes and swipes. "Thanks, sweetheart."

I place Finn on the bed next to Archer, which finally rouses him. Archer doesn't even open his eyes; he just peels back his covers for his brother to climb in beside him. Paris climbs up on the other side and squeezes in. I catch them like this in the morning all the time. It never fails to warm my heart and have me counting my blessings.

"Boys, I need you to wake up. We want to tell you some things before we go." I watch in fascination as all their eyes pop open. If only they would get up for school so easily! Hmm…maybe that will be Adrian's permanent responsibility when he's living with us full-time waking up my morning monsters. "Mornin', guys." They mumble their responses. "You know how I told you I was going to ask your mom to marry me?" They all nod. "Well, I asked her, she said yes, and we got married."

Well, that certainly cut to the chase. I told him I was nervous about telling them because I didn't want them to feel left out, and he told me to let him handle it, telling me he knew how to word it for guys. I stare at the boys, waiting for some reaction. Paris's eyes get big. Archer grins.

It takes a few seconds for it to sink in before Finn shuffles from under the covers and throws himself at Adrian, hugging him tight around the neck. "Can I call you Papa?" he asks. Adrian chuckles.

"If that's what you want. I like Papa."

"It's the only French word I can remember besides *merde.*"

My breath swooshes out before I spit out, "Finn Thomas Hebert! Do you even know what that means?" When his little mouth pops open, I throw my hands up. "No! Don't even say it. I don't want to hear that word come out of your mouth again, young man."

"Yes, ma'am," he says as he tries to hide behind Adrian's shoulder. Mmm hmm, he knows he's crossed the line.

"I like Papa," Paris says, bringing our attention back to the subject at hand.

"Me too," Archer agrees.

"Well, that settles that then. I'm Papa," Adrian says with a smile that he shares with each of us before speaking again. "All right boys, here's the deal. I can't go into detail now, but your mom and I are going to keep this to ourselves for a while. OK? I'm not asking you to lie to anyone, mind you. Just keep this our business for now. But if anyone asks, you should tell them to talk to your mom and let her handle it. OK?" They all nod. "Last thing I want to talk to you about." He blows out a deep breath and runs his hand back and forth over Finn's head. "I know you boys already know a lot about what is going on over there with the war and all, but you need to know that I'm very good at my job. It has been my honor and privilege to take care of my brothers, so you can bet I'm going to be taking care of business. I'm going to be extra careful now that I have you guys counting on me, OK?" Nods all around. "If you get scared, talk to your mom. Don't worry about me, though. This is my fifth time going to war if you can believe that. I'm experienced and smart and fast. Got it?"

"I want to join the Marine Corps, Papa, and be just like you," Archer says with a little hiccup. I have to look at the ceiling and swallow hard.

"Right now, Marine, I want you and your brothers to take care of your mom. You already do a great job, but you're really going to have to step up now that I'm not going to be around. Everybody good with that?" I look back down to four sets of eyes glued on me and lots of "yes, sirs."

"All right," Adrian says as he stands up and tosses Finn on the bed before picking him up by the ankles and dangling him over the bed. "Finn, quit messing around and get dressed," Adrian says over the boys' giggling.

WATCHING MY SWEET man move around the airport saying goodbye to everyone is heartbreaking. His parents don't show, and I'm beyond pissed. I mean, even if they're awful, they are his parents. The boys are keeping everyone entertained while we and the other families wait. Adrian's bandmates show up in full force and lighten the mood by alternating between their crude humor and touching remarks. Farah and her husband show up, of course. When Garner walks in and grabs Adrian and lifts him in the air, we all crack up. Garner drops him back to his feet but not before giving him a huge, sloppy kiss on his cheek that has Adrian giving him a kidney shot. I thought Garner was being his usual over-the-top self until he turned to Bonnie and I saw her wipe his eyes and then give him a small kiss.

All of this occurs without Adrian letting me get more than six inches away from him.

When the boarding call comes over, I feel a chill make quick work of my body and close those six inches to burrow into Adrian's side.

"I love you so much," he tells me. "Everything's going to be OK."

Before I can speak, I hear a woman's voice behind me and feel Adrian stiffen. Turning, I see the woman who has to be his mother. I've seen pictures of a younger, less tired version of her.

"Mom," Adrian says as he moves around me to hug her. "I thought you weren't going to make it."

"Of course. I wouldn't miss saying goodbye to my baby boy," she chokes out. "I tried to get your father to come, but he said he'd already told you goodbye. Anyway, that's why I'm so late."

"I'm glad you're here."

"Me too, son." He turns her around to face me. I smile nervously.

"Hello, Celeste," she says sweetly. "I hear you're quite taken with my son."

I laugh and look at my blues before looking back her. "Yes, ma'am. Quite taken," I confirm.

"Good, good. You're a good person. And Adrian deserves someone good."

I don't know what else to say but thank you. Thank you for being here, thank you for seeing the good in him and the good in me, and thank you for saying what he needed to hear.

Everyone takes that moment to give him one last, quick hug. He picks up each of the boys and hugs them extra tight and tells him how much he loves them before turning to me.

Tears shimmer in both of our eyes, so I smile and throw myself around him, hugging him to me tight. "I love you so much, Adrian. I'll miss you so much."

"I love you too, baby." He pulls back a little and gives me my blues. I frame his face and kiss him long and hard. I hear the last call for his flight and feel my best friends move in tight. I clutch at him and shake my head no a little as the thought of being without him overwhelms me before I finally tear myself away.

He pulls me back quickly, and his gravelly voice whispers, "I'm really gonna miss my *mimi*." I give a little bark of laughter through my tears. Locking eyes with me one more time, he grabs his duffle bag and backs out of the terminal to get on the plane that will take him away from us.

I lose him after he makes his way through security and through the gates. I let go of a deep breath and look to see the boys still waving. Bonnie and Farah are holding me from each side. I cross my arms over me and pat their hands. "I'm good."

Bonnie leans in and says, "Did he seriously just call you his pussycat? And in French?"

I can't respond for the huge grin that's on my face. Farah gasps, "He calls you his pussycat?" In French?" I smile at her and nod. Her mouth drops open before she breathes, "That's hot!"

The giggles that pour out of me at that point are the kind where you can't tell if someone is laughing or crying. I turn and give my girls hugs and say, "Thanks for that. I needed a good laugh."

"Thank your man," Bonnie says. "He certainly knows how to lighten up the mood."

"Yes, he does."

"Celeste, I cannot believe your families did not blow a gasket when they found about y'all," Bonnie says.

I blow out a deep breath. "Well, we probably would have made a bigger splash, but war has a way of trumping things. I think even our family realizes the severity of this situation and will probably save the theatrics and threats for another day."

It's the strangest thing afterward. No one is in a hurry to leave. We all just enjoy each other's company. Adrian's mom tells the boys Adrian story after Adrian story. They are a captive audience. Finally, we start to disperse and head out. When I look around, it's just us girls along with my boys and Adrian's mom.

"Celeste, is that your engagement ring?" his mom asks. I smile and nod. "It's beautiful, honey."

"It really is, Cel, I didn't want to say anything earlier and draw attention away from our goodbyes, but it's gorgeous," Bonnie says.

Farah picks up my hand and looks at it in detail. The wedding band is unique; it's covered in tiny diamonds and blends seamlessly with the two diamond bands encircling the engagement ring. It's a trio of bands, and it's hard to tell they're separate, which works perfectly, since we're keeping the official aspect of our relationship to ourselves for now.

"Thanks, y'all," I tell them.

"So when's the big day?" his mom asks.

"We're going to have a small ceremony at Holy Name two weeks after Adrian's return. That would put it somewhere around mid-April. We have to be flexible. You know how the military can be with dates." They all nod.

We say our final goodbyes. The girls offer to come over, but I insist that I'm fine. Adrian's mom makes me promise to bring the boys over sometime. I'm thinking I'd rather her come over to my house because of Adrian's father, but I don't say anything about that just yet. I'll cross that bridge when I get to it.

Farah hangs back from the others and says, "I'd like to tell you something real quick. I don't think that Adrian would mind now." I just nod. "Remember that night that I told you that he came clean to me in the club?" I nod again. "What he said…I'll never forget, Celeste. I called him on it when he said he didn't love you. I told him you were both fools, denying what you felt for each other. He finally broke down and said that the only thing that made him a fool where you were concerned was because you owned him. He said he didn't even exist without you. That he was an empty vessel and that you filled him and owned him until he didn't know where he ended and you began."

"Wow," is all I can utter when she finishes. "I…now…that's so beautiful that I just want him to come back so I can kiss him harder, longer," I say forcing myself to laugh so that I don't cry.

She hugs me tight. "I didn't want to make you sad. I just wanted you to know how much he loves you and has for a long time too."

Once the boys and I get home and take care of the chores that have to be squared away, we pile in the living room and watch comedy after comedy. Our laughs are slow to come at first. It feels awkward to laugh when our hearts are so heavy. After our third movie and some pizza that I had delivered because I had absolutely no energy to cook, my phone rings and we all jump for it.

"You're on speaker," I say when the call goes through.

"Well, hello, my little family. I miss you guys already. What are y'all doing?"

"Hey, Papa!" Finn yells before I can tell him that he doesn't have to yell. "We're having a movie marathon."

"Ah, what's playing tonight?"

Paris pipes up and tattles on me. "Ma made us watch the *Princess Bride* first."

"Hey, y'all love the *Princess Bride*," I say, affronted.

"Yeah," Adrian agrees, "y'all always laugh."

"But she always chooses that." Paris insists. I laugh because it's true.

"Adrian," Finn singsongs, "we're gonna watch your favorite comedy next."

"*Jaws*?"

Archer snorts with laughter. "No, the *Goonies!*"

"All right, boys," I cut in, "let me talk to Adrian real quick about what's going on. I'm sure he doesn't have long. Y'all go brush your teeth and then we'll watch the *Goonies* before lights out."

"Bye, Papa!" Finn shouts again.

Archer and Paris say their goodbyes.

I take Adrian off speaker and go to my room. "Hi," I whisper.

"Hi," he says back.

"We miss you already."

"I miss y'all too. I can't believe I'm missing movie night. I thought about all the things I'm going to be missing on the plane too. I'm going to miss all four of your birthdays and Christmas and every major holiday. That sucks."

"You'll be home for Easter," I offer.

"True," he says with a smile in his voice. "Look, I've got about two minutes. I have a question for you."

"Yeah?"

"Did you find anything in your pocket?"

I grin and pat myself down before feeling a little something in one of my back pockets. "I can't believe you were feeling me up in front of everyone," I say, thinking back to his wandering hands every time we would hug. He just laughs.

I work the little piece of plastic out of my back pocket and hold it up in front of me. "Did you read it?"

I swallow hard. Tears flood my eyes. I have to focus on breathing. "Celeste?"

I whimper.

"I mean it," he whispers fiercely.

Clearing my throat, I whisper back, "I know you do."

"Love you."

"I love you too."

Hitting end on the call, I toss the phone on my bed, lock my bedroom door, and go to my bathroom. I sit down on the bench and stare at the guitar pick he'd used on me that morning, reading it over and over again. *You hold my pick and my heart. Guard them.*

It doesn't take long for the words to become a blur.

-Twenty-

Our Life in Letters

THE NEXT SEVERAL months are spent thinking of every conceivable way to make sure Adrian knows exactly how much we miss him and we love him and how we treasure him. We send him care packages that he actually receives sometimes. I write to him every single day. I may mail them a few at a time, but every day I write him little notes even if some days I can only imagine a few lines. I stationed writing sets all over the house—on each of the boys' nightstands, in the living room, on the bar in the kitchen, in the office— pretty much everywhere—so that we could write to him as soon as we thought about him or had the urge to tell him something. Then, on the bar, we put a little mailbox that we decorated with Marine insignia for the boys to slip their notes into for me to mail. I told them if there was ever anything they didn't want me to read, all they had to do was put a little piece of tape over the fold and I would keep out. There was never any tape, and I was so glad because their letters never ceased to be a source of wonder and amusement for me.

We don't get to talk to Adrian much or email him very much because he's stationed on the front lines, which I try not to consider very often.

So our letters become our foundation of solace and happiness.

Wife,

I miss you. I love you. I can't fathom how hard these next few months will be, so I take it one day at a time. I focus on the mundane, like trying to get the sand out of my weapons and scamming to get some ranch dressing for my MREs when we go to camp for a few days. I finally did get that one package with all the ranch, by the way. I was in heaven.

Other than that, things pretty much suck ass. It's like I told you on the porch that night but worse. Do you remember? I don't want you to obsess over that. I just want you to know.

Tell the boys I love their drawings. Tell Archer his music looks perfect with the exception of the bridge. If he uses his metronome, he won't lose his beat. His song kicks ass. Has he played it for you yet? Does Paris realize that every picture he sends me of Skip looks the same? Turtles are not photogenic. Don't tell him I said that, though! Tell him I love them. Ah yes, and my man, Finn—tell him I put the picture of him in his flight suit in my helmet. I love it! Is he really making you call him Maverick?

Love you, babe,
Your husband

Husband,

The boys and I had MREs for lunch yesterday as an experiment. Did you know you could buy them on base? I bought them when we went to pick up Archer's & Paris's gear. Archer decided on jungle camouflage BDUs, and Paris picked up desert cammies. Finn's not coming off the flight suit. I have to wash and dry it while he sleeps. Anyway, I totally get your obsession with ranch now. MREs are disgusting. I don't know how you do it other than you'd have no other choice but to starve. The boys and I each got down about half before we gave up. If I were stationed in Iraq, I would be skinny!

Paris has earned another belt. But he told me he's over it and wants to focus on piano and pick up bass. I'm good with that. Archer has perfected his song that he has lovingly entitled "My Left Foot" because it describes the discordant sounds he plays up in his music. I didn't have the heart to tell him there's a movie called that. I'm sure he'll be thirty by the time he discovers it. Finn is not great right now. He's a little upset as I write this and is writing his own letter to you. I've tried to explain things to him, but you'll probably put it in "guy-speak" and make it all better.

I miss my blues,
Your loving wife

Captain,

This jerk at school told me that you are gonna be mincemeat when he overheard me telling Cooper that you're Force Recon and stationed in Iraq. I didn't know what mincemeat was but he said it in a real jerk way. Know what I mean? So we were gonna meet out back after school. Only thing is, Archer found out and told me I can't fight at school. I know what mincemeat is now. Is it really

THAT dangerous there?
Love,
Finn aka Mav

Mav,
Force Recon is not easy work, but it's very important work. It's a lot like what Maverick and his buddies do. We go and make sure the area is safe and secure before the combat unit moves in. We are incredibly safe and have tons of protective gear. My protective gear weighs about 80 pounds. To put that in perspective—you weigh about 60. It's like a chubby Finn-sized protective shield. Not too shabby, huh?

The deal with the jerk is this—he probably heard someone else, like his parent, say some crap (Don't tell your mom I said crap!) like that. He doesn't know what he's talking about. Remember—I'm smart, I'm fast, and I'm motivated. Can't wait to be home with you guys.

I love you,
Captain Adrian Hebert, USMC aka Papa

I love you,
Finn

252

Happy birthday Archer!

I hope you're enjoying being a teenager. We have a lot to talk about when I get home. I wish I could have been there, of course, but we're going to make up for lost time. Did your mom give you the gift I sent for you? (Well, asked her to buy for me.) Do you like it? Your mom said you've been taking your music real serious. That was very cool that you posted some online for me to see. Me and the guys crowded around one tiny laptop last time we were at camp. They said you were real good. Told you I wasn't the only one who thought so. Your cover of "Dream On" rocked, but when are you going to record "My Left Foot" for me? I'm dying here, dude.

Love,

Papa

Papa,

My song's not ready yet. I'm still messing with the bridge. A friend of mine, Taylor, has been coming over and jammin' with me. He's good. He plays electric, though, so after a while, Mom started making us play in the basement. She said she couldn't focus. She's been working a lot more now.

Everyone is jealous of my guitar strap too. No one else has a studded one with their name on it. It's very cool. Thank you.

Did you get your birthday package? We put extra ranch and beef jerky in it.

Love,

Archer

Boys,

My birthday package was awesome! Ranch, beef jerky, gum, wet wipes, Skin-So-Soft! You shouldn't have. Kidding! It was perfect and practical and everything I needed. Favorite part—those stellar report cards and awards. Honor roll all the way around, a few students of the month, some perfect attendance. Why didn't you have perfect attendance, Finn?

Love you all so much,
Papa

I was throwing my guts up. Mom made me stay home. It was three days before the end of the term too!

Dear husband,

I don't know what I did to deserve angels like you and Louis in my life, but I'm incredibly grateful for you both. Louis came over and we had a little too much wine while watching some old movies. He came clean and told me everything.

I can't believe that Tripp asked you to look out for the children and me. Why didn't you ever tell me? I had no idea. It makes me wonder if he knew that deep down we were drawn to each other. And the fact that you were there to bring him some peace of mind in the end makes me so happy. I think you didn't tell me because underneath that sometimes-arrogant exterior that I worship at you are such a modest man, and I love you so much for that. However, you can't keep information that substantial from me in the future. Remember: we are in this together.

I know you told me bits and pieces of what happened with you and the family, but I still can't fathom why you would put yourself so firmly in their clutches for me. You knew they wanted you for a tool to use against your father, and you entered willingly into the belly of the beast. And for me?

And the lengths Louis went to try to find me someone suitable— unbelievable. And you two—working together the way you did. I hate how it all unfolded, but I'm glad that Louis came to you when he saw my future was at stake. I asked him why that was since you two didn't really know each other. His response: he knew that you loved me and would do anything for me. He thought you loved me like he loves me, though. I don't know what I'd do without you two. I love y'all so much. I can't see the words on this page anymore. I have to go for now.

If I didn't say it enough—I love you. So much.
Tu me manques,
Your wife

Wife,
Never thank me for caring for you. I'll stop at nothing to protect you. Remember that.
Tu me manques, ma belle femme,
Your husband

Hiya Pops!

I know Archer and Finn like Papa. But I like Pops. I don't know if Ma told you, but Skip has moved on from this world. We're not sure what happened to him, but we gave him a proper ceremony and burial in the backyard. I want to get a hamster now, but Ma says no cause it's really just a cuter version of a rat. Will you talk to her for me?

Learning bass is awesome. Archer and I can play together more and his friend Taylor comes over with his electric. Ma is thrilled with our sessions. Not really! :P She does tolerate them, which is more than a lot of other moms would do.

Love you, miss you,

Paris

Dear Adrian,

I can't believe you had my car outfitted with an iPod port. You really know the way to my heart, don't you? The funny thing was when I told some of the other moms they looked at me like I was insane. One even said,"Is that what you wanted?" Umm...No, I didn't even know it existed, but somehow, someway, my amazingly generous husband who is thousands of miles away and who knows me so well did! Thank you, baby.

About the family, other than Louis, I really haven't seen them. The boys and are I staying to ourselves. Bonnie helps me quite a bit as does Garner, believe it or not. He's good with them too. I did meet your mother for coffee twice, though. She's got some definite issues, but she does love you and she's been really sweet to me.

I'm sure you've heard that the Dog Tags cut a song on request of some affiliate of a major label. I went to listen. They don't sound as good without you, in my opinion. However, they still sound really good. They're just not great without you. I may, however, be slightly biased. They're eager for you to get back.

I love you, baby, and miss you so much.

Celeste

Celeste, my love, my wife, my life...

I like it when you sign your letters wife. No, I don't like it. I fucking love it and don't stop.

Is the replacement rhythm guitarist as good looking as me? I know you have a thing for them. You know, as you practically fucked me with your eyes that night right before you attacked me and took advantage of me.

I'm happy you like your birthday present. I know how much you love your music. Did you get the iTunes card too? Did you discover some new artists to turn me on to?

Your love, your husband, your life,

Adrian

Dearest husband,

Shall I sign my letters Mrs. Adrian Hebert from now on? Would your claim on me be properly staked by that admission? Shall I turn my head while you piss in a circle around me? Wait, what century is this again? Kidding. I'll sign my letters however you'd like. I miss you that much.

What's with all the profanity?
And you know that no one is as HOT as you are.
Your love, your wife, your life,
Celeste

Wife,
Something about you calling yourself my wife turns me on. Speaking of, I thought you liked my dirty talk. If not, my sincerest apologies, madame.
   And I'm only hot because I'm in this damned desert.
Your husband

Husband,
Talk dirty to me.
Your wife

It was after this little note that I started receiving these guitar picks with his naughty little messages.

Misappropriate this.

Wants to hang out in my favorite spot.

Does this make you wet?

When he got closer to coming home, they turned sweeter.

-Twenty-One-

This Moment

FINALLY, THE LONGEST six months of my life have led to this moment. I'm almost giddy with relief and excitement as we make our way to the airport even though the boys are arguing over the silliest things like whose fault it was that the dogs were late in getting fed this morning and why Finn keeps repeatedly touching the backside of Archer's CDs and leaving fingerprints on them.

I look around and take in the beautiful spring day, trying to tune out their bickering. I know they are so excited to see Adrian and sometimes that excitement manifests itself in a strange way. I also like for them to try to resolve their conflicts before I step in, so I focus on the magenta azaleas and the Black-eyed Susans and the bright sunshine reflecting from the buildings.

I do this for several minutes, wondering what kinds of things we can get into in the city now that Adrian's home. One of the boy's comments crashes through my train of thought consisting of sunshine and rainbows and butterflies.

"What did you just say, Archer?" I enunciate each word carefully so that he understands this is a rhetorical question.

"Nothin'," he mumbles without looking at me.

"Archer, I'd better never hear that come from your little mouth again. Do you understand me?"

"Yeah," he mumbles again.

"What?"

"Yes, ma'am," he says with respect.

"Thank you. Now, you owe us an apology."

"I'm sorry, y'all. I shouldn't have said that. Finn, Paris, don't say that, OK?"

"OK, Archer," Finn says, "I forgive you."

I almost lose at it as I watch Archer's jaw tighten. I'm sure Finn had pushed his buttons and now was trying to sound all innocent. I sober. "Finn Thomas?"

"Yes, ma'am?"

"I don't know what you said to your brother," I say as I make eye contact with him in the rearview mirror, "but you need to apologize for goading him. A person can only take so much."

"Sorry," he mumbles.

"Finn."

"I'm sorry, Archer," he says sweetly. *Mmm hmm.*

"Look, I know you are all very excited about Papa being home, but we don't need to overload him with a bunch of bickering and fighting. I'm not saying don't show your excitement. I'm just saying tone down the brotherly love for a bit and let him get used to being around us again before overwhelming him with the nuances of your relationships."

"What's a nuance?" Finn asks.

"Finer points, distinctions, what makes us—us," Archer tells him.

I grin at him.

WE'RE EARLY SO I take the boys into one of the café's to wait. After they've picked out their drinks and snacks, we sit quietly and each do our own little thing. Archer and Paris are doodling, and Finn is playing on my phone. I'd picked up a Southern Living and was absent-mindedly thumbing through it not really paying attention to anything except my fantasizing about finally being able to make love to my hot Marine husband tonight.

I glance up when I hear the little noises the boys were making go silent. They're staring over my head awestruck. It's probably one of our famous New Orleanians. I turn around and immediately start grinning and weeping.

Standing behind the glass is a vision—a beautiful vision of a wonderful man. I can't believe it. I hear the boys rush around the table and watch as his eyes and his smile follow them until they all latch onto him at once. Their display of happiness causes lots of cheers and whistles. I can't help but smile with pride.

Who could not be affected by a man who's served our country being welcomed home by his children? I gather up our things, my gaze never leaving the sweet scene playing out in front of me. I'm dying to touch him, but once I start, I know I won't stop so I'm giving the boys their moment.

He looks so good yet so different. His complexion is darker, which makes those gorgeous blues pop even more. His hair is even shorter than when I'd cut it. His face is leaner, and I'm pretty sure he's gone up a size in uniform. His massive chest and arms fill out his BDUs quite nicely.

Once I have our things squared away, I make my way out to him, smiling the whole way. I cannot stop smiling. "Hi," I whisper when I get close enough. The boys stand back and make room for me to get to him. I hear Archer and Paris arguing over who will carry his duffle bag, but I block them out.

"Wife, my God, I've missed you," he says as his arms enfold me and he buries his face in my neck.

"Adrian, I've missed you. So much," I mumble into his chest.

He feels like a tree trunk compared to what he'd felt like when he'd left. "You're huge," I say.

"Nothin' to do but workout when I was at camp," he says.

I breathe him in deeply and I feel him shudder underneath me. "You smell so good."

"Baby, I've been travelling for two days. No way."

"Mmm hmm…You still smell like Adrian. Desert and ocean—hot and quenching at the same time." I lean back to smile up at him.

He laughs and pushes my hair back before kissing me lightly a few times. I hear the boys snickering behind me, and I roll my eyes. I kiss him in earnest for a moment and pull back to murmur, "Is it bedtime yet?"

He just laughs at me.

"ARE YOUR EYES closed?" Paris asks Adrian.

Adrian laughs and says for the third time, "Yes, my eyes are closed."

"Ta da!" Finn shouts.

Adrian lets his hand fall and his smile fades a little before becoming bigger than ever. "You made me a man cave?"

I look around and take in the gigantic TV that practically takes up an entire wall and the latest game system with a bunch of games shelved underneath. There's a mini-fridge and a small bar with a microwave. All the guy stuff you could possibly imagine. It looks as though the New Orleans Saints' merchandise stand has thrown up in here too, but the boys said Adrian would love that even if I thought it was over-the-top. I just wanted him to feel at home here.

"Do you like it?" I ask as I watch him move around the huge room that used to be a formal dining room.

"Do I like it? Babe, I can't believe you did this for me. Did you get cable?" he asks with a look of disbelief. "And what about your dining room?"

I laugh. "I hardly ever used it, but I worked it out. And, yes, we have cable," I confess with a groan. "The boys have a viewing schedule. Right, boys?" I get a bunch of begrudging "Yes, moms."

"Yeah," Archer jumps in to tattle on me. "There's a giant hole in the kitchen where Mom is expanding and adding to the sunroom to have another dining room."

"OK…So I'm still working it out," I admit.

"Adrian, look," Finn interjects, "this chairs rub your butt when you sit in it." We all share a laugh as we watch Finn's little body jiggle around in the massive massage chair.

After letting them all check out the foosball and air hockey tables, which were the only things I voted for in this room, I hustle the boys out to feed the pets and wash up.

Adrian grabs my hand and pulls me over to the loveseat. "And I'd like to know what this loveseat is intended for, wife."

I grin. He's seen right through me. "Lovin'," I tell him as he settles me in on his lap. He leans and plants kisses on my neck that have me aching instantly.

"God, I want you so bad. Even just holding you is everything I've hoped for. But I need to be inside of you so bad right now."

"I want you too," I whisper. "I missed you, baby. I've missed your beautiful voice." I run my fingers down his throat. "I've missed these lovely crinkles that I'm able to see when you give me that genuine smile that I love." I plant a kiss on the corners of his eyes.

I startle a bit when I hear the doors close to the man cave and Archer say, "Geez, Mom, close the door, why don't you?"

Adrian and I both laugh. I bite my lip. "Oops…"

"Yeah, are you sure they're cool with me moving in here right away?"

I shake my head at him. "Are you kidding me? They wanted to go over to your apartment and pack your stuff themselves. They're thrilled," I say laying my head on his chest. "I told them you needed to be the one to do all that. I've stocked up on all your favorite stuff to get you through the next couple of weeks until after the ceremony, and then we can get you officially moved in."

He's gone quiet and still, so I look up to catch a far away look in his eyes. He doesn't even seem to notice I've moved. "You OK?"

Rubbing my arm up and down, he nods. "I just can't believe this is real."

Tears instantly fill my eyes. "What do you mean, Adrian?"

He clears his throat and finally looks at me. I see tears swimming in his eyes. "Adrian?"

"I'm here. I'm right here," he says before he kisses me. Pulling back, he stands me up and says, "Let's get the boys fed."

"ALL RIGHT," I say as I hand Adrian his tea and sit down with him on the couch, "we're all set for tomorrow night. I've only invited our close friends over. Nothing too big, right?" He nods at me. "The other Dog Tags and their dates, Louis, Farah and Matthew—"

"I thought you said they were separated," he interrupts.

"They were for about five minutes. Matthew came to his senses, though. She's so excited. They're already trying to get pregnant."

"Good for them."

"I know. I want everyone to be as happy as we are," I tell him.

He runs his hand over my thigh. "Me too, baby. You know what would make me happy right now?"

"What's that?" I glance up to see desire shining in his eyes, and I smile a little before biting my lip in anticipation of what I hope he'll say. I'm not disappointed.

"I want my sweet wife to put all this," he raises his hands to all of my plans for tomorrow and for the house, "away and take me to bed."

I giggle and bite my lip again. "It would be my pleasure, sir. And all this," I wave my hand over the pile, "can stay right where it is."

I grab his hand and lead him into our room. He closes the door behind us and pulls me in. I kiss his neck and hum. "Oh, Adrian, I've missed you so much. I can't believe you're here and you're mine and you've moved in with me. And I don't have to say good night."

"I can say with absolute certainty there is nowhere else I'd rather be and no one else I'd rather be with," he says before kissing me into oblivion.

-Twenty-Two-

When Things Go Boom

IT'S OFFICIAL. MY children are trying to drive me insane. "Archer," I call.

"Yes, ma'am?" he answers as he enters the bathroom.

"What is this?"

"Umm…mud."

I take a deep breath. "This isn't just mud, son, it's mud and grass and water. And a huge mess. Why is this in the guest bathroom that I just cleaned yesterday?"

"I don't know."

"You just went outside and now this is here. Did you not do this?"

He shrugs at me. Shrugs! Is this normal teenage behavior? I wouldn't know since we weren't allowed to have opinions and bad days around my house. But this is ridiculous. "Don't shrug at me," I say after a minute of stewing. "Go get the broom and the mop." He turns around to march off. "And loads of paper towels," I call after him.

Everyone is going to be here soon, so I'm running through the house, tidying up real quick. I walk from room to room checking the vases and the candles and the candy bowls. I enter the kitchen to find Adrian and Paris making his favorite Buffalo Chicken Dip.

I smile at them. They make a pretty picture. I slide my phone out of my back pocket and snap one. They both roll their eyes at me. I'd probably taken a couple hundred pictures of them today. They'll get over it.

"I told you that I'd do that," I tell Adrian. "I want you to relax."

"I got it, babe. This is one of the only things I can make," he jokes.

Archer stomps through the kitchen, getting all of our attention on the way to the laundry room.

"What's going on with him?" Adrian asks.

"I told him to clean up his mess. Aren't I awful?"

He laughs and shakes his head. "Teenagers."

"I know, right? Archer, don't forget the mop," I call.

He reenters the kitchen about that time. "I got it. You don't have to yell. And I'm not five. I can remember to get the mop."

I can feel Adrian and Paris tense up from where I'm standing. This is not a side we've seen of my sweet little boy. Adrian says, "Archer, don't speak to your mother like that. It's disrespectful, and you're not a disrespectful person." *Good job*, I think. Firm yet respectful.

"I'm sorry, Mom. I just don't like it when you're redundant. I'm fully capable of cleaning a bathroom." I have to pinch my lips together to keep from grinning. Did I really encourage them in using elevated vocabulary and building sound arguments? *What was I thinking?*

"I accept your apology, Archer." I take his chin in my hand and tell him, "But that's twice today you've gotten in trouble for that smart mouth."

"Yes, ma'am," he says with a blush.

I let him go on his way and turn back to Paris and Adrian. "Paris?"

"Yeah, Ma?"

"Do me a favor. Stay ten, please."

"ADRIAN'S QUIET," BONNIE says.

"He's always quieter than the other guys," I reply.

Looking over at him, I think to myself that even though he's usually quiet he never has that distant look in his eyes that he has now. He's always present for people.

"Yeah," she says, "but he's quieter than usual."

He *is* quieter than usual. "He's probably just exhausted. I can't imagine being in the situation he was in for the last six months. He told me last night that at one point they'd had to sleep on the ground for six weeks. Six weeks. And that's when he was able to sleep. Sometimes he went two days without sleep. And all that while eating one or maybe two MREs a day." I tear up again as I think about how hard things were for him and his brothers.

Bonnie shakes her head. "Geez, that's insane."

"It makes me want to do something, but I don't know what. I feel helpless."

We gather in my huge sunroom so that we can accommodate everyone in order to give thanks and get dinner started. Adrian pulls me in front of him to lean me back on his chest. "I'd appreciate it if you didn't leave my side again."

Looking into those eyes, I see murky depths that trouble me. Putting my hand on his jaw, I ask, "Are you OK, baby?" He lets out a long breath and nods. I pull him to me and give him a soft kiss. "Are you ready to get rid of everyone?" He just nods again and I grin.

Louis gets everyone's attention and makes a little speech about duty and service and how proud we are of Adrian. I can feel Adrian cringing under me with every word until I finally look back at him. He's clearly uncomfortable. I grab his hand and squeeze it.

We move to start dinner and Garner stands up, which instantly makes me nervous. I've heard his rousing speeches before and there are children present. "Garner keep it G rated," I joke.

He has the grace to hang his head a little and give a nervous laugh before popping back up and raising his drink to Adrian. "Dude, I've never been happier to have someone home from war. I know it's tough listening to us talk about your bravery and honor, but just know that what you do, what you did, protects everyone and everything that we love. And I don't know about you, but I'm ready to get back to making music. I'd much rather make the world go around that way, wouldn't you, bro?" Adrian nods and grins at him. "Oorah!"

All the Marines say, "Oorah!" My future Marines aren't left out either.

I HEAR LOTS of shuffling around and shushing and know that they're trying to surprise me. It brings an instant smile to my face, and even though I'm exhausted, I drag myself out of bed to join them.

Entering the kitchen, I take in my men. They have an assembly line set up for making French toast. How adorable. I ruffle their heads as I pass them. "Hey guys," I mumble as I walk straight into Adrian's arms and burrow. What a fabulous way to wakeup.

"Babe, you were supposed to be sleeping in. The boys and I were going to surprise you."

I laugh and look up at him. He looks better today. More rested, refreshed. "I'm still surprised, Adrian," I say, planting a kiss on his chest. "You made coffee?"

"Of course. Go sit down. I'll make you a cup."

"Thank you."

Sitting at the kitchen table, I pull out my organizer and start checking off the details for the official blessing of our marriage. Adrian puts a cup of coffee in front of me, so I look up to tell him thank you but catch him frowning a little. "What's wrong?" I ask instead.

"It's going to be small, right?"

I tilt my head. "Yes, just our close friends and whatever family approves and a small reception here at the house. We still have two weeks before all that, though. Is that OK?"

"Yeah, that's fine."

"OK," I murmur as he walks away.

"All right, boys, make sure you get it coated real good on both sides with the egg mixture."

"Like this, Pops?" Paris asks.

"Yep, that looks perfect."

I hear a little crash and the sure sound of a spill and look up to see Finn's face crumple. Oh no, poor baby.

"I'm sorry," Finn cries.

Adrian starts toward him to help him out, "Dude, it's—"

"God, Finn, you're so stupid!" Archer says and rolls his eyes.

I open my mouth to get onto Archer. Before I can, Adrian snaps.

"Archer, everyone in this house is sick of your bad attitude and your smartass mouth," he growls. My eyes widen and I look at Archer, who looks like he's about to cry. I'm speechless. "You know what, why don't you just go to your room where no one will bother you? Cause I'm pretty sure we'd all like to eat in peace."

We all freeze for a moment. My home is not perfect by any means; however, we don't usually lose our tempers. The boys are certainly not used to me or even their dad, when he was alive, lashing out. Archer jerks out of his stupor first and slams his fork down and stomps away.

Adrian starts to follow him, but I jump up and say, "Adrian, how about you and me step outside for a second and cool down before we talk to Archer, OK?"

His gaze flies down to me and he says, "Did I do something wrong? Or are we gonna focus on that smart mouth that Archer's suddenly developed?"

"Oh, we're going to take care of that. I'd just like for us to be on the same page first," I say calmly.

He just walks around me and heads out to the porch.

"Paris help Finn clean up his mess, please. I'll be right back."

"Yes, ma'am."

I head out to the porch and find Adrian with his head down between his shoulders and his arms braced on the porch rail. I look out over the yard and see Mrs. Jones tending to her flowerbeds, so I give her a small wave. She's super nosey, so I'm glad I've noticed her.

Adrian hears me and turns around and folds his arms over his chest. Leaning back against the rail, he looks calmer. "I lost my temper."

"Yes, you did. I'm worried about you. Two years you've been helping me raise these boys and I've never seen you get angry with them. Frustrated? Yes. Angry? No."

"Cel, I'm so sorry. I'm sorry. I just...I don't know where that came from."

Taking pity on him, I cross over and wrap my arms around him, laying my head on his chest. "It's a little different now, going from being their cousin to their father. It's going to take some adjustments on all our parts. And really what you said to him was perfectly acceptable. I just take exception with how you said it is all."

"My dad used to cuss us out and overreact and I hated it. Used to cause me to walk around on eggshells. That's what I've always loved about being here. Everyone always feels so...comfortable. I fucked that right up."

I can't help but laugh. He sounds so pathetic. It's adorable. "Adrian, we're bound to have some growing pains. It was one incident. And Archer's been a little turd lately. We'll work it out. He had big plans to stay the night with Taylor this weekend. I'm saying that we take that away since he's usually so good and talk to him, of course. He's really only made his snide comments these last few days. Show him we mean business but don't go overboard. What do you think?"

"I think whatever you think. With this little smart butt exception, you've managed to raise some amazing kids. God, I hope Archer's not too mad at me," he says as he rubs his hands over his face.

I smile at him. "Thank you. Archer's an understanding young man, and he adores you. We'll work this out. I will say that I'm glad you're going out with the guys this weekend. You need to blow off some steam."

He leans and gives me a little kiss. "Thank you, babe. I love you. I'm sorry about that."

"I love you too. Let's go talk to Archer."

THE REST OF the week runs pretty smoothly. We're all in planning mode. The boys are planning for their spring vacation, and I'm planning our little reception, and Adrian's getting back into his music. We settle into a routine, and even though Adrian is quiet, he seems much better.

Tonight, it's boys' night out and girls' night in. Bonnie and Farah have come over and the guys have taken Adrian out. I'm pretty sure I heard "bar crawl" floating around.

The girls pop in *Bridget Jones's Diary* while I make margaritas.

The little boys play *Guitar Hero* in the back.

I start to pour a third and remember Farah doesn't always partake. "Farah, do you want a margarita, honey?"

"No, thanks," she calls casually, "I'm having a baby."

I slam down my margarita pitcher, sloshing margarita everywhere. *Whoops!* Rushing into the living room, I see Bonnie already all over her. I shake my head at her. "Thanks, what a way to tell me." I join in on the hugging and the tears and the talking to the baby who's probably the size of a pea right now.

Two down, one to go. Farah and I were both on top of the world. Now we just needed to get Bonnie there.

-Twenty-Three-

Protect At All Costs

MY PHONE WAKES me up from a dead sleep. Margaritas have that brain-numbing effect. Grabbing for my phone, I simultaneously put my glasses on and blink at the time and the caller before answering. "Louis? It's three o'clock in the morning." Looking over my shoulder, I register no Adrian.

"Cel, don't freak out, OK?"

"Now I'm freaking out," I say. "What's going on?"

He blows out a deep breath. "Adrian's been arrested and is being held for twenty-four hours. But he's OK."

"What was he arrested for?" Other than a noise violation, I don't think he's ever been in trouble with the law before and that was back in college.

Another deep breath released. "Public intoxication, public disturbance, simple assault and destruction of city property."

"Excuse me? Adrian doesn't get drunk."

"I know. I was pretty surprised myself. I would have told him to lay off, but it happened pretty quickly and probably because he doesn't drink very often."

"What happened?" I want to cry. I don't understand this at all. I know it's not the end of the world, but this isn't like him at all.

"We were at a club and some guy got violent with his girlfriend. Adrian intervened. The guy got mouthy with him, got in his face. Adrian warned him. Guy didn't stop. Adrian punched him. Once. That's all it took."

"Oh my God. What about the other stuff?"

"Well, that's where it got bad. The one punch we probably could've gotten him out of pretty easily, but when the cops got there, Adrian got pissed off because they were jackasses. So he started throwing some insults. They, uh, arrested him. Once they had him in the back of the cop car, the arresting officer kept being an asshole. Just taunting him, you know?"

"And?"

"Adrian kicked out the back window of their car."

I gasp. "What? Like the side window? Don't those usually have a cage on them?"

"Not the side window. The big back window. And, yes, there was a cage. That didn't seem to matter to your pissed off Marine."

"Louis, that's just not like him at all. He's been acting strange since he got back. Quiet, moody, and he was even short-tempered. I mean, he's an intense guy, yes. But this is different."

"Yep, I noticed something off as well. I just chalked it up to stress and exhaustion."

I run my hand through my hair, offering up a silent prayer on how to help my husband. "When can I pick him up? Do I have to bail him out or what?"

"Umm...he told me that I'm to pick him up. He doesn't want you involved."

"He doesn't want me involved?" I squeak out disbelievingly.

"Yeah, Cel, I think he's ashamed and doesn't want to hurt you."

I wipe at my eyes. The tears that are flowing cannot be stopped. My husband is hurting and doesn't want my help. "He's my husband. He hurts. I hurt," I whisper.

"I know, baby girl. Look, I'm going to get him tomorrow morning, take him to his apartment—"

"Don't you take him to his apartment, Louis. Bring him home to me."

"He asked that I bring him to his apartment. He said he's no good for anyone right now."

SITTING ON ADRIAN'S couch, all I can do is replay those words, "He said he's no good for anyone right now." And every time I do, I just want to cry.

I've been waiting here for over an hour. I'd looked around and noticed lots of pictures of the boys stuck here and there. I found his programs for the boys' events on his coffee table. All signs of a wonderfully supportive person who needed me right now, but it sounds like I might have a fight on my hands. I know that Hebert pride, and it was a force to be reckoned with. I've got news for him, though, I'm an Hebert too.

When I hear the key turn in the lock, my stomach turns right along with it. I'm a ball of nerves. I take a deep, calming breath and prepare myself. I tell myself to remain calm no matter what he throws at me.

His eyes find mine right away—despair, anguish, fear. I tear up again. "Hi, baby."

"Celeste, what are you doing here, babe? I told Louis to tell you just to give me some time." The jacket that he's holding has all his attention.

I swallow hard. He's calm. I'd gotten a "babe." The message is still clear, though. Stay away. "Adrian, that's not the way it works." He sinks down onto the chair opposite me but doesn't stop staring at his jacket. "You're my husband. It's my place to help you. Hell, it's my desire to help you. Something's going on. Is it this instant family you have?" His eyes finally fly up to meet mine. "Do you feel overwhelmed by us?"

"God, no. That's not it. Celeste, y'all are the best thing that's ever happened to me."

"Then what is it, Adrian? I can't help if you don't tell me what's going on. You didn't hide your feelings from me when we were just friends, and now's not the time to start."

He drapes his jacket over his chair and runs his hands over his face and over his head. "Do you want something to drink?"

"No, I'm good."

Getting up, he goes into the kitchen and I watch as he makes himself a glass of ice water. It's a struggle not to pounce on him and drag this out of him and figure out how to help him. He drinks it and then pours another damn glass and drinks it. Finally, he sets the glass down and comes back into the living room.

"Sorry. I was extremely thirsty."

"I bet. I heard you had a lot to drink last night. You're probably dehydrated."

"Do you mind if I take a shower?"

I shake my head no. I'm afraid if I try to speak that I'll cry. He's acting so cold, so distant, and so unlike my Adrian. He gives me a little smile and heads off to the bathroom.

Kicking my shoes off, I get up from the couch and go to the bathroom once I hear the water running. I crack the door and stand there watching him. He's so beautiful but looks so...pained. If this had been any other day, I'd pull my clothes off and climb in with him as quickly as I could. But this is not any other day. I'm afraid if I do, he'd push me away and that would crush me.

I ease back out and go out to the kitchen, take out the leftovers from last night's dinner that I'd brought with me, and heat them up for him. I'm sure he's starved. I'm placing it on the bar as he rounds the corner.

"You didn't need to do that," he tells me.

"I know, but I'm sure you're hungry."

He settles at the bar. "I am."

Before he can get started, I feel myself being propelled around the bar to pull his face to mine. "I love you, Adrian," I whisper fiercely. "Whatever you are going through, I can help you. We can work it out together." I kiss him, long and chaste. He's not there. *He's not there!* I sob and pull back. "You have to tell me what's going on. You can't pull away from me like this. I can't...I can't take it. You're breaking my heart," I say, my voice cracking.

He wraps his arms around me and buries his head on my chest, weeping. *No!* "Celeste, I don't want to hurt you. I'm not trying to hurt you. I'm trying my damnedest not to hurt you. But I'm...I need space and time. I'm not safe enough for y'all to be around right now."

"Adrian, what does that even mean? I don't understand."

Another sob. I run my hands over his head and down his neck, shushing him as I go. Leaning down, I kiss him over and over. I wish that my kisses held healing power and with each one, every sadness, every insecurity, every pain of his would dissipate, leaving behind the strong, compassionate man I'd come to know and love and cherish.

Finally, he pulls back. I run my thumbs over his tears and lean down and kiss them away. "I'm going to be staying here for a while." I shake my head at him. "Yes, Celeste, I don't trust myself right now. I have all these thoughts going through my head, uncontrollable but controlling thoughts. I don't even know how to explain them to you except to say that I don't feel...stable. I feel on edge all the time. You don't need someone like me around the boys right now. I need you to be smarter than that."

"We need you. We always need you. You make us whole. Do you understand me? Whatever you're feeling or going through we can figure out together, not apart!"

He stands up abruptly causing my hands to fall to my sides.

Pacing back and forth, he says, "I don't understand why the fuck you can't go and leave me to myself. I've been very patient. But I'm about to lose it, Celeste. I need you to go."

"No, you need me to stay and help you figure this out, Adrian." He's on me in a second, bracing both his arms on the bar behind me and pinning me in.

"I'm fucking broken," he punches out. "Do you have any idea what that means?" I shake my head because I don't. I don't understand. "It means that when I look at you, I see blood and carnage and blank stares of women who've been raped and mutilated and killed." I whimper. "Yeah, Celeste, pretty sick, huh? This is why I asked you to leave. But you want to talk, you want to listen, right? So listen to this. When I look at your boys, I see empty pits of despair and destruction. Do you understand now?" He's barely an inch from my face, his face is crumpled like he's in pain. Snatching my hand up, he taps the side of his head with it and tells me, "I'm not the same, but I don't know what to do to fix it. The only thing I know to do is stay away from you and your children."

"Adrian—"

"Leave, Celeste," he roars at me. I duck from under his arm and grab my purse and shoes. My sobbing and his heavy breathing are the only sounds I hear. All I can think is that I'm making this worse.

Heading for the door, I open my mouth to tell him I love him and I'll see him soon. I'm not going away for long, but I'm afraid of what he'll tell me in response. Pinching my lips together, I fight that instinct and close the door behind me.

"AND HE SAID that he has uncontrollable thoughts and he's been having flashbacks of the things he saw over there?"

I adjust the phone on my shoulder and click around some more on my laptop. "Yes, I came home and looked it up on the Department of Veteran Affairs website. He has Post-Traumatic Stress Disorder, Louis. I just know it."

"Doesn't that usually develop over time, though? Like months or years later?"

"No, it says here that every case is different. He's displaying most of the symptoms. I didn't realize that this week, but looking back, I definitely see them. He wasn't sleeping right, he was quick-tempered, withdrawn, quiet, not eating right, the drinking. Add to that last night's episode. I mean, what other proof do we need?"

"Well, what did it say to do about it?"

"He needs therapy and probably some kind of anti-psychotic or anti-depressant. But, I know Adrian; he's not going to take any medicine. It's a stretch to think he'll talk to someone. He's proud and stubborn and..." I break off in a sob.

"Shh, Celeste. We're gonna get him some help, OK?"

"OK. I think I'm going to let him rest tonight and go see him first thing in the morning. He hasn't slept, and I know that's not helping matters. Lack of sleep doesn't help with clear thinking. He's been texting me back since I left, so he's safe for now."

"Do you want me to go over there when I leave work?"

"Would you, please?"

"Of course, I'll call you and let you know how he is."

"Thank you, Louis."

LAST NIGHT WAS the longest night of my life. All those nights of staying up and watching Tripp slowly slip from this world had been the worst experience of my life. Not anymore. Not knowing whether or not Adrian would harm himself—definitely the worst feeling ever. I don't think for a second he'd harm himself intentionally. That's not it. I'd worried that he would go out, trouble would ensue, and then a hundred different scenarios play out from there. Louis had gone over with dinner and hung out with him, so I know he was safe for a good part of the evening. Louis said he'd acted like nothing out of the ordinary was going on. That he'd just been quiet, not apologetic or ashamed. Just quiet.

After dropping the boys off at school, I head over to Adrian's with some breakfast and coffee. I'm terrified of what I'm going to find. I know Adrian would never hurt me. I know he would never hurt himself. I'm more afraid of not being able to help him and of him running me off again. I'd been texting him off and on, and he'd been polite enough. Polite. My passionate man was being polite.

I'd always known loving him was never going to be easy, and with my eyes wide open, I'd been prepared to face many battles to keep him for my own. But I never thought I'd have to fight my husband for his love. A crippling pain fills my soul as that realization sinks in. As if he can't stand to be loved back by me, he has taken his love from me and is pushing me away. He's punishing himself. And I know that's what has brought this on—guilt and penance. Taking a deep breath in and releasing it, I steel myself to fight for my man. When I knock on his door, my heart is in my throat.

As he opens the door, my breath leaves me in a swoosh because he just looks beautiful. I feel like we've been apart forever, not just one night, and he looks so good to me. "Hey, babe."

"Hi." He opens the door and steps back to let me in. I want to hug him and kiss him, but I'm afraid of pushing. I pushed yesterday and that was no good. I walk past him and state the obvious, "I got coffee and bagels."

"Thank you. That sounds good."

"May I have a kiss?" I ask when he turns back to me.

He gives me that half-smile. The one that doesn't make the skin around his eyes crinkle. I despise that smile. I miss my smile.

Walking over to me, he places the coffees and bagels on the counter, turns around, and takes me in his arms. "I'm sorry about yesterday, Celeste. Sorrier than you'll ever know. I don't know what came over me, which is the problem—I can't seem to get a grip."

I smooth his t-shirt down over his shoulders. "I forgive you, Adrian. I only want to help you. And you know that. I'll do whatever I can to help you, baby."

"I know that. Thank you," he says again before kissing me lightly. "I missed you."

"Oh…I missed you so much," I mutter against his lips before deepening the kiss. He moans against my mouth, and I know that we need to stop and handle this issue, but I want him. I can't help but want him. Finally, I have the strength to pull back.

"Let's eat a little."

He just nods. Taking him by the hand, I lead him over to the couch and tell him to wait there while I get his breakfast.

While I get everything ready I watch him as he stares off into space. He doesn't attempt to make conversation or turn on the TV or anything. He just sits—still and blank.

We eat breakfast and I talk of light-hearted matters. He laughs in the right places, smiles when he should, and comments when necessary. All of it without one shred of real interest. We've slowly gravitated toward each other, and he lets me hold him.

A couple of hours pass this way, talking and sharing, until he finally dozes off in my arms. I look down at his long eyelashes resting on his cheekbones and those full lips. He looks so stunning lying here. Just like the man I sent to war, but I know that he's not that man anymore. Something fundamental about him has changed. It scares me so badly. After a while, I relax and doze off with him.

I can feel him staring at me, so I force my tired lids open. "Hey," I whisper. "Did you get some sleep?"

"Yeah, I did actually. Thank you for staying with me."

Oh great. We're back to polite Adrian. "Adrian, stop thanking me for everything. You're my husband. That's not going to change."

"I don't know, Celeste, I—"

I sit up quickly, swinging my legs around in front of me. "What do you mean you don't know? We're husband and wife. That's not changing." He shakes his head at me. "That's not changing," I repeat. "I've done some research, Adrian."

"Don't give me that PTSD crap, Cel."

"That's what's going on, baby. You've shown most of the signs." I list them for him. "All you need is to talk to someone about what happened over there, what has you so...overwhelmed. The doctors can help too with a little bit of medication."

He flies up from the couch and goes into the kitchen to grab a bottle of water and drains it before settling against the counter. "I'm not going to see any doctors and I'm not going to talk to anyone. I just need a little time and space. Two things you're not prepared to give me apparently," he says coldly. So cold.

"I would give you those things if I thought that would work, Adrian. I've read—"

"You've read," he sneers at me. He takes a deep breath. "You have no idea what you're talking about. I'd really like you to leave now," he says with no feeling.

"You'd really like me to leave now," I repeat flatly. Getting up, I move into the kitchen with him and wrap my arms around him. "I'm not leaving. You ran me off yesterday. I allowed that. I gave you some space. I'm not leaving today. I can help you get help."

"I just...I don't know what you want from me. There's nothing wrong that a little time and space won't help, and I'm pretty sure I've asked you for that."

"I'm pretty sure that I want my husband back. Not this machine," I say as I point at his chest, "or that ticking time bomb from yesterday. I want the man who grabs me and kisses the life out of me and then kisses it right back into me. I want the man who tells me what he is thinking, what he is feeling no matter the consequences. I want the man who loves me, who is willing to fight for me no matter what."

Grabbing my hair, he fists it in one hand and pulls my head back before he slams his mouth down on mine. I cry out but hang on. I've gotten a reaction, and it's not an entirely unpleasant one. He backs me into the wall and ravages me. "Is this what you want, Celeste?" he grinds out against my mouth. I can only groan my agreement as I reach up and force his mouth back to mine.

He pushes my skirt up with one hand and grabs at my underwear with the other. I hear ripping and can't help but be turned on by his enthusiasm. I hear his zipper and then he's inside me, grinding and pumping. "Put your legs around me," he demands. I comply.

Pulling my head back, I open my eyes to meet his but they're closed. "Give me my blues, Adrian," I whisper.

Instead he buries his head in the crook of my neck and drives into me even harder. I gasp at the pleasurably painful assault on my body. He shifts and buries himself in me so deeply that I cry out. Finally, his movements still but he is trembling.

He slips out of me and those blues finally meet mine. Steely. His eyes don't leave mine as he rights my clothes. "You got what you came for, Celeste? That's what you wanted. A piece of me, right? Everyone wants a piece of me. I hope you enjoyed it. And I hope it was enough to last you a lifetime." *What?* Tossing my underwear in the trashcan on his way out of the room, he barks, "Now, get out."

WALKING OUT HIS apartment is probably the hardest thing I've ever done . I stumble down to my car and know that there's no way I can drive. I pop open my hatchback and trade my shoes for my runners. Then I start the short walk to my house. When I get home, my breathing has returned to normal and some thoughts start registering. But before I can allow that, I need to get the boys squared away.

Taking my cell out, I dial Bonnie. "Hey, girl," she says.

"Hey, Bon. Can you do me a big favor and pick up the boys from school today? You can bring them back here if you don't mind and hang out with them."

"Cel, you know I will, but you sound terrible. What's going on?"

"It's Adrian. It's bad. I've got to help him," I say with a sob. "Can you help me with the boys while I take care of him?"

"Of course. They're off school tomorrow. I'll pick them up and we'll have fun and I can stay with them until whenever, sound good?"

"Yes, thank you. And let's keep this between you and me. He doesn't want anyone to know what's going on."

"Yeah, I won't say anything. But do you have help?"

"Yes, Louis is helping me with him. I don't mean to be rude, but I need to go take a shower and get a game plan together."

"Love you, girl."

"Love you too, Bon. Thank you."

I go into my room and kick off my shoes and pull my skirt and top off, thinking I'd like to burn that whole outfit. Stepping into the shower, I take time to wash my hair thoroughly and soap up my body to the point of ridiculousness. All this time, I hum a song, trying to keep my head clear.

Turning the shower off, I hop out and put on some fresh clothes and wrap my hair in a towel. I go into the kitchen and make a glass of tea and head out to my porch swing.

I feel my whole body relax into it before I allow myself to start contemplating exactly what had gone down between us. I'd given consent to him screwing my brains out and I'd enjoyed it, but when he pulled back and said those things to me and dismissed me, I'd never felt more used in my life. Like trash. He'd made me feel like utter and complete trash. A cut so deep, I don't have any idea how to staunch the blood.

Tears fill my vision as I consider what this means for us. Is this something I can get over? Being used and discarded like that. The way I'm feeling right now is a billion times worse than William ever made me feel. Is it because Adrian is essentially a good person and to have him treat me that way hurts that much more?

I'm losing my husband. I'm losing the love of my life. He's pushing me away with everything he's got and doing a damn fine job of it because for the life of me I can't imagine ever getting past what just happened.

Looking for comfort, my eyes search out my wisteria that's in full bloom. I take in the vines that cover the little sitting area in my front yard. Was it just four mornings ago that Adrian and I had sat out there and had coffee and smelled the fragrant flowers that I love so much? I curled up next to him and we'd watched the boys play in the sprinklers because that's how hot it was already in New Orleans. It was a gorgeous spring day that felt like a new beginning for my sweet family and me. Like the wisteria itself, the peace that I'd finally thought was mine was short-lived. A magnificent, wondrous thing that lasted a mere blink in time.

Before I can really consider what I'm doing, I'm across the yard, glaring at the wisteria. I reach up and start tugging and clawing at it. When I get enough petals in my hand, I crush them and throw them on the ground. The pungent, sickly smell incites me further until I've tugged and clawed and crushed almost all the petals from around the latticework. Exhausted, I let myself fall on my knees and I rock and I weep until a voice breaks into my little tantrum.

From across the fence, I hear my nosey neighbor, Mrs. Jones, as her words cut through my sobs. "Celeste, dear, what on earth did the flowers ever do to you?"

I can't help but laugh. She's right. I'm being ridiculous. I wipe my tears away and seek her out. "Mrs. Jones, those flowers had it coming."

She laughs back at me. "Did they now?"

Dusting myself off, I pick myself up from the ground and move over to the fence, snatching up the towel that had fallen off along the way. Looking at my hands, I see the purple stains and smell that magnified sweet smell that's making my stomach turn. I scrub at them a little with the towel. "Yes, ma'am. Those flowers were way too tempting. They bloom so quickly and smell so wonderful. They lure you in, insinuate themselves into your life, and then, in the blink of an eye, they're gone. And, of course, they're the most beautiful thing you've ever seen, but they just don't last."

She snickers at me. "You just gotta enjoy 'em while they're here. Appreciate them for what they are."

"True, but I think I'd rather crush them out than have them disappear on me."

She grins at me. "Does this have anything to with Adrian?"

I just nod.

"Ah, that's a good man—that one. I've never seen someone love another man's children like that. Always spending time with them. You can tell, too, the way he watches 'em. You know, a lot of folks act one way when people are watching and another when they think no one's looking. Not your Adrian. He looks at those boys like they're his entire world." I swallow hard and nod. That's not the issue. "That was until you and him got together, and finally, might I add. Now he openly includes you in that look too. Girl, you really held out there." I can't help but laugh at that. I sure did. "I'm impressed with your strength."

I squint through the bright sun at her and level with her. "I don't think I'm that strong, Mrs. Jones. I've never felt more scared or more compelled to give in and bury my head in the sand than I do right now. Adrian and I are having some…problems."

She nods at me. "Strength isn't the ability to feel strong, Celeste. It's the ability to overcome weakness. You may feel all sorts of ways, but that's not going to stop you from doing what needs be done."

Looking down, I scrub at my hands for a moment as I consider her words. No matter how hurt I am by Adrian, I love him and I'll do anything to help him. When I look back up at her, I smile big. I'm extremely grateful for her nosey nature in this moment. "You're right, Mrs. Jones. Thank you."

"Why are you still standing here, honey? Go show your man how strong you are."

"Yes, ma'am."

-Twenty-Four-

Merde

SHOOTING ANOTHER TEXT to Adrian while I'm in the elevator, I let him know that I'm going to be heading his way soon. Walking into Hebert and Hebert, I feel like a different person than I was all those months ago when I'd been summoned here. Back then I was just trying to weather the state of being in this family. Now, I wanted nothing more than what they could offer me, or more aptly, offer Adrian. Gladys's head flies up when she hears my angry heels clicking away on the floor. She gives me a smile before she takes in my look and then she frowns.

"Celeste, dear, everything all right?"

"No, ma'am. Where's my father?"

"He and the rest of the board are in the conference room. They'll be done shortly, I believe."

"Oh, no, that's actually perfect. I really need to see everyone. No need to announce me."

She gives me a knowing look over the top of her glasses. "You're sure about that, hon?"

I stand up straighter and strengthen my spine. "Oh, yes, quite sure."

She grins at me. "Well, go get 'em then."

Opening the door to the conference room, I cringe a bit when I see all these scary powerful men. My father looks up first. His look quickly turns from curious to astonished. He has no idea.

"Good afternoon, gentleman," I say, getting all their attention now.

Chip speaks first. "Celeste, what on earth are you doing here? We're in a meeting."

"I have something that trumps your little meeting, and if you cooperate, it won't take long. We have a family member in trouble and I need your help. I've never asked a single one of you for anything. With the exception of Louis," I say to him with a wink. He smiles back and stands up to regard me thoughtfully.

Chip opens his mouth to speak again, but I put my hand up and say, "Chip, like I've already said, this won't take long, but I will need you to hold on and hear me out. Adrian has come back from war as you all well know even though you couldn't be bothered to give a shit. I'm asking you to give a shit now. He's not doing well. He's not coping with what he experienced over there. I'm worried about him. He's drinking and pushing everyone he loves away. He needs and deserves our help. He's not going to go about this traditional route, but I know that you have ways around all that. I need you to put me in touch with a psychiatrist and a psychologist. He's going to need quiet, personalized care and all of our support. And you're going to get it and give it to him."

"Now, hold on here, little lady," Chip says with a finger pointed in my direction. "No one in this room owes Adrian a damn thing. That boy has gone and gotten himself into a heap of trouble and all on his own. The way I see it, you need to cut your losses." He shakes his finger at me. " I tried to tell you little girl. Like father, like son. Now that you've had your fun, it's time to move on."

I take a deep breath to avoid losing my temper completely. A tantrum will get me nowhere with these men. "Adrian is the *best* man I've ever know, and I can't cut my losses because he is more than just a good time, Chip. He's my husband, and we need your help." I look from face to face and see their shock register. "You heard me right. We married before he left for Iraq. I love him that much. I love him so much that I would defy all of you and the consequences be damned. Now are you going to help me do what is right for my husband, *your* family, without a fuss, or are we going to have do to this the hard way?" Silence. They just stare at me. Some with open looks of hostility. Some with shock. My father looks like he feels sorry for me.

Louis finally breaks the silence. He just doesn't do it the way I expect. Clearing his throat, he says, "I'm gay."

I can't help my sudden intake of breath and the instant smile that forms on my face. A laugh escapes me as I watch them all turn their looks of astonishment from me to Louis.

My father spits and sputters a little before he's finally able to ask, "What do you mean you're gay?"

"I'm attracted to men not women. I've been in relationships with men," he continues to explain as my father continues to look confused. "It means I'm a homosexual." He looks away from my father and locks eyes with me and grins. "I'm sorry, Cel. I didn't mean to steal your thunder, but I'm just so damned proud of you for sticking up for yourself and your feelings and for standing by Adrian. I was inspired." I just smile. I'm so proud of him.

"Now, son, how do you know you're attracted to men?" my father persists.

Louis chuckles and winks at our father. "Trust me, I just know. It's one of those things when you know, you know. Anyway, I told you that because you need to understand something. We," he points at me and then back at himself, "are done being pulled around like puppets. We're not perfect. We may not be what you envisioned, what you'd hoped for, but we are good people. We deserve your love, your support, and your respect. And we're going to start getting it. The one who needs us the most right now, though, is Adrian. He's in a bad place. A real bad place."

Louis pauses, grabs his neck, and looks up at the ceiling for a minute. Looking back at us, he takes us all in. "I promised him I wouldn't say anything, but you need to know what we're dealing with here. He told me where he was, which battle he was in. He didn't say too much about it other than it was bad—the worst kind of bad I could possibly imagine, but I went home and did a little research." He pauses again and looks at me with remorse in his eyes. "It was the place we'd all heard about. The one that's under investigation for war crimes because of the number of civilian casualties and the number of unethical tactics both sides are being accused of implementing. It's being called the bloodiest battle the U.S. has seen since Vietnam." I gasp. I had no idea. I'd heard of this, of course. But Adrian would never tell me where he was. He wasn't allowed to divulge his whereabouts while he was there, and he wouldn't say when he came home.

My father-in-law finally speaks up again. "You know, he has his own father and they've always done quite fine without us. I suggest you go and petition him for help. We're staying out of this mess."

My father tries to speak up, but I beat him to the punch. I'm done standing around trying to make them see reason. I've got to get back to Adrian.

"No, you're not staying out of it," I say, ice in my voice and in my veins. "And here's why. I gave you the opportunity to step up and help of your own accord." I smile a knowing smile. "I want you to remember that. Now you're going to help because you have to." Leveling my eyes at Chip, since he seems to be my main opposition. "Chip, Daddy, you'll be disappointed to hear that Tripp did not trust either of you to do right by me, and he left some information for me to use if you tried to hurt me or my children." I pause and bask in every second of watching Chip's face fall and rendering him speechless. "Several months ago I was approached and given some information that will bring you *both*," I emphasize and glance between them, "to your knees. And you both know what I'm referring to.

Now there are copies of this with the investigator who gave it to me and in various locations. If either of you try to acquire this information, I will release it as soon as possible. And if I'm not able, there are certain people who will release it on my behalf. Is that understood?" The look that passes between them is priceless. "Everything you've worked for gone and all because you couldn't treat your daughter and the people you are supposed to love with a little human decency. Your squabble with us over things that don't even concern you like who we love will be your downfall. It's not worth it.

"Are we on the same page now?" They just nod. "I don't want a damn thing from you other than for you to back off and leave me and my family in peace and to get me the help Adrian needs. Oh, and I want Adrian's arrest record cleared. Are we all in agreement?" They nod. "Great. Here's what I need…"

"HOLY SHIT, CEL. Am I proud of you! The way you stood up to them. Geez, baby girl. I didn't know you had it in you."

"Me either," I agree with a deep sigh. "I'm afraid that was the easy part, though. Getting Adrian to agree to my plan is going to be the difficult part." I check my phone, but he's not messaged me back.

"Yeah, you're right about that," he says as we step out of the elevator. "What do you have on them anyway?"

My burst of laughter bounces around the parking garage. My sense of humor gets more like Adrian's everyday. Leaning over the top of my car, I admit, "Nothing. I don't have a damn thing on them." His jaw drops. "I was bluffing. I do know someone who has something on them, but I don't actually have it. I can get it if I need it."

"Damn, girl. Remind me never to cross you. That whole room was scared of you. They had no idea."

Putting my car in gear, I turn to him before we take off. "You know I'm proud of you, right?" He just grins. "I'll do whatever I can to support you. I love you, Lou."

"I love you too, Cel."

"By the way, I've known for a long time you're gay. I've tried to discuss it with you several times over the years, but you always seemed so uncomfortable. I wanted you to do it on your own terms and when you were ready. So you may have had them fooled, but I've always known."

He gives me a confounded look. "I can't believe you knew. And how is that exactly? I've been very quiet about it."

I tilt my head and smile. "I don't know. It's one of those things when you know, you know," I say with a laugh.

USING MY KEY, I open Adrian's door a crack and peer in a bit, which is why I don't see *them* right away. Louis and I enter all the way and that's when I spot them. I take a deep breath. My insides burn. I hear Louis curse softly under his breath and ask if I want to leave. I feel his arm on my elbow and a light tug. Shaking him off, I move to stand behind the couch, and I can barely see through the angry tears in my eyes. I dash them away before I speak. Oh my God is it hard to speak. Speaking will turn this into my reality, and I don't know that I can handle it. I take in and then release a deep breath.

Using my key, I tap her on the shoulder. She looks up at me, surprised. "Get your ass up," I demand.

"What the hell are you doing here?" she asks sleepily. "Adrian said you were over."

I chuckle. "Did he now? Well, he's mistaken. Now, get your ass up."

The doppelgänger has the nerve to nudge Adrian and say, "Baby, do you want me to leave?"

Adrian's eyes open and he looks from her and up to me. "Shit, Celeste."

That's it. That's all I get? *Shit, Celeste?* Something's rotten in the city of New Orleans.

She sits up and smoothes her clothes down a bit. "I think I'll wait for Adrian to tell me to leave if you don't mind, Celeste," she says as she runs a hand down his chest and fists her hand in his t-shirt. When his hand comes up to clench hers, a fiery rage explodes in my chest. But she doesn't clue in and keeps talking. "Especially since he was so sweet when he invited me over."

I lean in and say with deadly calm. "Bitch. Get. The. Fuck. Out."

"Celeste!" Adrian admonishes.

Louis makes his way around the couch, grabs her by the arm, and begins to usher her out. "That's enough. Let's go. You don't want any part of this."

"Adrian, call me if you need me, honey," she rushes out before Louis has her out the door.

My eyes have never left his. He just looks blank, completely void of all feeling. Finally, he releases a deep breath and sits up. "I guess you should have called first," he says. "I told you we were done."

Knife to the heart, but somehow I maintain my composure, and I surprise him by smiling at him even though right now I'd love nothing more than to kick his ass. "Why, Adrian, we've only just begun," I say sweetly.

"What's that supposed to mean?" he asks.

Laughing, I grab his hand and lead him to the bathroom. He's looking at me like I've lost my damn mind. Maybe I have. "Take a shower. Clear your head. We'll talk when you get out."

He just shuffles past me and gives me a worried frown. *Mmm hmm, your little plan backfired.*

Making my way back to the living room, I close my eyes and collapse into the wall. Oh, my heart hurts so bad. I massage it a little and look up and say another prayer. I hear Louis come back in, and I look over at him.

"What did she say?" I ask.

"I can't believe you're not flipping out, Celeste. What the hell was he thinking?" He shakes his head at me. I know what he was thinking and that is the only thing that is keeping me from losing my fucking mind right now. I just raise my eyebrows at him. "She said that Adrian called her and asked her if she could come sit with him for a while. He told her that y'all were over, but that you wouldn't take the hint. Told her that nothing was going to happen between them, but that he would appreciate it as a friend. She said she's actually seeing someone and it's pretty serious, but that Adrian had always been good to her. She wanted to help him out. I told her that he's not doing well with being back home from Iraq." He lets out a deep breath. "She said she felt like something was off but didn't really understand. And to tell you that nothing happened between them. He asked her to lie down on the couch with him and that was that." That was enough, I think. "She also told me to tell you she was sorry."

I just nod at all that since I had pretty much figured all that out. I hear Adrian's shower cut off. "I need to see about him, and I'm not sure how much more fight he has left in him. He warned me, Louis." Louis gives me a questioning look. "He told me he would do anything to protect me, and that's what that was. He's trying anything and everything to push me away in order to protect me." Louis grabs me and kisses me on my forehead. I shake my head against his. "Thank you for finding all that out for me and for staying. It...helps. How long until the doctor will be here?"

He looks at his watch. "Thirty minutes."

"Here goes nothin'," I tell him.

Letting Louis go, I kick off my shoes and head down the hall toward his bedroom. He's pulling on his sweatpants. I close the door behind me, and he turns to me when it clicks.

"You're still here?" I swear I see a little relief mixed with his disbelief.

I actually laugh. He frowns. "Adrian, it's a good thing I'm smarter than you," I joke. Now he just raises those brows at me. "Mmm hmm, I know how much you love me and how you would do *anything* to protect me. Even if the threat is you. Even if you have to hurt me in the process. Not hurting me comes in second to protecting me, doesn't it?" No response. "You called her over here to make me angry in hopes that I would leave and never come back, didn't you?" I narrow my eyes and point at him. "And don't you dare lie to me."

He stares at me for a minute before collapsing on the floor beside his bed and leaning back against the footboard. "What's wrong with me that I could do that to you? How can you ever forgive me?" he asks through his hands that are covering his face. "Shit, Celeste, I practically assaulted you this morning and then I had another woman in my arms just now. Nothing happened between us. Nothing was going to happen. I wanted it to look that way so that you would leave me. Fuck! You should run and fast. I don't understand why you're not running."

"I know that. I knew it when I saw her even though watching you with her made me want to crawl out of my own skin. And I'm not going to lie to you, Adrian. The way you spoke to me after you took me in the kitchen…that hurt. It still hurts. You didn't assault me, though. I like it when you're rough," I joke. He barely cracks a smile, but it looks almost like a real smile. "It was what you said after. That's going to take me a while to get over."

"I'm sorry," he whispers.

I sink down in front of him and rub his jaw with one hand. "You're already forgiven."

He nods and grabs my hand, holding it to his face. "Don't leave me. I don't know what to do to fix this yet, but I know I can't live without you and our boys. I know that. I've been beyond stupid these last few days, but I want to fix me, fix us if you'll give me another chance."

"I'm not going anywhere, baby. I love you. And I know what we need to do." I pause before asking him to place his faith in me. I hope he remembers how many times I've trusted in him. "Do you trust me?" He nods and closes his eyes tight.

"THE BIGGEST THING," Adrian says, "is that there can be no record of my treatment. If the government found out, I could never serve in a combat situation again. I don't want that stigma following me around either. I know I've already told you, but I can't stress it enough. That's, uh, why so many people don't get help." I don't know that I want him to serve ever again, but we'll cross that bridge when we get to it.

"All right, Mr. Hebert, I understand. How long's it been since you've slept?" Dr. Patel asks.

"Uh…I've been dozing off for twenty, thirty minute intervals for the last several days. I, uh, don't remember the last time I actually slept."

"More than a week, less than a week ago?"

"More than a week," Adrian says, "Less than two." Geez, I know what it feels like as a new mother to go without sleep for a day or two. At one point, I'd actually wished I'd never had children. That's how crazy just a little sleep deprivation had made me. I run my hand over Adrian's back in silent support.

We'd been talking to the doctor for over an hour. It hadn't been easy, but Adrian told him how he'd been feeling and a few details of what he'd seen like what he'd screamed at me yesterday. He won't let me leave his side, so I'm praying this is a sign that he's done pushing me away. Dr. Patel had come up with a plan for getting him help, and privately. I want to weep with relief.

"Sleep is imperative in this situation. We can't move forward with anything until you've had it. The shot I'm going to give you will sedate you for quite some time, so I'll wait a few minutes and let you have a bite to eat before I administer it. Once I give it to you, you will want to be in a location prepared to sleep for a while, Mr. Hebert. Of course, you'll need to be monitored." I glance over at Louis.

"We're not going anywhere," Louis says. I smile at him.

Once we've gotten Adrian fed and in bed, Dr. Patel gives him some oral medicine to take. "This is a mild anti-psychotic. We'll start with that. I know you're not happy about the medication, but remember this is temporary but necessary for your speedy recovery."

"Yes, sir," Adrian mumbles. Dr. Patel gives him his shot and Louis sees him out with a promise that he'll be seeing us soon.

"Do you want me to stay in here with you?" I ask Adrian.

"Yes, please, baby. Don't leave me." His voice is dragging already.

I settle in with him, pulling the covers around us and placing little kisses on his head. He wraps me up so tight in his arms that I have a hard time breathing for a minute, but I don't care. I hear his breath begin to even out and his arms relax their hold.

When he speaks, it startles me. "Celeste, I'll spend the rest of my life trying to be deserving of your love. I can't even imagine the hell I've put you through these last few days, and the fact that you're willing to forgive me all that and stand by me...I'm blown away and humbled and in awe of you." He tilts his head back and captures me with my blues. "I'm ashamed that I doubted all of that. I'm sorry that my instincts weren't to trust in us but to push you away instead. God, how many times do I need to push you away before you'll finally go running? I swear that I'll never do that again. I'm glad you're strong enough for both us. Strong enough to see through my bullshit."

I kiss him lightly. "I believe in us, Adrian, and I knew that you'd do anything to protect me, even from yourself. It was hard to remind myself of that in the moment, but I knew if I could get through to you for a second and find a tiny crevice to force myself into that you'd let me in all the way."

He gives me a little kiss, but it is a weak one. He's starting to doze off.

Clutching his face in my hands, I tell him, "I love you, Adrian. Always. I'll never let you go. I'll never stop. You're mine." I kiss him hard even though he's barely with me. "And I protect what's mine."

-Twenty-Five-

Happy Anniversary

"MORNIN'," I HEAR him murmur against my breast. Instinctively, I arch into him.

I open one eye and look toward the window. "Adrian, it's barely light out. Why am I awake?"

"I want to make love to my sexy wife before our children are up and our crazy day begins," he says as he presses a little piece of plastic into my hand.

As his tongue tickles me, I laugh and angle the plastic so that I can read it. I grin. *Happy anniversary, wife.* "Happy anniversary, husband," I say.

"Today's going to be busy. I've got classes this morning and the kids to run around this afternoon and you've got your shoot, but this morning," he says with a nip that makes me moan, "you're all mine and tonight," he says with another nip that makes me groan, "you're all mine. Rock 'n' Roll, dancing, champagne, and hot sex on a school night. What do you say, *mimi*?" he asks as he devours my breast.

I grin big, knowing I'm about to rock his world myself. I grab his face and watch those blues focus on me. "I think that all sounds wonderful. I can't wait, but no champagne tonight."

"You love champagne."

"That's true," I hesitate for a moment before saying around my smile, "but it's not good for the baby."

He stills and I watch in utter fascination as hazy blues become alert blues. He sits up abruptly. "You're pregnant?" he asks.

"Yes, I'm only a few weeks."

"You're pregnant."

"Yes," I say with a laugh. "I'm pregnant," I repeat, hoping it will sink in this time.

"I thought you said it was a long shot."

I laugh again. Awestruck, he looks like a little boy on Christmas morning as he runs his hands over my belly. These little moments were happening with more and more frequency since our bad patch. Those first couple of months were by far the rockiest, but he'd worked so hard. The therapy sessions he'd had and that we'd had together were numberless, but one thing remained true—Adrian was committed to overcoming his demons. It wounded me that this beautiful, passionate man had been broken, but I was determined to help him put himself back together. I reach up and rub my hand over his scruff. This is the most excited and most animated I've seen in a long time. It helps my heart heal too.

We'd starting talking seriously about trying to have a baby a few months back. I'd been on birth control for so long that I determined that if we wanted to have a baby before I turned forty I should stop taking them immediately. I never dreamed I would get pregnant so quickly. Snapping out my trance, I say, "Well, apparently, our odds were better than I thought, or more likely you have very agile and determined swimmers."

He sits up further and howls with laughter before leaning back down and kissing me so gently that I fear I might break from the love that radiates from his lips to mine. "Celeste, I love you so much. You've made me a happy man."

He looks down my body and moves down to rest his head on my stomach. I run my hands through his wild hair and smile at him. "Hi there," he says. "Mommy and I can't wait to meet you, sweet pea." He glances up at me. "It's a girl. Her nickname's sweet pea. Got it?"

"I got it," I say with a smile.

He plants small kisses on my belly. "I love you, sweet pea." My heart melts. This man really knows how to bring me to my knees. "I can't believe it." He shakes his head in awe. "When do you want to tell the boys?"

"I'm thinking we might wait till I'm a little further along. I'm so old. I'm nervous that something could go wrong."

"Babe, you're thirty-eight. That's not old."

"In baby making years it is."

He smiles at me. "Our baby is going to be perfectly healthy. Right, sweet pea?" he asks my stomach before placing another kiss there. "You want to know how I know it's going to be a girl?"

"Yeah, how?"

He grabs both of my hands, kisses them, and puts them over his heart. "There has to be another woman like you in this world." I tear up immediately. "Kind, compassionate, generous, gracious, strong—"

"Stop," I whisper before I'm full on weeping.

"Brilliant, beautiful, sexy…wait, I don't know that I want our daughter to be sexy."

I giggle. "Don't forget she'll have some of your traits too—loyal, supportive, honorable, talented, determined, stubborn, bossy…"

"Hey," he says with a laugh.

"I hope she has these blues," I whisper as I rub his jaw.

"I hope she's the spitting image of you," he says kissing my palm. "I got you a little something, but it's not near as cool as what you just gave me."

"What's that?"

He doesn't answer me, he just pulls his shirt off and grins. My mouth drops.

I sit up and stare at the viney heart that covers his. It's beautiful —it starts at the bottom with my name in cursive and flows into a heart that ends with an infinity symbol resting next to my name. I reach out and trace it. It's almost completely healed.

"When did you get this?"

"Last week. You've been so pre-occupied. I can't believe you only asked me once why I was wearing a shirt to bed."

I laugh again. "That's because I'd suspected all week that I was pregnant, but I didn't want to tell you until I knew for sure. It was killing me." I trace the heart again. "Adrian, it's beautiful. I love it. Is that my handwriting?" I ask with a squeak.

"Yes, from one of your letters."

I laugh. "Oh, I guess it's a good thing I signed them more than 'wife' occasionally." I lean and place a little kiss in the center of the heart. His hand fits to the back of my head, holding me there for a moment. "I mean that much that you got me permanently etched on your body, huh?"

"Dumb question," he says with a kiss to my forehead. "You," he puts his hand on my belly, "and this family are the best thing that's ever happened to me. Every day when I wake up and when I lie down to go to sleep at night and about a billion times in between, I thank God for giving me y'all." He holds my face in his hands. "Mostly, I thank God for your stubborn nature and for the fact that you didn't give up on me."

I smile up at him, taking in those beautiful blues that give me my world. "You'll never be rid of me. You give me everything, Adrian, everything I've never had."

Epilogue

Adrian's Happily Ever After

"DADDY, YOU WANT dip it on 'em?" Hazel asks.

I throw my head back and laugh at my pretty girl, leaning down I plant a little kiss on her wavy black hair. "No, baby, even Daddy draws the line at putting ranch dressing on beignets."

"I thought Mommy didn't like beignets," Astrid says.

"Oh no, Mommy loves beignets. She just says that because she thinks they'll make her gain too much weight."

Hazel laughs along with me and says, "But today's Mommy's birthday, so she gets 'em."

"Yes, it is and we want her to feel extra special today. And we get to pick up your brothers today, so we've got a big day ahead of us." That gets some applause. "Astrid, hand Daddy that spatula."

Once I scoop up the fried dough and place it on the paper towels with the others, I unplug the fryer and grab the powdered sugar. I look at my girls sitting on the counter as they practically salivate over the donuts and smile at their eagerness. They can't wait to dig in. Passionate about food. I wonder who they got that from? "All right, who wants to help me put the sugar on them?"

"Me!" they shout in unison.

I look at them seriously. "Wait a minute...you girls sound the same and look the same and say the same things, so I couldn't tell which one of you really wants to help me."

"That's 'cause we're twins, Daddy," Astrid says and puffs out a little exasperated breath.

Hazel laughs with me. "Daddy's just kidding. He knows which is which. Right, Daddy?"

Scratching my jaw, I regard them carefully. I point at Astrid and say, "Hazel."

She folds her arms over her middle and gives me that pissed off girl look. "No, Daddy. I'm Astrid."

I laugh and kiss her on her forehead. "I know which one is which, sweetheart."

They help me shake the sugar over the French donuts, and then I help them down from the counter. They can barely contain their excitement. Putting the beignets on the tray with her coffee, I let the girls lead the way to our bedroom and open the door.

"Good morning, Mommy," they say again in unison. That never fails to amaze me. I slide the tray on her nightstand and take her in. Her black hair falls in soft waves around her shoulders. I watch as her dark brown eyes smile at our girls and then at me.

"Good morning, girls," she says as she lifts them and kisses the tops of their heads. She settles them beside her. "Good morning, husband," she says as she crooks her finger at me. I lean and kiss her softly.

"Mornin', wife. You look like you've been up."

"I was. I heard these sweet voices," she says as she tickles the girls, "and got up and made myself presentable for my surprise beignets."

"It's not a surprise if you knew, Mommy," Astrid chastises her.

"Oh, no, I was very surprised when I heard y'all whispering and getting things ready. And listening to my children and my husband's excited voices makes me so happy."

"Daddy said we have to make you feel very special because your birthday is so close to Christmas and it gets lost sometimes," Hazel rats me out.

She laughs at them and I laugh at her. Sometimes I have to laugh at her, otherwise, her beauty would break my heart every single time. "Did he tell you I am forty-three today too?" she asks them as she kisses their cheeks.

"No way." I interject. "I quit counting them like you told me to. You're still thirty-nine, and I'm still not on the naughty list." I wiggle my eyebrows at her and smoothe her hair from her shoulders.

She grins at me, rubs my jaw, and brushes the hair back from the girls' faces. "Look how lucky I am surrounded by all these gorgeous blues."

My heart twists. I'm pretty sure my "blues" are what won her over, so I thank God that he gave them to me. Snapping out of the trance she puts me in, I say, "All right, girls, let's go eat your breakfast before it gets cold and you can watch a cartoon before we have to leave to pick up your brothers."

"Thank you, girls, I'm going to enjoy my beignets so much."

I help the girls down from the bed and they toddle out. Leaning down, I wrap my hand around her neck and give her a little kiss. "Why don't you just relax here with your beignets and your coffee and your trashy romance novel that gets you all worked up." That gets another laugh out of her. "Then, I'll swoop in and make all your fantasies come true." That gets a groan.

When I come back into our room after getting the girls settled, I close the door gently and slide into the bed beside my gorgeous wife. "Did you enjoy your breakfast?" I ask her.

She looks up at me as she lays her book down. "I did. Thank you so much," she says as she brushes my jaw and my scruff. I dip my head and run it along her collarbone while she rubs my shoulders and plants kisses on my head.

"Mmm...that feels good," I tell her. It actually feels amazing, but what guy says that? "I'm glad you enjoyed your beignets. Happy birthday, baby."

"I sure did, but I'm afraid my pudge is getting pudgier," she says with a sigh as she rubs that almost non-existent "pudge."

I put my hand over hers on her belly and rub. "Baby, this teeny tiny little belly reminds me of the five little miracles we have. I wouldn't trade it for anything." *Sure as fuck hope I emphasized "teeny tiny" enough.*

She pulls my face up to hers and sears me with those eyes of hers. Those eyes that can always figure out exactly how I feel. Those eyes that assess and love and never fail to bring me to my knees. Then she kisses me deep. Pulling back a little she murmurs, "I love you, Adrian," against my lips. I feel myself getting hard. Laughing, I pull away and hop up to lock the door, eliciting a laugh from her. Reaching over, I throw the covers off and see that she only has on her silk camisole and nothing else. *Damn.* I groan. I run my finger down her middle, teasing her when I reach her hot center.

"I estimate we have about three minutes. Think I can make you feel good in three minutes, *mimi*?" I ask her, my voice sounds gruff to my own ears.

She rubs her thighs together and shakes her head. "There's no doubt in my mind, but I want you inside me," she says, her voice strained.

"Mmm, we'll see." I work my way down her body, but I only get to explore her with my mouth for a minute when I hear loud male voices. My head snaps up. "Shit! Louis is here. Do not fucking move," I order her.

"Yes, sir," she says with a laugh. Leaning up, I kiss her hard so she'll have that to think about until I get back. She groans. "Why did I give my brother a key again?"

I pop out of our bedroom but realize I have a raging hard on and two gay guys standing in my living room. Can't go making anyone jealous. Leaning around the corner to the living room, I say, "Hey, y'all. What's up?"

Louis looks away from watching Hazel balance on her tippy

toes and do her little spin. "Hey, man. We figured we'd follow y'all to the airport so we could help with the girls while y'all get the boys situated."

"Yeah, bro, that's cool. We've got the boys' welcome home dinner at the church afterwards. Y'all sticking 'round till then?"

Louis looks over at Chase who's holding Astrid and listening to her animatedly telling of her hamster babysitting duties. Chase nods and says, "Yeah, we can do that."

"Appreciate it. Y'all keep an eye on the girls for a few. We'll be out in a minute."

"No problem," Louis says. Somehow, I resist laughing out loud. *Looks like my girl's gonna get what she wants for her birthday after all.*

I go back in the bedroom, lock the door again, and turn to her. When I do, I almost lose it. She's flipped over on her stomach and appears as though she's had a hard time waiting for me.

"*Mimi,* get your fine ass up and get in the shower, and I'll scratch that itch you've got," I say as I smack her on that same fineness. "I just bought us some time so I can fulfill all of your birthday desires." She tosses her head back and focuses her hooded eyes on me like I'm her favorite person. I can't wait for her to get up, so I flip her over and pull her to me. She gives a little shriek. I grin. Sliding my arms under her, I lift her in my arms and devour her with my mouth as I take her to the shower.

I try to get the water temperature right while she works on driving me insane, nipping and biting at my neck and ears while rubbing her delectable body against mine. "Mmm…*Mimi,* are you trying to make me finish without you?" I tease her.

"Nuh uh, no way. I'll be good," she says with a laugh and steps back. I snake my hand around her thigh and hold her to me.

"Stay there. No more rubbing, though."

She gives an impertinent laugh and runs her arms around me and squeezes. I groan. Pushing my shorts down with my hands and then my feet, I turn to her and slip her silk over her head. I lean down and push her breasts together and up for my mouth and kiss and suck on them until I hear her panting. Letting her go with a pop, I grab her hand and pull her in the shower behind me.

"We have to hurry," she says breathless. "I don't want my brother to know what we're doing."

"Trust me, they know, they don't care," I assure her with a grin. I wrap one hand around her thigh and one hand around her neck and turn her head up to mine. I take in those big brown eyes that instantly consume me. Her fingers come up and she smoothes the skin around my eyes. That little act never fails to make me sober up. "I love you, Celeste," I whisper.

"I love you too, baby," she whispers back.

Leaning in, I nip and suck at those lips until she lets me in, then I kiss her until she's back to rubbing that body on mine. Sitting down on the bench, I rub my length again and again as she watches and bites her lip like she's holding herself back from attacking me. Turning her away from me, I back her up until she's lowered onto me. I widen my legs and feel her accept all of me. "*Mimi*, put your legs on the outside of mine," I whisper in her ear. She doesn't waste a second. I stretch our legs wider until I'm as deep as I can be.

Her moans are enough to get me off alone, so I try not to focus on that but on what I know will drive her crazy. With one hand, I move her back and forth over me and with the other I pinch and rub her tight little bud. When I feel her tighten and release a deep sigh, I let my hand slide over to her hip as she becomes lax in my arms. Mission accomplished. My *mimi* feels good. Her head drops back on my shoulder, and she starts kissing and biting at my neck. I clench her hips and move her over me hard and fast until I feel her building up again. I whisper in her ear, "There you go, *mimi*. Give it to me again, baby." Timing it just right, we find our release together.

WHEN SHE SLIDES her hand in mine, I give her a little smile, kiss her knuckles, and check my mirrors to make sure my girls are good to go. "All right ladies, are y'all ready to go get our boys back?"

"Yes!" they all agree. I just laugh. I've missed them too.

My gorgeous wife leans her head back on the seat and looks at me with wonder. "Do you think they learned any Spanish?"

"I'm sure they did, babe." I'm cut off when her phone rings.

She picks it up and groans. "It's Bonnie. I really don't want to hear it right now, but I know she needs to vent."

"Answer it then."

She releases a deep sigh. "Hey, Bonnie. What's up?" She listens, nodding at Bonnie's over the top ass. I feel her pain, so I loosen my hold on her hand and run my thumb over her palm and watch her smile through her gritted teeth. She tries to pull her hand away a little, and I watch her cross her legs. She's so easy to rile up and fucking insatiable. Lucky me. I let her off the hook and go back to just holding her hand.

"Well, Bonnie, you should have thought of that before." Pause. "I know you didn't mean for it to happen that way, but you're a grown woman." Pause. "You're just going to have to deal with it." Pause. "Stop it. You know I love you, but I'm not choosing sides." Pause. "OK, I'll see you later."

"That didn't sound good."

"No, she's nervous about seeing Garner." She looks back at the girls who look like they're dozing already. "She says it's the same every time he comes to town, and she doesn't want it to go down like that again."

"Mmm…well, you know where I stand on that whole mess."

She narrows her eyes at me and clenches her hand around mine. That's what she does when she gets pissy. She knows better than to let me go. "Yes, I know. Trust me, I wish I could stay out of it."

Her phone rings again. She sighs. I laugh. If she wasn't so gracious, they wouldn't call her with all their shit. She should just snap on their asses. I know she has it in her; she's sure as hell snapped on me when I've needed it.

"Hello, Daddy," she says. "Yes, sir. We're headed there now. I'm sorry. Oh, fine by me. No, that's great. See you then."

I tell her what I figured out. "Your dad's going to be there but not your mom. He's also had the displeasure of making sure Chip won't be there."

"You got it," she says with a snicker. She checks to make sure the girls are asleep. "Louis still doesn't want to be around my mother or Chip. He's not quite ready for that."

I visibly shudder. "I don't think I'd ever be ready to know that Chip was my biological father, and that he and my mother had been screwing right under everyone's noses for years." Talk about the shit hitting the fan. When Claire found out about Celeste and me and that Celeste's father was going to support us, she flipped her lid. Apparently her attempt to play nice was all a ruse.

We finally found out why she seemed to hate me more than she hated everyone else too. Her efforts at sleeping her way through our family had been thwarted when my father had refused her. In retaliation of her husband's "disloyalty," she blasted everyone's dirty secrets to the whole family. All the paid off politicians, all the prostitutes and their abortions for Celeste's older brothers, all the embezzled money, but the worst—finding out about William's victims. It made me crazy when I thought about how close Celeste had come to being one of many women who'd suffered the ultimate in violence at his hands. Claire and Chip had been the only ones to know about William's repeated acts of rape, but after her confession, Louis made sure William paid in the legal sense. My only consolation was that he was taking it up the ass multiple times a day at his new home in Angola State Penitentiary. The whole thing was nuts, but it put us all on an equal playing field, that's for sure. Nobody bothered with Celeste and me anymore.

Celeste lets out a long sigh. "I know. It's so hard to get used to the fact that my sweet baby brother was sired by that narcissistic pig."

I squeeze her hand. "You're not going to think about all that today. The boys have been gone for over a week. Our precious little girls are sleeping right behind you. Louis found a good guy in Chase and they're doing well. Your best friend and mine will work their own problems out." I catch her gaze and wink at her. "You got crazy hot birthday sex this morning and beignets. Life is good, babe."

PUSHING A DOUBLE stroller through the terminal is one thing I never thought I'd be doing . I have five beautiful children. That little thought never fails to stagger me. I watch as my oldest son picks up and spins my beautiful wife in his arms. He sets her down, and she is attacked with hugs from our three boys. I stand back and let them talk for a minute. There's nothing like watching a mama with her boys. After a minute, I push in a little closer and hug each one of their necks. I'm pretty sure Paris has grown because he's starting to catch up with me. Archer's been able to look me in the eye for a while, though. When Finn wraps his arms around me, I'm happy that I can still pick him up and jostle him back and forth a little.

"Boys, how was your trip?"

"It was awesome," Finn answers first. "I taught the kids how to play American baseball and football when we had breaks from working. I have a bunch of pictures too. I can't wait to get home and get them printed up and mailed to them."

I ruffle his hair and hug him to my side. "I missed ya, kid."

"Missed you too, Papa. The girls are knocked out," he says with a nod to the stroller.

"They got up early and made your mom breakfast, ate a bunch of sugar, and then went into a coma."

He laughs. "I thought mom said no more beignets."

"We won her over." I say with a grin.

Louis, Chase, and Celeste's dad make their way over and hug the boys. The boys regale us with talk of their mission trip for a few minutes before an excited Paris grabs a magazine from his bag and thrusts it in my face.

"Pops, look at this. Can you believe it? The Dog Tags on the cover of *People en Español*."

I laugh and look at my former band mates in all their glory. They've been kicking ass. I'm proud of them.

Archer pipes up. "I can't believe you gave all that up to hang out with us and our mom, dude. They're living the life."

I nod my head knowingly. "Yeah, I know exactly what kind of life they're living, and I wouldn't trade mine for theirs for anything in this world."

Celeste's dad pats me on the back and jumps in with his opinion, and my eyes almost bulge out of their sockets with what he says. "The work Adrian is doing with our veterans is commendable, boys. You'd do well to take note and remember that."

I look over at Celeste and my look of astonishment must mirror hers. Then we both grin. It had been better between us for a while now, but for him to outright state his approval was still unexpected.

His next question has me cringing for Archer. "Archer, you'll be leaving for college soon, son. Have you made your final decision?"

I'm impressed with Archer when his gaze doesn't waiver and his voice is strong. "Yes, Grandfather. I'll be heading to Annapolis. The Naval Academy has accepted me into their Cyber Operations program."

"Excellent. Navy or Marines?" Yep, there it is.

"Marines, sir."

"They'll be lucky to have you, son." Wonders will never cease.

Celeste doesn't hesitate to hug her dad right then. Acceptance—it's all she'd ever wanted for her and her family.

"Louis, how's entertainment law treating you, son?"

And that little change never failed to grate on my last nerve.

Bradford had put a good word in for Louis when Louis stepped away from the family practice, which meant Bradford was around a lot more since they were such great friends. Which meant that I had to pretend not to want to punch his face in every time I caught him checking out my wife. If he were just admiring how damn gorgeous she was, I could handle that. But, no, he looked at her like if I stepped one tiny fucking bit out of line, he would whisk her off and nurse her wounds. Bastard. He needs to get a woman of his own.

Louis rubs the back of his neck and grins. "It's good. More relaxed pace. A little more traveling. I'm enjoying it."

"Well, someone's got to do it, but I never thought it would be you with all your brilliance."

Louis just laughs. "They need brilliant people too, Dad."

"Well, at least we still have Chase around the firm," his dad says with a sigh.

I see the girls stirring and their brothers are on top of it. They abandon us and lift them from their stroller, hugging and kissing and passing them between the three of them.

My eyes burn at the sight of them. I feel Celeste burrow into my side and look down at her. Tears shimmer in her eyes, so I hug her to me tight and lean down and kiss them away. "Happy tears?" She just nods. Planting a long kiss on her forehead, I murmur, "Thank you for this family, baby." I feel her hiccup, so I squeeze her ass to make her laugh.

"All right, family. We've got a long day ahead of us. Let's get going."

GETTING THE TWINS settled takes a heck of a long time, so when I get to the sunroom I'm whupped. But when I see her sitting there in her little blue silk camisole and shorts, I get a rush of energy. I walk over and pull her up so that I can sit and then pull her back down on my lap.

"Hey, baby," she murmurs.

"Hey, yourself. How's this for a hot birthday date? You, me, and this loveseat?"

"This loveseat holds some of my best memories, so I love it right here. And you're taking me to the concert tomorrow, so I'm good."

I lean in and get a little taste. "Mmm…you're better than good."

"Today was a great day," she says as she runs her hands through my hair. "I'm so happy to have the boys home."

"Me too. And your dad blew my mind, by the way."

"I knew he'd come around eventually, baby. You're amazing. I just happened to be the lucky one who saw it first."

"You weren't always so lucky," I say, thinking back to how I'd put her through hell for a while. It still boggled my mind that she was strong enough and loved me enough to see what I needed and to do something about it.

She runs her fingers over my neck, massaging me. "Baby, that's all behind us now. You asked me how I could forgive you, how I could put my trust in you. It's so simple—you give me everything, Adrian. It's only fair that I give it all right back."

I run my hands up her jaw and bring her face close to mine. I pray that she can see it all in my eyes—all my love, all my respect, all my awe—because I know that my words could never do my feelings justice. "You're my life, my love, my heaven," I pause for a second before I give her words back. Her words that rocked my world. "My everything I'd never had," I whisper.

Playlist

Everlong - Foo Fighters
Baby Did a Bad Bad Thing - Collide
In Your Eyes - Jeffrey Gaines
Crazy for You - Madonna
The Blower's Daughter - Damien Rice
Someday - Harry Connick, Jr.
My Hero - Foo Fighters
Wicked Game - Phillip Phillips
So What - P!nk
Comedown - Bush
Criminal - Fiona Apple
Kiwi - Maroon 5
Missing You - John Waite
Can't Take My Eyes Off You - Frankie Valli
Breakaway - Kelly Clarkson
I Never Told You - Colbie Caillat
Stay - Rihanna
Just a Kiss - Lady Antebellum
Amazed - Lonestar
Bridge Over Troubled Water - Simon & Garfunkel
Imagine - John Lennon
Everlong—Acoustic Version - Foo Fighters
What I Got - Sublime
Hold You in My Arms - Ray LaMontagne

Stay - Sara Bareilles
Brown Eyed Girl - Van Morrison
The Reason - Hoobstank
One Thing - Finger Eleven
Home - Phillip Phillips
Bed of Roses - Bon Jovi
One - Creed
Breathe Me - Sia
Hurt - Johnny Cash
I'll Stand By You - Pretenders
Make This Go On Forever - Snow Patrol
Hide and Seek - Imogen Heap
Love the Way You Lie (Part II) - Rihanna, Eminen
Bleeding Love - Leona Lewis
Brave - Leona Lewis
Glitter in the Air - P!nk
Then - Brad Paisley

A Note from the Author...

Post-Traumatic Stress Disorder is a topic that hits close to home for me. This being a romance novel, I don't go specifically into all that is required and endured for treatment. In essence, I brush over the details but the gist of the matter is this—PTSD affects more people than we know. Know the symptoms and never quit fighting for those afflicted. We (civilians) could never understand what our men and women in uniform go through, but there is treatment and the stigma associated with it is beginning to fade. I thank them so much for their courage and bravery in the face of the many evils this world has to offer.

Everything I've NEVER HAD

BY
LYNETTA HALAT

Chapter One

The Kiss

– THE WAY ADRIAN SEES IT –

WITH A STUPID ass grin the size of Texas plastered on my face, I watch mesmerized as she throws her head back and loses herself in the music. Since she's obsessed with the band Bush, I'd asked the other Dog Tags if we could cover more of their songs tonight. I'm glad we did. It's been good to see her relax and cut loose. She's been through hell, and no one deserves to have fun more than she does.

I give a chin lift to my buddy who's been moving in circles around her all night to keep all the douche bags away from her. I hope she's not wondering why no one is hitting on her. I don't want to make her feel bad about herself, but I'm not ready for that. Five fucking years I've loved this woman. The last year and a half—I've been *in love* with her. I'd promised my cousin, her deceased husband Tripp, that I'd take care of her. And I know she needs to move on from losing him and find someone, but she won't meet anyone who is even a tiny bit deserving of her in a dive like this. Just her being here raises the value of this place a million times over.

We wind down "Everything Zen," and I lean over and shout our next song to Zach. He gives me a funny look but doesn't argue. I never order him around this much, but I want to play this song while I watch her and pretend. I've imagined myself with her while listening to this song so many times that it's fucking ridiculous and it hurts like a bitch, but I'm a glutton for punishment.

She's been smiling at me all night, so when I play the opening notes to "Everlong" and she shoots me a pained expression, I know immediately that something's wrong. Was this her and Tripp's song or something? Nah, he hated rock music. When she whispers to Bonnie and throws me another desperate look, I panic. Is she sick? I would've noticed if she'd drunk enough to be sick. I watch her fight her way to the back of the small club and toward the back door. My buddy gives me a questioning look, but I shake my head, letting him know that I've got her. I'm already tapping Zach on the shoulder and yanking my guitar off. A couple of girls try to grab at me as I follow her out. I shake them off quickly, and by my look, I'm sure they can tell I'm in no mood.

Standing at the door for a few seconds, I stare in fascination as her whole body trembles in that sexy outfit that had every man in this club hard for her, especially me. I despise that outfit; it shows entirely too much of her tan skin that seems to glow almost. I push the door open and let it slam behind me as I breathe in deep along with her, inhaling her unique scent. My instinct to devour her has never been stronger.

Hoping she won't hear my pulse racing in my voice, I ask, "Celeste, everything good?"

Even though I know she's tough as nails, she sounds so small and fragile when she replies, "Umm...yeah, what are you doing out here? Doesn't your band need you?"

Baby, the world could need me to stop a giant asteroid from crashing into it, but if you needed me, I'd fucking be there. That seems a little dramatic. Settling, I say instead, "They'll live. You're more important."

When she spins around, she takes my breath away. She looks determined and fucking fierce. Again, I'm fascinated as she strides toward me. Moving doesn't even cross my mind because she's never really gotten in my space before. I'm expecting her to stop so when she doesn't and is close enough to breathe me in and capture me with those lust-infused big brown eyes, I'm powerless and couldn't move even if a damn hurricane washed ashore right now. My eyes widen with disbelief—does she want *me*? *No fucking way.*

Her hands suddenly shoot out, pulling my lips to hers quickly. Gut says—devour her. Brain says—don't you fucking dare. Don't you react. She doesn't mean it. In no way could someone as pure and as good as Celeste care about you. No way could she want to be with you, knowing everything she knows about your family. Since I'm not really reacting, it feels like my first kiss all over again. I want this, want *her* more than anything, but I don't know how to handle it so it's mostly awkward.

When her tongue brushes my lip, I'm done for. Mach speed, taking me beyond lust, beyond passion, and dumping my ridiculous ass right on love's doorstep. I'm in love with this woman, and for now, I don't care that she could never love me. I don't care that she'll crush me when this moment passes. I just need to taste her. Right the fuck now. So I let her in and move in for a taste of my own—just a little taste. And little's all I get before she breaks our kiss and backs away from me.

What the hell did she do that for? I was just getting started. I need her mouth back on mine like I need my next breath.

"Adrian, I'm so sorry. I...I don't know what I was thinking." Her tremble is what does me in. "I wasn't thinking, I guess."

So it's like I thought. She's feeling vulnerable and it's not really about me. Gut shot. I should walk away right now. No, no, fuck no. If I only get one opportunity to kiss her, it's going to be a hell of a lot better than that one timid kiss. I have to kiss her back. I want her to know how I feel. I need her to know, but I can't, can I? *Pussy!*

Shit! If I kiss her, I run the risk of losing what we've built. I can't lose her and her boys—they're my world. What would I do without my fucking world? The absence I feel at the imagined loss staggers me.

Yet that thought wars with the thought of never tasting her again. Fuck it! I'll blame this song and the booze. She's had a couple. I've had a couple. I start toward her, and if I didn't love her so much, I would laugh my ass off at her frightened expression. What does she think I'm going to do? Fuck her right here on this porch?

I don't waste any time because I don't know when she'll snap to her senses and run me off. I capture her mouth with mine and thrust my tongue into her pliant mouth. Before I can register exactly how incredible she tastes, I run my hands down her back and draw her to me completely, overwhelming all my senses. God, so good. So perfect. Her body fits to mine like a second skin. Like she was made to mold herself around me. Her little whimpers in the back of her throat drive me mad, and I can't get enough of her. I take her deeper, willing her to give herself to me completely. And my gut pinches when she does. She's mine.

When her shaky hands pull at my hair, I groan. I want her sweet little hands all over me. Want her to explore me while I explore her. Fuck. One taste will never be enough.

I pull back and place gentle kisses on her sweet mouth. Knowing I'll never get enough of her, I try to savor how amazing she is before I have to end this. Before she ends me.

When she says, "Mmm...Adrian," I feel that need to consume her again and know that I have to stop or my taking her right here, right now will become a reality.

With one more tender kiss, I pull back and gaze at her. She's got her eyes closed, but I can see the corners of them turned up. So I glance down to take in the smile resting on her beautiful face. And it hurts. It hurts that that smile can never really be mine. God, please don't let me have screwed this all up. I swallow hard and try to push past my fear.

When her eyes flutter open, pleasure spills from them, but that look is quickly replaced by panic and her swift intake of breath. Fuck. She rights herself and stiffens. I brace.

"Adrian—" Nuh uh, no way can I take her letting me down gently.

"No, that's all on me, Celeste. I'm..." I run my hand through my hair. Shit. I'm nervous as a prepubescent boy getting caught looking at his first bit of porn. "Shit...I'm sorry. I'm a shit. It's just..." *Think fast, dickhead.*

"I've had too much to drink," she blurts out. "This is the first time I've been out, and...I was just having fun but started feeling lonely, and I had too much to drink."

Yeah, I'm drunk too. Drunk on her. As if I didn't have it bad enough, now I've felt her, tasted her, turned her on. God, I thought it was impossible for her to be any more gorgeous, but she was even hotter turned on. And the fact that she was turned on for me—mind-blowing. Even if it was for one brief moment that I'd never get back or experience again, the pain that has ensued is worth it. I'm crippled to know that I'm not enough for her. I scrub my hands over my face, trying to rid myself of all feeling and come up with something to say.

Blaming it on my genes always seems to work. Blowing out a deep breath, I say, "Yeah, and pig that I am, I took advantage of all that."

Her voice is so sweet as she declares, "You're not a pig. As a matter of fact, you couldn't be any further from that if you tried." She doesn't know the half of it. She sees only good. "And, to be honest, I really needed to be kissed. So...thank you."

Poor thing. She looks mortified. She's so fucking innocent. This thought troubles me because it means that I'll have to play protector while she finds herself a new man. "So, we're good then. No, uh, awkwardness?" I've turned into a stumbling fool over her. *Fanfuckingtastic.* For years, I've been controlling this, and now it's all out there for her to see.

"Of course. I'm not one of your simpering groupies. I promise not to stalk you and demand any more kisses," she says and a blush immediately consumes her precious face. I'm dumbfounded. Did she really just compare herself to a bunch of barflies?

I can't help but to reach out for her and try to show her how much more than that she is, how much more she means to me. She doesn't jump from my touch, but she might as well have for the way her shifting away has me reeling. It's worse than I thought. She's going to hate me. I'm screwed.

I put my hands in my back pockets to keep from trying to touch her again and rock back on my heels, shooting for nonchalance, when all I feel is sheer panic. "You ready to come back inside then?" *Come let me play you a kickass song and get this bad memory out of your head.*

"Umm...I just need another minute. I'll be right in, OK?" she says with a small smile. That's better.

"OK," I agree. I turn to go, but then wonder if she just doesn't want to be around me. Damn. I turn back and confirm, "See ya inside."

"Yep," she agrees.

Making my way back inside, I grab a beer and head up to the stage even though we have a few minutes. I need to clear my head, and I don't feel like having some random girl shoving her tits in my face while I do.

How many times have I imagined that kiss? I don't even know, but I do know it was beautiful and perfect. She is beautiful and perfect. I'd give anything if...*nah, man, don't set yourself up for that.*

I'm going to have to talk to her tonight. I can't let her stew. Damn, it's not my week to cut grass and the boys are in the country. What do I do? Just show up there groveling like a little bitch? Yeah, I'd grovel for her. *Ain't too proud to beg.*

I lick my lips before I take a swig of my beer and taste her again. So fucking sweet. Taking a pull from my beer, I look out over the crowd and realize she still hadn't come back in unless she was in the bathroom. I spot Bonnie and Farah. Don't girls usually do that shit together? Farah's got her back to me. And Bonnie's ogling Garner, so it takes me a second to get her attention. I motion to her with my finger. She scrunches her face up at me before coming over.

"Geez, Adrian, you've pulled me away from one hot piece of man." She turns and looks back to see some blonde bimbo sidling up to Garner. She lets out a hiss. "This better be earth shattering, or I'll be forced to castrate your fine self," she grumbles as she turns back to me.

Oh, it's earth shattering all right. I ignore her little threat. "Where's Cel? Bathroom?"

Her brow furrows and she shakes her head at me. "Oh, no. She just shot me a text, saying she was grabbing a cab. Isn't that strange? I tried to catch her, but she was long gone. Sent her another text, and she said she's fine," Bonnie says with a shrug. "Just wanted to get home."

I drop my head, shaking it. It's worse than I thought. She can't even stand to be around me. "I should've fucking known better," I mutter before turning back to get ready for our second set.

Acknowledgments

To my soul mate best friend, Bobbie Myers, yes you are first again. How could you not be when you spend countless hours on the phone, online, and travelling with me in order to help me achieve my dream? Not to mention reading my manuscript eight times over and analyzing one sentence with me for God only knows how long? I know you do it because you love me and you believe in my work, but know that the blessing of you is beyond appreciated. I'm so grateful that you spoke to me that day in the bleachers of our sons' baseball tryouts even though I was praying that no one would because I was on death's door and didn't have the energy to put any make-up on. I love you to pieces.

To *my* everything, my husband…you believe in what I have to offer this world and support me in every way possible. I am ever so grateful. And how awesome is that my husband follows book blogs now so that he can keep abreast of all the latest happenings? Love that man!

Thank you to my children for not guilting me too much when I went AWOL while finishing this book. Your support and love mean the world to me, Austin and Nolan. I hope you are as proud of me as I am of you.

My entire family has been incredibly supportive of me. I wish I could name them all here, but I have to say that my mom, Marie McAdams, is beyond amazing, and I am so grateful that she used to drop me off at the library on Saturdays rather than making me run errands with her. To my aunts—Velina, Sandra, and Iva—you are such strong women from whom I am constantly learning, and I love you all so much. Thank y'all for making my first book signing a success!

Thank you, Amanda Conine, for gifting me the name Archer. I'll never forget the day while we were in between class periods and you were talking with your mouth full and mumbled your husband's name. I said that's a cool name—Archer—and you remarked, "Yeah, it is cool but I said Richard." Priceless!

Thank you to a great friend, a huge supporter, and excellent New Orleans fact checker, Tammy Vizzini. Let's go have that Goody now!

Liz Murach from Sinfully Sexy Book Reviews, I cannot thank you enough for listening to me ramble about how much I love the Foo Fighters, sharing in that obsession, and researching and sending me the links to get permission to use their lyrics for "Everlong." Those lyrics are Celeste and Adrian's love story set to music, so they are priceless.

To my awesome beta readers—Megan, Elle, Debi, and Stephanie—thank you so much for the invaluable feedback and falling in love with my story and my characters. Your insights and hilarious comments made revising a blast!

I've said it before and I'll say it again—my Dragonfly Divas rock! I'm so grateful that you love Every Rose enough to tell others and help me spread the word. I couldn't do this self-pub thing without you.

I have so many writers whom I adore and who inspire me, and I love being a part of our writing group, Indie Gals. Those who support me to the ends of the earth, I have to say thank you so much. Wendy Ferraro, Mel Bellew, Kimi Flores, Melanie Dawn, T.L. Manning, Chelsea Camaron, Liz Upton, Scarlett Metal, LK Collins, L. Chapman, and Beth Michele—I love you all so very much.

Without you, my readers, my book would just be a thing and not the living, breathing organism that you make it when you love, connect, remember, and share it. Thank you.

Book bloggers—without them this indie thing would be so much more difficult and not near as much fun. I have so many bloggers who love and support my work, but a few in particular really "get" my books and me and go above and beyond in promoting them.

Kristy Louise from Book Addict Mumma, your love and support mean the world to me. You were one of my first ever readers, and I've been so happy to share my journey with you. Thank you for the book trailers!

Stephanie Oursler from the Boyfriend Bookmark, I don't think I've ever had to ask you share a single thing for me. Your love and enthusiasm for *Every Rose* is unparalleled, and I'm so grateful. And you are so genuine that it makes my heart hurt.

Angie McKeon from Angie's Dreamy Reads, thank you so much for organizing my blog tour for EINH and for championing this book. I've loved your blog from the start because of your passion for books and their authors and your ability to engage readers, so 1 am thrilled that you decided to take me under your wing.

Maureen Sytsma from the Scarlet Siren, boy I am glad you liked my *Every Rose* reader beware statement! Your twisted sense of humor and eagerness to make graphics for me are beyond appreciated. You are one talented and ridiculously beautiful woman!

Stacy Nickelson from It All Started with a Book Blog, I'm so grateful that you found *Every Rose* and connected with it on a fundamental level. I don't know what I'd do without you. You are a class act.

Chris Carmilia from Chris' Blog Emporium, thank goodness for Goodreads and your gorgeous review of *Connected*. We bonded over that, and I hope it's a bond that never breaks.

To my favorite lovers—Natalie, Dina, Meagan, and Jennifer— at Love Between the Sheets, thank you for loving my books and me. Y'all are the most genuine group of girls I've ever had the pleasure of fangirling with!

Ava from Book Nerds Anonymous, thank you so much for your love and support and for sharing your story with me.

Laura Voss from Stephanie's Book Reports, your love and support has been unwavering. Thank you for falling in love with Michael and wanting to see his success as much as I do.

Thank you to all the bloggers who took a chance on me, joined my blog tour, or promoted my books—Crystal's Many Reviews, Booky Ramblings, Sweet Sassy Sexy Book Blog, Book 2 Book, Beauty Brains and Books, Hooked on Books, First Class Books, Sparkling Pink Bookshelf, The Rookie Romance Blog, Musings of a Misfit, Mary Elizabeth's Crazy Book Obsession, Kiss And Tell Reviews, #BookNerd, Escape Into A Book, Bridger Bitches Book Blog, The Blushing Reader, Reviews by Tammy and Kim, Curious Kindle Reader, Swoon Worthy Books, Love Between the Sheets, Group Therapy Book Club Blog & Review, Kassie's Book Thoughts, Smokin' Hot Book Blog, Mean Girls Luv Books, Whirlwindbooks, Fiction's Our Addiction, G & C Book Blog, For the Love of Books, Read and Share Book Reviews, The Autumn Review, True Story Book Blog, PEACE LOVE BOOKS, Three Girls and a Book Obsession, Reading is My Time Out, Books Coffee and Wine, My Secret Romance Book Reviews, The Book Enthusiast, Maria's Book Blog, Chapter Break, Bookaholics Blog, Thoughts and Reviews, The Book Avenue, Mackable Book Babes, Stories and Swag, Sofia loves books, I'll Be Reading, Love Words And Books, Read More Sleep Less, Morning After a Good Book, Rude Girl Book Blog, Tabby's Tantalizing Reviews, I <3 Books, Flirty and Dirty Book Blog, Totally Booked, and Maryse's Book Blog.

About the Author

For as long as she can remember, Lynetta Halat has lived to read and has written countless stories and plays since she was a young girl. An avid reader, she'd has always dreamt of penning books that people could connect with and remember; and her first novel, *Every Rose*, was the perfect catalyst to launch her into the world of publishing, and now she has followed that up with an adult romance in *Everything I've Never Had*. Her love of the English language prompted her to pursue a master's degree in English from Old Dominion University in Virginia. A self-proclaimed "Coast Girl," she lives in Mississippi with her adorable husband, two amazing sons, and two loveable dogs. She is currently at work on third book.

For more information about Lynetta and her books, visit:

FACEBOOK

https://www.facebook.com/LynettaHalatAuthor

WEBSITE

www.lynettahalat.com

GOODREADS

http://www.goodreads.com/author/show/6969980.Lynetta_Halat

TWITTER

https://twitter.com/LynettaHalat

Made in the USA
Lexington, KY
14 April 2014